An Empty Cradle

S.L. Broadbent

PublishAmerica
Baltimore

PublishAmerica has allowed this work to remain exactly as the author intended, verbatim, without editorial input.

ISBN: 1-60813-281-1
PUBLISHED BY PUBLISHAMERICA, LLLP
www.publishamerica.com
Baltimore

Printed in the United States of America

Dedication

This book is dedicated to my daughter, Jamie and my husband, Nigel; who always seem to support my dreams, no matter how half-baked and crazy they might be.

Acknowledgements

My great thanks to all the people at Publish America who have helped me to see one of my many dreams come to life.

Chapter 1

In a tangle of overgrown shrubbery the hunched form of a man stood wrapped in darkness. Less than twenty feet away a young couple sat close together, their bodies molded into one dark figure as they sat on the small park bench. The man from the shadows gazed out at them, his body swaying slightly from an overindulgence of whisky in his system, yet he was able to steady himself by grasping his thick, callused hands onto the thin, twisted trunk of the rhododendron next to him. The build of his body and the condition of his hands marked him as a working man, a laborer. The man he watched so intently had a strong jaw line with broad, square shoulders made all the more so by his formal charcoal wool coat. Definitely *not* the build of a laborer, but the capability was there. Affectionately he stroked the woman's red hair, his body close to hers, his gaze lost deep within her own. There could be no mistaking the genuine affection they had for each other, no denying that they were lovers. Anyone who would have stumbled across their late night meeting would have assumed they were a happily married couple out enjoying the crisp night air. Their conversation was low and slightly muffled by the cold wind that blew from the west, but the dark figure that stood in the darkness could hear just enough of their quiet conversation to bring a murderous rage to the surface of his heart.

"Our son will be here soon. You need to make the provisions to leave here with me before his arrival or I fear for the boys safety. There is no way that your husband will believe the child is truly his once he sees him" The man said, his hand tenderly lifting up her chin in order to bring her gaze to his.

"Are you sure we can't stay here, at least until he is born? The doctors here are so caring, so understanding of my current condition. Besides, Dr. Sims has been my doctor since I was a young girl. I think *he* at the very least could be trusted. Perhaps I could even deliver the child in his office, after hours." The woman rubbed her stomach, her gaze settling on the dark row of distant trees that lined the opposite hillside.

"There is just no way that you will be able to give birth in the traditional sort of hospital, we've discussed this before. I don't feel that even Dr. Sims office would be safe. Don't cling to the human practices of birth, there is too much at risk here. I have friends, colleagues, in England who are more than capable of helping with the delivery; proper medical doctors who understand the importance for complete and utter secrecy." He paused for a moment, trying to quiet his growing impatience. "My people can have the plane tickets ready and waiting at your word, but I do feel we that it is imperative that we leave soon." He rested his hand on the large, swollen orb that was the woman's unborn child. "Do you think it's possible that he already suspects that the child is not his own?"

"No, if he did I'm afraid I would already be dead. I tell you he has it in him you know, the ability and the mind set to kill me and the girls. I can see it in him when he is angry, when he is on the brink of spilling over into total madness." She glanced around them, as if half expecting him to be there, to jump out of the bushes and savagely attack her. "He's been watching me lately, acting suspicious of everything I do, and asking ridiculous questions. I almost didn't make it out this evening but he said he had to run to the store for a case of cigarettes. He'll be gone for hours, he always is. He's even started drinking again. The late nights out, the smell of whisky on his breath. He frightens me sometimes. The way he looks at me, the hate I see in his eyes," she turned from him, her gaze drifting down to the parking lot and his black Mercedes that was parked next to her old red doge. The glaring incarnation of their opposites of class made her smile nervously. Two sides of the social circle parked one next to the other much like themselves in a way. She wondered if they stood out as differently in the public eye as their cars did in the parking lot. Such deep contrasts. She gazed at him for a moment, her confidence waning. What *did* he see in her? What could she give him that another woman more his social and economic equal could not? Her desire to ride away with him became almost overpowering; what if he were to suddenly realize his mistake? He would be better off with a woman of wealth, a woman without so much baggage; a husband, two kids. But the girls, he said he loved the girls because they were a part of her, but did he really? Could she just be fooling herself into thinking someone like him could truly be interested in a poor girl from the wrong side of town? Cinderella she was not. "He's even started to become verbally abusive and violent with the girls. He smacked Deanna in the face yesterday for slamming her door. She's just at that age, there was no need for him to treat her like that. They're both afraid of him now. *I* can't even hid what he is to them any longer. They are too old and too smart for it to do any good now." She kissed him deeply, moving closer to him and holding his hands. Wanting to feel the safety of his arms, *needing* it like a coke addict needs a fix.

The hunched, dark form of the man moved closer to them, his manner agitated, his body leaning forward, straining to hear more.

"You haven't forgotten your promise to me that you would take the girls too? I could never live with myself knowing that I left them behind with him, not with his temper." She shuttered at the thought of him hurting her children. "We can't leave them with him. Jack is sure to make them pay for what *we* have done. I can't leave with you if it means leaving my other children behind. They deserve a good life with us. They deserve to be safe and loved."

"Don't worry. Have I ever gone back on a promise that I've made to you? I told you that the girls would be safe and I meant it." He flashed that amazing white smile at her, the one that made her knees buckle. Instantly she felt foolish for even questioning him. "I have already made the arrangements needed for them to join us, there is no way that I would leave them behind to be abused by their father. I had to make sure that their needs could be satisfied first and I assure you that I have done so, although with considerable effort. I have arranged for them to finish their schooling abroad in Germany. It's a fine school. I even had a chance to tour their facility a few weeks ago. The girls will love it there and the schools level of education far surpasses that of any in the United States." The man with her looked around him…he smelled something, something that had caught in the wind but then quickly passed. "I know you want the girls with us but I think it will be best if they are schooled away from home until we are sure the girls will be able to accept the child's differences." He turned away again, trying to pick up the scent of that lingering odor that he had just caught, but the wind began to pick up and washed it away. "Everything will be fine, they will have the finest up-bringing that wealth and class can offer them. I promise you that the girls will never want for anything"

"Tonight then." Her eyes sparkled in the fading light. "Let me get the girls and some of their personal belongings together and I will meet you back here in an hour." She smiled brightly at him, her hands clasping the sides of his strong face, her thumbs tracing the soft curve of his full, strong lips.

"My driver will be the one picking you up tonight, it can't be helped I'm afraid." He smiled at her and nodded toward the setting sun. "My appointment has already been set and the time grows near, I must be leaving soon. We will have to make some provisions for the coming nights together, as I'm sure you're aware. You have nothing to fear from me but I don't think the girls will be able to handle it. You can stay at my hotel until morning when we will be able to travel, after that we will have to make further arrangements until the children can be settled in their new school. The flight to England isn't long and all the proper papers have already been filed. A business partner of mine has been kind enough to secure passports for you and the girls. There will be no problems for you and the children entering the country."

With that he kissed her and taking her gently by the hand they both left the relative comfort of the park bench. He led her a few steps down the broken cement path that wound its way through the trees and on into the parking lot below. A few tufts of grass had sprung up from the uneven cracks, missed by the grounds keeper in his weekly mowing. The evening lights that scattered the parking lot and each wooden pavilion had just come on and their cars were illuminated in the distance.

"Come, I'll walk you to your car," he pulled playfully at her fingers.

"No, I want to stay a bit longer, take in some of this wonderful night air. You go on."

"Very well, but don't stay out here too late. I don't want to have to worry about you being out here all alone in the dark." He pulled her closer, their lips almost touching as wrapped her in his strong, warm arms. He held her there for a moment, feeling his son move strongly inside the womb of his lover as he gazed deeply into her eyes, and then kissed her good-bye. Reluctantly he made his way down to his car, stopping once to wave to her before pulling the Mercedes door closed and starting the engine in a roar of gasoline and a spark of ozone. She waved back, watching as the red glow of the car's break lights flashed as he disappeared into the distance. She was once again alone.

The young mother stood there for a moment enjoying the coming night's promise of spring and the cool breeze as it kissed her face. Silence enveloped the small park as chill ran up her spine, she wrapped her arms around her stomach protectively, the coming night would be colder than she had expected. The possibility of a late snow crossed her mind. Never the less she smiled to herself and the thoughts of her and her young family's soon to be fairytale life.

She almost didn't dare to believe that she could be so happy, not when she had resigned herself to a life of near poverty and self regret. She would finally have a chance at real happiness, of real love. Her young family's life had truly become wonderful.

It was at that moment that heard a rustling of bushes behind her and she turned to see a man appear out of the darkness to her side. Fear grabbed at her soul as she recognized the lumbering form of her husband. She saw tears streaming down his face, his hands had become clenched into tight, white knuckled fists that swung loosely at his side like clubs.

"Jack," her voice cracked. Stepping back she could clearly see the dangerous intentions in his dark, bloodshot eyes. The newfound hatred he had for her had intensified.

"How could you! You're nothing but a fucking whore!" He spat at her through clenched teeth. His face became a deep purple-red and saliva foamed at the corners of his mouth as he spoke. He looked more like a rabid dog than her once loving husband.

"It's not what you think Jack. We're just friends." She spoke softly, trying to defuse the situation she was in but knowing deep inside that she couldn't. She backed up farther, her eyes searching for someone, anyone near enough to hear her scream. In her heart though she knew no one was there. Her lover had gone and the parking lot was vacant except for her own red car. No one else existed at that moment except her, her lovers unborn son, and her murderous husband Jack.

He stepped closer to her, unsteady and shaken on his drunken feet. He stumbled over to one side, groping out into nothingness, but then managed to gain some stability. He was close enough to see the fear that he brought into his wife's eyes. Close enough to see his own ugly reflection, his own disgust of what she had become staring back at him. With a clenched fist he struck her full in the face. The face that had become nothing more to him than that of a liar and a whore. He could feel fine, small bones of her face collapse under the force of his swing. Laughter escaped his twisted mouth as her pregnant body was thrown to the ground in a spray of blood. Visions of her lying naked with another man, of fucking him, blurred his vision He towered above her, straddling her with his legs as he stood there and spit down into her bloodied face as she tried to roll over onto her side. Pain shattered through her face and neck as she lay on the ground, desperately she fought to stay conscious She tried to cry out, to scream, but her jaw was badly mangled. Nothing escaped her lips except her own haggard breathing. Clutching at her stomach with one hand and her face with the other, she feared not only for her unborn child but for her own life as well. She was at his mercy and mercy was one thing that Jack had little of. He stopped for only a second and hope rose in her broken heart that he would stop, that he would leave her and go back home to sober up. Instead he bent over to pick up a large chunk of concrete from the broken ground and with the swing of a man cutting wood he struck her. Over and over he smashed down upon his wife's face until there was little left for anyone to identify with any accuracy. Blood and brain matter saturated her once fair red hair and began to pool around her limp body. A slight gurgling sound escaped what should have been her mouth as her last rattling breath escaped her. She lay still, no longer fighting against him, no longer trying to defend her broken body. Her blood stained hands slowly slid from her stomach to the soft ground beside her.

In a daze of fleeting sobriety the man finally stood from her tortured body. His wife's broken and lifeless form sickened him. What he had done to her and child he loved began to register in his drowning mind, like the slow motion film of a man pulling a snake out of the grass instead of a hose and watching as his brain begins to recognize it. In his horror he fell backwards, dropping the bloody rock next to her battered body as if he were surprised and shocked to see it in his own hands. His own body shook violently from the release of so much hatred, the adrenalin churned in his stomach and vomit rose quickly into his mouth, burning the back of his throat and spilling out onto his shoes. Wiping the splatters of blood and vomit from his face he turned to run, the horror of what he had done to his family reaching for him and gripping at his soul.

He stopped. Something was behind him. Some-*thing* was towering high above him in the darkness. His brain shut down. He tried to focus his mind, to truly *see* what was before him. Seconds passed, his vision cleared. There before him stood a hulking, dark creature that one only heard about in dark, twisted fairy tales while huddled around camp fires as a child. He was sure it was the Devil himself; come to take him home to the tortures of Hell for killing his wife and her bastard of a child.

"It was you!" Jack pointed a crooked, bloody finger at it. "You did this to me! You brought me here to kill my wife! You fucking bastard! Only the devil himself could twist my mind in such a way to make me do such a terrible thing!"

He screamed out at the creature, his eyes wild, spit flying from his mouth as he shook his head and wept.

The creatures red eyes narrowed in on him, its filthy teeth bared. The sour breath of Hell itself poured from deep inside its belly as he gazed down on him. Jack began to laugh uncontrollably, his arms spread wide as if asking for his own deliverance from evil. The unholy beast paused only momentarily as the night air whipped around and brought with it the smell of blood and death. The creature's jaws lashed out, ripping the man's throat from his quivering body in one fierce bite. For a moment the man stood there, blood pouring from his open mouth and flowing like a gothic waterfall down his neck. Jack fell to his knees, blood spouting from his neck with every beat of his slowing heart. With an angry swing of the creature's mighty arm Jack's head left his body and rolled into the darkness, coming to rest just under a clumping of near by maple trees.

The dark legions of Hell surely walked that night and with it came the swift prosecution of the damned. The beast paused briefly at the woman's shattered body before disappearing deep into the woods beyond. Moment's later one lone howl emanated throughout the night air full of anger, pain, and loss.

Chapter 2

Fifteen years later…

Deanna lay in a pool of pink linen sheets half asleep and listened as Seth's silver BMW roared into life and pulled out of the driveway. Vaguely she remembered that he was on his way to the airport.

They had been married less than a year and she usually saw him off with a kiss, but this morning she had slept in and he had not bothered to wake her. Not sure whether to be annoyed with him or delighted; she took the rare opportunity to soak in the peaceful silence and the warm morning sun as it made its way across to her pillow. She stared up at the ceiling, watching the reflection of fine lines that the oak tree had scattered across it's vast whiteness, much like the boney hands that had reached out to her moments earlier in a dream. She turned away, still too close to the night and the on slot of dark dreams that she had just woken from to look too intently at them.

Her gaze drifted to her wedding photo that sat wrapped in silver casing next to the bed and a smile touched her full, pink lips. She missed him already. Deanna pulled the sheets up to her chin, she could still smell the lavender water that she had sprayed on them the night before to help her sleep. Her dreams had become increasingly disturbing the farther along her pregnancy became Hulking, dark monsters pulling at her, wanting to steal her unborn child in the dark of the night. They had become a nightly occurrence, so much so that she had started fearing them before she even went to bed, making sleep difficult if not imposable. Often she would wake in a pool of sweat, her heart pounding and her mouth as dry as cotton batting. She had to resort to natural sleep remedies to help her grab even the few hours that she did manage to squeeze out of the night.

She snuggled a bit deeper into the lavender scented comfort, trying not to dwell too long on the dark figures that haunted her sleep; scattering the dust of their memories from her troubled mind. Huge, hairy monsters with hideously sharp teeth, reaching out for her from the dark corners of Hell.

She tried to rationalize it all and had even read in one of the many pregnancy magazines that littered her living room that it was perfectly normal to have such horrifying dreams purely due to the stress and insecurities of the new mother-to-be. As she lay there, the thought of spending the entire morning in bed crossed her mind briefly, but she remembered that the five apple trees she had ordered from the local nursery had arrived late the night before. They desperately needed to be planted and if *she* didn't do it, she knew that it would never get done.

Over the past month, due largely to her increasing size, Deanna had found it difficult to get the normal day to day business of running a household completed in just one day. Seth had offered to hire a housekeeper but she had declined on the grounds that she enjoyed running the house. If for nothing else than to keep her mind occupied and her hands out of the refrigerator. The tragic reality of it was that she didn't want to share her new husband and their new home with a stranger. The possibility that the stranger might even be thin and beautiful froze in her mind, there would be *no domestic help*. Then of course there was the swelling of her feet, the constant fatigue, and the periodic nausea that had made the last several weeks difficult to say the least. There would be no denying it, the simple fact was that the new and improved size of her stomach made doing *anything* difficult. Even sex.

Reluctantly, and only after her bladder demanded it, Deanna sat up and slipped her feet into her pink fuzzy pig slippers, dreamily making her way to the bathroom to pee. Not halfway down the hall she could feel the now daily movements of her overly active child pushing heavily on her already overloaded bladder. She picked up the pace and barely made it to the bathroom before the tide broke. The doctors that Deanna had been seeing on the fairly regular basis since she first realized she was pregnant all had told her the same thing; that the baby was *very* strong and *very* healthy. She had even started to wonder if they were mistaken about her due date, which was impossible since Deanna knew that they hadn't had unprotected sex until they were officially married. She had been adamant about that, she didn't want Seth to believe that she was a risky investment, not if she were ever going to get him to commit to a *real* relationship. In the end Seth agreed to marry her and start a family the right way, and even though it was true that the child had been moving around much more than she knew most did at an early stage in the pregnancy, Deanna just chalked it up to never smoking and Seth's obviously well formed genetics.

Deanna stood in front of the mirror and sighed, she looked positively puffy. If she put her chin down to her neck three chins popped up. Well, almost. It didn't matter the number, just that there were more staring back at her in the mirror than there should have been. With a sigh of disgust she pulled her eyes from the plump vision of herself and instead tried pulling her unruly red hair back into an off-center bun, but only managed to catch about half of it. A huff of air escaped her full lips, pushing up a red single curl from her brow line. Relinquishing her grip on the mess of curls she tried again, this time with a bit more success and managed to make a half decent bun. She stood there watching as the hot water pulsated from the faucet causing a swirl of steam to coil up and cloud the mirror. She was starving, her stomach began to growl loudly as she pulled the stopper for the sink and filled it with steaming water. With a few pumps of her favorite apricot face scrub she washed away the nights worries and focused on more important things, like breakfast.

Had she looked up at that passing second when her head was bent down and she was scrubbing away the dullness from her skin she would have seen the dark form of a woman as it pushed against the glass, its smoke like hand slipping through the confines of the glass and then floating down to gently caress the back of Deanna's head. The figure lingered only a moment and then in a puff of smoke dissipated into nothingness, leaving only the reflection of Deanna popping up from the sink with a soggy face and blindly groping for a towel to dry it.

She suddenly felt strange. Like someone was in the room with her, watching her. Quickly she dried her eyes and cast a nervous glance around the room. Nothing. She stepped tentatively out into the hallway to listen for something, but what? Had someone knocked at the door? No, that hadn't been it. She would have heard that clearly enough. This was more of a perceived feeling than an actual sound. Deanna waited and listened, still nothing.

Slowly she stepped back into the bathroom and this time locked the door. Normally she never even bothered to close the door while she was in the house alone. Today however she needed the extra security of the door not only being closed but also locked. Deanna suddenly felt the aching need to have Seth at home with her in order to not only keep her company but also to protect her.

There was no doubt that he could make her feel less alone and vulnerable.

She looked at her reflection in the mirror.

"You're being silly old girl. You're letting those nightmares into your waking life. Before you know it you'll be checking under all the beds for the Boogie Man." Deanna didn't like the way her words seemed hollow, how they seemed to bounce back off the walls with a flat, lifeless sound.

Quickly she brushed her teeth and plucked a few unruly eyebrow hairs before she made her way back into the bedroom to dress into something warm. Deanna had planed on planting the apple trees she and Seth had picked out from the local home improvement store only the other day. She told him that she wanted to catch as many days outside as she could before the winter snow set in so he had reluctantly agreed to let her do it herself. He had seemed a bit worried about the possibility of her over exerting herself but she assured him that she would take her time and have plenty of breaks in between trees. Hell, there were only three of them, not an entire orchard to plant and she managed to assure him that he was only being silly. After all, she was a big girl and she knew her body's own limitations. Deanna grabbed her rubber gardening boots out of the closet and headed down-stairs for something that at least resembled breakfast.

She had a good appetite even for that of a pregnant woman, but she admitted that her selections were not always healthy. Protein, and lots of it was high on her list of 'got to have it' foods and rare stake had become a staple in her once vegetarian diet. The animal rights activists that she had started to donate to on the monthly bases would be ashamed of her right now. Every time she bit into a thick slice of meat or devoured an almost raw slice of bacon she felt the despair and sorrow that the poor creature must have felt on it's way to the slaughter house. Her new animalistic taste buds however couldn't help but salivate for more, so she had started to donate more money for the cause. Her own form of redemption so to speak.

As she came to the bottom of the landing Deanna could see her husband's briefcase sitting on the floor, its black form propped up next to the small oak table in the house's main entrance. He would have normally stopped there to put on his coat and gloves and she would have held it for him had she been awake to see him off.

Deanna could play the scene out in her mind like a movie, his strong body moving with ease under his dark black suite and coat. Let's not forget the blue cashmere scarf that he always wore, setting off his steely eyes that burned into her like blue flames. Deanna had always had a *thing* for well dressed men, and Seth had to be the best she had ever laid her hungry eyes on. She pouted a bit at the thought of missing him. She knew she should have set her alarm and gotten up with him that morning and not lounged in bed like some sort of ripe watermelon. Her only excuse had been that she was so tired the night before that she'd decided to forego the normal morning ritual for the soft comforting allure of her bed. She chastised herself now, Seth wouldn't have left his briefcase behind if she had been there to see him off.

Deanna had already started to miss the intoxicating feeling of her husbands strong body against her own. She began to long for the secure feeling that she got when his arms were wrapped tightly around her, as if the whole world could dissolve around them and yet she would still be safe and loved. Her body's temperature jumped a few degrees at the mere thought of him.

She stood there with the large black leather-bound case in her hands, the leather soft and cool against her skin. She leaned her body against the small table, debating on what to do next. Absent mindedly she began to play with the case's zipper as each scene played out in her mind like a movie of the week. She thought to call him, but there would be no way for him to get back in time to get the case and then drive all the way back to the airport in order to catch his flight. Without a second thought she pulled her boots on and her over-sized plaid coat from the closet and grabbed her purse. She would try to catch him at the airport and not only deliver his briefcase that he had left behind, but also get the good-bye kiss that he had so shamefully neglected to give her as well.

Not more than five minutes down the road Deanna caught a glimpse of herself in the rearview mirror and immediately had second thoughts. She glared at her reflection, no make-up on and her hair was beginning to fall in wild ringlets from the loose bun she had it in. Looking like this was no way to make Seth miss her, not at all.

"Well, at least I remembered to brush my teeth," she commented half to herself and half to the tattered looking reflection that stared back at her in the rearview mirror.

Fifteen minutes later Deanna pulled her Champaign Mercedes into the short-term parking lot of the Pittsburgh International Airport and walked to the front entrance as fast as her over-burdened body would carry her. She made her way as quickly as she could past the countless travelers and their baggage, and politely pardoned herself all the way down the escalating sidewalk until she came to the main gates where only the people with actual tickets managed to get through. Deanna made her way as far up into the crowed as possible without actually entering the line. There she just skimmed the lines outskirts as she popped her head in and out of the clusters of people saying their good-byes.

All around her there was the low hum of background conversations punctuated with the occasional shrill cries of a child. The periodic thunderous roll of baggage as travelers rolled them tap-tap-tap down the tiled floors or rode past slowly on carts driven by men in dark blue uniforms with flashing bright blue lights. Deanna's mind swam through the muck in search of her husband. Just then, she caught sight of the back of his head. There was no mistaking him for anyone else; he was tall and broad shouldered, not to mention impeccably well dressed. His sandy blonde hair with a slight wave to it singled him out above all others.

She felt the familiar flutter of butterflies in her stomach as she gazed out at him, her body suddenly becoming warm and relaxed now that she held him in her line of vision. Deanna had been lucky enough to find him in time, he hadn't boarded the plane yet.

She smiled out at him. Early on in their relationship Seth made her feel like a young, awkward school girl that had managed to date a boy far out of her own league. In the time that elapsed since their marriage however Deanna was beginning to feel that she had somehow out grown the girl she used to be. She no longer thought about the differences in their social and economic background. She loved him and she knew without a shadow of doubt that he loved her back.

Deanna yelled his name out only for it to be stopped dead in its tracks by the impervious wall of noise that stood between them. She then tried rather successfully to maneuver her overly pregnant body through the crowd of people towards him. There she was stopped just as dead in her tracks as her voice had been.

Deanna's heart was shaken to its core and the smile she had worn only seconds before vanished from her quickly paling face. Seth had turned just enough to one side to make it possible for Deanna to see whom he was so intently listening to. The proverbial blonde bombshell with a sultry look in her eye, practically melting into him as she bent his head down to her mouth with a slender manicured hand. She spoke to him and smiled, her lips were close enough to lightly graze his ear. She lingered there suggestively before playfully pulling away. They were clearly traveling together, there was no doubt that they *knew* each other. Seth had never mentioned anyone ever accompanying him on his flights to and from England before, so Deanna had just assumed that he had been traveling alone all this time. Deanna now realized that she had assumed incorrectly.

Deanna was no longer conscious of the noise or the people around her, her surroundings blurred and shook with emotion. Her mind raced to find a logical, rational explanation for what she had been unfortunate enough to witness, but none came to her. Deanna's face was suddenly hot to the touch, her vision became a porthole size lens that had become focused solely on the couple in front of her. The seemingly perfect traveling companions that were lost in an intimate conversation of their own and interested in no one else in the world but each other. The pounding of her own heart beat out the screams of her mind to confront them, to push her way through the crowd of people and what?

Scream?

Cry?

Blatantly make one hell of a scene in front of thousands of people?

No. Somehow, someway, he would turn it back onto her. Turn it like he always did, at every opportunity he ever had. She knew he would, he was Seth Toumbs, and he could make *anything* her fault.

Right now all Deanna wanted to do was to get as far way from there as she could before he saw her and began his torrent of lies and evasions. Before that...that *woman* saw her, looking ever like the doughty housewife that she suddenly felt she had become. With tears running full tilt down her now burning crimson face, Deanna made her way to the nearest ladies room with Seth's briefcase still clenched tightly in her arms, all but forgotten.

Once safely inside Deanna rushed straight to the sink and washed her pulsating, hot face with cold water. The harsh florescent lights that burned from a multitude of softball sized bulbs made her squint at her reflection. Deanna looked around, for the most part the restroom was empty. Two stalls were occupied out of about fifteen. She clutched the side of the white porcelain sink to keep herself from collapsing as the cold water rushed down the drain like a geyser, after several moments her breathing began to steady. She waited like that for what seemed like hours until the last two ladies left her alone in the stark light of the restroom. She set the briefcase down in a puddle of water next to her on the large expanse of white tiled sink and continued to wash her face with cold water, sobbing deeply into her hands each time they came up and cupped her face. Her eyes and cheeks stung from her tears, the cold water slowly bringing calm to her body and the baby that had begun twisting in protest to the sudden rise in her blood pressure.

The two ladies had left hardly noticing the blotchy skin and swollen eyes of the woman washing her face, not caring really who she was or if she needed help in any way. Deanna suddenly felt horribly alone. She waited, no one else entered and after a moment she closed her eyes to compose herself, to think of what she would say to her husband. Then looking up at the mirror for a last supporting glance from her earth shaken reflection, she dialed Seth's cell phone.

The phone rang twice and his deep, heavy voice answered. "So you're awake. I thought for sure you'd still be dreaming away the morning hours."

You fucking cheat…how I hate you…

"The baby woke me," she managed to get out without being too affected by the warmth of his voice. "I was just about to drive up to the airport. You um…you left your briefcase. Do you think there is still enough time for me to get there?" Her voice broke a bit at the end, but not enough for him to notice, at least he didn't seem to anyway.

"No," he said quickly. "Don't worry yourself about that darling. There is nothing in there that I don't already have a copy of in my laptop. I just like to keep a back up in case I lose one of them. Just put it in the office for now and I'll update it when I get back. Too bad you didn't get up with me. I wouldn't have left it behind then. No problem though, as I said."

There it is…he's twisting it, making it all my fault.

There was a slight muffling over the phones receiver, as if he were covering it up with his hand. She could hear a woman's voice but couldn't make out what was being said. Her eyes welled with tears, her chin shook.

How could he do this to me…now…

"Must be a lonely flight," she managed to gasp out. "Seven or eight hours with nothing to do. I'm sure I would go crazy flying all alone, with no one to talk to." Her eyes narrowed waiting for him to say he was with someone this time; that he wasn't all alone this time and that he *did* have someone to talk to.

"The time goes fast believe it or not. I guess mostly because I manage to keep myself occupied throughout most of the flight. Speaking of which, you should too. I'm sure that if you kept yourself busy it would feel like I was home before you even had a chance to miss me."

There was the boom of the loud speaker as a woman's voice announced that flight 245 out of Pittsburgh International to Gatwick Airport was now boarding first class. Deanna wondered if the voice echoed on the phone, if he realized she were actually there in the airport. "I have to go now Deanna; they are starting to board first class. I'll see you in five days time. Take care of that baby for me while I'm away." Without waiting for a reply Seth hung up and the line went dead.

Deanna burst into a flood of tears. Seth was lying to her about being alone. There could be no doubting that he *was* having an affair. If he hadn't been, there would've been no reason for him to lie. No reason at all.

Take care of the baby... what about me?

After what seemed like an eternity in emotional Hell Deanna managed to pull herself together enough to leave the confines of the bathroom and go home. She couldn't help but think that it was going to be a long five days. Five days of her mind playing wicked games on her, evoking all sorts of dirty, adulterous deeds between her once loving husband and that cheap whore that he now seemed to favor over her. The vision of him gazing down at the other woman resurfaced itself in her mind, the look in his eye was unmistakable. She knew sexual desire when she saw it, and boy was it there. Was the woman she saw him with merely the flavor of the week or did they have a long standing relationship? Deanna fought back the desire to vomit, and wondered if he had even bothered to use a condom when he was with her. Her life was falling apart and now she had to worry about catching some God awful disease from her own husband.

She pulled off the highway at the first exit, her knuckles white with the amount of pressure she was exhorting as she gripped the wheel like she wanted to grip his throat and drove straight to her sister's house. As she opened the car door to get out she lost the battle to keep her stomach contents where they belonged and vomited in her sister's gravel driveway. Not much to worry about, after all she hadn't even had breakfast yet.

Her sister as usual was still asleep. She worked at a local nightclub until about five in the morning so it wasn't unusual for her to be in bed well past noon. Even though her sister Bridget was two years younger than she was, Deanna always felt she could depend on her to help her through anything, even this. Bridget was smart when it came to men…years of experience, she thought sourly. Bridget always did seem to have an excess of men hanging around her. Growing up she couldn't remember a Friday night that Bridget sat at home. Deanna on the other hand had plenty of Friday nights plopped down in front of the T.V. with their grandmother watching boring movies until Bridget finally staggered in around three a.m. drunk and disheveled. Deanna told herself it was because she had her standards, something her sister seemed to lack. If it had a penis and money Bridget was interested.

Even at that Deanna knew that she had to talk this out with her sister before Seth came home or she would surely lose her mind. Bridget would help to put things in perspective; she had always been good for that too. Perspective was one thing, but sympathy was quite another. Deanna knew her sister was more apt to play the roll mistress than that of the doting wife. A quality that had always made their already rocky relationship even more difficult, if that were even possible.

After about the fifth ring of the obnoxiously shrill doorbell, Bridget finally opened the heavy, multi-paneled door. Her hair was a mess of strawberry blond curls and her skin was it's normal alarmingly pale tone. If Deanna didn't know her she would have assumed Bridget was ill, but that was her normal color. She was forever that 'two hours dead' shade of grey-white, and refused to get any sun. The sun caused cancer, her sister had commented once when Deanna asked her to join Seth and her at the beach. That was months ago, *before* Deanna was showing her pregnancy so much that she didn't dare even step into a swim suite, let alone ware one in public.

There was a sparkle of left-over green glitter on her sister's left cheek, drawling attention to her fine facial features. There was not doubting that she was a beautiful woman, her paleness just seemed to make her look fragile and weak. Perhaps men liked to feel they were keeping her safe, protecting her; as if *she* needed protecting. Bridget could be as hard and as cold as the marble she resembled.

As she looked at Bridget the thought of her sister doing more than just dancing crossed her mind like it had done so many times before. She stood there in wrinkled pink kitty-cat pajamas that weren't buttoned properly, but she still managed to look like someone out of a Playboy centerfold.

Bridget squinted her eyes against the autumn sun. "What the hell are you doing here so early," she asked, leaving the door open behind her as she slowly retreated back into the darkness and warmth of the living room. If her sister would have gotten there just twenty minutes earlier she would have seen *them* leave, and she would have never been able to live it down. Last nights bonus left her sore all over.

"It's hardly early Bridget, it's past ten o'clock." Deanna closed the door behind her and immediately opened the heavy drapes that darkened the room, causing Bridget to moan in disgust.

"You know Deanna, I hate to break it to you but not all of us live in Never-Never land. Some of us actually work for a living." She grumbled.

More like get pounded for a living, she thought dimly to herself. *But it pays well.*

"What is it?"

There was no other way for Deanna to say it other than to just spit it out.

"I think Seth is having an affair."

That did it. Now she had Bridget's full attention.

"You have *got* to be shitting me," her look was one of both surprise and bewilderment. "I can't imagine *Seth* cheating on you. Hell, he's such a straight laced ass, I didn't think he had it in him." She couldn't help but chuckle a bit at the thought of him picking up some hooker in his new Mercedes and asking her not to touch anything, but then she managed to quickly pull herself together for her sisters sake. "What I mean to say is that he can't ever seem to get enough of you. Even now that you're pregnant he's still all hands." She made a squeezing gesture with her fingers and then curled up in a ball at the far end of the sofa, far enough back so as to be out of the harsh light of morning and tried desperately to hold in some of the warmth from the bed she had just reluctantly left. As she pulled her legs into her chest her body instantly flinched in pain. No matter, Deanna was too caught up in herself and that 'stick up the ass' husband of hers as usual to notice anything about her.

Deanna closed her eyes and thought about how much Seth had always been so turned on for sex. He still was, but only now it was with someone else.

Her stomach flip-flopped.

Never a night would pass when they didn't make love, even in her current condition and his sexual appetite was at times hard to quench. Her husband's darker desires weren't always granted and she wondered briefly in the back of her mind if the blond bitch had agreed to do things that she just couldn't bring

24

herself to do. Her face reddened in anger. Maybe if she *had* done what Seth wanted she wouldn't be going through this right now…maybe if she had been more like her sister. But that was unfair of her, Bridget was many things but she was still her sister and right now she needed her. In an act of total surrender Deanna threw up her arms and sat down next to Bridget and sobbed uncontrollably for a good five minutes.

"Maybe you should start at the beginning and tell me everything." Bridget pulled herself from the sofa and slunk to the front window, pulling the curtains shut just enough to soften the light from her eyes. "Do you want some coffee? I can make it strong enough for you to tell me what the hell happened between you two. I can even add some Bailey's if you like. I know it helps to clear *my* head."

"I'll pass on the Bailey's for now. It's still a bit early for me." Deanna tried not to sound *too* condescending but was unsuccessful.

Bridget let it pass, she knew her sister was in no condition to hide her true feelings about her right now so she let her have that one for free. She did however still make a mental note of it. Payback can be such a bitch.

Without skipping a beat she said, "did Seth tell you he was having and affair or did you bust the bastard doing it with someone?" The thought almost made her smile but she managed to hold desperately onto her poker face until the feeling passed. Bridget got up and went to the bar to pour herself half a glass of bourbon before heading into the kitchen to start a pot of strong coffee. She had only been sleeping for two hours and the thought of starting *this* conversation sober was absolutely unthinkable.

The vision of Seth trashing around naked in bed with another woman pulled on her mind. Even *she* had to admit that he wouldn't be the first guy that cheated on his pregnant wife. In her porthole sized view men were pigs, plain and simple. The wife got fat, and they went hunting…nothing new or remarkable there.

"No", her sister squirmed in her seat like a woman on the witness stand in court. "I followed him to the airport to bring him his briefcase and kiss him goodbye. He had somehow left the case behind this morning by the table in the foyer. That's when I saw him with some woman crawling all over him like some sort of sex crazed animal." Deanna almost snorted with disgust.

"Maybe she was just one of his clients, or perhaps even his secretary." Bridget looked down and noticed that the buttons on her pajamas were miss-matched and began realigning them, careful not to show the quickly purpling bruises on her breasts.

"I met his secretary, her name's Grace. She's old enough to be our mother. Besides, what *normal* woman acts like that if she's not sleeping with the guy. No Bridget, you should have seen him with her. The way he touched her, the way he looked at her. There is no way that she was *just* a client to him. Anyone with eyes in their head could've seen that." Deanna's focus drifted back to the harsh memory of the airport. Her eyes seemed to glaze over as if she were about to have an outer body experience that would end up going horribly wrong.

"I can't believe this is really happening. I'm still sort of waiting for my alarm clock to start ringing…if you know what I mean?" Bridget came back into the living room. "The coffee will be a bit longer. Do you want something to eat? There's half a dozen Danish in the kitchen. I'm a firm believer that there's nothing quite like a sugar high early in the morning to get your body moving."

"No thanks, I don't think I could keep anything down right now. The baby has been upset all morning. He hasn't stopped moving since I saw Seth at the airport with that woman." Bridget rubbed her belly. "I was thinking on the way over here that maybe Seth just can't handle the thought of becoming a father, he's still quite young after all. Maybe the thought of being someone's father has pushed him into the arms of another woman. A woman *without* any responsibilities of her own. He wouldn't be the first guy to go screaming off into the distance after realizing his whole life was about to change. Diapers and bottles at four in the morning could be enough to send the steadiest man running for the hills."

Bridget stood there looking at her sister, searching for the right things to say but was having a hard time coming up with anything constructive. They were far from close but she still felt a sort of sisterly tie to her and she didn't want to come off like she didn't give a rats ass one way or the other. Besides, it was hard for her to sound caring for a sister that she had no respect for. Deanna had been such a strong woman before she met Seth. Now she was like some sort of lapdog waiting for a scrap of meat or a pat on the head. She made her sick.

"I just don't know what to tell you Deanna. Seth is the last person I would suspect of fucking around with someone else. But if you suspect there is more going on here than just business to client relations then you're probably right. Most women usually are right about that sort of thing I'm afraid. Hell I should

26

know really, I'm usually the one they're seeing on the side." Bridget sat down next to her and draped her arm around her shoulder, her arm came up slower than it normally would have but Deanna didn't seem to notice. "I suppose some women just choose to look the other way and ignore their womanly intuition all together. Sometimes I think it must be easier than a messy divorce, not to mention the husband is usually so gilt ridden that they buy their wives all sorts of expensive gifts. You would be surprised just how many of them choose the trinkets over their husbands fidelity. Especially if they have been married for a long time. It's almost like after a while the wife actually *expects* her husband to cheat on her and therefore she somehow manages to find it in her heart's to excuse him for his sudden laps in good judgment. Crazy really if you think about it."

There was an awkward, almost physical pause between them. Bridget could hear the clock above the bar in the living room ticking away as they sat there in silence. The grinding seep of the hands began to grate on her worn out nerves and she began to wonder to herself how much longer she would need to console her sister before she finally decided the only resolution to her problem was to just go home and wait for him to return from England so that they could have it out in private. Either that or she could just ignore the problem all together and chalk it up as one of life's little slaps on the ass while you're not looking.

Deanna was the one to break the mind numbing silence. "I think he may have been seeing her all along you know. Sometimes late at night I would hear him leave the house. At first I used to be frightened, so I asked him about it. He assured me that it was nothing and that he just needed to think…to clear his head, and the best way for him to do that was by taking a walk at night when everything was quiet. He always had so much work to do, deadlines and demanding clients, that I never really questioned him again after that. He never took the car, so I never imagined until now that he could be seeing another woman. After today though I imagine that he probably met her somewhere close. Perhaps even at the local park since it's just at the bottom of our hill and then went on ahead to her place. Early the next morning when he finally came home he would head straight into the shower before I even had a chance to see him and stay in there for ages. No doubt washing the smell of what I would imagine to be her cheap, foul smelling perfume from of his body.

"He stayed out all night and you didn't think that was important?" A critical look passed over Bridget's face, but she managed to reign it in. "I'm not sure if that's stupidity talking or naivety."

Deanna looked at her, the hurt from her words reflected in her eyes.

"I'm sorry Deanna, it's just that you've had a bit more warning than just today's little incident, and yet you sit here acting totally shocked by the whole thing."

"I feel so stupid Bridget. You're right of course about everything. Why didn't I confront him when I had the chance? Why didn't I at least follow him to see where he went at night?" Deanna's eyes welled up again with tears that threatened to spill over at any moment. "I don't know what I will do if she takes him away from me. I can't raise this child on my own. I'm not single mother material, I'm just not strong enough."

After a few quiet moments of inner conflict as Deanna struggled with herself as to the best route to follow for not only herself but for her family she finally resolved her mind to the only thing that seemed at the time to make any sense. She had to enlist the help of her sister. Bridget would in essence become her eyes and her ears. She would do for her what she could not do for herself in her current condition.

Deanna sat up with a determined look plastered squarely on her face and turned to Bridget. "I want you to follow them."

"Bridget half laughed. "You have got to be kidding me Deanna. I can't just pick up and go chasing after your husband. I've got work obligations and a life of my own; not to mention Buster needs looking after."

They both looked over at the overfed and under-exercised black tomcat lounging on the other end of the sofa half asleep, half listening to snippets of their conversation. His head perked up a bit at the mention of his name, but realizing it wasn't going to be accompanied by anything interesting to eat; he lay back down and thoroughly ignored them.

They both sat in the suddenly stark silence of the room, mulling over their own thoughts as the smell of rich, dark coffee filled the room.

"I think the coffee is done," said Bridget with a sniff of the air, but neither of them attempted to move.

"I need you to do this for me Bridget. Take some time off; I know you must have some vacation days coming to you. There are other singers, other acts at the club that will gladly cover for you. I can stay here with Buster and make sure he is well taken care of while you're away. I'll even pay you for your lost wages. I need you to find out if my marriage is a lie. I need you to help me get my life back. My life *and* my pride." Deanna's tone was flat and hollow, like a woman about to accept the worst in life as just that…life.

Bridget sat there considering her options. What options? There were none. None that she would be able to live with, at least not with any form of pride. Her big sister, check that, her *pregnant* big sister was sitting on her sofa practically begging her to find out what was going on with her tattered marriage and she was even willing to pay for everything. A free holiday abroad and all she had to do was check up on Seth. The only thing that stuck in her craw about this whole thing was that fact that her sister just assumed that she would be willing to drop everything and do this for her. It's not like they were that close anymore. But she figured that after all Deanna *was* her sister, and isn't that what sisters are supposed to do? Help them to fix their totally fucked up lives.

"Okay, I'll do it. But how am I supposed to find him? It's not like I know my way around England."

"I still have his briefcase that he left behind in my car. It has all his addresses, phone numbers, and contacts in England I swear Bridget it won't be difficult at all and I'll pay for everything."

"That's the least of my concerns right now Deanna. What if he sees me? What if he finds out I've been sent there to spy on him by you? How am I going to explain my being in England without telling him everything?" She went to the bar for another glass of bourbon. This was becoming far too complicated, far too quickly. Just like everything else in her life these days.

For a moment Bridget considered not only going to England, but never coming back. The thought of reinventing herself sparked something deep inside her. She could make herself over into someone new and interesting and never feel the need to look back. It's not like there was anything there for her, not really. She could even change her name if she wanted to, the possibilities were endless.

Deanna pulled her back into the moment. "Just make sure that doesn't happen. I'll be right back, just let me get his briefcase from the car. Then I will call the travel agent and get you a plane ticket. You should call work now; I need you to leave tonight."

Deanna will never change will she? Always the bossy little bitch, demanding that things be done her way and in her time. That's one thing I won't ever miss. thought Bridget.

Bridget doubted that there was any way for her to get out of going now even if she wanted to, not that she did. It might even be kind of fun chasing down Deanna's husband like some sort of seedy, back ally bounty hunter. There seldom seemed to be room for Bridget's opinion in anything when it came to her relationship with her sister, but this time she was willing to let her have her way.

"Okay sis it's a deal. I'll check on him for you if you promise to watch Buster and foot the bill." Bridget toasted her sister and gulped back what was left of her bourbon and smiled. Today just might be her lucky day after all.

Caught in the whirlwind that was Deanna's life, Bridget picked up the phone and dialed her employer. She managed to come up with some half-baked story of a relative in trouble and that she needed to leave town tonight, not far from the truth really. She was reassured that there wouldn't be a problem to find a fill in for her, even with such a short notice vacancies were filled almost immediately. Work was money and "performers" like Bridget needed all the work that they could get.

Just as Bridget was hanging up the phone's receiver Deanna came back in and handed her the leather-bound briefcase with all of Seth's business information in it. "I looked through it while I was sitting in the parking lot at the airport to see if I could find the name of the woman he was with, but I didn't find anything. It does however have the address of the hotel where he always stays on the second page, along with the phone number there and a few other contact names. All of which I noticed are men. I'm beginning to wonder if that's just his way of keeping me happy, all the *male* names I mean. Maybe they are really all *women* he is meeting out there and he has just changed the names to trick me into believing that these trips of his are only business related when clearly they are not. I can't help but wonder if maybe the last year of my life has been nothing but a horrible joke at my expense."

She is really grasping at straws now. Somehow I don't think Seth is that smart, thought Bridget smugly.

No matter how hard she tried, Deanna couldn't shake the memory of him bending down and listening so intently to the woman standing next to him at the airport. The way he looked at her, the way she touched him and smiled. The baby kicked violently inside her as her temperature began to rise as the vision danced in front of her. She had been so foolish to trust him.

"Let me use your phone for a moment, I need to call the travel agent and get you a ticket for the next available flight. You will be able to pick it up at the check in counter at the airport. That's the way Seth always does it." Deanna made the call and paid for the ticket with her visa card, arranging for Bridget to pick it up at the check in desk under her name.

"You are going to have to travel under my name. Luckily I always have my passport with me so you will be able to take that along with you and don't forget that you'll be using my credit cards while you're over there as well. We look enough alike that there shouldn't be any trouble."

"Let's hope so anyway, there is no way I would be able to get a passport tonight unless it was a fake, and possibly not even at that." Bridget sat there looking at her sister who had all but recovered from her ordeal. "Well, I guess I should go and get packed then. What *does* one wear to spy on a cheating husband in England at this time of year?" She smiled and hugged her sister, trying desperately to fight off the suddenly overwhelming feeling that they were both making a terrible mistake.

"Black. I'm sure any spy worth his weight would be dressed in black." Deanna hugged her back; she always could make things better for her. Even when there was no way of making anything good come of something, Bridget always managed to make her feel like she could breathe again.

"Thanks Bridget, I really don't know what I would have done without you here to help me."

"You would've had to hire a private eye like the rest of the world, that's what." Bridget remarked and left the room to pack.

Deanna filled the time by having her calls forwarded on to Bridget's phone so that if Seth did call he wouldn't have any reason to suspect anything, not that he would. She would stay at her sisters until she was certain that everything was okay. If it wasn't, she decided right then and there that she would have all the locks in the house changed and her divorce attorney on speed dial. There was no way she was going to let Seth get away with this and not have the foresight to provide for herself and her child.

Finally alone in her bedroom Bridget quickly made the bed, rolled the several used condoms that had littered the floor in toilet paper and threw them in the trash. The cash that was left of the dresser she counted again, four hundred dollars. Not bad for one nights work, a bit on the rough side but nothing she couldn't handle. Which was far more than could be said for her sisters

31

situation. The thought of Deanna sobbing over a cheating husband made her want to puke.

Bridget had always been a practical woman, use who you can, when you can, and don't be surprised if it all turns into shit in the end. Her sister on the other hand was a fucking romantic. Who needed love and family anyway? From the looks of what was currently happening to her sister Bridget figured it wasn't much different than what she did. The one vital difference between them was that Bridget *never* cried over a man. Never.

Within seconds Bridget's handcuffs and mouth gag along with a vast array of sexual devices were safely packed away from Deanna's prying eyes. Bridget wasn't ashamed of what she did, at least that's what she told herself, but she wasn't going to risk her sister nebbing through her private belongings. Hell, because of her profession Bridget's house was already paid for and she never wanted for anything money could buy. But the mere thought of Deanna judging her from where she sat so high up on that golden throne of hers was more than she could stand. Besides, Bridget preferred that her sister believe she was some sort of a starving performer. It suited Bridget's sister rather well to feel she had done better than she did in life. At the same time Bridget was content with knowing that wasn't the case at all and that if you really took into consideration all aspects of their lives, it was actually Bridget that came out on top. After all, she wasn't the one begging her sister to follow her cheating husband while she stood by helpless and pregnant with his child.

She went to her closet and took out her new Louis Vuitton matching luggage and chose to take only the small carry on. She couldn't imagine there would be much need to over-pack, after all she was sure she wouldn't be there for long, and if she *did* decide to stay there and never come back she would just call a few of her friends and have them send the rest of her belongings over. Bridget had more than a few people that owed her on a rather large scale. She figured that even the sale of her house would be rather simple when it came right down to it.

One or two nights would be all it would take to find out if Seth was up to no good. Bridget threw in some warm, comfortable jeans and a few shirts. Four changes of panties and two bras. She already had a separate travel case of make-up that she took with her on "extended ventures" so she just tossed that in along with everything else. She was packed and ready to leave in under thirty minutes.

Bridget went back into the living room to see how far her sister had gotten with her flight arrangements. Deanna was sitting on the living room sofa scribbling down some of the contact names and phone numbers from Seth's briefcase, she had obviously finished with the flight reservations and had continued on with other things.

"I'm all packed and ready to go. I guess I'll just catch some sleep on the plane if I can. What time is my flight?" asked Bridget, setting her overnight bag on the sofa next to Buster.

"Not for another four hours." Deanna got up from the sofa and stood in front of her sister. The paper she was writing on still clutched tightly in her hand. "Why don't you jump in the shower and freshen up? You look like Hell." She smiled at her and touched her sister's arm. "Besides, that way I can finish jotting down some of the information in his book, just in case you need me to follow you out there. I can't imagine why you would, but you never know. Better safe than sorry mom always used to say. Now I want you to call me as soon as you get in, and then again when you find Seth." Deanna stood there for a moment. "Promise not to keep anything from me Bridget. I want you to tell me everything. I *need* you to tell me everything."

"I promise that I will find out all I can about what's really going on, and don't worry. I won't hold anything back." Bridget looked down at her cat. "Just don't let Buster starve."

"Don't worry, I stress eat as I'm sure you remember so Buster will probably gain even more weight." She looked over at him, a deep hum of contentment radiating from his enormous body.

"That is if it's even possible for him to get any bigger. Why don't you put that thing on a diet?"

You're one to talk Deanna, can't say you're looking too slim these days, thought Bridget.

Bridget glared at her. Buster might not be her *kid* but he was as close as she was ever going to get and the fat remarks were beginning to get under her skin. If she recalled correctly the last time her sister decided to grace Bridget with a visit she made the same sort of derogatory remarks about her poor cat Buster. Bridget decided right then and there to make a mental note to let her sister know just how fat *her* kid was when the little tubo was born. Then she would see how *she* liked it.

"Yah, well…I guess I'm going to hit the shower then. Feel free to put the tube on, there's ice cream in the freezer if you feel you need a little frozen dairy therapy. I know it does wonders for me."

With that said Bridget left the room to get a shower and Deanna went to the freezer for a mega serving of ice cream. Bridget always kept a well-stocked freezer of what she liked to call "frozen dairy therapy" At any given moment one could find at least four kinds of ice cream sitting there just waiting to cure anything that ailed you from blind dates gone horribly wrong to menstrual cramps rough enough to make you curl up in bed and stay there for days. This time though Deanna was sure that not even all the Ben & Jerry's in the world could make her feel any better.

Chapter 3

Two hours later Bridget was standing in line waiting with Deanna to claim her flight ticket for United Airlines flight 622, nonstop to Gatwick Airport. Bridget hadn't imagined that her first trip to England to be a spy mission, but there she was, waiting in line half asleep and sore as Hell from the night before.

All of this running around just to track down her sister's cheating husband, if he even *was* cheating that is. Deanna had always had a way of exaggerating things so out of proportion that Bridget was sure that Seth didn't even *know* the woman he was being accused of sleeping with.

Seth had always seemed to her to be a stand-up sort of guy. He never made a pass at *her* anyway, not like some of the slime balls Deanna used to bring home before landing this one. Bridget had always been careful not to ever let them get very far with her. She *did* however make sure to let them get just far enough to prove to her big sister that they weren't worth the toilet paper that she wiped her ass with. Bridget didn't think that her sister resented the fact that her would-be boyfriends always seemed to be attracted to her. It wasn't as if she did anything to lead them on, not really anyway. But who really knows another person, or for that matter, how *anyone* other than themselves thinks or feels? Still, Bridget thought she had to trust her a Hell of a lot more than she thought she did to send her out after her husband. Even though a private eye would have done a much better job and without any possible form of personal interest or involvement.

After producing Deanna's passport and credit card as her own and being granted not only the ticket but a courteous smile from the booking agent, Bridget and Deanna took the escalator to the second floor to find the right terminal for her flight. It was at this point that Deanna could no longer accompany her sister and they said their goodbyes.

"Make sure you call me as soon as you get to the hotel. I have written down all the information you will need on this paper. I've decided that I should

probably keep Seth's book with me just in case something should happen."
Deanna handed Bridget the tattered looking paper she had been scribbling on
and hugged her awkwardly.

"No worries. I will call as soon as I get a room and let you know how the
flight went." Bridget folded the paper and stuck it in the back pocket of her
jeans. "I'm sure everything will turn out to be just one big misunderstanding."
She smiled and turned from her, making her way through the crowd of travelers
as quickly as she could so as to break the uncomfortable static between them.

In a matter of minutes Bridget had filed in line behind an on slot of weary
travelers and waited her turn as the line moved slowly ahead. Everything that
happened there on the second floor seemed to move rather quickly and luckily
for her without any baggage to check, and only a small carry on, she wasn't
stopped to have her luggage x-rayed or even searched. Which was more than
could be said about the large family in front of her with three kids and about
ten bags. I'm sure someone must have seen them as a national threat since they
were escorted to the side to have their belongings searched and their body's
scanned. Thank you Homeland Security.

Unfortunately though for her before she knew it Bridget was smack dab
in between the small window of the plane and a guy with enough aftershave
on his body that she could *taste* him before she even had a chance to sit down
next to him.

"Well *hello* darlin', this must be my lucky day!" The man grinned at her,
his eyes scanning every inch of her as she passed by him and slid into her seat.
"My name is Earl...Earl Jenkins." He licked his lips. His eyes never really
made it to her face since they seemed stuck on her ample cleavage.

Bridget didn't skip a beat but flashed a bright, friendly smile at him and
buckled her seatbelt.

"Nice to meet you...Earl is it?"

"Sure is." The man nodded, his gaze finally coming up for air from being
locked onto her breasts.

Bridget locked onto his bloodshot eyes.

"Well Earl, I hate to be a bother but do you think you will be needing your
air sickness bag?" She pointed over at the white paper bag that was sticking
out of the pocket behind the seat directly in front of him.

Earls smile began to fade.

"Well, no..."

"Would you mind give'n it to me? You see I suffer from the most *horrible* motion sickness. Hell I can't even watch car chases on TV without a bucket next to me…Projectile vomiting, if you get the picture."

Earl quickly handed Bridget the bag and looked down the isle behind him in search of an empty seat. Obviously he *had* gotten the picture and it was more than he had bargained for.

"You keep it."

"Thanks Earl, you're a doll baby." Bridget flashed another smile but Earl was no longer interested. He was still scoping out the back of first class, hoping to find that empty seat.

Bridget sank back into her seat and put her headphones on. There were enough movies to watch on the small screen in front of her to kill seven or eight hours easy. Two Dramamine pills and a glass of white wine later Bridget was fast asleep, dreaming of dumb bimbos and sleazy husbands.

Chapter 4

Seven and a half hours later when Bridget's plane touched down at Gatwick International Airport her new friend Earl was nowhere to be found. He had obviously found another, more accommodating seat elsewhere on the plane. Perhaps even one that didn't come along with the risk of being vomited on by some woman. Bridget smiled to herself, it was good to know that that little trick didn't just work in cabs.

They all waited there for another forty-five minutes for them to do whatever it is that pilots do before they finally let you off the plane. Bridget imagined that they all just sat around up front talking and laughing without anything more important to do than find out what bar they were all going to hit as soon as they were off. Finally they were all instructed to leave the now smothering confines of the plane and Bridget, along with the other passengers, lined up in single file in order to get out, and on with their boring earthbound lives.

Bridget, along with about two hundred other tired and hungry people were herded like sheep down a ramp and through a poorly lit winding hallway, who's carpeting had become soiled and worn with age, only in order to line up again to collect their luggage. Moments later the conveyer belt sprang into life, dutifully spinning around on its silver metal cables the wares of forlorn travelers, thus allowing them to pass on through to customs. The mass of people stood there in small, abstract clusters around it's perimeter. Young couples cuddled together, their hands in each others back pockets wearily leaning against each other for loving support. Older couples opted for the surrounding benches, content to let those in a greater hurry than themselves to retrieve their belongings first. Families with sleeping tots tossed over one shoulder, the stress of the long trip weighing as heavily on their faces as their kid's did on their body's. Men and women dressed in all branches of military uniforms stood with "stuffed to the seams" duffel bags, each returning home from far off locations stood along side tattered looking college students with not much more then the clothes on their backs. All of them could be coming or going, it was hard to tell which. Each with that same distant look splashed across their faces, the look that said that they would rather be *anywhere* but here.

When it came time for Bridget to make any declarations (whatever that might mean) and to tell the man standing behind the counter in a rather bland uniform, why she was even there in the first place, she just couldn't help but blurt it all out. To air her dirty laundry, as her mother would have said. Never the less it gave her great satisfaction to say it out loud to another human being.

"I'm here spying on my sister's husband if you really must know," she smiled as brightly as she could muster under the circumstances. "She wants *me* to drop everything and fly all the way over here to see if he is really cheating on her with this blond she saw him leave the States with "ON BUSINESS" but somehow he had neglected to inform his wife that he had an attractive female traveling companion." She even made the little quotation marks with her fingers when she said "on business." Bridget was rather impressed that she managed to say it all in one haggard breath.

What could the man say in response to that? The bland man in his bland uniform looked at her for a moment with a sort of half smile on his face and then stamped her passport. "Happy hunting," he said in a not so happy voice. "I hope you enjoy your stay here in England." Honestly, what more could be said?

"Thank you. I hope everything turns out to be just one big misunderstanding." She winked at him in her usual seductive way. Taking her passport from his grasp she headed out to the main lobby and on to exchange her dollars for pounds, find some real food, and then perhaps look into getting a taxi to the hotel.

Bridget looked around the cramped airport. Newspaper and gift shops littered the place from one end to the other, each with their own offerings of food and drink. Almost none of them were familiar to her, and since she had never really had British food before she opted for a McDonalds. Something familiar was just what she needed. Two cheeseburgers and a triple thick chocolate milkshake later she was feeling something close to normal again. The slight bout of nausea that she had suffered at landing had all but vanished as she slowly regained her land legs. Bridget decided that some fresh air would help to extinguish the suffocating feeling she was beginning to have sandwiched in-between all those people as she made her way through, and out of, the tightly packed airport.

Well over an hour after landing she was finally standing outside the airport waving down the next cab driver that came along.

"Can you take me to 2121 Fairfield Circle? Laurendale Manner, at least that's what I think it's called. Do you know where I mean?" Bridget leaned over in order to have a bit of eye contact with the taxi driver. He seemed to enjoy the view of her ample cleavage as she rested just outside the window.

"Sure, I know where it is, nice place…if you have the money that is," he wasn't looking at her face. "I'll have you there in no time, get in." The driver gestured to the back seat and started the meter as Bridget got in. The back of the cab was amazingly clean. Not at all like the ones she had on occasion ridden in on nights when she needed a quick and efficient ride home. Randomly throughout the ride she would catch him watching her from the rear view mirror, his eyes always migrating towards her breasts. She had to bite back the normal reflex of asking if his problem was that he had never seen *real* breasts this large before. Instead of being vulgar towards him, since this *was* a sort of vacation after all, she just tried to ignore the old fool as best she could.

The road trip, which Bridget was sure had taken much longer than necessary, wound it's way through a vast array of small hamlets and tight knit communities that ran along a great stretch of windy, single lane country roads until she could see the large manner rise up as if out of nowhere. It's somber magnificence perched high on a rural hill and surrounded by a patchwork of farmer's fields. It most assuredly had been at one time in its long and prosperous existence a castle, or at the very least the home of some important and influential diplomat. Now it had become nothing more than a stuffy old meeting place for businessmen and their "women".

The vision of Deanna sitting on her living room sofa and breaking down into a fit of hysterics burst into Bridget's mind again like it had done countless times before on the long trip over from America. Skirting that thought, but just outside her perception, was a great deal of deep seeded resentment. As displaced as it was, it was still there. Still leaking its poison into her thoughts. The vast part of her really *did* wish to help her sister. But never the less, the quiet, more subtle part of Bridget wanted nothing more than to be left alone and to leave her sister to deal with her own problems.

The exterior of the estate looked as if it had been expertly chiseled right from the very stones of the surrounding hillside itself. Had Bridget been able to walk the perimeter of the grand old manner she would have seen where the rear of the house did indeed vanish into the hillside surrounding it, like a cancerous tumor on the earth. In a somewhat futile effort to soften the homes hard lines, blood red canvas awnings had been installed over every window, but the only improvement that they had succeeded in was to help splash a little color against its otherwise dull brown exterior. The equally dull, but never the less sufficient, brown gravel drive that wound its way up to Laurendale Manner was flanked on either side by a guard of tall, impervious evergreens, giving Bridget a feeling of being boxed in by living walls. It was positively claustrophobic.

Was it keeping something out or keeping something in, thought Bridget.

With the hour growing late and the sun beginning to set in the deep violet sky gas torches had been lit intermittently along the way to the house. Each one casting long, dancing shadows against the opposite dark walls of living greenery. Finally the taxi came to a stop and Bridget got out, the night air had become cold and damp. As the evening wind picked up Bridget pulled her heavy, green cable knit sweater closer about her neck, covering the taxi drivers view of her breasts. A vague look of disappointment appeared on his face as he unloaded what passed for her luggage from the trunk of the small cab. Bridget pretended not to notice and instead rifled through her purse in order to produce a small, brown leather wallet from which she pulled her newly acquired British pounds. After some mental deliberation on her part she paid him the amount that showed in glowing red numbers on the meter, plus a nice tip.

The old man counted his money and smiled. "Here's my card Miss. When you're ready to leave this place you just give me a call. Old Mac will make sure to get you where you need to go." His face seemed a bit more weathered in the fading light than it had before, more vulnerable.

"I'll do that. Thanks." Bridget smiled back at him.

Taking the small overnight bag from him and putting its thin, brown leather strap over her shoulder Bridget made her way up the torch lit walkway to Laurendale Manner's grand front door. The air became even damper and smelled vaguely of earthworms as she neared the front door causing a deep chill to run down her spine, catching on every vertebrae of her back on its way down and spreading like icy finger tips over her body in a wave of goose pimples. Somewhere, not far off in the distance crows cried out to each other in the fading light of day, breaking the silence like thin glass in the heavy, confining air that seemed to hang around the place like a deep depression.

The front door was massive; solid Carpathian oak, with black iron hinges the size of Bridget's fist. Bridget had barely made it onto the large, brown stone slab that doubled as a patio, when the heavy door slowly swung open, assisted by a tall, porcelain-skinned woman. Her long black hair was held back from her face in a tightly wrapped, smooth bun, accented by a strikingly beautiful hair clasp made of pewter or silver from the look of it. When the woman turned her head Bridget thought it reminded her of a warriors shield that had been decorated with fine jewels. The woman herself was quite beautiful if not a bit on the dark side of conventional beauty. Her eyes were the palest shade of blue that Bridget had ever seen and her skin was so white that it too had a shadow of blue to its smooth surface. She was dressed in a long black dress of heavy fabric, possibly a wool tweed, no doubt to help keep the damp chill out. It made the woman look painfully prim and proper from head to toe. The one true spot of color on her was the blood red lipstick that graced her full lips. Bridget began to feel the uncomfortable twinge of jealous embarrassment as she thought of how she must look in comparison to the creature before her. She reassured herself that she had been traveling and that no one looked good after eight hours on a plane. Even so, she figured that if the boys back home saw *this* dark beauty she might lose a customer or two. She had the look of a dominatrics if she ever saw one, but what did she care? The woman standing in front of her might look the part but not many women could play such a demanding part, at least not very well at any rate. Even Bridget, for as emotionally hard as she was, felt more comfortable playing the slave. Domination wasn't one of her strong points, although there had been plenty of times when she wished it had been.

"Welcome to Laurendale Manner," the woman smiled, stepping back into the foyer she led Bridget into the large estates main hall, closing the heavy door behind them with a dull thud. "Do you have a reservation?"

The heaviness that Bridget felt outside became amplified by ten when she walked through the front door of the old manner. The air was stale and lifeless, almost sour, like milk that had been sitting out in the summer heat. She wrinkled her nose unintentionally as she fought back the desire to breath through her open mouth.

42

Bridget never noticed the massive creatures that lurked behind the counter, watching her, smelling her, their black, hunched forms would have only been visible in the low light of the room if they had moved. Their eyes seared into her flesh; bright blue eyes like nothing from this world. Not human, not really, yet too intelligent to be animal in origin. They sat as still and as lifeless as the furniture that surrounded them. Watching and listening to their new guest intently, her smell as sweet and as enticing as honey dripping slowly from the cone. They began to salivate.

"No, I'm sorry, I haven't got a reservation. I hope that won't be too much of a problem." Bridget couldn't help but think there wouldn't be any problem at all; not another living soul could be seen or heard in the vast emptiness of main hall and no other cars were parked outside on the wide gravel parking lot.

"We have over twenty-five, well appointed suites here at Laurendale Manner. There is almost always *something* available to fit in a last minute guest. Luckily for you, at this time of year we are more apt to be a bit on the empty side of things, what with the weather changing so soon." Her accent, although clearly not American, also wasn't English, as Bridget had expected it to be. She thought it was perhaps more European; but seeing as Bridget had never really traveled outside her own borders; it was hard for her to place it.

"Well, it's a good thing for me then that you *do* have a room available. I'm sure that my ride has already left, he didn't seem like the sort of guy who would hang around for too long." Bridget's smile was wide, she brushed her bangs from her eyes in order to see the woman better. Bridget followed the dark beauty to a large, oversized desk of intricately carved dark wood. She couldn't help but think that while the outside had been softened in an effort to make the place look a bit more approachable, the inside had somehow been grossly overlooked. It definitely was *not,* in any way your typical hotel lobby, the main hall looked dark and unwelcoming, perhaps even intimidating, not the kind of place you would see splashed across a vacation brochure summoning the wife and kiddies out for a weekend in the countryside.

"If you will just sign the registry, I will call the boy down to show you to your room. May I assume that it will only be you that is staying with us? A single bed perhaps?" A small, thin smile crept across the woman's crimson lips.

"Yes, it's just going to be me. I'm not exactly sure how many nights I will be needing if that's all right? I'm on a bit of a fact finding mission for a friend really." Bridget handed the woman her credit card and within a few moments she was on the phone, calling for someone to come down and help Bridget with her bags and see her to her room.

The woman handed her back the Visa card and smiled.

"My name is Eva; if there is anything I can get for you while you're staying here with us there is a phone in every room. Just dial zero." Eva glanced down at the registry, "It's nice to meet you Mrs. Toumbs…Deanna is it?" A curious look passed over the woman's face, as if she knew she wasn't Deanna. Impossible, she was just feeling guilty. It wasn't as if the credit card was stolen.

Bridget quickly nodded in response; at first she had almost forgotten that Deanna had insisted that she go by *her* name. The fact that she was using her sister's credit cards and passport would have made it impossible *not* to do so.

"Can you tell me if I have I been unfortunate enough to have missed dinner? I'm a bit starved to be honest, I could eat just about anything. The food on the flight over was less than satisfying," grumbled Bridget. Her stomach growled in agreement. She could have eaten just about anything at that point. Even the mystery food from the crowded airport would have tempted her now. The smell of it had been rather tantalizing to her stomach, it was her brain that managed to get in the way. Suddenly 'Shepherds Pie' sounded marvelous, even though she wasn't quite sure what it was.

"Dinner will be served in about an hour from now. The main dining hall is through there and to your left." Eva pointed behind Bridget to a hall leading out of the main lobby. "I will send the boy up to get you if you like when it is ready? If you're not sure if you can wait that long you can just tell the boy and he will show you what to do."

"Is it possible to get something sent to my room and skip the dining room all together? I'm really very exhausted and would like to just relax tonight if at all possible. Maybe even take a hot bath if the room has one?"

"All the rooms are fully equipped with tubs and showers for your convenience. The boy will show you where to find a full list of foods that our chef can make for you at your request. The number to the kitchen will be in your room, they will be more than happy to have whatever you like sent up to your room if that is your desire."

Within moments a young, dark haired boy, possibly not even out of school yet, joined them and without a word took Bridget's single overnight bag from her shoulder and led her through the main hall and up an immense wooden staircase that formed a high arch over the center of the dimly lit hall below. Tall, white marble Grecian statues flanked each side of the balcony, gazing down with lifeless eyes onto the door below, welcoming guests with their own special brand of hospitality. Most of the walls that Bridget could see were covered with dark, knotty wood paneling to a height of about four feet, the rest of the way up the wall had been hung equally dark colored wallpaper. Running at six foot intervals down the hall were hung heavily ornate brass sconces that cast a warm, soft glow against the wall, illuminating the deep carrion red of the wallpaper and then fading again into heavy darkness. The gently worn carpeting that ran its way up the entire length of arching steps and down the far reaching halls at either side was dyed a deep claret. The pattern of which mimicked that of the wallpaper with its tan vines that twisted into a virtual sort of life, becoming almost three dimensional at first to Bridget, that is until her eyes were able to focus better. Then they became just another regular, everyday, lifeless pattern that could be found on any hotel floor.

From the top of the stairs where Bridget now stood she could clearly see the front door and the great expanse of main hall beneath her. She had started off after the boy when Bridget was stopped dead in her tracks as she caught sight of the door as it began to swing slowly open and saw none other than Seth Toumbs coming in out of the damp night air. Draped on his arm was none other than the curvy blonde that Deanna must have been so upset about. From first appearances she was right to be upset, the woman was all over Seth. The woman's hands and lips made more contact than a politician seeking re-election, and Seth didn't seem to be in too much of a hurry to form any sort of formal protest.

With a snort of pure disgust Bridget quickly ducked out of sight and followed the boy to her room. She would still have to call her sister and let her know that she made it to the hotel in one piece, but she hesitated at the thought of telling her what she had just witnessed. Promise or no promise, she needed to find out a bit more about what was going on with Deanna's husband before she flew off the handle and blabbed everything to her sister. She just couldn't bring herself to do it, at least not yet. Besides, Deanna wouldn't be expecting her to find the love birds so quickly. Bridget would have more than enough time to do a little eavesdropping of her own and then later when she had gotten all the juicy details she would be able to find the right way to tell her. That is if there even *was* a right way to tell her sister that she was right to suspect that her husband was cheating on her with a cheap imitation of Marilyn Monroe.

From somewhere deep inside Bridget's mind the whispers came that perhaps her sister deserved what was happening to her. After all, Deanna had more than enough time to call Seth out on his strange nighttime behavior; his late night walks that lasted well into the morning and his immediate hot showers that followed. Bridget couldn't help but think that Deanna had brought it all on herself really, and that if it had been *her* husband that had been acting so strangely she would have had it out with him ages ago. She would have confronted him, maybe even followed him on one of his late night trips and had it out with *both* of them in some horribly embarrassing public display of hysteria. Bridget had never been one for quiet subtleties or innuendo, she was the kind of woman that got up front and in your face when it came to her feeling for men and what she wanted from them. Bridget had also never gotten any of the seemingly lucky ass breaks that her sister always just managed to fall into, time and time again. Although now Bridget could finally feel a bit of equality drifting gently back into her meager life like a glass bottle gradually washing its way back onto a sandy shore. This time though it wasn't Bridget's life that was in the proverbial shitter, it was Deanna's, and she couldn't help but smile a bit at the novelty of it all.

Bridget's mind was becoming increasingly intoxicated by the smug rivalry that had taken over her normally nondescript feelings for her sister. She had never fully confronted the resentment she harbored for her sister and now it seemed as if it were libel to take over her whole personality if she didn't somehow reign it in and control it under the weight of traditional family obligation.

So instead of gloating openly about Seth's obvious involvement with the woman she instead insisted that there was no way in the world that the floozy was going to get away with seducing her sisters husband, even if he *was* much more than a willing candidate. And even if deep down in her heart of hearts she didn't want to give Seth even the slightest opportunity to talk his way out of it, she decided that she did at least want to give him the benefit of the doubt and the chance to prove himself capable of adhering to his wedding vowels, for now anyway. Bridget's tarnished mind chimed in that there was no denying that they *did* in fact know each other, and that they were indeed sharing a suite together, and that soon they would be breaking the sheets in with great enthusiasm. As her grandmother would have said, had she still seen it fit to walk the earth; anyone with eyes in their fool heads could have seen *that*. Unless of course, they didn't want to.

Chapter 5

When Seth Toumbs opened the door to 2121 Fairfield Circle he caught the sent of a familiar musky perfume. While it was true that it was *not* the perfume that he had expected to have someday entice his senses here in the musty halls of Laurendale Manner, it was still one that he had become distinctly familiar with over the past year none the less. A sense of curiosity, perhaps of excitement even, touched his bones. He smiled as he closed the door behind him, delighted in the knowledge that the game had taken an interesting turn for the best.

Eva looked up slowly from the registry book as he and the buxom blonde entered the main hall. There was the slightest hint of the narrowing of her eyes as she gazed out at them, as if to burn them both with her cold blue eyes right where they stood, but instead she managed to slid a thin smile of welcome across her full, crimson lips. She had to bite down hard on her tongue in order to keep it in line.

Seth had to steady his guest several times before they even managed to reach the heavily carved desk in order to keep the woman from toppling over in her four inch silver heels. She slithered over him like some sort of sex starved lizard, not the least bit shy about where her hands traveled over his firmly muscled body.

Without any form of introduction Eva broke the silence with a roll of her eyes and said. "You have *another* guest. One of the boys have just taken her to her room. I am quite certain however that she is *not* your wife, although it is true that she has signed the registry as such. She is *not* the woman you had me keep an eye on, and although there are some striking similarities between the two, she is not pregnant."

"Thank you Eva," he said, glancing at the open registry book and reading his wife's name. "From the musky perfume that the imposter is wearing I would have to say that it is none other than my sister-in-law, Bridget. I do believe that she has been sent here to spy on me. I thought I caught the sent of Deanna at the airport, I would have expected no less from that overbearing wife of mine. Deanna always could talk her sister Bridget into doing anything for her, no matter how ridiculous." His smile was dry and humorless.

"I'm sure you are correct, but there is little that can be done about it now. Unless you would like me to get rid of her in my own way?" Eva said, her eyes gazing up the steps where only moments before the woman claming to be Deanna Toumbs had just walked.

"I'm sure that won't me necessary Eva, at least not yet anyway. Besides, this might prove to be rather fun. I can't wait to hear what she has to say to me. She'll probably stomp her pretty little feet and call me a cad." Then Seth's face hardened a bit, his nostrils flared. "I *told* you to keep them in the lower level Eva. You know we can't afford to have someone see them here." He leaned forward, his voice agitated but he spoke softly. "If they were to get out it would be catastrophic for the entire household!"

"I'm sorry Seth. I will make sure that they return to the lower level immediately." She glanced behind her into the darkened alcove. There was a slight flutter of movement and then a heavy stillness. Two pairs of unearthly blue eyes, similar to her own, glowed back at her and then lowered in a submissive gesture as she gazed back at them in the darkness.

Eva turned her gaze back to Seth, and there was the unmistakable sparkle of something deep within those pale blue pools of hers, something of warning swam in those cool waters. Seth either didn't notice, or didn't care to.

The two dark forms that slunk behind Eva didn't however seem to show any form of submissiveness towards him as they gazed out from their hiding place, and instead their eyes hardened upon Seth like stone. The eyes that stared out at him held something much different than before; resentment, perhaps even hatred? Seth broke visual contact with them and settled his eyes back on Eva's cool face, seeming to care little for their quiet, unspoken protest.

"Whhhat are you...talkin' 'bout darling," demanded the blonde. Her words were slurred as she stumbled forward to look vaguely in the same direction that Seth had been studying so intently but saw nothing there but the heavy drapery and muted darkness.

"Nothing to trouble yourself with my dear." Seth turned to her and kissed her full, drunken lips. "Eva's...pets are not permitted in the main living quarters, that's all." He took the blond by the arm and led her slowly upstairs to his room. The woman leaned the weight of her body into him, kissing his neck and gliding her hands over his ass, squeezing it slightly and giggling with drunken laughter. Halfway up the stairs he stopped and looked back at Eva where she still stood watching them with her usual cool and expressionless face. "We will be dining at seven tonight. Make sure the others are made aware." His voice had become impatient and irritable as the woman with him stumbled backwards and almost fell down the stairs. He grabbed at her swiftly and gritted his teeth into a tight smile. "Forward darling, we are moving forward."

"Yes Seth, as you wish." Eva smiled thinly at them, forcing her cold laughter down into the pit of her stomach. She then waited until Seth and the woman were gone before she turned her attention back to the two faceless creatures behind her in the dark.

"I'm sorry my darlings, he didn't really mean what he said. It was cruel of him I know but you know how temperamental he gets when he brings a new friend into our group. He knows what you two mean to me, to us. He was just thrown off by Bridget coming here; perhaps you should go to my room and wait there until he has a chance to cool off. You know that he never stays for very long anyway and then you may come back out and have your usual run of the house."

Obediently the two black forms withdrew into the folds of darkness and disappeared from her view. A fleeting grey shadow of anger passed over her face as she watched them leave but she managed to take control of if swiftly. She knew better than to let it out, to let her anger get the best of her. Things would happen, things she would regret later when the dust had settled and the bodies were counted. In her effort to gain control of her emotions she had clenched her fists so tightly that a drop of her own blood fell to the floor, vibrating through her head like a warriors battle cry. The acidic smell burned her nose and she opened her fists, blood ran freely down her pale wrists. She watched it for a while, lost in the simplistic beauty of her own flesh and the allure of her beating pulse. Eva licked the palms of her hands, her crimson red lips pushing deep into the cuts as if they held the most sweet and luscious of nectars. When she finally pulled them from her mouth the wounds had sealed themselves so completely that it was as if the blood had been from someone else and that she had just merely wiped them off. Hesitantly she made her way into the kitchen to tell the staff when dinner was to be expected and that two additional guests, along with Seth would be joining them.

The staff that ran the large manner like a pristine and well oiled sailing ship consisted of half a dozen adolescent boys that were mirror images of each other, right down to the very way they moved. All of them could be described as having black, fine hair that hung in bowl cuts right above the nape of their necks. Each with their own matching pair of small, deep set eyes that were black as pitch and skin that had a certain pale transparency to it, not unlike wax. They worked and lived in complete and utter silence and while they understood every order given to them no expression was ever observed on their tight lifeless faces. Eva explained bluntly what was expected at the dinner table and at what time it was to be completed, all nodded silently in response to her domestic demands and then continued droning on with their usual daily cleaning and polishing that they had been seeing to prior to Eva's new set of orders.

As Eva was about to leave the busy confines of the kitchen the phone rang next to her on the wall making her jump slightly.

"Hello?" She said, then there was a short pause.

"Yes," Eva said into the receiver, "that won't be a problem. I always have some on hand." Another slight pause, then, "Yes Seth, I will make sure that it is taken care of that immediately." Eva sighed, rolling her eyes in disgust.

She placed the heavy, outdated receiver back on its hook and spoke to the nearest boy, touching his shoulder first to get his attention. He turned to her, focusing on her words with deep interest.

"Seth would like a bottle of wine brought up to his room, take him the chardonnay '65 and something sweet from the pantry for that *girl* he has with him. Not that I can imagine she needs it from the size of her thighs, but take it to her anyway."

Nodding quickly, the boy disappeared into the small darkened wine cellar that adjoined the industrial sized kitchen and flicked on the light.

Enough food could be prepared for over a hundred guests with little effort in this room, and it had been, countless times. Although the days when large parties had been held at the manner were long gone, Eva could still remember them clearly. As it was, only one, of the two professional sized stoves was ever used these days and most of the dishes that were piled high on the white open shelved cabinets that lined the stone walls now only collected dust. The long expanse of black granite countertops that lined the perimeter of the kitchen were now only sparsely used and the lighting had become dim and out-dated three decades before. Cobwebs clung tightly to every darkened corner and mice or other, less acceptable creatures, could be heard gnawing at the old bags of rice and flour that sat piled on top of one another under the central workspace with its butcher block top and massive, turned legs of solid oak to hold its immense weight.

Eva remembered, although not without the harsh pang of longing, when the daily life at the manner was very different, the large estate practically hummed with both human and supernatural life alike and the frivolity had gone unmatched since then. She remembered fondly the lively costume parties that were held there every year during the summer solstice and again at the coming of winter. Doors wide, the summer breeze carrying the sent of jasmine and the sound of laughter, or the winters snow brought in on the backs of visitors only to melt quickly in the heat of the great fire that graced the main dining hall.

But that was then, back before Seth had returned to her, back when it had only been her and the girls. Back before she grew to love him too much and her children were born. *Her* children that were never accepted by him, but instead made him brood and stomp his foot throughout the vacant house in anger. Now only the occasional guest stayed within these walls, usually his, and then never for very long. Seth had become short tempered and secretive in his day to day life. He hadn't even bothered to mention to them that he was bringing a woman back here to Laurendale Manner. His intentions with this new woman or his sister-in-law for that matter were unknown to Eva and her trust in him began to falter. She was becoming weary of him.

With a sigh of longing for what used to be, Eva left the busy memories of the kitchen behind her and only after bolting the main door tightly against the darkness of the night, she withdrew to the confines of her own room. There she would gather the items Seth had requested and ready herself for dinner. It was sure to be an interesting, if not enlightening evening.

Chapter 6

Once they had entered her room Bridget tipped the boy what she felt was an acceptable amount. She figured she could have carried her own bag up the steps to her room if he had just let her. Although she would have never been able to *find* her room since she wasn't given a key, or even a room number for that matter, so she figured the kid did come in handy in that respect. When they got to the door there wasn't even one of those brass room numbers nailed onto it, so it just blended in with the countless other doors that lined the darkened hallway. That being said, it wasn't as if the kid killed himself dragging a ton of luggage up the stairs in order to constitute a big tip. Although he did look a bit pale and pasty like he was coming down with the flu bug or something. She hoped for his sake that the poor boy was just in desperate need of some sun and fresh air. In her well intentioned, yet short sighted opinion, kids his age should be out running the streets and causing trouble, not indoors working their young lives away making what had to be shit pay.

It wasn't long before swift and total exhaustion overtook her and Bridget was literally forced to lay back on the bed, her entire body shaking with fatigue and her mind becoming a torrent of tight and uncomfortable thoughts.

Bridget was torn between telling her sister the truth, just as she had seen it played out in front of her, or delaying the inevitable pain of the situation for a bit longer. Before she knew what was happening Bridget was dialing the phone in a sort of automatic daze as her thoughts continued to skip from one outcome to the other.

"Hello?" Deanna's voice seemed strained and weary.

Hearing her sisters voice on the other line, so full of anticipation and worry, forced the decision for her; she would hold off on the truth and stall for a bit more time. How could she find a way to explain away what she had seen with her own eyes? She was having difficulty explaining it to herself, let alone her sister.

"Deanna, it's Bridget. I made it here in one piece." She tried to sound upbeat.

"Thank God, I've been worried sick about you! I thought for sure you were stranded in some far off corner of the world where they don't speak English and you would never find your way home again," said Deanna with a heavy sigh. "Have you caught sight of Seth yet? Is he there with that…woman?"

"No, I haven't caught sight of him just yet," she lied. "But he *is* registered, so I'm bound to come across him sooner or later." Another lie, she hadn't seen his name on the registry, but he could have signed in under the woman's name he was with, or he could have even used an alias. Bridget just assumed that was what *all* cheating husbands did when they finally broke down and shacked up in some cheap and dingy hotel with a nice little piece of ass; at least that's what she did. Mr. and Mrs. Smith, or sometimes Jones. It had become kind of a running joke really, no one ever really bought it, but it made life so much simpler.

"All I can say Deanna is that I'm glad *you're* paying for this place and not me, it's not exactly the Ritz. Don't get me wrong though, it's definitely huge and expensive looking but it smells kind of funny and is about as charming and upbeat as a funeral home. It's not really the place I would imagine a guy would take his mistress, at least not if he wanted to keep seeing her." Bridget said, looking intently around her room. Drab and chilly, *definitely* not the Ritz.

"Maybe not, but I really don't think they are going to be too interested in their surroundings Bridget. I can't seem to stop this nagging feeling that I have in the pit of my stomach that this is all going to end badly." Deanna whined, grating on the last of Bridget's tired and worn out nerves.

"Don't give up the marriage license just yet Deanna. I'm sure things will work themselves out for the best in the end. Just try and give me a bit more time to find out what's really going on here and then I'll get back to you. Oh, and don't forget about the five-hour time difference."

"Alright…but call me the minute you see him. I just *have* to know what's going on between him and that woman before I lose my mind." Deanna was beginning to work herself up, Bridget could hear it in her voice.

"Look, I'm going to take a hot shower now and get ready for dinner, I'm absolutely *starved*. How about I call you in the morning, once I've had a chance to look around the place and find a few people to talk to; that is if there *are* any here to talk to." The last bit was more to herself than to Deanna.

"Alright, I'll let you get some rest and something decent to eat, but make sure you call me the minute you find anything out."

"I promise. I'll talk to you later. Goodnight." Bridget hung up the phone and reclined back on the bed to rest her aching back.

Laurendale Manner was much more aged than she had first realized when she walked in the front door, and a Hell of a lot more creepy. Bridget figured that the less time she spent in this drafty old hotel, the better it would be for her health, both physical *and* mental.

So far Bridget wasn't enjoying her trip abroad as much as she hoped she would. Why couldn't Seth run off with some woman to someplace warm like Spain or the south of France? No, that would be too romantic, he had to go and pick someplace cold and damp. Bridget had to keep reminding herself thought that she wasn't the one paying the bill, *that* at least made her feel *slightly* better.

The *one* time Bridget had actually managed to brake free of her normal day to day life and was able to finally travel somewhere outside her own borders, she was stuck looking after her sisters husband like some overgrown babysitter. To make matters even worse, at least from what Bridget could tell, the place didn't even have so much as a one stool bar to get drunk in. The thought of being forced to drink alone in her room like some sort of leper made her brow wrinkle in weary contempt for her sister and her insignificant marital problems.

Bridget sat up on her elbows and surveyed the room. The décor was like something out of the late seventeenth century. The bed was a king size, four poster monstrosity, made entirely of solid mahogany wood with intricate carvings of deer being relentlessly hunted down and killed by a roaming pack of wolves.

How very pleasant, thought Bridget rather dryly.

Dark themed tapestries hung from almost every nook and cranny of the rooms walls in an attempt to soften the hard lines of stonework and wood. The dark wooden floors were covered with hand tied Persian rugs of fine, intricate designs and lavishly dark velvet pillows softened every ridged wooden chair. Heavily lined velvet and damask drapes flanked either side of the time worn, leaded glass windows of the rooms ancient French doors. Their fine silver inlay framed the early evening sky and led out onto a stone patio that overlooked a great expanse of lawn. The patio itself was adorned with an assortment of potted plants and flowers that were nearing their time for replacement as the weather turned colder.

But the true centerpiece of the room, had anyone ever bothered to ask for Bridget's opinion, was the oversized stone fireplace on the opposing wall from the bed, complete with breathtaking crystal candelabras and hand chiseled stone lions that stood guarding each side in highly polished marble. A freshly made fire crackled in its full, gaping mouth and warmed even the farthest corners of the room with a soft orange glow. Bridget pulled herself reluctantly from the center of the bed and sat up, her feet dangling like those of a school child from its great height, and opened the side table's single drawer.

Inside was a brown leather menu with a short list of interior house numbers and a large food list; from the look of the rather large selection of meals and side dishes the estate had a kitchen that was better equipped than most five-star restaurant. To Bridget's delight there was not only a wine list at the bottom of the well-worn pages but also a list of good, old fashioned, hard liquor. While there was little chance of her getting a burger and fries during her stay in this fluffed up graveyard, the prospect of actually being able to wash whatever she *did* eat down with a warm cognac, seemed to make it all worth while. Rather high on the list of possibilities was elk steaks and ostrich, not Bridget's usual fare but well worth a try, since she wasn't going to be footing the bill for it that is.

From her vast experience of hotel rooms, no prices on the menu usually meant that the food was too expensive, if not teetering on the side of insane. In her profession though that also meant that they guy was willing to spend some serious money, something that was always a plus in her book.

She called down to the kitchen and ordered the elk steak, red skinned mashed potatoes, asparagus with butter and pear sorbet for dessert. Then went about the task of unpacking what little clothing and make-up she had brought with her. Part of Bridget hoped that she would not be there long; if Seth wasn't fooling around it would be hard for her sister to explain the extra charges on their credit card. Then again, if he was, and it looked like he was, she was sure that Deanna wouldn't mind sticking the bastard with the bill.

Bridget considered the very real possibility that she would just stay here indefinitely. In England that is, *not* Laurendale Manner. And while the weather *was* turning cold and she hadn't seen much, if any, real sunshine, she was sure that England had its own strong points. She could go to London and work there.

The possibilities were truly endless.

Bridget entered the small but luxurious bathroom and began to put away her toiletries. Just then there was a hard knock at her door.

"Just a minute," Bridget yelled. "You must have the fastest room service I've ever seen!"

Setting her make-up bag down on the counter she quickly made her way into the bedroom, fixing her hair in the back where it had come loose from its twisted bun along the way. She opened the door and froze, the smile vanishing almost instantaneously as she gazed out at her visitor.

"Seth!" Bridget's face instantly flushed with embarrassment at being caught in such a ridiculous manner. His big smile widened even more at her obvious shame. Her one and *only* consolation was that he was missing his blonde girlfriend.

He bowed down in front of her with a great sweep of his arm like some sort of over-stuffed diplomat and smiled sleazily up at Bridget. "It's customary for me to welcome all the new guests that stay here while I'm in residence. Now imagine for me if you will my great surprise when I saw not only my own wife's name scribbled there on the pages of the registry book, but also that the payment for said room, had been made by *our* joint credit card. I'm sure that even you can see that I couldn't help but come straight here to welcome her. How you've changed Deanna." His smile was hard and cruel.

Bridget's obvious embarrassment had suddenly changed into full blown anger.

"Deanna saw you at the airport. Who is she Seth? And don't lie to me, I saw you two come in together. My God Seth, she was practically humping your leg in the lobby!"

"That's what I like about you most kid, you always did cut straight to the point, no pussy footing around. May I come in?" He waited patiently by the door until Bridget finally nodded and moved away.

She let him slither his way in like the snake he was and then quickly crossed the room to the bed in the center of the room and sat down, putting as much distance between herself and his slimy personality as humanly possible. The desire to slap that smug smile off his face right where he stood was getting to be more than she could stand. Seth had shown no remorse, no guilt for what he and that woman had been up to. If anything he seemed to beam with childish glee at her discovery. Her shoulders slumped, her eyes desperately searching for the man she *thought* she knew.

"How could you do this to Deanna? She loves you so much, and I *thought* you loved her."

Seth sat down on the bed next to her; putting his arm around her shoulder as if to console her. "Tell me little Bridget, do you always do everything your sister tells you to?" He smirked. The warm light from the fireplace cast a long, dark shadow across his face, making Seth seem suddenly sinister to her, almost inhuman there in the fading light.

She shrugged him off. "You didn't see her when she came to me, when she was falling apart standing there in the middle of my living room. Deanna begged me to come and look for you, to see if what she thought was happening between you two really was. To be honest Seth, from what I've seen tonight she was right to suspect the worst of you."

"It's good friends like Michelle that keep Deanna in the house we live in and the expensive diamonds around her beautiful neck. Without her...and women like her...Deanna wouldn't be able to afford to buy every little shinning bobble that strikes her fancy." His face hardened a bit. "Your sister couldn't live hand to mouth like you can, although I know for a fact that you have been doing rather well for yourself lately. She's not as strong as you are Bridget, she's not a fighter."

She chose to ignore what he was hinting at and said, "So it's true. You *are* cheating on her with this Michelle woman, for what? For money?" She looked at him in desperation. Seth had always come across to her as a man above reproach. Was he telling her that he was some sort of gigolo?

"A woman such as yourself shouldn't be so quick to judge. I tell you what, come to dinner tonight with the rest of us in the main dining room and I will introduce you to Michelle and the others. I'm sure once you meet them things will begin to clear themselves up rather quickly for you. By the way, I've taken the liberty of canceling your dinner order so if you choose not to grace us with your lovely presence you're bound to become rather hungry." He pushed her bangs back to look into her eyes. "Be a sport and come downstairs in about an hour so that we might all dine together. I promise you it will be well worth the inconvenience of leaving these four lovely walls."

"How dare you! I can't believe you had the nerve to actually cancel my dinner order. What makes you think that I would even *want* to eat with you and your little whore?" She stood up and walked over to the open door and leaned on its brass handle; at this point she was quite certain that nothing could shock her. Then she paused a moment and looked back at him, the realization of what he had said earlier finally striking her. "And what did you mean exactly when you said that you meet all the guests personally when you're in residence? You act like you own the place or something."

Seth got up and joined her by the door, sliding his large hand down her arm. "I do own the place Bridget; it's my home away from home." Smiling at her he pulled the door closed behind him.

Bridget stood there in utter disbelief. How could it be that her sisters husband owned this place? She knew they had money, but this place must have cost a small fortune. Bridget was also certain that Deanna knew nothing about it, or she would have been sure to rub such an extravagant possession in her face. How does one keep a secret like that from their own wife?

Bridget had come to the conclusion that Seth was rather good at keeping all kinds of dirty little secrets from a great many people. She hadn't seen him up until that point as a cheat and a liar, but there it was, glowing in her face like a red neon sign in the night. He had practically admitted to the affair with that woman of his, Michelle. He even made it sound like he did it all for the money. Granted, she would be the last person to throw stones for taking part in carnal pleasures for the simple fact of making money, but it wasn't as if *she* were the one that was married. Seth could go on with this ridiculous charade and act as if he were simply sleeping around with attractive wealthy women for no other reason other than to keep his wife Deanna in expensive furs, but she knew that was a lie. She knew her sister well enough to know that she would rather have a faithful and loving husband than a new BMW in the drive-way every year. And no matter what Seth claimed to the contrary, she knew he was out fucking around because he liked it. Like a dog that has an itch that he just can't ignore, and Seth was doing all he could to scratch it. Besides, Seth had a successful import-export company that she *knew* existed. She and her sister Deanna had visited Seth at his corporate offices several times before they were even married, the place was huge and filled to the rafters with merchandise.

She would go with him to dinner tonight, as he had requested, and *somehow* make him see the light. She wouldn't have to tell Deanna anything if he agreed to stop seeing this Michelle woman of his and probably countless others. Come to think of it, he had said "them" when he asked her to join him at dinner. Bridget's stomach flip-flopped. There had better be something strong to drink with dinner or she was certain that no matter how good it all tasted, it wouldn't be staying down for long.

Bridget went to the bathroom to finish unpacking her small bag of toiletries and to take a quick shower in an effort to wash away the dull ach of extended traveling from her exhausted body. As the warm shower beat down on her tired mussels she stopped to think about Deanna and the baby. There was more at stake here than just Deanna's happy marriage. There was a child involved this time and that made it all the more serious. Seth had to snap out of this illusion he was living in and step up to bat, he needed to take responsibility for this glaring mistake of his.

Bridget turned off the water and stepped out, wiping the cloud of steam from the mirror so that she could see herself better and began brushing her teeth. It was only then that she noticed a small streak of what looked like blood on the white porcelain sink by the drain. She immediately dismissed it as some sort of cleaning product that hadn't been washed away thoroughly. Granted, the place was a tad bit on the creepy side, but it was hardly what she would consider to be the hot spot for murder. Suddenly the shower scene from 'Psycho' shot through her mind like a runaway bullet. She had sat through that movie on more lazy Sunday afternoons than she wished to confess but it never seemed to have as much impact on her then as it did at that moment. She began to feel the hairs on her arms stand up and she shook them from her body vehemently. Bridget pulled her tired mind from coasting down that black and white cinematic road in an effort to keep her sanity. She figured that line of thinking was probably not something that she should be exploring if she ever expected to get *any* sleep while she stayed in her outdated, but sufficient accommodations; alone.

Forty-five minutes, and three outfits later she made her way down to the main dining room. She was thankfully the first one to arrive, which gave Bridget the perfect opportunity to scrutinize whoever came through the door next, and man, did she plan on giving Seth's little home wreaker the once over.

To her surprise there was only one long, linen covered table that graced the large dining room. The great expanse of dining space was lit at the far end by a roaring fire and then again towards its center with three silver candelabras, each had at least twelve long white tapers slowly burning in them and the group of them cast enough light and heat to warm the entire room.

The young boy that had originally shown her to her room now entered with a large soup tureen.

"Do I just sit anywhere, or are there assigned seats?" Bridget asked.

He didn't speak but instead set down the white porcelain soup tureen that he had been carrying and pulled the richly upholstered chair out that sat just to the left of the head of the table. He waited quietly there for her to sit down and then pushed her in to a comfortable eating distance from the table. Not once did he speak or make even the slightest attempt at eye contact with Bridget. The boy's demeanor was shy and unnaturally reserved. He made Bridget think of a boy she once knew back in high school, Tommy Bowen, who had been physically and mentally abused by his father for years. *He* had acted that way. That is until one night after a particularly harsh beating he stuck the hunting riffle in his fathers face that he had lifted from his neighbors house and pulled the trigger. Tommy killed the bastard in a spray of bullets as he lay there on the living room sofa sleeping off a fifth of Jack Daniels and a six pack of Iron City. After that, it was like the kid had been liberated or something. Liberated and incarcerated on the same day. Pity too because Bridget had always liked him. She had even gone to visit him once afterwards to see how he was dealing with life behind bars and to drop off a few of the comic books that she had seen him reading and all the kid could talk about was how wonderful life was now that his father was six feet under ground and rotting. Creepy kid really.

Bridget was suddenly pulled back to the present when her attention was caught by another young boy entering the room. At first her mind didn't register that he was the exact twin of the one now sorting out silverware and folding napkins into little swan-like birds. Then he passed close behind the other boy and she flinched.

It wasn't as if it was totally unheard of that twin boys should want to work at the same hotel together, not really, but what *was* unheard of was the pulled and translucent quality of their skin. Before she had seen only one of them in the rather diffused light of the hallway and her room. Now however the two boys stood smack dab in front of her in a blaze of candle light prepping the table for dinner and she couldn't help but think that they looked like two walking corpses that had been totally drained of blood. Normally when someone is that pale you can see a bit of color on their cheeks or around the hollows of their eyes, but not with these boys.

One left briefly only to return again with a large platter of what looked like roast beef and potatoes. Bridget was unsure if she were even hungry anymore.

She looked down at the soft skin that lined the inside of her arm, the blue veins started at her wrist and crawled in lazy curves up her arm where they then branched off and disappeared from view under her flannel shirt. She had been quite pale all her life yet she had always had them.

Bridget gazed at the two boys that stood working quietly before her but they were dressed in long sleeved, white dress shirts made of crisply starched cotton fabric and it was impossible for her to tell if they had them also. Either way, Bridget couldn't help but think that these two were looking more and more like wax dolls with every passing minute. And while she *could* believe that there was a possibility that one of them could be ill it was rather unlikely that they would both be ill at the same time.

Their pale and sickly skin *had* to be from being overworked in this damp and moldy death trap of a hotel and Bridget made herself a mental note that she would talk to them later that night and see it they were interested in *anything* other than working.

Still though, she was beginning to feel the slightest bit uneasy as she sat there, alone in the room with them.

Sunlight was all they needed, and then they would be two, normal, quiet, creepy, *twin boys that worked together in a hotel*, she thought.

Finally in an act of total mental desperation Bridget forced her focus away from the two boys and instead studied the entrance of the dining hall, hoping to see another guest enter the room and release her from the unnatural hold they seemed to have over her. *Anyone* to break the overwhelming feeling that she was having that the boys weren't even *real* would have been welcomed; even Seth and that woman of his.

After what felt like an eternity the strange pair finally left her alone in the room and she instantly began to feel more at ease. Gradually she sat back and enjoyed the closeness of the fire.

Bridget felt rather lucky to sit so near the fire, she still felt chilled to the bone even with the multiple layers of clothing she wore. The cold dampness of the house had become inescapable.

After roughly another fifteen minutes of sitting there alone the first person, other than herself of course, appeared for dinner. There would have been no way for Bridget to have mistaken the slim lined, dark haired woman for anyone else; her features were that distinct. It was none other than the woman Bridget had first met upon entering the old manner just a few hours earlier; her name was Eva Van Cruse.

Her attire was completely different than when she first set eyes on her, and if not for the fact that she recognized her striking blue eyes she might have at first guessed her to be another woman entirely.

No longer stuffy and proper, the woman was now dressed in a red, silken gown that showed far more skin than it covered up. Her fine, long neck was wrapped tightly with diamonds in the form of a cuff-like necklace and her ears dripped with rare stones in a cascade of brilliant color. The hair that she had earlier, rather prudently, worn up in a tight bun now cascaded freely down her porcelain white shoulders in black, rolling waves of silk and settled at the small of her bare back.

She was *amazing*.

Bridget had to almost *physically* close her mouth as it dropped open at the remarkable transformation that had been revealed before her. She suddenly, and quite painfully, became aware of her own, now utterly inappropriate, attire. Instead of high end evening ware Bridget sported a cream turtleneck, plaid green-flannel over-sized button down shirt and comfortable, yet faded, blue jeans. Her face warmed at her own embarrassment. Then to make matters even worse, Eva sat down right next to her.

Bridget tried to study the woman's strong features as unobtrusively as possible. The thought struck her, as she made casual glances in her direction, that she didn't even seem to have pores on her face, as if her body had been painstakingly carved from fine, milky white marble. Bridget suddenly began to get the feeling that she was the ugly duckling who had been unfortunate enough to be seated next to the beautiful and sophisticated swan.

Damn it.

"I guess we're early," Bridget smiled, absentmindedly touching the coolness of her bare hands against her now very warm face in an effort to reduce the redness that she could feel beginning to burn there.

I knew I should have brought something formal to wear. My God, my hair isn't even done properly.

"Not really, the others just like to be fashionably late. They would do it every night if we had visitors more often. Though I must admit, this place has felt entirely too much like a morgue lately." She smiled faintly at Bridget in an attempt to make her last comment seem somewhat humorous. But Bridget didn't feel the slightest bit like laughing.

As Bridget's mind danced around the flesh crawling effect that Eva's poor choice of words had had on her entire physical being, two women entered the room, hand in hand like little children. Both of them were dressed in gently flowing, emerald green evening gowns that had to have been made of the finest of silks as they gently skimmed the fine contours of their bodies. And while the gowns that they wore matched in color and material, they each had a slightly different cut to them, drawling your attention to different aspects of each of the women's small, but well made bodies. One had a deep, plunging neckline that ended just below her finely jeweled bellybutton. The other had a high colored neck and then plunged down in the back to reveal every one of her small vertebra down to the curve of her buttocks. Both gowns were floor length with an all too revealing side slit that started at the floor and ran to the top of their shapely hips, although on opposite sides of each other. And *both* were adorned with an exquisite array of fine jewelry, similar in style and quality to those of Eva's. The women, not much more than girls in this case, were exact twins in every way, from their mocha colored skin that glistened and sparkled down to their thick, black pixie haircuts.

They wore a distinctly familiar perfume that filled Bridget's senses as they entered the room; sugar cookies. It reminded her of a stripper she knew back home.

Although they were dressed like adults Bridget was having a hard time believing that they were of legal age to be putting out to Seth, or anyone else for that matter. Their faces seemed so young, so innocent, and yet here they were looking like two professionals. God only knew what else Seth had them doing. Bridget imagined them seducing old, graying men of their life long pensions for a quick, yet satisfying, romp in the sack. They looked as if they could get the job done and make the guy swear he got his moneys worth, no matter what the price was in the end.

Quick on their heels were the ones Bridget was most interested in, Seth himself; and draped lazily over his arm was the woman she had seen him with earlier that evening, humping him like some sort of animal in the main hall of this gaudy whore house. The woman he had called *Michelle*. Her womanly temper began to rise.

"Ah, I'm so pleased you decided to join us Bridget," he smiled charismatically at her. "I suppose I should have mentioned that dinners here at Laurendale Manner are *always* formal." Seth stood beside Bridget and stared down at her with that stupid smirk on his face. Bridget's hand itched to smack it.

Bridget felt as if the temperature in the room had gone up about twenty degrees. "Yes, well, no matter. I didn't pack anything formal anyway. You will just have to make due with me as I am. I'm sure my appearance isn't *that* offensive." She pushed her hair back slightly with the palm of her hand in a sort of indignant snap.

"You look positively…charming." Seth turned from her and gazed around the table. "Now that everyone is here allow me make the introductions."

His thick, manly voice had that sultry effect that would have normally made Bridget go week in the knees had it been directed solely at her, and in some dark and lonely corner of the house. At least it had that quality to it *most* of the time anyway, but Bridget was having a hard time feeling its subtle effects tonight. Most of the time she would have readily admitted to Seth's own brand of playboy charm; even if it did consist mainly of the slimy type found typically in Hollywood movie agents and smarmy Vegas lounge lizards.

Seth escorted the curvy blond by the hand and stopped just across the table from Bridget's seat so that she could get a good eye full of her. "This exquisite creature will from tonight onwards be known to us simply as Michelle. She's one of the last remaining members of a grand old family in the States and she simply can't wait to spread her wings and become part of *our* tightly-knit little family."

Michelle stood by his side and beamed her bleached white, dentist perfected smile at each woman that sat at the table. "It's so nice to finally get to meet all of you. Seth has already told me so much about you all that I feel like we are truly sisters," her eyes sparkled with self-importance.

Bridget couldn't help but think that her little speech had been heavily practiced in front of the bathroom mirror. She smiled to herself as she imagined a pull cord sticking out of Michelle's back. Just pull the string and see what the dumb blonde has to say. Michelle was a fake, pure and simple. Bridget also knew that if you pushed them hard enough, all the sweetness washed away like wet paint in a thunderstorm. Just one more reason for Bridget to hate her, as if she needed any more. The pure fact that she was fucking her sister's husband was more than enough for her to hate her all the way down to her pretty little painted toes.

Bridget was still focused on Michelle and that false smile she had plastered on her face when Seth began introducing the other women at the table to Michelle. "Candice and Jessica are sisters, twins to be exact, as I'm sure you've noticed. They came here many, many years ago along with Eva from the darker…less sophisticated corners of Europe. They have helped to make Laurendale Manner a home, and not merely a resting place for my tired old bones."

Bridget couldn't hold it in anymore, before anymore fake salutations could be muttered, Seth was abruptly cut short by her furious outburst.

"I'm sorry; I don't mean to interrupt this twisted little party of yours but what *exactly* is going on here? Is this some sort of sick joke or are you honestly running a whore house Seth?" Bridget half stood up but Eva touched her arm in reassurance.

"It's nothing like that my dear, although I can see where it might seem that it is. We are as Seth said, a family." Eva poured Bridget a glass of red wine from the silver pitcher that sat just to her right and handed it to her. "I think you need a stiff drink."

"That's not exactly what I had in mind, but thanks none the less." Bridget drank the whole glass of wine in one go and then took the pitcher from Eva and refilled it again for herself. "I'm sorry Eva, I don't mean to be rude but how can you expect me to believe that."

"Don't misunderstand me Bridget; we're not the *traditional* sort of family."

"No, I didn't think you were."

"We are *better* We choose who we invite into our family and we care deeply for each other. We are as loyal as any blood family has ever been, possibly even more so."

"So who are you supposed to be Seth, their daddy?" She looked at him with contempt. "You can't tell me that your relationship with these women is purely plutonic." She looked around the room; none of them seemed offended by her statements. Hell, none of them even looked surprised.

"I never said *that*," Seth smiled. "They are all faithful concubines that grant me every wish a sexually robust man like myself could desire. And in return for such a wonderful and selfless gift they are granted an opulent life here in Laurendale Manner, are given every luxury money can afford and are safe from the drudgery and horrors of the outside world." Seth said it in a matter of fact tone, like someone reading a shopping list out loud. His whole attitude was shockingly laidback and casual. He leaned over to kiss Michelle, taking her face in his large hands. "Michelle here can't wait to get settled in and become part of our family." He caressed her cheek, his hand trailed slowly down to cup her heavy breast and then lower, to slide between her legs causing her to purr in delight.

"You have got to be fucking kidding me!" This time Bridget did get up, but only momentarily. She staggered a bit and then sat back down. The room suddenly became darker at the corners and then seemed to double in on themselves. Bridget had to force herself to focus on Seth and Michelle, her ears were ringing like church bells in her head.

I didn't drink that much, what the hell was in that wine?

"Have you forgotten Deanna," she slurred, "and the fact that she is pregnant with *your* baby right now?" She tried to steady herself in her chair by holding onto the sides of the table, but it wasn't working.

"Oh, I would never forget that Bridget. You see, that child is *the* most important thing that I possess. You see he is not only important to my future, but to the future of my entire race as well. He is something that I could *never* forget."

What the hell is he talking about...has he lost his fucking mind...?

From what she could only describe as from a great distance Bridget could hear Eva's voice enter into her mind. "You will soon be privileged enough to join our family, we are women of great strength and courage. You will fit in well here. We like you Bridget. We want you to become part of us."

The last thing Bridget saw as she began to lose consciousness was Seth slipping the knot that kept Michelle's dress up around her neck. The fabric quickly spilled to the floor in a pool of blue silk, her naked body coming to rest in front of him on the table like some sort of sacrificial offering to a long forgotten God. With Michelle's head tilted back in pleasure Seth took her in his arms, his mouth buried in her ample breasts, his hands penetrating the soft flesh between her thighs. Bridget collapsed on to the floor with the fleeting thought that she would never be able to explain away what she had just witnessed. Not to herself, or her sister.

Chapter 7

Bridget lay there, sprawled out on her bed, waiting for her eyes to focus. She was back in her room from the look of it and the fierce pounding of her head was a good indication that she had too much to drink. Even though she couldn't remember having more than two glasses of wine at dinner, a simple fact that would have normally not even been enough to give her a half decent buzz on any other night of her life.

Eventually the bed finally stopped spinning and she sat up, noticing only then that someone had changed her clothes. In place of her sensible, warm flannel was a sheer, pale green, silk gown that was more like something she would wear on stage than in her real day to day life. After her mind came to grips with the fact that someone had changed her clothes, she then noticed that she no longer had anything on underneath. She was completely commando.

She went to move, her body ached viciously and moisture flowed from between her legs. She had been raped, or drugged enough to agree to sex with Seth. Her body shook as her mind tried to remember what had happened. Nothing but the dull ach of terror entered her clouded mind.

How could he do this to me? How could he drug and rape me...

She sat there in bed as snippets of the previous hours viciously poked there way into her brain. She remembered Seth carrying her up to her room, darkness, the weight of his body against hers and the overwhelming desire to be with him. To drink him in, to let him seduce her. Bridget remembered that it had been her that had undressed first. That it had been her that had wrapped her naked body around his and demanded him to enter her. Bridget remembered the sweet taste of him in her mouth and the liberating feeling of him thrusting himself deep within the folds of her body. She hadn't been raped, she had been fucked, and quite happily too.

Bridget tried to rationalize the possibility of the drug in her wine being more than just there to knock her out. Maybe it was given to her in order to make her more pliable, not to mention agreeable to Seth's advances? She sat there looking at the pale green gown she now wore in utter disbelief. Why were her clothes changed? She couldn't remember that part of the evening. Every time she closed her eyes and tried to remember she saw only the visions of her and Seth, thrashing around the bed like to two starved sex addicts. The visions that entered her fuzzy mind were anything but reassuring. Even more importantly *and* disturbing to her, was why they wanted to drug her in the first place? Because that was the only explanation she could come up with to explain how two glasses of red wine knocked her on her ass the way it did. What did they think she was going to do? Then she knew.

Seth was caught with his hand in the cookie jar, he's terrified I'm going to tell Deanna...but now there is no way I can tell. How can I confess Seth's infidelity without confessing my own?

Just then there was a sound of a turning key in the door; she was a prisoner too from the sound of it.

Eva entered the room with a tray of food. "I thought you would be awake by now. I'm sorry we had to drug you, Seth carried you to your room after you passed out. We couldn't have you calling Deanna just yet. I'm sure you understand. You missed dinner. I thought you might be hungry."

Fuck no I don't understand !! But she kept her thoughts to herself.

It was Bridget's stomach that did all the talking; she was starving.

"Yes, thank you," said Bridget. "You seem like a rational sort of person, do you mind telling me what the hell is going on here. I realize Seth must have put you up to it, but you look smart enough to know that this could be construed as kidnapping. I'm sure it's illegal in merry old England just as much as it is the States." She stood up and shakily walked over to the tray of food. "Do you mind telling me who changed my clothes?"

"Oh, that. Seth didn't feel that what you were wearing complimented you, so he had me find you something more attractive. The twins are about your size so I borrowed that from their closet. Seth has taken the liberty of ordering you some new clothes, something to suite your complexion. They will be here in the morning from one of the many local shops that he is fond of."

"It seems Seth is used to taking all sorts of liberties when it comes to others," her mind was practically on fire. She couldn't remember a time when she was more angry at the thought of letting her overactive libido get the better of herself. But it was amazing, her mind had begun to clear and she couldn't help

68

but wonder if it was the drugs or if Seth was really that good in bed. In a rush of self-loathing she pulled her mind from the damp, rumpled sheets and focused on the food in front of her.

Bridget surveyed the selection of food on the tray Eva had brought in with her. It all looked tempting and without much thought at self preservation she took a mouthful of Elk steak and then paused before swallowing it. "This isn't drugged too is it?"

"No," she smiled, "there is nothing in there except too much pepper for my taste. Seth didn't want you to waste away to nothing, he likes a bit of curve to his women."

No shit. Bridget thought with a small, inconspicuous smile.

Bridget swallowed the meat in her mouth and drank most of the large glass of milk before continuing.

"This is all a bit extreme don't you think? He obviously doesn't care about Deanna or his baby for that matter, so it must be the money. Pennsylvania is a community property state, making Deanna entitled to half of what Seth owns." She made a passing gesture with the half empty glass of milk at the room and its wealth of objects. "And from the look of this place it's more than either of us were aware of. From what I see here he stands to lose a great deal when I call my sister and tell her what a disgusting pig her husband is, which is exactly what I plan to do." She swallowed the rest of the milk and slammed the glass down on the table a bit harder than she intended to. The sound made her head pound in protest. "He will lose custody of his child for this you know," she said holding her fingers up to her forehead in an attempt at keeping her brain from seeping out. She only hoped that Eva didn't know about her little intercession with Seth, or else all this threatening would get her nowhere.

"You're assuming Deanna will divorce him. I assure you, it will never come to that."

"You act like there's nothing wrong with what he's doing." Her eyes widened and she put down her fork. "You can't tell me you're the type of woman who walks ten paces behind a man and expects whatever chauvinistic impulses cross their tiny little minds."

Eva didn't say anything at first but sat down on the bed next to her.

"Hardly," her eyes seemed to roll a bit when she said it. "I just know when to push an argument and when not to. Sometimes it's in a woman's best interest to look the other way at a man's…indiscretions."

"You can't *really* mean that? You're telling me that Deanna should just turn the other cheek and let Seth continue to whore around behind her back. For what? For money? Or do you think she should stay to keep some make-believe family alive that she *thinks* she needs?" Bridget's temper began to rise again. The thought of any woman going along with such a load of bullshit, let alone believing it was in their own best interest, made her want to shake Eva; shake her and slap her.

Eva smiled and placed a hand on Bridget's thigh. "You will learn what his touch can mean to you in time. You will come to realize that you just can't live without it, not happily anyway. He has a way of getting under your skin, into your blood so to speak."

You're not kidding lady, I could fuck him all day...

Bridget gently pushed Eva's hand from her. "No one is that good in bed honey," her expression soured. "I should know."

Eva left her side and went to the door. "He will be in shortly to talk with you. We are all *very* intuitive here Bridget. We can all feel the heat you have for him even if you don't realize it yourself. It's only a matter of time before you act on it."

It's too late for that darlin'...been there, done him.

She left the room, turning the key in the lock as she went.

Bridget sat there for a moment trying to clear things up in her mind. Seth was everything Deanna had suspected him of being and more. To top things off, from her current position, he was also a kidnapper. Unfortunately for her, Eva had been right about her feelings for Seth. She always fought she kept her feelings well hidden, especially when it came to her sister's husband, but all that was water under the bridge now. She had *slept* with her sisters husband. Bridget had no right to feel anything but disdain for him and for what they had done, but all she wanted now was more of him. The thought of his touch made her shake. She had to stop this, now. Seth had cheated on her sister and drugged *her*; he was not a man worth the obvious reciprocations of letting her desire for him override her otherwise good sense. This was one time she knew it was better to keep her knees closed and her feet planted firmly on the ground. But could she?

She picked up the phone, nothing. Not that she expected a dial tone, but it was worth a try. She went to the French doors, they opened easily enough but where could she hope to go in a slip of a dress and no shoes, even if she did manage to get down to the grounds below from that height. Just then a key turned in the lock of her bedroom door. Bridget knew it was him but she also knew this wasn't going to be as easy as she had originally hoped.

Seth entered the room, his tie was off and his shirt was only half buttoned, calling attention to the soft tufts of chest hair underneath. Bridget could have done without seeing that. Quickly she looked away.

"You must be furious with me Bridget. I can't say that I blame you. Cheating on your sister, not to mention drugging you. Hell, I even stole your clothes." His smile was wide and warm like a child's though she knew not as innocent. Bridget studied the floor, her jaw clenched. She could feel her temper rising with every word that slid from his sweet, luscious mouth. "Eva has good taste in clothing don't you think? You look *amazing*. Much better than that doughty old outfit you had on at dinner. Why on earth would you cover yourself up in such constricting clothing?" He crossed the room and stood in front of her, his eyes not shy about where they traveled. "But then again, you were quite happy to take them off for me. Quite happy indeed."

Again the overwhelming urge to smack that smug smile right off his pretty little face sprung into her mind. She needed a drink.

A nice bottle of wine and I might even be able to laugh about this, she thought.

Bridget crossed an arm over her body in an attempt to conceal her breasts from him, the fabric was too sheer to be modest and the coldness of the room made her nipples push against the thin fabric.

"How can you be so glib, so uncaring about Deanna? You lied to all of us. I thought better of you," her voice cracked toward the end, her eyes welled with tears. "How can you do these things to me. What the hell has happened to you?"

"Don't be too righteous Bridget. We both know that what happened between us last night was initiated by you. Not that I'm complaining mind you, I have always wanted you to be more than just a sister-in-law to me, more than just a occasional presence in my home. I must admit though that with all your foot stomping and name calling I didn't think you would be so quick to act on your true feelings for me. Then again, a woman of your profession isn't really into any form of sexual restriction, even if it does mean coming on to your sister's husband. I'm sure if Deanna knew what you did for a living she would have never sent you. Never in a million years."

He reached out with a large, steady hand to hold her face up to him, hesitantly she tore away, not wishing to make eye contact for any length of time. Afraid he might truly be able to read her thoughts somehow.

"You're disgusting. I don't know what the Hell you're talking about. I'm an actress, a singer; nothing more." She turned her body away from him as best she could without laying back to far onto the bed.

"Don't lie to me Bridget, I know you better than you know yourself. I know what you do to make all that extra money; the parties you attend. Those positively *delicious* private parties that your boss insists you go to. You tell yourself it's for the money, as if that makes it more acceptable to your Protestant mind. But we both know that you do it because you like it, the thought of all those writhing naked bodies there for your touch, the men, the women…it turns you on like nothing else in this world." He grabbed her by the arms and pulled her up to him; eye to eye she couldn't keep the dirty truth from him. His laugh rang out harsh and uncontrollable, bringing tears to her eyes. "And from the bruising on your body it looks like you don't mind the rough stuff either," his hands bit into her, causing her to squirm in his vice like grip. A small puff of air escaped her lips, making him smile.

"You're wrong, tonight was a mistake. A mistake brought on by the drugs you slipped into my wine. I can control myself, especially when it comes to *you*." she sneered at him. "I'm not some sort of animal."

"Oh, that's where you're wrong Bridget, you are an animal, a human animal, and that's what appeals most to me."

He pulled her closer, she could feel him against her thigh, she tried to move so that he was no longer touching her, his body not so hot against hers; but he held her there in his grip. She began to feel her own body's temperature rise. The warmth that radiated from the darkness between her thighs betrayed her. He smiled, his eyes burned into her flesh.

"What is it that you *think* you owe your sister?" he whispered. "She has treated you like her lap dog since you were kids, long before your parents were killed. She relies on you for everything. Why isn't *she* here Bridget? What makes it your responsibility to come all the way over here to another country to spy on her husband for her? You risk *your* job, *your* livelihood for what? Because she dismisses everything you are and makes you no more than a servant to her whims."

Seth was right, she knew that everything he said was true, but she resisted opening up those feelings of resentment, of hatred that she harbored for her sister for all these years. The sister that always made her feel unimportant, uneducated, and unnecessary unless it was to do her bidding. She softened in his grip, her eyes widened in what she felt at that moment was true understanding.

"She never has appreciated everything that I have done for her you know. College, friends, perspective husbands, all lost in her desire to keep me at her side, to keep me under her control." She dared to touch his face, the new roughness of his unshaven skin caused an explosion of warmth to erupt in her body. What a mistake.

"You can take everything she has Bridget. You can have everything you have ever desired and more, there is no shame in taking what should have been yours to begin with." He pulled her into him, drinking from her lips and scorching her skin with his touch, his hands tightening around her quivering body like iron vices. "You can become like the other woman here, or you can become more to me than you thought you ever could. I haven't quite figured out where I need you in my life just yet. Should you run with me at my side, or should you help to create the future?"

She lost herself in him, lost what little loyalty she had left for her sister as she felt the heat of his body against hers. Bridget wanted her sister's life, so she decided the best place to start was with her husband.

"Yes," she confessed. "I want everything Deanna has, everything that could have been mine. No, I take that back. Everything that *should* have been mine. I want you Seth, and I promise to be whatever it is you need me to be."

It was liberating to admit to herself what she truly wanted, even more liberating to act upon it. She pulled him to her; desperate for his kiss, his touch. The thrill of acting on her desires without the excuse of drugs made her impatient for his touch. Heat radiated from her body, threatening to burn her alive in one adulterous wave of passion.

"I can make all your dreams come true sweet little Bridget, even the darker ones," he looked at her knowingly. "But I need you to come to me willingly."

"I do."

"Yes, but you also need to come to me with a full understanding of what I am, everything that I become. Only then can you truly be mine."

It was at that moment that Seth took her gently by the hand and led her out the door and into the softly lit hall. Gathered outside the room the rest of the women of the manner stood waiting for her to join them.

Chapter 8

The hall itself was rather dark, and although candles were lit intermittently along the walls, it was still difficult for Bridget to see clearly. From what Bridget could make out each woman was dressed in a similar gown as herself. The only exception was that they were all in what looked to be black, although in that light it could have easily been any dark color. The one real striking difference being Michelle, she was wrapped in a white silk robe with a gold clasp that met just under her heavy breasts. The sheer fabric that hugged her body didn't quite meet in the middle, revealing a gap in the soft white fabric. In those few inches where the fabric became separated Bridget could see flashes of Michelle's naked body beneath as she moved.

Bridget began to feel strange; just mellow enough to think that she had been drinking, but not so much as to not understand what was going on around her. The thought that she had somehow been drugged again resurfaced, Eva could have quite easily lied to her about the food. Bridget was starting to wonder if she could trust anyone in this house...including herself.

Bridget was fairly certain that she wasn't dreaming, but her body was light, as if she could have floated down the hall with little effort. Michelle on the other hand was obviously heavily sedated. Her eyes were partially closed, her body loose and clumsy to the point that the twins, Jessica and Candice, had to support her on either side to keep her from falling over. Not that Bridget wouldn't have found it to be hysterical, but with the somber attitude of everyone around her she was sure that it wouldn't have had the same effect on everyone else.

Seth gently touched her by the arm and to her amazement she glided along with them down the corridor without any formal protest. Bridget's senses were screaming that something was wrong, but at that exact moment she felt as if she had spoken her words would have fallen to the softly carpeted hallway unheeded, as if the words themselves held little or no meaning. Bridget couldn't help but be led by Seth, let out into the darkness that surrounded them.

They made their way as a tight knit group down the steps and into the main hall where Bridget had first entered Laurendale Manner. Off to the right side there was a door leading into what looked to Bridget to be the house's study.

The room itself was dark but the fire that burned fiercely in its stone fireplace helped to illuminate the walls, two of which were lined with bookcases that almost overflowed with dark leather bindings of old and yellowing pages. An intricately carved desk held center stage, the majority of its body bathed in darkness with only a fraction of the golden light reflected off its smoothly polished surface. Large tapestries of ancient battle scenes adorned the upper walls, much like the other rooms of the great manner in a failed attempt to soften the hard lines of stone and wood that dominated the old house.

Three young boys stood nearby and watched as the party moved toward the center of the room. Their faces void of expression and Bridget felt a chill run up her spine at the look of them, so alike as to be triplets. The shadows that were cast upon their faces made them look haunted. Their eyes dark and deep set, unseeing and inhuman in every respect. Bridget remembered them as the boy who helped her to her room and again as the twin boys who helped to set the dining room table. She had assumed that there were just the two of them. Yet here in the darkness she was confronted by three mirrored images that made the hair on her arms stand on end. Then came the unsettling feeling in the pit of her stomach that not only must there be more of them, but also that they no longer seemed real to her. The nauseating feeling of being in real danger had begun to creep into her spine and there it settled down to nest like rats in her bones.

Seth momentarily released his hold on her and slid a large bronze statue of a naked woman, her body wrapped in the coils of an immense snake, from where it sat on the corner of the desk, taking along with it as he did a good deal of dust.

It struck Bridget again how old and tired the house seemed to be. How it practically moaned with the passing of time, as if it had been crouched on this very spot for eons and was now eager to leave and find a new venue to live out the remainder of its days.

Seth stepped back, moving Bridget with him as he did to make room as the desk rose up slightly and glided smoothly back to touch the wall behind it. The firelight only licked the outer edges of the gaping hole that had secretly nestled beneath it, barely casting enough light for Bridget to see the top step. Smooth, time worn stone steps led spiraling downward into it's unknown depth to where unimaginable deeds had gone unchallenged for centuries. It was there that Bridget and Michelle were led.

After several moments of being escorted down the steep steps, a small glow of light could be seen coming from the next corner. Bridget could feel the slow but steady change in temperature, but instead of being what one would have expected to be cold, the air was actually very warm and heavy. It made Bridget think of a sauna that had been set on low and she could feel the beads of sweat begin to form between her breasts and run down the smooth plain of her stomach.

It wasn't long before the small group had gone deep underground and to Bridget's surprise the tight winding stairwell opened out into a great open room. The ceiling was lost to blackness, and the walls that lined the brown stone room were roughly carved. A thick pelting of fine dirt lined the floor like sand and the perimeter was dotted with smaller cells that housed...what? Supplies? Food? Or something much more sinister?

In the center of the room lay a large flat slab of black stone buffed to such a high shine that it looked like a dark pool of water. On either side of the stone, large, hand made torches were lit that cast down flashing shades of orange and red against everyone and everything that came within striking distance of their finger like flames. Along the perimeter of the room where the several small chambers waited without doors or bars, only now Bridget could make out the vague movements of something within them, impatiently pacing their doorways and wanting nothing more than to get out. Seven openings in total she counted, all of them stark black holes set against the warm brown of the walls. Each one looking as if they had been chiseled from the ground itself by human hands. The strong smell of urine stung her nose from where it hung heavy and acidic in the damp air.

On the opposite side of the stone platform stood a mirror that had to be at least ten feet high and ten feet wide. It stood upright; no supports from any side could be seen, and it reflected the party glumly in its ragged seams as they entered the room. The edges were raw, no frame encased it's immense silvery form. Bridget could tell even from where she stood in Seth's hard grasp that it had to be even older than the house itself from the magnitude of waves and imperfections that it held there in the depths of its glass.

Seth handed Bridget off to Eva as if she were some sort of naughty child that needed watched and went to stand with the twins and Michelle where they had traveled farther into the dim light of the room. Together the three of them led Michelle onto the stone slab and knelt her down within its smoothly polished, onyx center. On either side of the flat stone were two waist high, smoothly carved alabaster vases where Jessica and Candice went to stand, their hands caressing the contours of the vases like lovers. The young girl's faces became starkly illuminated by the light of the torches and suddenly seemed to become wicked and ancient to Bridget in the harshness of the light.

The cool white vases were plain and unadorned, their simplistic pale beauty sat in great contrast to the darkness of the rest of the room. They practically glowed with their own inner light as if alive in some way. At first glance Bridget thought she could see movement from deep within their semi-transparent silhouettes, a dark form that slithered eagerly against it's paleness, casting wicked shadows against the vases thin sides. As her eyes began to adjust to the light of the room the movement from deep within them seemed to vanish; perhaps it was merely shadows cast by the light of the torches with nothing more menacing hiding deep within them than spiders spinning their crooked webs.

As Bridget watched the scene unfolded before her like a poorly rehearsed local community play, Seth knelt with the barely conscious body of Michelle in his arms in the center of the platform. He draped himself over her like a warm blanket, kissing Michelle deeply and spreading her arms up and out to either side to form the shape of a cross forged in human flesh. Michelle offered no resistance, not that she could have anyway, and lost herself in his kiss, her body moving easily with his passionate touch. He removed her robe gently, all the while never relinquishing his grasp of her body. Michelle moaned loudly with pleasure, her eyes mere slits as he pulled at her body, his mouth traveling the length of her in a warm and passionate frenzy of teeth and tongue. Seth caressed her flesh with his hands, bringing her to climax with the soft but firm expertise of his fingers, her naked body ached high in the air as she vibrated into him. Sweat rolled slowly down her body like nectar from a flower, at that very moment Seth owned her.

Bridget watched the perverse play unfolded in front of her as if she were in some way disconnected from her body. She could see everything going on inside the sparsely lit room from the safety of her mind where it balanced itself steadily between fantasy and reality. Her own groin ached for his touch, *she* wanted to be the one on the platform, *she* wanted to be the one to feel his touch. Bridget tried to step forward, to move closer to the erotic play before her, but Eva held her tight. The woman's grip was amazingly strong for her size.

As Bridget stood cemented to the spot by Eva's firm grip she watched as Jessica and Candice reached out towards the alabaster vases. Each girl rested her forearm against the lip of the vase and in unison, ran the long, tapered nail of their index finder down the inside of their wrist. The twins were slicing open their own soft flesh and as they did so, caused their blood to flow like dark wine into the pale vases gaping mouths. They too began to sway, mimicking the others love making as they moved in time with them. Each girl seemingly unaware of the wounds they had inflicted upon themselves as they lost themselves to Seth's sooth and sultry rhythm. As the last drop of their blood fell, the two girls pulled their arms back, licking their opened flesh like children licking ice cream.

The white alabaster of the vases had turned a deep red from the girls blood offering and they both began to vibrate. From deep within each cylindrical vase shot out a long, woody brown root. Each thick and earth soaked root was followed by dozens more as they danced and slithering their way to Michelle and Seth as they continued on with their lovemaking. As the roots began twisting themselves slowly up Michelle's body and around her long, swan like throat Seth released his hold on her. Gently the vines caressed Michelle's face and body, holding her lovingly like Seth had; unnoticed by their heavily sedated prisoner.

The mirror's reflection started to change; it began to bubble and warp towards it's once smooth center. The group's reflection turned and twisted within its glassy confines. Bridget could feel the horror begin to well up into her throat where it became lodged somewhere in the darkness. Her voice was held there, unable to escape it became constricted and then reluctantly fell silent. Something horrible was about to take place, something wicked.

In the center of the mirror it began to ripple as if someone had stuck their finger in a pool of placid water causing it to stir. A bubble formed and then popped, then more followed. From somewhere deep inside a long, black claw pushed its way through, trailed by a thick blue-black finger. The women began to chant softly at first, but as their desperation grew, so did their voices until it became a mind numbing scream.

Seth's voice rumbled out deep and throaty. Bridget couldn't take her eyes from what was happening in front of her, no matter the terror that beat in her human heart she dared not look away. The creature that immerged was nothing less than terrifying. Its large, muscular body was that of a man, his face, reptilian. The unmistakable smell of death and rotting flesh that he brought along with him was overpowering. Bridget started to gag, her eyes caught sight of dog-like creatures immerging now from the seven rooms that lined the massive hall. They were all the size of healthy tigers, although some more slight of build than others, as if there were different sexes, or perhaps different ages in their group. Their black furred bodies arched and drew near to the platform, saliva running from their gapping mouths as they paced back and forth, watching the scene unfold in front of them with amazingly *human* eyes; blue eyes.

Michelle was to be a sacrifice. Would she be torn from limb to limb or would she be eaten? Bridget fought back the desire to vomit, her eyes still firmly glued of the horror before her.

The creature on the platform now with Michelle and Seth must have been at least nine feet tall; its smooth, rubber like skin was blue-black, flecked with silver as if made from the very mirror it stepped from. Heavy scaling flared from its massive tail to the ridge of its grotesque head, adorned with heavy, black horns on each side, curving in to just touch the beast's face. Around its thick neck hung human teeth on a thin rope made of sisal and leather wrist bands were wrapped tightly at each limb. As it came towards her, she must have come out of the deep trance or drug she was on and a blood-curdling scream escaped her lips. She leaned back, as far as she could from the creature. The roots that bound her held tight, the thick root that had twisted itself around her throat tightened, cutting off her screams; she fell silent, her eyes bulging with fear. The creature's blood red eyes glanced at Seth, and then at Michelle. Seth removed himself from the creature's path and backed to the far end of the platform.

"My Lord Grumhold, please except this offering we bring to you. Help her to pass smoothly from this life of human frailty, and bring her soul to your bosom. Make her one of your unholy servants so that she may rid this world of the vanity of man." He gestured toward Michelle who had by this time lost consciousness. Bridget also seemed to be having trouble keeping on her feet, her legs had suddenly become like rubber. Seth had become inhuman.

The creature flashed a smile of fangs as it bent over the now limp body of Michelle. With one touch of the creatures hand on her skin the roots that had once kept her prisoner released their hold on her. Scattering to the sides of the blackened platform the roots began to weave themselves into a living cage around the two. The pale, weakened body of Michelle now dangled in his arms as he took her by the throat, subduing her screams as she awoke.

Michelle looked to Bridget to be under some sort of spell and no longer feared the unholy creature before her, either that or her mind had completely shut down, no longer capable of dealing with the events that were going on around her. At any rate, she had even reached out and touched the arm that held her, the creatures long, black claws digging into her soft skin. But even then Michelle showed no sign of fear or pain. She actually *let* him touch the roundness of her breasts and caress her between her long legs. To Bridget's disbelief Michelle began moaning in pleasure. She reclined back on the stone slab and let him enter her, screaming out as much as in pain as in pleasure. They molded into one, his body thrusting deeply into hers and it was only then that she began to change. The skin that was once a bronzed tan began to darken into the blue-black that mimicked the creatures. Her once soft tresses of blond hair became black as pitch, and her soft human body became one of a monster, although still very much in the female form.

As Bridget watched in terror, Jessica, Eva, and Candice also changed before her very eyes. They too became like the others, blue-black skinned with straight black hair. Their once soft, curvy bodies had became taunt and muscular. The women shed their own gowns and swayed to the others lovemaking, purring and moaning with delight.

At some point Seth must have left the platform unnoticed because before Bridget realized it he was standing right next to her, the heat of his breath sliding down the shallow curve of her neck. Bridget could feel his strong arms encircling her waist, her mind still a haze of confusion and worry.

"In a few moments you will see what it is that makes it possible to have all your desires, all of your passions realized." He kissed her deeply, and then released his hold on her to gaze deeply into her wide eyes.

Fear gripped at Bridget's heart; she could feel the perspiration begin to form on her top lip, her forehead. The hair on her arms and the nape of her neck stood on end. The terror, the realization that *she* would be next gripped and tore at her heart. The horror of being dragged to the platform, of being raped by the monster before her made her vision blur. A low, deep growling sound now came from the hairy throats of the dog-like creatures. Fangs reached from over extended jaws and saliva dripped as they circled the stone that held Michelle and the creature. Eva stood to the side, disconnected from the small group. She stroked the wide, ugly head of the largest of the dog-like creatures that seemed content to stay by her side. Eva caressed him like a woman would caress her child.

It was only then that Bridget realized that Seth had changed, she was so busy watching the horror unfold in front of her that she didn't realize how her own life was now in jeopardy. The danger she feared did not come solely from the visions before her; but by the very near monster that now stood beside her. Seth's body loomed over hers, his form now stood at least two feet taller than before and its entirety was covered in black, coarse hair. His once charismatic smile had been replaced with long, pointed fangs that mirrored those of the beasts that now guarded Michelle and the *thing* as they melted into one monstrous creature. Their body's thrashing about wildly in their violent alien lovemaking. While Seth didn't resemble the towering creature that erupted from the mirror or the creatures that paced the floor, she was certain that he was related to them in some unnatural way. She knew deep in the pit of her stomach that *this* was the family that Seth had so proudly spoken of, and *this* was the family he wanted her to join.

The room darkened around her as she began to loose the last remaining threads of her consciousness. Seth bent his hideous form down towards her and caught her body in his monstrous grip before her now useless legs had a chance to crumble under her weight, his sour breath coming in heated waves against her flesh. His eyes burned into hers and it was then that she finally found her voice, soft at first, as if it had come from someone else in the room, and then suddenly increasing in decibels until she was sure the sound was truly coming from deep inside her. It was Bridget Manning that was screaming in horror. It was Bridget Manning who's heart beating wildly in her chest, and who's mind was throbbing at the sight and sound of the events as they bared themselves to her openly and uncensored.

The beast that had once been her sister's husband bared a mouthful of razor like teeth and lunged viciously out at her, grabbing her by the shoulder as she turned to run and sank its teeth deep into the softness of her flesh. Pain shot through her body as she collapsed to the ground under the weight of the monster. Seth didn't release her, but dragged her now limp and bloody body into one of the seven rooms; the weight of his massive body over hers was almost suffocating. She could feel the dirt from the floor in her hair, sticking to the sweat and blood that beaded down her back as he dragged her. The creature then released her and the pain pulsated dully throughout her body, his sour breath panting down in her face. He growled at her and his voice was thick with the animal that he had become, but she could still make out what he said.

"I have chosen you to become my mate Bridget. You will not become like the other creatures that you see around you. You will become so much more to me, you will become my equal. Tomorrow night when the full moon rises over the estate you will understand the privilege I give to you now and join me in the hunt for human flesh." He reached down and ripped the blood soaked gown from her body with his claws, putting his full weight over her. Bridget gasped to breath. She couldn't move, couldn't think, the pain was immense and a torrent of silent tears began to stream down her face. The monster that Seth had become was raping her and there was no one in the world that could help her now. Nothing could be done but lay there and hope for it to be over quickly. Blackness was coming, threatening to swallow her up in it's velvety curtain. Her ears began to ring, her mind drifted to the stark whiteness of the operating room. Back to the day she had the abortion, that horrible day so long ago. The day that spun her life in a different direction, the day that brought her to this very moment in time. Restitution would be made tonight.

If the monster killed her in this nightmare that she had been hopelessly trapped in Bridget wondered briefly if her own *real* life would be over? After all, this was a dream…things like this just didn't happen. Things like this just didn't exist. As the blackness took over her senses Bridget was certain that even her own *real* death was better than waking up and finding out that this wasn't just a dream and that it had all actually taken place; *much* better.

Chapter 9

Candice and Jessica were instructed by Seth to take Michelle to her room and wait for her change to be completed. Michelle would be physically dead for some time while her human soul was literally pushed out and replaced with that of a Succubus. A creature, Bridget would later find out, that was of a womanly form and lived off the essence of men. Literally sucking them dry of life as they slept. Their sleeping body's taking on a life of their own while their testosterone filled minds lye dreaming of perversions too compromising and illicit to suggest to their wives or girlfriends. The Succubus was irresistible to men, and men were irresistible to the Succubus. They were in a way connected, both feeding off the needs and desires of the other until only the Succubus remained. The victims would grow to anticipate their nightly encounters, to even long for them, causing them to lose focus on their day to day lives. Sometimes resulting in the loss of jobs and eventually even friends and family to the demands of their sexual nocturnal fantasies. Separating the men from the rest of their lives made it easier for the Succubus to take over and dominate them, making the men slaves to their passionate, frenzied touch until there was nothing left of them but a dried out human carcass. Only then would the Succubus move on to her next victim with a pang of regret for the loss of yet another human, another lover. She was pushed along by the rumbling of hunger in her stomach and the ach of desire in her groin until she found her next lover, her next meal.

While Grumhold had planted the seed of the Succubus deep within Michelle's body it still needed time to take root. During which time period the body was no more than an empty vessel to which it became susceptible to all sorts of dangers. The least of which was the possession from other, less favored, demonic spirits that were not welcome in the house. She needed to be watched carefully until the Succubus was able to fully transform and take up permanent residence within the confines of her body. If the seed did not germinate quickly enough, and some *other* being managed to set up housekeeping in Michelle's body, the girls were instructed to kill her immediately.

Michelle had been designated the well appointed bedroom directly across from Seth so that he could monitor her comings and goings until she became more established in the family group. Normally Seth didn't make additions to the house, at least not successfully. In fact, the last successful additions to the house had been all Eva's doing. Jessica and Candice had been brought there from the back allies of Paris several decades earlier and in the relatively short time that they had spent there in the lavish confines of the house, they had all managed to become rather close. While Seth often enjoyed their company like the strong, virile man that he was, he however had nothing to do with their arrival, or the subsequent living arrangements. However, this time Seth had been quite taken with this new woman and the curve of her body tempted him so much that he eventually decided to risk Eva's profound displeasure with him and added her to their small group without her prior consent. While it mattered little to him if Eva approved of Michelle or not, he did want to make sure that she interacted well within the group. If Michelle didn't, if she caused turmoil in the house, Eva would be sure to use it as an excuse to dispose of her as she had done so many times before with his playthings.

As it stood now Seth was digging himself out of a rather deep hole when it came to Michelle. From the tight lipped reaction from the rest of the house Eva and the girls were not very pleased with the fact that Seth had made a female addition to the house without their prior knowledge. That, along with the fact that Bridget arrived the very same day put the entire house in an overly abrasive mood. The calorie ridden icing on the cake had to be the very real possibility that Seth's other wife, Deanna, would be joining them at some point in the very near future along with her child.

Jessica and Candice seemed unsettled by the day's events and while they were not totally accepting of Michelle they had at least been open to the possibility of new blood in the house. Unlike Eva, who seemed to retreat into herself even farther. She had become quiet and distant from Seth and his desire to discuss the matter with her seemed to fall on def ears. She wanted no part of Seth's new toy.

In the confines of Michelle's room in the early morning hours her body suddenly sat up. Michelle's lungs began sucking in the air around her with an urgency, like someone fighting to breath again after having the wind knocked out of them. Her eyes bulged wildly with fear, her hands grasping at the bedding around her as her lungs slowly began to fill with air. Gradually she calmed; her breathing became normal, steady.

The Succubus form that sat before the twins, new and unknowing of this strange world, was in deep contrast of Michelle's former self. Her once wavy blond hair had been replaced by a think black main that fell straight, just past the high peaks of her breasts. The flesh of her body that had at one time cast a healthy, sun-kissed glow now shown blue-black with the shine and texture like that of a diver's wet rubber suit. Once azure eyes now stared back predator yellow, and there was no mistaking that they *had* become the eyes of a predator.

"Am I dead? Surely the beast has killed me." Moaned Michelle, her voice thick as if from a deep and lengthy sleep.

"Only in the spiritual sense of the word," said Candice. "Your body is still very much alive."

"I feel strange, like someone has been sitting on my chest." Michelle pressed her hands against her chest. "And I'm so thirsty. I cant remember a time that I've felt so *dry*. I must have something to drink."

"The feeling of heaviness will soon ease once the blood starts to circulate a bit better. The thirst however will need looking after," said Candice. As she moved towards Michelle she motioned to Jessica for help getting her out of the bed and onto her feet.

Jessica took Michelle by one arm and Candice took her by the other in order to steady her as they helped her off the bed. Michelle's body still felt heavy and sluggish, she needed help to even stay on her feet, let alone walk.

"My feet feel like they are stuck in mud. I can barely move them." Michelle slumped against Jessica.

"You just need to circulate the body's blood a bit more, that's all. Your heart was stopped for quite a while and it takes time to get things running smoothly again. It's kind of like starting a car on a cold winter morning. Besides, it'll take you some more time to get used to your new body. That's why we're here to help you." Jessica pushed her back up to a standing position and steadied her again.

After several moments of stagnant movements and near collapses they were finally certain that she could stand on her own two feet without any need of their assistance. Only then did they bring her to stand before the most exquisite mirror she had ever seen in her life. Heavy silver framed the liquid soft perfection of the mirror before her. It's lustrous form was embellished with cherubs that winked from behind clouds, and doves that sought to play on outstretched wings. Michelle was mesmerized by its sheer beauty, finally having to physically tear herself away from its casings to see the strange new creature staring back at her from within its center.

Gasping, she recoiled back from her reflection, but shock quickly turned to curiosity. She leaned in and touched her reflection as if making sure it was her own, and then smiled. Michelle now had a certain wicked beauty about her, one that intrigued and delighted her. Michelle was no longer the dumb blond that she was normally classified as being. Her human body had never matched what she felt to be truly *her* on the inside, but now it did; and she liked it. All her life people assumed she was too stupid to hold more than a single dim thought in her head, let alone carry on an intelligent conversation. Their ridicule based merely on the color of her hair and the curve of her body. All that would change now. Now the world would fear her just like she had always wanted it to. As a smile spread wide across her full, lapis lips, she saw for the first time that the inside of her mouth was full of the most deadly looking, razor sharp teeth that she could ever have imagined.

"The better to eat you with my dear." she laughed, her head tilting back in pure joy as the deep sound bellowed from her throat.

Jessica and Candice couldn't help but laugh along with her. They hadn't initially been drawn to her. The fact that Seth just brought her into the house without any explanation or prior consultation with any of them had put the girl's backs up. They did however get the feeling that she would make a truly successful Succubus; with the right training of course.

"So you say my soul is dead. But I feel the same as I did before, only stronger, more alive."

"Well, perhaps dead is an overstatement. What I meant to say is that your human soul is no longer in your body. When Lord Grumhold takes you as one of his own the coupling destroys your human soul," said Candice, pushing a strand of Michelle's hair from her face in order to admire her new features better.

"Yes, your human *soul* is dead, but your body...your body is alive and ten times stronger than it ever was. Grumhold planted a Succubus inside you when he took you. His seed is very powerful. It has germinated deep inside your human body and has made you what you are now." Jessica smiled, admiring the great beasts work.

"I'm just a shell of my former self then?" Puzzled Michelle.

"I guess you could say that. The truth is your memories…your likes and dislikes, Hell, your whole personality, has been imprinted into the Succubus like a fingerprint. You are as you always have been, just much more deadly." Jessica looked at her, it wasn't hard for her to believe that Michelle had always been a bit deadly. Even without the seed of the Succubus rooted deep inside her belly.

"Amazing." Michelle turned to admire herself in the mirror again. "I'm even more beautiful than I was before."

"Yes, much more beautiful." The two girls looked at one another and rolled their eyes. Jessica even snorted, but not loud enough to make Michelle notice. She was far too busy looking at herself to notice much of anything else anyway. The room could have crumbled down around her blue ears and she wouldn't have noticed.

"Now Michelle, about that thirst you complained about earlier. We can fix that for you now if you like." Jessica gestured towards the mirror as she and Candice changed into their Succubus forms in a fluid ripple of movement. Michelle's eyes opened wide by the ease in which the girls changed.

"You're like me now…sort of." She looked both girls up and down, assessing their beauty against her own. Michelle clearly the winner in her own eyes. Modesty was never one of Michelle's strong points.

Ignoring Michelle's condescending overtones Candice felt a need to put her at the back of the line where she belonged. Michelle was feeling too sure of herself. "We all have our place here. That is, we are all unique in our own way. Take Eva for example, she is very different, in ways that I couldn't even begin to explain. She has great powers, powers that even Seth himself is careful not to toy with. Eva can do great evil if she wishes, or great good."

Michelle seemed interested, and was about to ask for more details but Jessica changed the subject, giving Candice a disapproving glare.

"Bridget, on the other hand is not a Succubus at all, she's a Werewolf, like Seth. Seth took her as his mate at the very moment Grumhold took you. I believe it was because he felt she would suit him better as his hunting partner, than she would merely as his concubine." Jessica looked at her hard, wanting to see if the words stung as venomously as she intended them to. There was not much in the form of an outward reaction, but enough to prove her point, if only to herself, that Michelle was a jealous woman. Something they could all live quite happily without.

For a moment Michelle turned to herself in thought.

Has Seth deemed me too dimwitted to be his partner in life, and feels these two young girls are more my equal? Does he feel something more for Bridget than he has led me to believe?

She turned back to the girls, her fake smile planted firmly on her plump lips. While the thought of Seth choosing Bridget over herself enraged her beyond belief, she held her emotions in check, at least for the time being. Michelle was certain that the problem of sharing her lover with these other women would eventually work itself out in her favor. If not, she would merely assist the process along with the help of violence, but for now, she was content enough to let it slide.

"Back to your thirst, watch and learn," smiled Candice.

The twins stood opposite the gilded mirror and closed their eyes. There bodies, although similar to Michelle's in every conceivable way had their own slight differences. Their build was slight, and lean where as Michelle's was full and curvaceous even in its new form. Either way Michelle would be hard pressed to admit that their beauty was in any way equal to her own.

Nice, thought Michelle. *But hardly as well suited to the form as myself. They are still no more than teenagers. Their form hasn't yet matured into womanhood. Where as I on the other hand command a mans attention by the mere curve and maturity of my body.*

As the girls rested their hands lightly on the mirror it began to glow from deep inside and a fine, pale blue smoke began to cascade down the wall and out of its depths. Its reflective glass began to bubble and churn within its casing of silver and filigree. Soon it steadied and the glass surface became no more than a window. On the other side framed within its confines lay a man sleeping. His dreams troubled, he stirred, moaning something incoherently. Candice and Jessica stood close to the newly opened porthole, their faces almost touching the glass as they breathed deep, like someone smelling the most delectable array foods. Without any effort of their part, or any words spoken, their young, slim bodies became translucent like smoke and filtered through the porthole to the other side. Michelle watched in amazement as they stood by the man's bed, their bodies solidifying as easily as they had become transparent only seconds earlier.

They bent down and caressed the man, pulling the sheets from his tired body. Their hands gliding effortlessly over his glowing skin, his body still tossing and turning as if in the throws of a menacing dream. After several moments of their gentile caresses he began to settle, half awake, half asleep, as if caught somehow between the two planes of reality He reached out and reciprocated the caress as they joined him in bed, his mind was sleeping yet his body was awake and fully aroused. He pulled them to him like a man possessed, his eyes closed, he kissed them each in turn losing himself in the softness of their female flesh.

The man was young, perhaps no more than twenty, with a smooth, hairless body and taunt young muscles. Jessica mounted him, her monstrous form moaning in delight as she rode him, sweat glistened on his body as he drank fully the kisses of both women. Several moments past, Jessica had taken much of the mans seed deep into her body, yet their feeding had not been satisfied. Relinquishing her grip on him Jessica moved forward onto his chest, his mouth buried in the small mounds of her breasts as Candice took over, her mouth sliding down his body, her lips gripping him, taking him as he shuddered, his strength growing weaker as she drank from him, his breathing became shallow and troubled.

Michelle could now see a blue haze come from off the man's body and enter into the air. Dancing and swirling about, the man's essence came to the surface of the mirror and pulled Michelle in, demanding that she take from him. The ach of her body became as strong as her thirst.

Candice pulled herself reluctantly from the man, her desire to continue feeding had become hard to control. They had visited the man on the nightly basis for the past month and he was beginning to show signs of illness. Soon he would need to be replaced, but he was young, and strong. They were certain to get several more weeks out of him before his untimely death. He would be missed, like all of them were. In the end his body would fail, his soul would be broken and his seeds would be used to forge countless unions between Hell and earth. Demons would be born and the world would be one step closer to utopia.

Smiles of satisfaction crossed the girls' faces as Michelle entered the room. Again she marveled at how exact their looks were, even in their succubus forms they were impossible to tell apart.

"Your turn Michelle. Take him deeply, drink his seed so that we might help to create another race of demons to walk the earth."

She stood over his weakened body. His pulse was quick and his breathing had become uneven and raspy. Michelle did as she was instructed. She could feel the steady flow of semen into her body. She could feel it settle into the deepest corners of her womb where it would wait to be impregnated by the demon Grumhold. To her delight it was the most thirst quenching and refreshing feeling she had ever experienced. Her body took him deeply, taking so much from the man that she felt heavily intoxicated when she was finally pulled away by her two young instructors. Their bodies were then transported back through the mirror and into Michelle's room. The mirror grew dark and returned to its former vocation of showing Michelle her own reflection. She felt ten years younger and immensely strong and vibrant. No drug she had ever taken, no alcohol she had ever consumed came even close to this feeling of total empowerment. She was hooked, this was no ordinary sex, this was soul quenching and earth shattering. Highly addictive.

"Just remember to only take what you need to satisfy yourself or you will kill the human too soon. Killing humans too quickly, although not totally distasteful, will limit your daily feedings and thus cause you some discomfort should you be unable to fill the void that a kill will make. My sister and I have been feeding off this young man for some time, but we can not keep this up forever. Soon it will become imperative that we move onto a new, fresh human male. We try not to kill unless we are certain that the space will be filled. So be certain that you do not kill unless that is your desire," smiled Jessica.

That was her desire, thought Michelle. She nodded her understanding. To kill had always been her deepest desire. "Now what?"

"Now we visit with Grumhold where we will complete the process. You have felt his touch once already, at your taking. Now you will be able to enjoy the deep satisfaction that comes with knowing you are helping to further the demon race. The seeds that you have taken from the man rest deep within your body. Now when Grumhold takes you he will change the genetic makeup of the semen, causing it to mutate and penetrate deep into our own eggs. Within an hour after conception your body will produce several thousand eggs which you will lay in his lair where he watches over them until they mature and grow into our brothers." Jessica crossed the room and opened the door.

Michelle purred at the thought of so many sexual partners. "I think I can handle that. All this sex *and* money. What more could a girl ask for?"

Chapter 10

Still below in the humid air of the catacombs Eva had stayed behind to talk to Grubb, her eldest wolf-child. While he could not speak verbally, they were connected on a much deeper level; telepathically. Their minds were connected and they spoke freely to each other on the daily basis. A secret that she had managed kept to herself. Not even trusting Seth enough to ever let him know of their ability. Along with that secrecy came the ability to learn about a great many things that took place in the manner. None of which she was particularly pleased with.

I don't like the smell of this new one mother…this Michelle, thought Grubb, standing to one side of her and leaning gently against her thigh.

What do you mean my love?

She smells off. Not right in the head I think. I don't trust her. The others sense it too. Grubb nuzzled her gently. *"I think she should be watched. She's the type that would slit your throat while you slept if given half a chance."*

Eva rubbed his head, *"While I trust in your instincts my dearest Grubb I doubt that I will be able to sway your father to see our side in this matter. He is quite taken with this one for the time being. I'm certain however that his desires will start to wane in time, like they always do, and then he will see her true nature. Once he is able to see past his own desires and to more rational, level headed plain of thinking I will then be able to dispose of her as I have all his other play things. I will however heed your words of warning and keep a close eye on her until then.*

Thank you mother, thought Grubb. Reaching forward with his front two legs the great beast stretched out his spine to it's fullest extent. *Mind you…I wouldn't mind having a taste of her first.* He smiled as only a wolf could and Eva smiled back.

I don't doubt that for a moment my son.

Stroking Grubb on the head she kissed him goodnight as she made her way back up to the main floor of the manner, deeply troubled by the warning her son had given her.

Eva was becoming weary of Seth's constant desire to run the manner like some spoiled rock star. He had become more and more demanding and arrogant in the last hundred years and Eva felt that perhaps now was the time for change.

As Eva made her way down the hall to her room she heard hushed voices coming from behind her. She slid into one of the alcoves to listen; it was the girls and Michelle. From the sound of it Michelle's first lesson at being a succubus had been a successful one and they were on their way to the lower level to complete lesson two.

Grumhold would be pleased.

He had a taste for curvy, full-figured women like so many other males did, weather they be of the human or demon type.

She smiled faintly to herself.

At least he would be able to enjoy her for a bit longer. She owed him that much anyway. In the end though, she was certain that Grumhold would see things her way and help to remove her from the house.

Unlike Seth, Grumhold knew that what was important to Eva, was important to everyone.

Chapter 11

Bridget's first thought of consciousness was one of fear. While the suffocating weight of the werewolf had left her body she still felt his presence somewhere in the room. She could hear it, panting and pacing in some distant corner of the room. Her first thought being that if she moved he would want more of her; and that was not something she wanted to deal with.

Not awake.

She cold feel the warm fluid of him on her, *in* her. She fought back the desire to wipe her hand between her legs, to remove it's vulgarity from her body. He was watching her, she could feel his eyes burn into her as she lay there naked and covered in blood and dirt.

"You're awake," the beast grunted, "I was hoping I didn't kill you."

She flinched at his voice, animal and yet so human. She pulled her body up to a sitting position, her mind screamed out in pain. It was more than his seamen that ran from between her legs, it was blood, her blood. He had injured her in his desire to mate with her, rape her, she began to shake.

"You were smaller than I had expected, I have remedied that," the beast almost smiled with contempt. "You will not bleed for long." He walked over to where she lay huddled in the corner of the room, the dirt grinding into her ass, sticking between her knees she pulled her legs up to her chest. He smelled her, his muzzle coming close enough to the side of her face for her to feel him drawl in the air around her. She squeezed her eyes shut, waiting for him to strike out at her.

"Please," she whispered, "don't."

"You forget yourself Bridget, you belong to me now. I can take you whenever and however I wish. You are like me now, and by this evening you will see what it means to rule the night, to live without the fear of dying and to taste the heavenly flavor of soft human flesh."

Without another word he left her alone in the darkness and the stench of the catacombs beneath Laurendale Manner. Alone with her thoughts and her nightmares. Alone with her ever growing regret of her life she bled into the dirt; alone with the mind numbing realization that she had been bitten by a werewolf.

She would turn into that *thing*, isn't that what he had meant? She would turn and become like him, a killer. She would murder and...*eat*...innocent humans. Her stomach turned, it flip-flopped over itself and she could feel the sour burn of vomit rise up in the back of her throat. She quickly fell to one side, her elbow holding herself up far enough to spill the contents of her stomach and not have to lay in it. She was a monster like him now, her mind reeled. What the hell was she going to do? She couldn't tell her sister, Deanna would never believe her, not without showing her, and then what? What if she killed her, what if she couldn't control the animal that now coursed through her veins, penetrating the very being of her soul.

Bridget rolled to the other side, away from the sour stench of her own vomit. She couldn't live the rest of her life being a werewolf, doing the terrible things that she knew in the pit of her stomach she would be *forced* to do. The terrible things she would *want* to do. There was nothing left for her now, nothing. Bridget's mind latched onto the only thing it could. The only place she could find to lay blame. Deanna.

Why did you do this to me Deanna?...you ruined my life. Why couldn't you just leave me alone?

Bridget pushed herself to her feet, her body resting against the cold surface of the stone wall. Her nakedness pressed against it, she could feel her thickening blood as it oozed its way down her shoulder and over her breast. Her hand felt for it in the darkness, the pain was numbing, the bite that Seth had left behind felt huge in the darkness.

It was true, the creature had not lied, she *would* become like him. Tears began to well in her eyes, spilling over they mixed with the dirt on her face. She could taste their saltiness as they touched the corners of her mouth. Bridget pulled herself from the darkness of the room, following the suddenly harsh light of the torches that still lit the way back to the steps. She needed to get back to the upper floors of the manner where she could wash the filth and blood from her body.

Bridget looked cautiously towards the mirror and the highly polished stone platform, expecting to see the monster Seth waiting there for her, waiting to ravage her body again.

The room was empty.

Everyone had gone, even the monster that had taken Michelle and made her into that nightmarish creature that thrashed about in the darkness. Was what happened to Michelle worse than what had happened to her in the quiet darkness of the cavern? She wasn't even sure Michelle was still alive, for all Bridget knew the monster dragged her helpless body back into the mirror from which it came only to devour her in some ritualistic feeding.

The brutal vision flashed across the corneas of Bridget's eyes causing her to gag.

The only thing Bridget knew for sure at that exact moment in time, the only thing she could count on, was that her life would never be the same. She wiped the tears from her eyes and began to climb the steps. Each time Bridget pulled the weight of her body from one carved step to the next she was certain that her battered flesh would pull itself apart and that she would crumble to the ground in a sort of human slurry.

Strangely enough as she continued on up the steep incline she felt stronger, each step had ceased its painful torment and she began to feel almost normal. By the time Bridget's naked form reached the top of the roughly carved steps, and stood there alone in the darkness of the study, she felt better than she had in the past ten years of her human life.

It was the poison in her system, she could close her eyes and see it moving slowly through her veins. The filthy virus that made her into the same beast as Seth had also made her stronger, more resilient to pain and fatigue.

Bridget made her way from the study to the main hall and stood poised by the oversized front door. She could leave this place, make her way to the nearest main road and get help. In her current condition she was sure to draw attention to herself and in a matter of moments she could be far away from these horrid people and their dark Gods.

But she didn't.

It was at that moment that Bridget cast her old, tarnished life aside and chose instead a life of bloodshed and murder. A life where her most exquisite desires would be freely granted and where her unmatched physical strength was suddenly more important than her prowess in bed . Bridget stood silently in the main hall of the Laurendale Manner, to her amazement she could smell and hear things she never could before. The first thing that became caught like a fly in the spiders web of her newly tuned senses was that of Seth Toumbs.

Bridget could smell the heat of him from where she stood. He was different from the others in the house, almost sweet like candy. Her thighs ached painfully for him, but she pushed him forcefully from her mind.

Bridget ran to her room now, taking two steps at a time she cleared the vast openness of the staircase easily and then on to her darkened suite where she closed the door behind her with a thud.

She stood for a moment, her breath easy and unburdened as her mind raced with the endless possibilities of her new life. As Bridget went to turn the small light on next to her bed she realized how easily she could see about the room, even now as it lay in complete darkness. If this had been only a few hours earlier she would have been fumbling around the room, unable to see anything. It was as if Bridget were wearing some sort of night vision goggles, much like the ones you see flashing across the screen of war movies as the enemy takes aim. The room was in total darkness but she could still make out the shapes of objects that were scattered about the room clearly.

Bridget smiled to herself, a dangerous smile that she knew the meaning of all too well. She knew that she had already accepted Seth's offer before she had even made it to her room. Bridget *would* be his, and she would turn her new life into something she had never had before. The vast possibilities opened up to Bridget like a flower in the coolness of a spring shower.

She turned the small table light on and went into the bathroom, her reflection in the small mirror was one of both disarray and strength. Bridget's hair fell to her face in tired ringlets of dirt and sweat. Her face had become streaked with dried tears and dirt. Her shoulder gaped openly at her, the bite of the werewolf stood out grotesquely against the paleness of her bare shoulder. The pain had all but subsided and Bridget now touched it curiously with her left index finger. It gave slightly under the pressure of her finger and blood began to flow slowly again from the two matching holes causing her to grimace in pain.

Bridget looked down at the rest of her body, the blood that had run from between her legs had all but dried, leaving behind burgundy streaks that ran down the length of her inner thighs. The ordeal that she had just lived through suddenly seemed to be nothing more than a distant memory, like the glimmer of lost summers from her childhood. It had become no more important than that of a dream, a nightmare. Without anymore thought on the matter she turned the shower on and stepped inside.

The hot water washed the dirt and blood from her body, stinging the open flesh wound on her shoulder, but the horror of the night had passed. Bridget no longer felt the overwhelming desire to run from the old manner and leave her sister, Deanna, to deal with her own marital problems.

She washed her hair, the soft perfume of the shampoo suddenly strong. Bridget hummed softly to herself. She was content to stay here, to become Seth's new lover and nightly companion.

Through the steady beating of the water against her skin and the tiled walls of the shower itself Bridget heard someone enter her room.

Amazing.

She wasn't surprised or frightened. Bridget took her time, not rushing as she would have before. She turned off the water and left the warm confines of the bathroom and entered into the stark coolness of the bedroom where Eva stood waiting for her.

"I think I understand now what you meant when you said I would desire his touch. About how important it would be to me," said Bridget, without even trying to hide her nakedness or the severity of the wound on her shoulder.

"It's like a drug, a drug coursing through your veins." Eva stepped a bit closer, her body relaxed and smooth in it's movement. "I like you Bridget, which is more than I can say of every woman Seth brings home. You have the possibility to really connect with the rest of us here at Laurendale Manner, don't waste it." Eva smiled warmly at Bridget as she welcomed her into the family. "You are welcome to stay here Bridget; you are welcome to spend an eternity here if you wish."

Bridget caught the heady sent of a man…and something deep within her was suddenly forced into life by a blast of electricity.

Chapter 12

Deanna awoke with a start. She had fallen asleep on Bridget's sofa while waiting for her sisters phone call that never came. To make matters worse, she even ended up having some of the worst nightmares since their parents murder. Most of which were about her sister, her naked body covered in blood and heartily dining on the corpse of a young man.

Not something she wished to experience again, at least not in this lifetime.

Her dreams were becoming increasingly vividly and more and more disturbing each time she fell asleep. The quicker she put that nights cruel visions out of her mind the better. Sleep was steadily becoming something to dread at its coming, and something to regret at its leaving.

Deanna gazed at the bar. One good drink would help her to sleep soundly; possibly even without the continued nightmares.

But the baby...

A ridiculous idea really, she pushed it from her mind, although with some degree of difficulty.

It was a little after nine o'clock in the morning so she calculated it to be after two in the afternoon now in England. Deanna mused about what her sister would be doing at that time, why she hadn't called her as expected. Perhaps Bridget was out following Seth as expected, or perhaps it was nothing more than she was having a late lunch and hadn't gotten to a phone just yet to report her findings.

Then Deanna's mind began to ebb back to her dream, her nightmare. What if her sister really *was* in trouble and needed her desperately? She should try to contact her, she should try to do *something.*

But no, Deanna would wait to hear from Bridget. Her sister could handle herself better than anyone else she ever knew, of that one thing she was sure of.

A low wave of nausea welled up from the center of her being. The baby was hungry, Hell *she* was hungry and soon the thoughts of Bridget and even those her latest nightmare were growing dim in her mind. Hunger had replaced those thoughts, and it was no less demanding than the terror that had just recently occupied her mind. Deanna was desperate for something to eat, anything would suffice, and from the equally desperate look on Buster's face as he sat there gazing intently at her from the deep folds of an olive green, chenille throw, so was he.

Now that she was fully awake and moving around, Deanna also began to realize that the sofa was no place for a pregnant woman to sleep through the night. Her entire body ached, from head to toe, even her hair hurt. She made her way slowly to the bathroom to pee and splash some cold water on her puffy eyes. Every painful step reminding her to sleep in the guest bedroom during the upcoming night.

Her sister, although she had left in a hurry, had always made a point of offering her the use of the spare bedroom whenever she came for a visit. At least that was the way things stood before Deanna had married Seth, and she couldn't imagine that the invitation could have changed much since the last time they spoke.

Deanna crossed the hall from the bathroom to the guest room and stood in it's open doorway, the room was small but adequate. A full size brass bed, much like the ones they had while growing up at their grandmother's house, stood out against the soft pink wallpaper of the far wall. An old fashioned white dresser and night stand with shinny glass knobs were the only other pieces of furniture in the room. They too brought back memories of a woman long dead and the painful reasons for living with her in the first place.

Still, it was a comfortable room and the ach in her back reminded her of the real reason she needed to suppress those foul memories of loss and murder. She needed a good nights sleep and she wasn't ever going to get on sprawled out on Bridget's sofa.

Deanna sighed and rubbed her stomach, her child would never have the chance of knowing either of his, or her, Great Grandparents. If either of them had still been alive the child might have suffered from terminal smothering due to extended kissing. Death by love. Deanna smiled to herself and patted her large overgrown stomach.

"You just squeaked by that one my love." Her words echoed down the empty hallway making her jump at the sound her own voice made in the stillness of the house. She was restless.

Deanna walked a bit further down the hallway to Bridget's bedroom and opened the door. She had never really been in her sister's room before and she was rather surprised at its grandeur. Hardwood floors the color of black coffee and buffed to a high sheen nestled under ornate Asian rugs. The drapery that hung from the two large windows were heavy enough to block out any offending sunlight (imperative, she imagined, when one worked nights and slept during the day.) and rich in texture. Bridget's canopied bed was immense, and took up quite a chunk of the large room with it's thick, oversized mattress that came just below Deanna's no longer visible waistline. Expensive crystal figurines adorned the nightstand and dresser and an old family photo of them all before the tragedy sat framed in silver next to her bed.

Deanna sat on the edge of the bed, the old photo now resting in her hands as she remembered the day it was taken. It was Easter morning and they had just returned home from Church. Even back then they only went during the holidays, they never did seem to make it every Sunday like their mother would have wanted. From the snippets of memory that flashed through her mind even their father Jack had been in a good mood that day, something in those days that was a rare occasion in itself. Deanna remembered how they had all stuffed themselves with ham and chocolates until they thought they would burst. Bridget couldn't have been more than eight then.

Life was so good that day. If only…

She put the photo down, not wanting to tarnish the memory of that moment with the dark and dismal years that soon followed. Not long after the photo was taken their mother had unexpectedly become pregnant and their father became withdrawn and violent…even with the two of them.

Deanna pulled herself from the painful memories of her past and went back into the kitchen to examine the contents of her sister's refrigerator. As she had suspected, there was nothing in there that particularly caught her eye and from the sparse collection of dried out leftovers and old take-out containers she wasn't even sure if she *should* eat any of it. From the limited selection her choices consisted of foods from the nearby restaurants; General tso's chicken with fried rice, half a case of Pepsi and four tired looking slices of what looked to be cheese pizza; not even so much as an egg or half a gallon of milk could be found in the recesses of her sister's barren ice box.

She had to remind herself that Bridget was a single woman, and that she really didn't need to keep that much food in her fridge. Besides, her sister probably ate out quite often, and more than likely she wasn't even the one paying the bill. Deanna's imagination was rather vivid and she stood there, leaning up against the kitchen counter, envisioning Bridget dressed in some seductive evening gown and getting into the back of a shinny new black Cadillac with some dried up old man. The two of them on their way to some five star restaurant topped off with desert at her place. Deanna shook her head, she really needed to stop thinking that way about her sister. Bridget was helping her after all and she had no real proof that her sister did anything else but sing and dance. No proof what-so-ever.

More importantly, Deanna would need to call for groceries sooner than she had expected; she was starved.

Deanna gazed intently around her sisters living room, it was much like the bedroom she had just left, it had the same expensive feel to it. She was not sure now why she had always just assumed that Bridget hadn't made a success of the entertainment business, looking around her now Deanna had to admit that she must have, at least that is unless she was up to her well shaped eyebrows in debt. She took a long, hard look at the leather furniture and what seemed to be original artwork in her sister's home. None of it was cheap, none of it worn out hand-me-downs or third rate knock offs. The leather was real enough, the paintings grand enough. None of what Deanna saw in her sisters home came from bargain outlets or discount warehouses, at least not that she could tell.

It's not like they lived in the fast paced, bustling cities like New York or Hollywood, but still, it looked as if Bridget *had* done rather well for herself, she just hadn't really noticed it before.

There was that nagging thought in the back of her mind again that suggested that her darling little sister did more than sing and dance down at that club of hers, she wished the negative thoughts would stop surfacing, but there it was like a flashy red and white bobbin floating on the surface of her mind. Deanna tried to stop her mind from spinning off in ten directions at once…prostitution, drugs, gambling…the mob…she reminded herself that Bridget was a big girl now and that she could make her own decisions, or mistakes, whichever they may be, and that she had no business interfering with her life. But the nagging kept surfacing at the back of her mind that her sister was in over her head, perhaps even in danger. Again she pushed it down, suffocating it, silencing it.

Not so deep down Deanna had always wished her little sister would grow up and take a little more responsibility for her actions. Bridget had become so wild after their parents murder; so rebellious. She couldn't help but wonder how differently her sister's life might have been if it had never happened. But it did, it *had* happened and she needed to find out just what her sister had gotten herself into, how she could afford to live like this on a dancers salary.

Deanna's eyes had started to open, to reveal the truths about her, and the people she loved. The truths that she had turned a blind eye to for so many years, and she was finally beginning to see what the world was truly like around her. In a way she wanted to thank Seth, after all it had all started the moment she saw him at the airport with that woman.

That woman...

Tears began to well up in her eyes again, her forehead throbbed with each beat of her heart as if it had suddenly moved from her chest to her head and was too big for such a confined space. Deanna regretted not being a stronger person, she knew it wouldn't matter at the end of the day if Seth was having an affair or not; just so he came home to her and the baby in the end. Deanna was so in love with him, she even briefly considered calling Bridget at the hotel and just telling her to come home, that it didn't matter anymore, not now, not once she had a night to think about it. That was the truth, she did, she *had* thought about it and in her effort to force Seth from her heart ended up having one Hell of a lonely night. The thought of spending an eternity without him, and eternity *alone* scared her. Deanna had given herself enough time to realize what she could lose if she pressed the matter of the other woman any farther.

I love him so much... and yet...

But what *would* she lose?

My husband... my child's father...

A cheating husband wasn't much of a loss if she stopped and thought about it, not much of a loss at all.

He slept with her, I know he did. And now he's with my sister...

Deanna went over to the small, eighty's style bar in the corner of the living room where she had seen Bridget put what had looked to be an appointment book during her last visit.

There it was, tucked out of sight along with a thick stack of credit card bills and shopping receipts by the sink. In her current condition Deanna figured Bridget must have assumed this would be the last place her sister would be poking around, it's not as if she was the type of woman that would drink during her pregnancy. The book itself was bound in a soft, smooth leather, dyed a dark burgundy, the color of a good, hearty wine. The pages were covered in gold edging with a thin braid of matching gold floss that was used as a makeshift marker. Deanna glanced through the book, names, numbers, and locations. Most of the names, but not all, were those of men. *All* of them however had what looked to be a grading system next to their personal information. The crude grading system was in the form of dollar signs. Deanna's brow deepened in worried thought, she didn't like the look of it, not at all. When Bridget was younger and still living at home Deanna had come across a similar grading system in one of her sisters books. When Deanna had asked Bridget about it she had become angry, telling her she had no business looking through her personal things. She had used stars back then, and they had *all* been guys names, guys Deanna knew she dated on and off, and others she had never even heard of before. She had worried back then too.

In the back cover of the book was written "Pigglie's Bar" with the number and address under it written in gold metallic ink. Her mind instantly latched onto it, had her sister ever mentioned it before? For that matter, had her sister *ever* really mentioned *where* she worked other than a night club downtown. Deanna looked at the name again, Pigglie's Bar. It sounded so…sleazy.

Just then the large, heavily furred body of Buster the cat rubbed up against her leg and brought her back to her current situation. At first Deanna had managed to tune out his obnoxious demands for food, but now his constant, ever demanding meowing was becoming annoying even to her. Deanna went back into the kitchen, as her bare feet touched the cold, tiled floor it sent a chill through her entire body causing her to grimace, reluctantly she emptied a carton of what looked like shrimp-fried rice in his empty bowl and warmed up the remaining cheese pizza for herself.

"That should shut you up for a while. Don't tell Bridget I gave you that either." She stood there watching him as Buster purred into his bowl, lost in the joys of old shrimp and cold rice as only a cat could.

She would definitely need to call for some groceries, and soon too. There was no way she was going to risk having to eat anything else out of there, she needed some protein. Just the thought of biting into a juicy, rare stake set her mouth watering. Deanna looked down at Buster and her mind suddenly wondered what BBQ sauce would go with cat?

"You better hope they deliver this far out…or you might be on tonight's menu." Deanna laughed out loud at the thought of dicing up poor old Buster, but a part of her wasn't really joking. She had briefly wondered what he *would* taste like slathered in some good old K.C. Masterpiece. "Just the pregnancy talking old girl, you wouldn't really eat your sisters cat." She looked down at him and felt she needed to amend that last statement. "Or *any* cat for that matter." Deanna left the room with her pizza, the more space she kept between the two of them the better, she was hungrier than she realized.

For now she wasn't risking calling anyone and tying up the line until she heard from her sister, not even for food. Forty-five minutes and half a pizza later Deanna decided she couldn't wait any longer and called the hotel herself to see what Bridget had managed to find out, if anything, about Seth and that woman.

"Laurendale Manner," soothed a female voice, "Eva Van Cruse speaking. May I help you?" The accent was heavy but Deanna had become so accustomed to hearing it since Seth had started staying there so often, that she understood the woman perfectly.

"Hello, can you connect me to...Deanna Toumbs' room?" She had almost forgotten to ask for herself.

"But of course, one moment please."

The phone in her sisters room rang several times with no response, eventually Eva returned to the line. "She must have stepped out Madame. Would you like to leave a message for her?"

"Yes thank you. Could you please ask her to call her sister when she gets back in?"

"I will leave the message for her hear at the front desk. I will be sure she gets it as soon as she returns."

The phone went dead along with Deanna's hopes of speaking to her sister, of finding out just what was going on there. The thought of asking her just what she had been doing lately to pay the bills crossed her mind, but it would be too easy for Bridget to just hang up the phone and avoid the question all together. Deanna knew that Bridget wouldn't be inclined to talk about her private life, she never had been one for sharing intimacies, but even she had to realize that they were family and that she would have to come around sooner or later with the truth.

Deanna sat there in the dim morning light of the living room brooding, she was having a hard time figuring out what was more important to her at this point; finding out what her husband was up to while he was so far away, or finally knowing the truth about what her sister did for a living. Either way, Deanna knew that all this was going to end badly, she could feel it in the pit of her stomach like bad food just sitting there, heavy and uncomfortable, waiting to be puked up. She knew she would feel better by bringing it up, by forcing it out into the open, but it didn't make it any easier. Deanna decided that such decisions were better made on a full stomach so she headed back into the kitchen for the rest of last nights chocolate fudge ice cream and note pad to jot down what groceries she would need.

As Deanna opened the freezer a cold rush of white, smoky air rushed out at her and sliding down the side of the refrigerator like it was coming out of a fog machine. She reached in and pushed past the yet unopened carton of Rocky Road in order to finish up what she had started the night before. While there wasn't much left she felt that it was only right to dispose of it entirely before breaking the seal on the next flavor. Deanna fished a large spoon out of the side drawer, removed the lid from the ice cream and tossed it into the trash. There would be nothing left this time. She grabbed the small, pink note pad and pen that sat next to the phone in the kitchen and returned to the living room with the carton of ice cream resting on the top of her overextended belly. Deanna began to dig into the frozen concoction before she even had a chance to sit down.

Deanna sat there for some time, stuffing mouthful after mouthful of ice cream into her now frozen mouth and considering her limited options. Her thoughts returning again and again to the address she had found in the back of her sisters contact book, sprawled out in gold lettering, daring her to go there, daring her to find out what her sister was up to.

Pigglie's Bar.

It wasn't that far, not really, she could be there in a matter of minutes. Perhaps going there and talking to the people that worked there would help to shed a little light on the matter, perhaps that was the *only* way she would ever really know for sure. Maybe it was just a hang out, a place to go and talk with friends. Just because it was in her book didn't mean that she had to work there. It didn't *mean* anything.

Deanna looked at the clock; not even noon yet. She would wait a while longer to hear back from Bridget and then she would go and see where it was that her sister spent her time. She might even bump into some of her friends, they could talk, she was bound to find something out. Someone there *had* to know her. It looked so important, that address in gold ink in the back of her book, so important that someone *had* to know her sister.

Minutes slowly turned to hours and Deanna finally decided she had waited long enough. Her sister was out for the night, probably enjoying London's night-life. Deanna figured it was time for her to do a little investigating of her own. She wasn't prying into her sisters personal life, she was watching out for her. It had been a long time since Deanna played the big sister card, but it was never too late to prove to Bridget that she cared. And that's just what it was too, Deanna cared. At least that's what she told herself as she grabbed her car keys off the kitchen counter and locked the door behind her. She cared and that was all there was to it.

Deanna stopped briefly at her own house to change and grab her make-up bag and some extra clothes. The house seemed foreign to her, her shoes clanking loudly in the empty silence of the rooms. Deanna was beginning to feel like she didn't belong there, it was a house that had until yesterday held the promise of a wonderful future. Now it only reminded her of the vast differences between Seth and herself. They truly came from two different worlds.

By four-thirty she pulled her car into the parking lot in front of Pigglie's Bar. Her face soured, the look of the bar matched it's name; sleazy with a capital S. Deanna sat in the warmth of her car debating on whether or not she really wanted to go in. It looked a bit rough, a bit risky, and the clientele that came in and out while she sat there milling it over didn't look like her kind of people.

I have to know.

Deanna pulled open the heavy metal door and was instantly struck with a disgusting mixture of cigarette smoke and booze, followed closely by the mind numbing sound of music. Her stomach flip-flopped, but she ignored it as best she could and "Bellied up to the bar."

The bartender, a rather hard looking woman with heavy makeup and a barrage of piercing looked her over. Deanna thought she looked worn and a bit used up, but still, she was thankful it was a woman behind the counter and not a man. Any way you sliced it, Deanna always found it easier to talk to other women.

"If you're looking for a phone honey ours is out of order." The woman motioned to the dirty black pay phone that hung indignantly on the far wall. A yellowed and wrinkled portion of receipt paper was taped over the receivers handle that read "Out of Order" in bold black ink.

"No," Deanna glanced awkwardly at the naked dancers that flashed intermittently from behind the woman and tried to find the words she needed. "I'm looking for Bridget Manning, I was wondering if you might know her?"

The woman seemed surprised at first, maybe even defensive, but then she softened a bit, as if suddenly remembering it was her job to deal with the public.

"Look honey, I don't want any trouble. If your husband has a hard time keeping it in his pants maybe you should have a word with *him* and *not* one of my girls," she emphasized her meaning by pointing a long, darkly painted nail at her chest. Then she turned to fill the drink of an old man seated to the left of her, his eyes never leaving the girls naked bodies as they gyrated to the heavy pound of music in front of him.

At first Deanna blushed.

How did she know about Seth?

Then the realization of what the woman was really talking about hit her like a ton of naked bodies. Bridget *worked* here, and from the look of the naked ladies wrapping their bodies around silver poles on stage and the half naked ones that trolled the floor serving drinks and enjoying the occasional grope, she had a rather good idea of *exactly* what that entailed.

"Oh, no…it's nothing like that." Deanna yelled over the pounding beat of the music. "I'm a friend of hers. She told me she worked her and that next time I was in town I should meet her here for a drink…is she going to be in tonight?"

The woman shook her head. "Sorry, your out of luck tonight, Ms. Manning called off. She said there was some sort of family emergency she needed to take care of. She's bound to be out for a few days from the sound of it. Too bad, Bridget is one of the favorites around here. Sorry I couldn't be anymore help than that."

Before Deanna could thank her the woman moved to the far end of the bar to where a tall man in his late forties had waved her over with a wad of cash. Poised against his leg was a young woman, not more than twenty, her nakedness rubbing against him as he spoke quietly to her. The woman behind the bar took the money and once she finished counting it, pointed to one of the back rooms. It looked to Deanna that a bargain had been struck, and paid for, as the girl led him back into the darkness to collect his prize.

Deanna suddenly felt sick.

This is what her sister did, *this* is how she made her living. But was that all? Surely she couldn't make that much money here. Maybe there were things that even Deanna had no business knowing, she nodded to the woman and made her way towards the door. The sound of the music and the stench of stale beer had suddenly become overwhelming and the need for fresh, clean air pulled Deanna from the confines of the bar and out into the stark brightness of the parking lot where she abruptly vomited the fleeting remains of chocolate fudge ice cream and cheese pizza.

Chapter 13

It wasn't until mid-afternoon of the following day that Bridget finally placed the call to her sister.

"Thank God you're alright. I left a message with the woman at the desk yesterday to have you call me as soon as you got in, but you never did. I was starting to wonder if something terrible had happened to you," sighed Deanna. "I don't like not knowing what the Hell is going on, but I assume you're okay then since you called today. Were you able to find anything out about that woman I saw Seth board the plane with?" The desperation in her voice was thicker than she wanted it to be but there was no getting around it. She *was* desperate, and she hated feeling that way, even more than the gut wrenching thoughts of her husband in the arms of another woman. She had become a weak, watered down imitation of who she used to be.

"Calm down Deanna, I didn't call you last night because when I got back from town it was far to late and I would have only woken you up. Besides, I don't think you have anything to worry about anyway, at least not with your marriage. I've spoken with Seth and you were right about only half of what you *think* you saw. The blonde you saw him with *was* traveling with him. He said it was an unusual circumstance that caused them to have to actually travel together. Most of the time business ventures can be worked out over the phone, unfortunately this time the stakes were rather high and the company insisted on sending out a mouthpiece of their own, you know, to watch out for their own interests. Anyway and from what Seth has told me she does seem to have developed a sort of *thing* for him, but he assured me that it's definitely not reciprocated. He can't very well be rude to her, not while the merger is taking place. Seth told me he has made it clear to her that he is happily married and anxiously awaiting the birth of his first child."

"You spoke with him? Good God, what he must think of me. I really was hoping that all this sneaking around could be done without his knowing you were even in England." Deanna suddenly felt uncomfortable with the fact that Seth and her sister were staying at the same hotel. The thought of them spending time together grated on her nerves. That irrational, childish voice from deep inside her head reminded Deanna of what her sister *really* did for a living.

Deanna wanted her to come home…now.

Was it possible that Bridget might suddenly find herself attracted to Seth? There they were, two healthy, mature adults, thousands of miles away from prying, judgmental eyes. No one would ever be the wiser if one night they snuck away together, snuck away under the dark cover of silk sheets for a little one on one hospitality.

The very real possibility of Bridget coming onto her husband forced itself into her mind. She could see him with her, touching her, loving her. With some effort on Deanna's part she pushed the vision aside; after all, they were sisters. Bridget would never do that to her, no matter what their relationship had become. Nothing could ever change the fact that they were sisters; nothing.

"There was nothing I could do about it Deanna. I had to sign in under *your* name don't forget, and well, I guess he must have seen it when he stopped at the front desk. What did you expect him to do once he thought you were here?" Bridget asked, there was a hint of growing irritation in her voice.

"You're right of course, I suppose it couldn't be helped. We can't change things now anyway. Did he seem upset that you were there?" Deanna had begun pacing the kitchen floor as her anxiety grew.

"No, lucky for you I'm a quick thinker. I managed to smooth things over with him, blamed it all on your wild hormones. He was really quite understanding."

"And you're sure about the woman then? I don't know Bridget, the way he acted towards her at the airport, he just seemed so damn…*interested*."

"Trust me, it's all just an act. Seth assured me that it's purely a business relationship, nothing more. He would have acted the same way if she was three hundred pounds and sporting a full beard. Business is business."

Deanna paused for a moment as her mind processed, and then gradually accepted the information her sister had passed on to her. Her gut on the other hand told her differently, there was no way that was just a business relationship. But in all honesty Deanna couldn't come up with one good reason why would her sister lie for him. Not one.

"I imagine you'll be on the next flight home then? I feel silly I suppose, I can't even begin to imagine what Seth thinks of me." Her face grew hot at the thought of what their conversation must have been like. She could imagine Bridget's less than wonderful portrayal of her; the crazy sister who is too high strung for her own good and now hormonally imbalanced to boot. Deanna imagined she came out looking like a real wack job.

"Really, there's no need to worry about anything sis, he understands. What with your hormones running ramped and all, I told him you were bound to think something was going on. To answer your question though, no, I'm not coming back just yet."

Deanna's heart stopped.

How could I have been so stupid?

"Seth has invited me to stay a while, that is at least until his business meetings are over and the merger goes into effect. In fact, he even said last night that he wants you to come too, we can make it a sort of mini family vacation, just the three of us."

You were with him last night?

"He feels bad for neglecting you Deanna. Mind you, it's not because he wants to, it's only due to all of his business obligations lately. Seth said that if you two spent more time together, maybe then you would realize just what you mean to him."

There was a slight pause on the line as Deanna tried to sort through the sludge pile of emotions she was going through. "There is just no way I can come to England, I'm in my third trimester. I really don't think I should be flying anywhere until after the baby is born. Why don't you two just come home and we can talk everything out over here." She didn't want them alone together, not now, not ever. Deanna couldn't help but think there was something going on between them that her sister was neglecting to mention, she could feel it in the marrow of her bones. She could feel herself begin to lose control of her mind, *and* the situation.

"Hold on, hold on," said Bridget impatiently, "let me put Seth on. I'm sure *he'll* be able to talk you into coming over."

The phones receiver was exchanged and Seth's deep, calming voice came through loud and clear.

"Hello darling, Bridget here tells me that you think that I've been up to no good with another woman. Really Deanna, you should have more faith in your husband. Not to worry though, I probably would have thought the same thing." he lied. "*If* the situation were reversed that is, although I can't see you flying off on business any time soon."

"I'm sorry Seth, I just don't know what came over me. I saw that woman all over you at the airport and I just panicked. All sorts of things have been running through my mind since then. I should have known better I suppose, like you said, I should have had more faith in you."

I still don't have faith in you, I know you are up to something.

"It's not as if you've ever given me any reason to suspect you of anything like that before, so why should I think that now?

Maybe because now my eyes are finally open to what you are, what you are doing.

"My only excuse is that my hormones are out of control and that it was probably just the pregnancy making me feel the way I did." The words came out so easily, but Deanna didn't believe in a single one of them, not one.

"So it's all decided then and no more jealous behavior on your part. You will fly over here, and the three of us will all have a few nice days in the country side together. That is, once my meetings finish up and the merger is in effect, it shouldn't take more than a few days at the most. The fresh air will do you and that baby boy of mine some good."

He had already made the decision for her, just like he always did, and now it didn't matter *what* she said or *how* she felt about the long flight over; Deanna knew was going to England.

"I would love to come to England you know that, only what about the baby Seth? It could be unhealthy for the baby flying this late in my pregnancy. What if something happens on the plane? You know, some sort of complications with the baby, you never can tell just what might happen and I think I would feel better staying here at home." Deanna talked but she was certain that Seth wasn't listening. She hoped that the mere thought of something happening to Seth's child might force him to see her side for once. That hope was short lived.

"Don't be silly darling, you really are a nervous creature aren't you? The best way to get over your unsubstantiated fears is to face them head on my dear. I will call my doctor here in England and arrange for him to see you as soon as you touch down. You *know* the doctors in this country are far better than the ones you're seeing now. And if that's not enough to put your mind at ease then you should call Dr. Galliker, right now if you like, and get the okay from him first. If he says you shouldn't fly then I will support his decision one hundred percent and come home as soon as I'm able."

"Alright, I've always wanted to go with you to England, although it never seemed like the right time." Deanna was staring down at Buster, defeated.

She still didn't think it was the right time to fly half-way across the world, but who was she?

"I suppose it *would* be good for us to spend some quality time together, in a more relaxing atmosphere. And you know how I've always wanted to see London. Maybe we could even take a drive up to Scotland, if we get the chance that is." Deanna rubbed her belly, "the baby does miss your voice I suppose. Okay, yes. If Dr. Galliker gives me the go ahead to fly I will catch the next available flight."

"Great, it's settled then. We will be expecting you shortly then. Would you like to talk to Bridget again before we hang up?"

"Yes please, put her back on. I love you Seth. I guess I'll be seeing you all soon then."

"I love you too Deanna. Wait while I just put your sister back on the line." There was a strange rustling sound as the phones receiver switched hands and Deanna's mind instantly locked onto it. It sounded familiar, but she couldn't place it.

"I'm so glad that you've come to your senses and decided to fly to England and join us Deanna," said Bridget when she got back on the line. "You won't be sorry. The place is absolutely fabulous! You might even find yourself never wanting to leave."

Deanna couldn't help but think she *would* be sorry; *very* sorry indeed.

"Thanks for doing this all for me Bridget, for dropping everything…your life, your job, and running off to England to save my sanity. I really do appreciate it. It's good to know I have a sister I can count on. A sister I can trust." But she didn't trust her; not now anyway. Not after finding out what Bridget *really* did for a living. "Just one other thing though Bridget, what do you want me to do about Buster?"

"Oh, that's nothing really. There is a little girl next door, Angela is her name, she absolutely adores him. I think that she must be part of his weight problem you know. I've caught her giving him tins of tuna on more than one occasion. I can only imagine how many other houses he stops off at for handouts. Just give her the key to the house and ask her to feed him and clean his litter box for me until we get back. Tell her I will pay her twenty dollars when I get back for her trouble."

"Alright then. I better get going and give the doctor a call or I will never get there." Suddenly she felt that there *was* an urgency for her to be there. No matter what argument to the contrary that entered her mind she still didn't like the idea of Bridget and Seth being alone together. "I will call you right before I leave to give you the flight number and my arrival time. I guess I will be seeing you all very soon then."

"Yes, see you soon."

They both hung up, and as the line between them was severed Deanna suddenly felt drained and exhausted. The simple fact that Seth had told her that he wasn't having and affair made little difference to her. She still felt that something was wrong with Seth's well thought out reasons behind his unsavory behavior at the airport. Her sister was supposed to watch him, *without* being found out, so that he couldn't just lie his was out of this one.

There was something else though, something in the pit of her stomach that soured and twisted at the thought of her conversation with her sister. What was the noise that she heard over the line when the phone had been passed back to her? It was wrong, out of place, and it nagged at the back of Deanna's tired mind.

She didn't trust Bridget, not lately at any rate, and maybe she never really did, but only hoped that she could.

Bridget had lied for how long about what she did for a living? Was it months or years? Deanna knew that Bridget wouldn't, couldn't be proud of what she did but it didn't stop her from doing it. Prostitution was a dangerous business to be in, women were murdered everyday doing what her sister did…turning tricks. What made Bridget think she was any safer? Deanna would confront her, tell her what she knew to be the truth about her profession and see if their relationship was strong enough to make her stop. If not, she would be forced to remove Bridget from her life and that of her family's. She couldn't let her child become associated with such criminal and vulgar acts and the people it attracted. Deanna was finally beginning to see the people around her for what they truly were, and along with that came a whole new understanding of the world around her.

After being placed on hold by the attending nurse for a good five minutes Deanna was finally able to explain her traveling worries to her personal physician. Without what seemed like much thought on his part he cleared Deanna for take off. The only stipulation being that she agreed to move about the plane's cabin as much as possible and to drink plenty of fluids during her flight.

Dr. Galliker had commented that Deanna's baby seemed much stronger than most and that any underlying feelings of misgiving or eminent doom should be ignored.

Ignored? Should any *mother ignore her instincts?*

It was only her hormones talking.

He's sounding more and more like Seth.

The child would be fine.

How can you be so sure?

The mere mention of a doctor waiting to examine her upon arrival in England seemed to seal the deal for her doctor. Deanna had been given the go ahead from everyone but herself. She thanked him and hung up the phone. Buster lay basking in the hot sun that streamed through the open curtains, the tip of his tail tapping to some unknown tune that played out in his soft feline head.

Deanna sat there feeling confused and off track, her life seemed to be snowballing out of control. It was then that she promised herself that things would be better between her and her husband. Better now that she understood how the world really worked, better now that she realized just what she had to do to keep this family together. Deanna would *fix* whatever it was that had gone wrong between them and she would overlook his indiscretions.

She had to.

Deanna had so much more to think about than just herself these days. She had a baby on the way, and kids need their father, they need a strong male figure in the home or they were libel to grow up unbalanced. Deanna wouldn't let things ever get out of control again; they were going to be a family soon. She would pick up the pieces, mend what needed mended and carry on. She was a strong woman, a strong woman that was feeling lost and weak.

What else can I do?

Young families needed stability, everyone knew that.

I love him, but ... I don't trust him.

Chapter 14

Bridget reached across the great expanse of bed and hung up the phone's receiver. Her naked body enveloped in a casing of liquid grey silk sheets and Seth's strong, supple arms. She snuggled closer to him, feeling the heat of his body radiate into her own, his warm breath flowing down her neck as she passed over him, his hand sliding up the curve of her back. Bridget smiled down at him, her hand slowly leaving the phones receiver as she let the heaviness of her breasts glide smoothly across his chest. Seth's eyes never left the curve of her body, his hands coming up to caress her full breasts, bringing them to his mouth he kissed them, suckled them like a newborn cub. Bridget purred with delight at his touch, her body arched towards him, needing him, wanting him. She slipped her thigh over him, his arousal complete she let the sheets fall from her body as she sat upright. He slid into her smoothly, her breath caught in her throat as he pushed his fingers into the soft tuft of hair between her legs, amplifying the sensation of him. Bridget rocked her body against his, slowly, forcefully until their passions exploded simultaneously in a rapturous flood of vibrations. Slowly as if in a drugged state she pulled her body from him, and slipped into the warm alcove of is arm. Bridget had never felt so invigorated, so *very* much alive.

It had been raining steadily all afternoon, the soft spray of icy water rushing against the leaded glass of the windows in cold grey waves, but neither of them had noticed. Neither had cared. Their eyes never traveling far from the others body. The horrors of the night before had diminished with the light of day and Bridget's new found vitality had spilled over onto Seth and he was eager to reciprocate the feeling. It had been a lifetime since he had quenched his sexual thirst with another werewolf, and it had been better than he had remembered. Much better.

How Bridget had been able to find her way into his bedroom she was not sure. Fragmented flashes of memory plagued her mind, she vaguely remembered walking from the heat of her shower and smelling him from a great distance, and then as if by some sort of teleportation she suddenly found herself naked in his arms.

Bridget tried to remember now, not that it was particularly important to her, but because she was never one to favor inconsistencies in her own memory. In her profession it paid to remember who you were with and why; call it a slight quirk in her genetic make-up. The last thing she remembered clearly and without any form of vagueness on her minds part was sitting down at the dining room table and waiting for everyone to arrive for a late dinner. Eva had come in some time after her and sat down next to her, it was at that point that things began to fade. The only memories that had managed to surface after that were when she remembered waking in the basement, full of pain and fear and climbing the hand chiseled steps that led from the deep caverns of Laurendale Manners *other,* much more satanic life. It was what had happened *between* those two events in her memory that had become nothing more than stagnant, muddy water.

Bridget ran her hand up the smooth plain of Seth's body, the musky sent of him still *very* intoxicating to her, still *very* desirable. She lay there trying to pull together the strings of unconnected memories that had become frayed in her mind but she was still unable to knot them together in any sort of chronological order. When Bridget had reached the top of the stairs last night, after waking in the filth of the basement where she had lane naked and covered in her own blood and the trailing remains of the monsters semen, her first idea was to what?

I can't remember.

To get away?

But I didn't, I stayed.

By the time Bridget had reached the top of the stairs she had changed. Both her body *and* her mind had gone through some sort of miraculous evolution. Everything that had previously made Bridget Manning *who* and *what* she was had shifted drastically.

I feel electrified, reborn.

Bridget gazed up at the ceiling, her mind buzzed lazily like a slow moving bumble bee in the heat of late summer, the importance of what had been missing from her memories slowly began to fade. What did it matter to her what had happened in the shadows of the night to make Bridget feel the way she did now? The events were over now, and nothing that had been locked in the far corners of her mind out of sheer necessity, could cause them to suddenly become reversed or changed.

Bridget felt like a new woman.

She had bedded her sisters husband without so much as a second thought or flutter of hesitation. Bridget cared nothing for Deanna's feelings, at least not at that exact moment in time, and even her own, deep seeded reasons for committing such a horrible act against her sister had become lodged deep down in her gut where it became translucent and unimportant. Sisterly love had been replaced by the simple need to fulfill the animalistic lust that she felt for Seth, and the feelings of regret would no longer be something that she dwelled on.

Bridget pulled herself up on her elbows and looked around at the pure grandeur of the room she now shared with her sister's husband. Rich red tapestries lined the walls portraying barbaric fights of medieval times long ago. Expensive Persian rugs covered the highly polished wood floor and an immense stone fireplace took up most of the opposite wall, sending out a warm and sensually pleasing heat that radiated throughout the room. It's dim orange glow reflected off their pale, naked skin, making them seem to move even while they rested motionless. Seth's bed that rested atop a small raised platform was larger than any Bridget had ever seen.

I can have all of this and never have to suffer through some stinking, sweaty, three hundred pound man fucking me until I can't breath. I will never have to fuck anyone, or anything, that I don't want to again.

Lying back in the warm crook of his arm, the heat of Seth's body against her own, she couldn't help but think he was truly an amazing man. Bridget had always been rather fond of him, ever since the first time Deanna had introduced them over two years ago. She had always felt that he was different, special in his own dark and brooding way. Although she never imagined just how different and special he really was. The simple fact that he had super-human strength and the ability to change into a massive, hulking beast; a *werewolf* none the less, made it all the more mind blowing to her.

The slow but gradual realization that due to Seth's carnivorous bite, she too would have the ability to change into a beast, a *werewolf.*

Then what?

At first the mere thought of it, of changing, her bodies tormented breakdown and then reforming terrified her, eventually it began to settle in the deep crevices of her chest. Bridget let her gaze travel over Seth's opulent body. He suffered nothing from the change, at least nothing that seemed to last. His body was strong and firm, to which she could attest from the fierceness of their lovemaking. Fear was quickly being replaced with curiosity and the slight tint of guilt that had lingered in the back of her mind for bedding her sister's husband seemed distant, becoming almost nonexistent as she lay there in the safety his arms.

"Deanna will be here early tomorrow morning I would expect," Bridget mused. "That is if she manages to get a flight right away. I don't think my big sister likes the idea of us being alone together. I could hear her suspicions in her voice, she has it in her head that we have already been unfaithful to her."

"I have already spoken to Dr. Galliker and he understands our position. There will be no problem getting the approval for the flight over, none what so ever. As for my wife's mistrust," he pulled her closer and kissed the gaping hole that he had earlier inflicted in her shoulder. "I fear she is quite right about that." His smile was wide and playful. He rolled her over onto her stomach and pulled her to her knees so that she faced away from him. His strong hands guiding her hips back into him as he stroked the dampness between her legs. Seth waited only seconds before pushing himself into her, her hands reaching out into the softness of the bed to support their weight. The deep, penetrating thrusts that Seth sent into the softness of her body forced a long moan from her lips. His sexual appetite rivaled her own, if that were even possible, and the desire to be taken by him over and over again filled her with seething desire. The fierceness and velocity of their lovemaking was stronger and more intense than any Bridget had ever know in her lifetime.

An hour later they lay next to each other exhausted but fulfilled, sleep weighing heavily in their minds. Before sleep had taken too great a hold over her, Bridget considered the coming night and what it meant to her…and to her body.

"When you change from this…magnificent human form into that of the equally magnificent werewolf…does it hurt?" Bridget's brows pulled together in deep furrows. The thought of her body going through such dramatic changes was, to be quite honest, beginning to frighten her.

"Not now, the change has become swift and painless. I no longer even stop to consider the changes that pass over my body, it has come to be second nature to me." Seth cupped her face in his hand and stared down at her. His heart beat faster as he lay there, gazing upon her fine features, than it had in ages. "Although, I must admit that when I was first infected with the blood of a marauding werewolf that hunted the grounds of northern England things were much different. It was there on that cold and rocky ledge that divided my country from that of Scotland I thought I had lost my life to the beast. I will never forget it, to this day I sometimes wake at the sound of footsteps falling rapidly behind me in the dark. My eyes straining to see who, or what is hunting me. It was over quickly, dawn had risen suddenly on the eastern side of the mountain and the beast retreated into the thick cover of forest. I can only imagine that if dawn had not been so near, he would have devoured me instead of make me one of his children. Luck as it seemed, at least that night, was to be on my side."

"So at first it *is* painful. Great." Bridget snuggled down deeper in the sheets, not wishing to dwell on the fast approaching night and it's full moon.

"Yes, at first it *is* quite painful, but it doesn't last and eventually the body gets used to the change, almost welcoming it, until it is no different than I would imagine waxing your beautiful legs to be." Seth ran his hand up her thigh, gently touching the warm, soft hair between her legs in a playful manner.

"That painful huh?" she teased, smiling up at him. Bridget tried to remember if she had seen Seth change into the beast that had taken her. Her mind searched for some fragment of memory but nothing surfaced, she only remembered waking up next to it...him...in the darkness and fearing him. Those overwhelming feelings of fear were also starting to fade, along with what had happened to her earlier that evening. Bridget couldn't even remember how it was that she had even found herself to be in the dark catacombs beneath Laurendale Manner in the first place. Her head was beginning to ach.

Seth playfully grabbed her lips with his own and removed the small frown that had appeared on them, pressing gently against the sweetness of them and pulling at them gently before he released.

Bridget could have stayed in that moment for a lifetime, but like most things in her life it seemed to flutter by with the swiftness of a sparrow.

There was a soft knock at the door.

"Come in Eva," Seth said. Sitting up a bit more in bed and pulling the pillows behind him so that he could rest his strong back against them.

Eva entered with a small bowl of green, rank smelling water and a small cotton rag.

"I've come to see to Bridget's wounds. I'm sure you wouldn't want them to leave a scar. Her skin is so pale and perfect, just the way you like it." She lovingly caressed Bridget's shoulder and arm, smiling down at her from where she stood like one would a younger sibling. Eva sat the bowl down on the nightstand next to the bed and examined the holes left behind by Seth's teeth. "At least you were careful not to tear the flesh this time," she looked down at Bridget's open wound. "Sometimes he has a hard time controlling himself. You might be surprised to know just how carried away he can get, or maybe not, since you two have spent the majority of the day locked up inside this bedroom." Eva eyed Seth sternly, "some of the newer family members might not be as understanding as the rest of us."

"I am sure Michelle is busy learning the new tricks of her trade. I will go to her in time," said Seth as he moved over to let Eva take a closer look at the wound in Bridget's shoulder.

"I am sure you are right Seth." Eva looked at him like he was anything but right, although she continued on with what she was doing without bothering to mention it. Instead, Eva sat down on the side of the bed next to Bridget and gently patted the dampened cloth on the gaping holes in her flesh. The liquid that Eva administered was thick and slimy in consistency like raw eggs and it pooled inside the deep marks left behind by Seth. There was a slight foaming around each of the holes and Bridget could hear a hissing sound coming from deep within her body as the medicine took hold of the infection. After a few moments a small stream of black smoke rose up from where the large canines had punctured deep into her flesh and had left behind holes the size of nickels, seconds later each hole had sealed itself back up and only the palest of pink circles could be seen left behind in her flesh.

"Don't worry my dear, after your first full moon they will disappear as well," said Eva.

"Eva has been good enough to take care of most of my own injuries. You are immortal now Bridget, like myself, but that is not to say that you will not sustain injury and pain, it's just that now the vast majority of them are incapable of causing your death. Eva has the remarkable ability to make *most* of the wounds that you are liable to suffer from to heal…but not all. The exception of course would be a wound dealt by anything silver. I'm afraid that would prove fatal. Another fact to remember is that if one were to be attacked by *another* werewolf that could also prove to be fatal. That is, if those injuries were sever enough."

Bridget gazed intently at the pink circles left behind by Seth's bite as she listened. She couldn't help but think that this was Seth's way of making it perfectly clear to her that even though she was now an immortal like himself, he could still end her life at any moment if he truly wanted to. A thought that didn't go unnoticed, but instead tucked away in the back of her mind so that she could dwell on it later.

As Eva sat the small bowl of liquid on the small table Seth pulled her playfully onto the bed next to him, kissing her and caressing her slender, strong body. Her nipples hardened at his commanding touch as they stood out against the thin, soft fabric of her gown, her body arched towards his in mutual desire. No matter what her mind had intended at that moment her body had already made it's own decision as to whether or not to accept his touch.

"Eva has been with me for a very long time you understand. We know well what each of us needs, and wants from a lover." His eyes never left the smooth contours of Eva's body, for the moment she commanded his full attention.

Bridget smiled; there was no jealousy to be had, no resentment that boiled just under the surface of her skin. She knew she wasn't any less important to Seth than Eva. If anything *she* was his new play thing in town, and he desired her more for her freshness. Bridget also knew that nothing had really changed in her life, she was still only another ring in a long chain of women that catered to the whims and desires of men; *other* women's men. A personal and professional flaw that Bridget had spent a lifetime realizing *and* accepting. The country might have changed, but she hadn't, and neither did her profession. At the end of the day, Bridget was still a prostitute no matter what her intentions had been.

Then Seth made love to them both, basking in the liberties that he had become so accustomed to.

The passage of time moved quickly and soon the black veil of night replaced the gray dullness of the afternoon. The evening sky had actually cleared somewhat, showing the night's constellations brightly in the distance. The moon hung low and heavy, barely topping the distant row of trees at the far end of the property, a ring of silver encased its fullness.

Bridget was the first to wake, Seth and Eva had fallen asleep on either side of her, their arms and legs wrapped tightly around her. The group had formed an intertwined pattern of erotica that normal men only dreamed of in the coldness of their own empty beds.

The moon called to Bridget, she slowly unlocked her naked body from the small group and stood by the window, mesmerized by its beauty, her heart pounded in her chest. The feeling that Bridget could just reach out her hand and touch it overwhelmed her to the point that she held out her fingers and traced its haunting outline on the window's glass. Her body ached for it, her mouth began to salivate and open slightly as if her mouth desired nothing more than to kiss the smooth orb like a long missed lover.

It was then that a popping sound suddenly echoed throughout her head as her jaws were forced out of their sockets and outward, pulling and ripping the skin from around her face. Pain seared through her head and down her spine causing Bridget to collapse to her knees. Screaming out in terror and unmerciful pain she woke her two sleeping lovers, causing them to abruptly join her by the window. Eva crouched down next to her on the floor and stroked her back, trying to ease her fears.

"Shhhhh darling, it will be over quickly. Don't fight it, just let the animal rush over you." She watched as Bridget lost herself to the wolf that now resided deep within the caverns of her body.

Bridget's body arched backward and then extended forward onto the floor as she was engulfed in a series of seizures that shook through her entire body. Thick, coarse hair, russet in color now pushed their way from every pore on her body, forcing the human skin from her quickly growing muscles in a bloodless explosion. The skin from her body merely falling away to the floor like dried corn husks that had been caught in the wind. Bridget could now hear the popping of her other joints and the cracking of her bones as she was pulled apart and then reshaped into the animal form that she had only read about. Bridget began to grow not only in size but also in strength. Deadly, razor sharp claws had replaced her once womanly painted nails; she was no longer human.

Lost to everything that was happening around her Bridget hadn't noticed that Seth had also changed, although not nearly as dramatically. His large, black body loomed over hers, watching with what could only be described as pride at the way she took her first change.

Bridget had done well.

Eva opened the leaded glass French doors that led out to the cement balcony and the cool breeze that bust through filled their senses with the smells of wet earth, earthworms, sheep, and yes; humans. The last sent made the new werewolf point her nose to the night sky and begin to salivate.

Her new streamlined, animal body was only slightly smaller in stature than Seth's, who still managed to make a strikingly handsome male form, even when not in his human shape. With only a single look back at his new mate Seth sprung from the second story balcony and down to the grounds below. The only sound he made as he landed was a muffled thud as he hit the soft ground below.

Unsure of her own powers at this point and still a bit clumsy on her newborn feet, Bridget at first hesitated. With an optimistic nudge from Eva she too sprang from the stone balcony and joined Seth below on the great expanse of wet lawn. The soft ground gave way under her heavy paws, forcing mud to squeeze between her toes. The cold water from the days rain splashed at their underbellies as they swiftly made their way to the outlining hamlet of Odiham, Bridget close on the heels of her new master.

On either side of Laurendale Manner were large farms that consisted mostly of sheep, turnips and potatoes. A few large estates followed that and then the small hamlets main street with its pub, post office, and chemist rounded out the surrounding area.

Seth preferred to hunt in the larger cities like London or Basingstoke, where the subways and parks held a vast array of unwanted and destitute vagrants. Here, in this small, well off community the people would be missed, and it could cause trouble if their disappearances were ever traced back to the halls of Laurendale Manner. Seth had already set it in his mind that perhaps one of Eva's children could be sacrificed to the public, if for nothing else than to keep himself and his new wolfen bride safe. His mind was also set in the knowledge that Eva must never know of his plan, or else there would be much more than just Hell to pay. Even Seth knew just how powerful Eva was, and he knew it would be in his own best interest if one of the beasts had just "mistakenly" gotten out at the wrong time and was unfortunately killed by one of the local police. Fortunately for him, he had a great number of what he considered to be important connections in town, and in London, that were sure to see things his way. Seth knew that if a killing of one of the local townspeople were ever to be traced back to the manner, all that would come of it would be that he would have to pay a small, inconsequential fine for keeping such a dangerous creature on the property. What they did with one of Eva's children was of no consequence to him, he cared nothing for them. Seth had even considered killing one of them himself and making it look as if the creature had merely stumbled upon his lands before being killed by someone else and that he had absolutely nothing to do with the beast.

What *was* important to him was that Bridget got her first taste of human blood as soon as possible. He wanted to seal their union together with a kill, chaining her to him with the common act of murder.

At about 1:00 a.m. he and Bridget settled into an ally on one of the side roads that lead out of town and waited for any late night opportunity that happened to pass by. Not long into the early morning hours a small group of men burst from the well lit interior of the local pub, spilling clumsily onto the darkened sidewalk. The Black Swan's wooden sign swung freely in the cold breeze that tore its way up High Street taking along with it the last remaining scatter of brown leaves and an empty candy wrapper. The small group of drunken men reformed and slowly headed back to where they had parked their cars earlier in the evening, their voices echoing off the opposite wall of buildings as the shouted loudly to one another. One man, not more than thirty, must have lived in one of the small cottages just outside of town since he didn't join the others, but instead said his good nights there on the sidewalk and headed down the street on foot. The men pulled off with a beep of the horn and a holler and in no time they were down the road and out of sight. The man left behind on the street stumbled forward a few feet and then leaned up against the cold metal of a nearby post box in order to light his cigarette, a red glow briefly illuminating his face, immediately followed by a great white cloud of smoke. After a few solitary puffs on his cigarette the man carried on his way up the street, muttering something to himself about the chill in the air and the sudden need to pee. He paused briefly at the corner chemist, looking intently at the vast array of items in the well lit display window and then continued on, loudly humming to himself in the darkness as he went.

Two shadows passed behind him.

Their blackened forms crouched low and close to the tightly parked row of cars by the side of the road, letting their presence go unnoticed.

Not more than five minutes later he was no longer on the town's well lit High Street but on one of the more quiet country roads that was only lit by the occasional street lamp. Houses at this end of the hamlet were farther apart than in the center of town, and the tree line stood out heavy and dark as he weaved along the side of the road. A small pond lay at the entrance of a towering country estate where he stopped to finally relieve himself of the four and a half pints he consumed at the Black Swan. His humming echoed flatly in the night air as he stopped the get his bearings.

Across the street, in the low lying growth of the surrounding fields he thought he heard movement, his body tensed as the night suddenly seemed to close in on him from every conceivable direction.

Something ran swiftly across the road ahead of him.

The hair on the back of his neck and ridge of his spine began to rise but his senses were still dulled to almost nothing as he crushed the butt of his cigarette in the mud and walked from the light of the last street lamp and into the surrounding darkness. The night had become deathly quiet.

The pale light of the moon as it dipped lower in the late night sky outlined what he thought were two large dogs crouched ahead of him in the darkness, not more than ten feet from where he stood on the side of the road, probably loose from a neighboring farm. His fear subsided, he had thought momentarily that he was about to be mugged, instead, it was nothing more than two marauding dogs out for a bit of sheep meat He stooped to pick up a large stick from the heavy row of trees that flanked either side of the country road and yelled for them to go.

They didn't move away, they moved closer.

The two large dogs inched their way slowly down the ridge at the side of the road, their eyes never leaving the man's face. Again the man yelled, this time swinging the thick stick back and forth in the air making a low pitched swishing sound.

The two dogs stopped.

Rising up from their crouched positions in the darkness the creatures towered over him by a good three feet, fear sobered the man in seconds but it was already too late. In one flashing moment the largest of the two lunged toward him and ripped the mans throat out with one clean swipe of his teeth The smaller of the two seemed weary at first, nudging the quickly dieing body before it and then, as if suddenly sure of the relative safety, or perhaps only unable to control itself any longer, began shaking the mans limp body viciously and dragged him into the deep cover provided by the deep overgrowth of trees and woody vines.

Seth watched as Bridget began tearing at the mans body. Her smooth ruddy snout buried deep in the mans chest cavity, pulling cords of skin and fat and devouring it in loud, sucking gulps. She tore down lower, the intestines and stomach slid smoothly from his gut as she ripped at him, swallowing them hungrily.

Music to Seth's ears.

He joined her, pulling from the ravaged body what he considered the crowning glory of a kill, the mans heart, warm and palatable in his mouth he chewed it slowly. Seth left most of the body for her, making little effort to take more than a few select pieces that she would have not appreciated as much as he. The brain, liver and heart were delicacies that only a seasoned werewolf like himself would know to consume quickly after a kill. All were organs that contributed to the strength and vitality of even an immortal like Seth.

Blood seeped from the quickly disappearing body, mixing with the already damp earth around them. The smell was intoxicating to Bridget. She was overcome by the warmth and sweetness of the flesh, the almost fruitiness of the lungs and intestines and the rich beauty of the blood itself. As Bridget ate, her human memories were pushed to the deepest corners of her mind. The more she consumed human flesh, the more she desired. The need to eat became maddening and her stomach began to ach for more as she and Seth sat licking the last remaining flesh from the bones as they stuck out from the earth like bleached sticks.

In what seemed to Bridget to be only minutes their thick animal coats had become caked with congealed blood and bits of human flesh and organs. In the end nothing but the blood stained bones would be left behind. Seth instinctively dug a shallow grave and pushed the mans few remains into it, covering them from view. The only remaining evidence that a misdeed had been committed was a patch of blood soaked earth that would soon be washed away by the early morning rains.

Less than an hour later they had returned home to Laurendale Manner, naked and bloody in their human form.

It was dawn.

Chapter 15

Deanna spent over half of her trip to England in the small, cramped confines of the plane's only toilet, vomiting up cold pizza and something the flight attendant claimed was chicken cordon blue, although she had her doubts. She remembered reading somewhere in the paper that in reality airplane food was really rather good, that is, if you ate it while still standing on good old Mother Earth. Something about the high altitude and the compressed air makes your taste buds commit their own sort of Hari-kari. Deanna figured that was either true, or the flight attendants only easy way out of having to explain just plain bad food at ridiculous prices.

Her feet, she surmised, must have swollen to what had to have been twice their normal size. The desire to remove her intensely constricting shoes had become overwhelming.

She didn't however.

Deanna knew full well that if she had, she would never manage to get them back on again; at least not in this lifetime. So she only loosened them. She did this by asking the ever present flight attended to relieve some of the pressure by giving her a small footrest. In order to do this she was moved to first class free of charge.

An older flight attendant, no doubt with children of her own, had given Deanna a stern look on more than one occasion. She, much like Deanna herself, thought that no woman in her right mind would risk flying so late in her pregnancy.

But she *had* risked it. Why?

Because I'm an insanely jealous ass, that's why.

Was it *really* that important that she and Seth have their little family vacation right now?

No.

Deanna knew the real reason for her agreement to fly so far; it was because of her sister, Bridget. Deanna was almost ashamed of herself for thinking the way she was, but she couldn't shake the thought of her sister seducing Seth. The thought that the last thing she needed right now was to have the two of them alone together and thousands of miles away. Deanna hoped however that her feelings of dread were nothing more than her hormonal imbalances hard at work, brought on by her future son or daughter.

Finally the flight came to an end and she bid the helpful stewardess a fond goodbye and vacated the plane as quickly as her swollen feet would carry her. But nothing happens as quickly as one hopes they will. So, after what seemed like days of standing in an unmoving, ridiculously long line at customs she was finally able to reach the luggage pick-up area and collect her fashionably matched belongings. Deanna was then ushered quickly along with the pulsating flow of other passengers into the main lobby of the airport where they spilled out into a great hall. Unfortunately for her, even her pregnancy didn't save her from being pushed and prodded like a lazy steer into the outlying edge of the crowd by the faster, more agile people in the group There she was shoved along until she found herself wedged up against the farthest wall along with the elderly and those few passengers that were unfortunate enough to have traveled with small children. Not that Deanna disliked children, just traveling with them. Long trips and young, easily distracted minds just didn't go well together.

The stress of being alone, of traveling such a great distance in her condition, and without the guidance of her husband throughout the length of the entire trip finally escaped her chapped lips and floated into the vast emptiness that hung above the crowd. Desperately Deanna began searching for a familiar face in the blur of travelers that swirled around her like a multifaceted typhoon of human figures.

From what Deanna could make out, most of the other passengers from her flight had disappeared shortly after their arrival, first in large, clustered groups like escaping sheep and then sporadically, with the last few drifting away into the surging flow of people until she no longer recognized anyone. By contrast, it seemed like an eternity before she managed to catch sight of Seth and her sister standing among the other thousand or so people mulling about the airport. At one point she had even wondered if perhaps she had given her husband the wrong flight information. It was easy enough to do in her current state of mind but it was also something that Deanna knew would cause this little vacation of theirs to turn sour rather quickly.

Deanna quickly ran her tired fingers through her hair in an attempt to smooth out the possible fatal mess that clung hotly to her face. What she wouldn't give for a nice long shower and a clean set of clothes. She had found them, or they had found her, and Deanna couldn't help but release the tensions of the day in a flood of salty tears. Now she could finally relax, sooth the tensions from her swollen, tired body and let Seth take control of everything, the way he always did. He flashed his best salesman smile at her and crossed the busy room to stand by her side, Bridget followed close behind on his heels, with a rather charismatic smile of her own plastered across her pretty face. They suddenly reminded Deanna of two gaping hyenas closing in on some defenseless pray; unfortunately the pray seemed to be her.

"Traveling rather light I see Darling. No matter, we will pick up anything you might be missing later," said Seth, handing the two small bags to the chauffeur that stood beside them like some brooding bodyguard. The thought that he was already chastising her for not packing the way he would have wanted her to crossed her mind, but she quickly swept it away. There would be time for arguments and innuendo later, right now she just wanted to hold him.

Deanna hugged him tightly, breathing in the sultry smell of him, enjoying the comfort his body gave her as he returned the hug. "You rented a limousine," she said as she stepped back and released him. "You didn't need to go out of your way for me. I'm sure a taxi would have been just fine."

"To be perfectly honest my dear, I didn't. The limousine was supplied by my company and is solely for my use while I'm here on business every month. Fortunately for you, it was still at the hotel when Bridget and I extended our reservations and arranged for you to join us. Besides, there is much more room in the back for you to spread out and be comfortable than there ever would be in a taxi." He leaned over and gave the chauffeur a pat on the back. "Mark here has been with me for years, he knows the least bumpy roads to travel on for a woman in your condition." He winked at her, flashing that charismatic smile at her they way he always did. This time however she had the oddest feeling it was more like the flashing of animal teeth.

Those damned hyenas again...something has changed.

Deanna couldn't help but think his smile *had* become a bit darker, toothier, than she had remembered it. The high polish of his charms seemed to be fading in the harsh florescent lighting of the airport, but perhaps it was only her perception of it. She *was* rather tired after all.

"Well that's good, I don't think the baby and I can take much more jostling about." She giggled and rubbed her stomach, the child kicking strongly where her hands rested.

Deanna only giggled when she was nervous.

What do I have to be nervous about? The baby seems fine, he hasn't stopped moving since the plane touched down.

Bridget picked up on her sisters nervous giggling right away and moved closer to her. "It's great to see you Deanna, it will be so nice for us to finally get to spend a bit of time together, as a family."

The small group made their way as quickly as possible through the crowd of travelers and out into the heavily packed parking lot. They waited under one of the many side canopies that jutted out from the side of the building while the chauffeur, Mark, went to get the limo from where he had parked it in some far off corner of the lot. They didn't wait long. There was a flash of light as the mid-morning sun was reflected off the cars windshield as the long black limo turned the corner and pulled up along side of them. Deanna's body felt instantly better, in mere seconds she knew that she would be able to remove her shoes and leave them off for the remainder of the day. She climbed awkwardly into the back of the long black limo, sliding her still numb ass over the cold leather of the back seat, at the same time letting her shoes fall to the floor with a light thud.

Freedom.

She wiggled her toes in delight.

Bridget slid in behind her sister, although she made sure not to sit too close to Deanna. Instead she chose to give her the room to spread out a bit more if she needed it. Bridget was certain that the long, confining flight was more than only a *little* strain on Deanna's body and didn't wish to add anymore to her sisters discomfort. While she cared very little for Deanna herself, Seth had explained the very great importance his unborn child had on *both* of their futures and how it was in their best interests that the child be healthy.

Seth slid in last next to Bridget. An act that didn't go unnoticed by his wife, who felt rather strongly that he should had sat next to her.

"I'm sure you'll just *love* the hotel, it's a grand old place, full of character and charm. Fortunately for us it's practically empty right now too. Seth said it's because of it being the off season right now, so we will have the place practically all to ourselves for the next *two* weeks." Bridget smiled and held her sister's hand as if they had suddenly become the best of friends.

"Two weeks? I didn't realize we would be here that long. I figured a few days at the most. I didn't pack enough things to last me that long." Deanna was surprised, she had never been told their little vacation abroad would be that long, then again, she had neglected to ask.

"Oh, don't worry about that, Seth will take you into town to get whatever you need." Bridget practically beamed at her.

Deanna thought that her sister looked younger somehow, her skin was glowing and refreshed. The little vacation to England had agreed with Bridget, she only hoped it agreed with her the same way.

"Have you colored your hair or something Bridget? It looks redder I think." She tilted her head back to get a better look and studied her sisters features. Her hair and her skin looked better than it had in years. Then there were the new clothes she had on, Bridget looked like she had just stepped off the cover of *Cosmopolitan* magazine. "You really do look amazing, they must have the most wonderful spa treatments here." Jealousy sparked in her chest, Bridget was indeed a beautiful woman.

"Well, I can't say that I've colored my hair, but I do think it must be the clear air out here or something, I feel *amazing* Not to mention I have been getting some great sleep, it's *so* quiet at the hotel." The tone of Bridget's voice suggested that she was teasing Deanna, and she began to feel uncomfortable.

"I don't know much about Bridget's sleeping patterns, but I can attest to one thing; she's eating better." Seth patted Bridget's thigh. "You won't find any of Bridget's usual garbage being served where we're staying. The staff at Laurendale Manner have to be, without a doubt, some of the best in the entire country."

Deanna's eyes hardened. *What the hell was that about?*

Bridget and Seth looked at each other with a sort of knowing connection between them that didn't escape Deanna's notice, along with that overly-familiar pat on the thigh that Seth had just administered to her sister. She didn't like the way this was going.

Close on the heals of her anger Deanna felt a wave of nausea filled exhaustion wash over her body. Normally she would have gladly started an argument at that very moment, asked Seth straight out what the Hell he was doing touching her sister that way, but suddenly all she wanted to do was to get to the hotel and lye down. The thought of collapsing into a soft bed actually brought tears to her bloodshot eyes.

Deanna would work out what was going on between the two of them in her mind later; once the jet lag had subsided and she was able to think more clearly. She reminded herself for now though that she was just being silly, like she had been at the airport, nothing unseemly was going on between the two of them, she was just being…hormonally challenged so to speak. Deanna assured herself that once she had the baby, things would be back to normal, *she* would be back to normal. She also needed to remind herself that they both loved her as much as she loved them, to think anything to the contrary was just plain ridiculous.

The limousine ride was long, but comfortable. Seth had even been kind enough to bring her some sandwiches and milk to tied her over until they were able to eat something more substantial at the hotel, a sort of picnic in the back of the car. It reminded her of the way things used to be between them, so easy and carefree. Deanna must have fallen asleep at some point during the long ride back because the next thing she remembered after eating her ham and cheese sandwich was the car pulling into the driveway of a weathered old manner and Bridget nudging her awake.

"We're here," she whispered.

It wasn't exactly what Deanna had expected. The place had a heavy, ominous feeling to it that settled in the pit of her stomach. Bridget had described it to be a "grand old place," but all Deanna could see was the *old* part. There was nothing in her opinion that was grand about the place in the least.

"Sorry, I must have been more exhausted than I thought. The trip *was* very long," Deanna stretched and rubbed her stomach as she looked out the open window. "At least the baby has finally calmed down. I thought he would never stop poking about."

"Well, if he's that boisterous in your belly, just imagine all the running about you will be doing once he's born," said Bridget.

Deanna was helped from the car by Seth and the driver and then on into the main hall of the hotel due to the fact that her shoes refused to go back on, and she had to be carried. As she stood there with her bare feet on the cold hard floor of the hotel she couldn't help but think that her sister had been right when she said it was the "off season."

The place was dead.

No one sat by the large fire that burned in the hotels main hall, no one lounged in the array of high end furnishings that graced the dark, overbearing room, sipping bourbon and conversing quietly with one another, and no one commanded the obnoxiously ornate desk that stood alone in front of the lobby. The mood was heavy, the air stagnant, and Deanna couldn't help but think they could use with opening a few of the buildings old windows to let some of the outside air in. She supposed however that with as damp as it was outside, it would prove to be of very little help in the end.

"It's like a morgue in here," she said, half feeling like it truly was. "I'm surprised they bother to stay open this time of year if it gets *this* slow. Trying to run a hotel at even a small profit when its this empty must be a nightmare. I can't see where this can be good for the owner's bottom line."

"It's my understanding that the owner has more than enough money to keep this place running rather smoothly with or without guests." Seth took her by the arm and helped her up the steep flow of stairs and on into their room. Along the way Deanna couldn't get past the feeling of being boxed in, of the walls closing in on her, of suffocating her. She had to breathe deeply in order to keep from panicking.

It's the jetlag, nothing else. It will pass in a few days and then everything will be fine.

The long hall that they walked through in order to get to their room was dimly lit by old fashioned glass lanterns and Deanna had the feeling of stepping back in time. Seth opened one of the many doors that lined the hall and entered their room. She gazed through the open door and was pleasantly surprised by its grandeur, even if it was a bit outdated and the carpets had become thread bare in patches. While the timeless beauty of the room was not totally lost on her, exhaustion was quickly setting in and her legs began to buckle under the weight of her body. She dropped her shoes to the floor with a dull, toneless thud and leaned against Seth for support.

"I guess I didn't realize just how tired I was," she pushed her unruly hair back from her face as she spoke. "I'm really not feeling very well Seth," said Deanna, as Seth rested the majority of her weight on the edge of the bed next to him. Her face had suddenly paled and tears welled in her eyes as they sometimes did when she let herself become over-tired. There was a slight glow of perspiration on her skin even though there was still a chill in the air. "I might need a bucket."

"No buckets I'm afraid, but the bathroom is right through that door." Seth pointed at a slim door to the right. "Why don't you just lay back and take a nap. I'll call Dr. Landau and have him check on you as soon as he is able." He helped her to lay back on the bed and turned the light out that sat next to her. "Would you like me to close the curtains?"

"No, the light's not bright but I would like to be able to see my way around the room. Just in case I need to rush to the bathroom."

"Very well, as you wish," he patted her hand gently and kissed her on the forehead like one would expect him to treat his ailing mother, not his wife. "There's no need for you to worry about the baby Deanna. I will call the doctor from the main hall downstairs so as not to disturb you. I will let him know that you're here and that you're not feeling like your old self."

She was asleep before he had even left the room. Lying on her side facing him, he could see that she was resting deeply. Her breathing even and steady. The sedative he had slipped her in the glass of milk that she drank on the car ride over was working better than he had expected. For a brief moment he worried that he might have given her too much, but dismissed the thought quickly. Deanna was a strong woman, she had to be, or he would have never chosen her to be the mother of his children.

Daylight had quickly slipped into night and the nightmares that had followed Deanna across the sea had only become stronger, more lifelike than they ever had before. It was only now in her dream state she was finally able to recognize Laurendale Manner for what it truly was, the radiating factor…the beacon so to speak, behind her nightmares.

As Deanna now lay sleeping within it's bosom she dreamt that she had been awake earlier, as the long black limo had neared the hotel, but she knew that to be a falsity. She knew that it had been Bridget that shook her awake after the car had come to a stop and the door had opened to reveal the hotel, the old estate that was known to her as Laurendale Manner. It was in this new dream of hers that she was finally able to see the dark towering manner that had haunted her sleep for months, and much more clearly than she ever had before.

It *was* Laurendale Manner.

In previous dreams, when Deanna had watched its dark, ambiguous form growing from the very mountainside itself as the car pulled onto the gray gravel driveway, it had been too dark for her to see it clearly. It was also in those distant dreams that the cold, damp air of evening came rushing in at her from the open window of the limo to brush their frozen hands across her face, further blurring her vision as her eyes watered against their cold sting. Each time she visited this place, Deanna's dream world would refuse to cast enough light on the vision before her in order for Deanna to make out the identity of building clearly.

Deanna had dreamed of the very place she now slumbered in many times before, and yet she had still failed to make the connection when she first arrived at Laurendale Manner. Her mind *still* blocking the vision as she looked up at its aging facade from the limo's open windows.

The cold air *had* blurred her vision.

Deanna's nightmare had finally begun to spill over into her walking, talking life.

It had become *real*.

Chapter 16

When Deanna woke from her nap in the early morning hours of the next morning the room was still bathed in darkness and the open window merely a lighter shade of gray. She lay there for several moments in a state of near panic trying to remember exactly *where* she was. As Deanna's eyes finally began to focus in on the darkness that surrounded her, helped in part, by the pale orange shimmer of early morning light that had filtered it's way in through the partially open window where it outlined the aging hotel room around her in gold; she remembered.

She was in England.

In a flash of memory like the burst of ignition on a gas burner, she remembered the long, uncomfortable flight over the Atlantic and the subsequent fatigue she had suffered soon after arriving. Seth had been kind enough to carry her from the car so that she needn't worry about attempting to get her swollen feet back into her shoes. He had also brought her straight to their room and then promptly left her alone to rest. Deanna's heart began to beat more steadily as her panic subsided.

He should've been back by now.

Seth should have been sleeping by her side or at the very least been somewhere in the room with her, but she was alone, and that old familiar feeling began to slither back into her mind that perhaps Seth *was* being unfaithful. As she began to sit up there was a soft knocking at her door.

"Yes, come in…I'm awake now," she called out, assuming it was Seth. The door opened and the illuminated form of her sister and an older man in a tweed suit were outlined in the hallway.

"Sorry if we woke you, but the Doctor is here to see you. Seth said you were exhausted from the flight so he has taken another room down the hall." She showed the gentleman in and turned the small light on next to Deanna's bed causing her to squint up at them.

"There was no need for him to do that, I would have much rather him stay here with me," Deanna began to pout like a child.

Why on Earth would Seth think that his sleeping in another room would make me happy? The only reason I'm even in *England in the first place was to spend time with him, and at his request to boot.*

Her mind began to wonder again in the direction of infidelity, and the possibility that such infidelities might even be with her sister, at least that's the feeling she got from what she had witnessed between them yesterday, but then stopped. The old man had pushed his way into the room and now stood towering over her bed. She had suddenly became very aware of the good Doctor and his little dark bag of goodies

"Mr. Toumbs and I go way back my dear. As per our agreement Mr. Toumbs called me as soon as he saw you to your bed, and I came as quickly as I could to furnish you with an examination and peace of mind. Unfortunately, Mrs. Martin decided last night was the night to make yet another addition to her ever growing family…hence my unforeseen delay." He brushed an old weathered hand through his thick white hair and rummaged through his bag for a small flashlight and long black stethoscope. "I'm sure you're just fine, but…seeing as you're so far along in your pregnancy it doesn't hurt to take a look. Besides, Seth was good enough to mention that you were a bit nervous about traveling such a great distance in your current condition, so I agreed to come and pay you a visit. If nothing else than to put your mind at ease," he smiled down at her, causing the wrinkles around his eyes to deepen. They were a clear, steely gray that flashed with the youth and intelligence of a much younger man.

"I don't wish to be any trouble, *really.* It's just that this is my first pregnancy and I've had such terrible dreams," Deanna looked at Bridget. "Not to mention that since my arrival here I've hardly been able to keep my eyes open. I was never like that before the flight." She tried to smile back at the good doctor, but found she couldn't. Her mind was still fully locked onto Seth and his separate sleeping quarters.

Where is he anyway? A wave of nausea washed over Deanna again. *Shouldn't he be the one here seeing that the baby and I are okay, instead of my sister?*

"I'm sure you've just caught yourself a mild case of jetlag…it will pass in a day or two, and then I'm quite certain that you'll be back to your old self again." He took the small flashlight from his bag and looked into her eyes and throat. The old doctor then asked her to sit up as he slid the stethoscope down her back and listened to her breathe and then gingerly took her pulse. All in all a normal, run of the mill, quickie check up that one would expect from their old family doctor without much desire to find anything seriously wrong with you.

And of course he didn't.

The last thing he did was to listen to the baby and gently press on her stomach. "Sounds like a good, strong baby in there Mrs. Toumbs. Nothing seems out of the ordinary, except perhaps for a bit of dehydration on your part."

A glance that lingered slightly longer than it should have passed between her sister and that of the good doctor, Deanna began to feel unsettled again. In one smooth motion he turned from both of them to rummage through his black leather bag. In seconds he retrieved a small vile of clear liquid from it's dark depths along with an individually wrapped syringe. The new age of hygiene hadn't passed by even *this* old world, country doctor.

"What's that for?" Deanna glanced at the doctor and then quickly at her sister where she sat at the opposite corner of her bed, her face a mask of iron. No emotion settled on her sisters fine features.

"Well, you *are* a bit too dehydrated for me to feel that only a cold glass of water is enough to do the trick, so this will help give your body, and the baby I might add, the boost you both need. Just make sure you drink plenty of fluids over the next few days and I'm sure there will be no need to see my old face again." The doctor licked his lips nervously and then dried them with the back of his hand.

"I'll make sure she gets plenty to drink Doc," Bridget said, leaning in to touch her sister's hand and smiling, her face suddenly full of warmth and kindness.

With a rub of alcohol and a jab of the needle the doctor left the room and disappeared down the hallway. Bridget took the small, clear glass water pitcher from the bedside table and disappeared into the darkened bathroom. Deanna could hear the sudden rush of water as she filled it under the tap and then returned to the room. Deanna's eyes already scanning her sisters face for the warmth that was there only seconds before, but had suddenly disappeared.

"I hardly think it's necessary for Seth to sleep in another room, don't you?" Deanna waited for her sister to say something, *anything*, but she merely filled the glass with water and tried to hand it to her.

"Drink."

"Can't you go to his room and tell him that I would rather that he stayed here with me?" She made no attempt to take the glass of water.

"Drink." This time Bridget took her sisters hand and placed the glass in it. "The doctor said to drink...so drink."

Deanna brought the glass to her lips and drank as much as she could of the lukewarm tap water, she grimaced, and then quickly handed the nearly empty glass back to her sister.

"Where *is* Seth anyway? Not that I'm ungrateful Bridget, but don't you think that it's only right that my *husband* should be with me right now?" Deanna was past being upset with Seth, now she was just plain angry.

"I'm not really sure *where* Seth is to be honest," she set the glass down on the table. "Anyway, I thought my time of babysitting your husband for you was over, now that *you're* here." Bridget said it rather sharply, and then turned away from her sister as if to regroup her thoughts. "Look, we're all a bit tired and on edge. I didn't mean to snap at you." She turned back and looked at her sister, that old bit of warmth returning to her face. "I'll go and see if I can find Seth and have him come and talk with you about the sleeping arrangements." Bridget went to the door and opened it, flooding the room with light from the hallway.

"Thanks Bridget, I mean it...you've done so much for me." Deanna sank back into the comforts of her bed and looked at her sister. Bridget had changed somehow, and it was much more than just how she looked on the outside, although that was proof enough that something significant had happened to her. It was more like something had *changed*, really *changed*, deep inside her being.

"I'm sure you would have done the same for me, if the chance ever came up. Besides, we're sisters aren't we? What else could I do?" There was a strange look that passed over Bridget's porcelain white face, a look of hatred.

Deanna caught onto it again, that tone in her voice that was sharp and agitated. Her sister's personality had done a complete and utter change for the worst, and she was feeling the full brunt of it now.

Deanna almost said...*You cold have said no*... But stopped just before the words reached her lips. Her sister *had* said no, or at least a version of it, and she had chosen to just ignore it. Deanna suddenly realized that she hadn't given Bridget much of a choice, not really, and the realization also brought with

140

it a pang of guilt. Perhaps that was the reason behind Bridget's sudden anger towards her, the fact that she had dismissed her sisters wishes to stay out of the mess between her and Seth, to just mind her own business. But how could she change things between them now? They were already thousands of miles away in England, not to mention that she was in no condition to have it out with Bridget just at that moment. Deanna would find a way to smooth things out with Bridget, she always did.

Instead Deanna said, "I know I would have the same for you Bridget, but I just wanted you to know how much I appreciate what you've done for me...really." She meant those words right down to the bottom of her soul, but they seemed to have little effect on her sister's new personality.

"Sure sis, I know you would. But it was no biggie, really." She paused before closing the door behind her. "If I don't see you again until dinner, make sure you drink all that water I brought you. I don't think you would want anything to happen to the baby just because you didn't listen to the doctor and stay hydrated like he told you."

There was a strange, shallow expression that passed over Bridget's face that made Deanna all the more sure that something *had* changed her sister. Bridget had changed right down to the inner most corner of her being, and it wasn't for the best.

Chapter 17

Deanna lay awake for some time after her sister left, drinking the water she had left behind for her and brooding over Seth's irrational insistence on sleeping in another room. Her initial intention had been to get up and look for him herself, only the heavy vale of sleep came over her body rather quickly and she lost her determination to the downy comfort of the bed.

Deanna slept for several hours until she was ripped from her sleep by the sudden overwhelming pains of childbirth as they started to wash down the entire length of her body. The pain seared through her hips and back, contracting her leg muscles so strongly that they began to shake wildly with adrenalin. Terrified, she reached for the phone that sat next to her on the bedside table, nearly knocking it to the floor in her urgency.

"Hello? Hello? Please get my husband, Seth Toumbs. I'm not sure what room he's staying in…but tell him his wife needs him immediately. I think the baby's coming."

The woman on the line calmly agreed to send him up just as soon as she were able to reach him. Deanna thanked her and hung up the phone. She was unsure how long she had slept but she had been waiting for Seth half the day and she began to wonder if Bridget had even *tried* to find him for her as she had promised.

"For Christ sake, where is he!" Cried Deanna, as sweat began to bead across her forehead and down her back as the pain filled her body. "It's too soon!"

The labor pains flooded her body again, this time bringing with it the flow of warm water from between her legs.

Please God, no!

Her water broke.

Deanna began to cry, she *was* having the baby, and from the look of it, she was having the child alone and without the benefit of a doctor. She felt the urge to push but denied it, causing her hips to scream out in pain. Her teeth clenched tightly together as she called out desperately into the empty room.

"Seth! Seth! Where the Hell are you!"

After several terrifying moments alone, Seth finally entered the room, trailing close behind him was her sister, Bridget.

"Where the hell have you been!" she screamed, tears had mixed with sweat as they streamed down her face and disappeared into her pillow. "The baby is coming *now*! For Christ sake someone call the doctor!"

No one moved, they both just stood there watching her for a moment like two complete idiots. Then without saying a single word Seth opened the drawer of the bedside table and took out a small vile of green tinted liquid and a syringe.

"What's that," she glared at the needle, "Seth you *really* need to call the doctor! The baby is coming and it's too early!" Deanna was close to hysteria now and Bridget came to her side. A real, if only brief, look of concern placed firmly on her face.

"Don't worry Deanna, it's just something to help you relax. The baby will be just fine." She smiled at her but the look that crossed her face was anything but comforting to Deanna. It was nothing short of cold.

As another contraction shook through her weakened body Seth stuck the needle deep into the flesh of her arm. A wave of heat radiated from the puncture wound, blurring Deanna's vision and numbing her lips. She found it impossible to speak or to scream.

What is he doing...I can't move!

Her body had become heavy and immobile, her heart pounded loudly in her chest until the only sound she could hear was that of her own labored breathing.

Seconds later Deanna began to periodically lose consciousness between her contractions. Each time the pain of her body would force her awake the visions around her would change. Each time her eyes would slide open she would fight to stay conscious, only to lose herself to the darkness that surrounded her again. As the night progressed she awoke to find herself naked and lying on the bed, surrounded by woman she had never seen before. Each one of them helping to push her body up in response to every painful contraction, helping her to push the child from her numb body.

Deanna's drugged and poisoned body had become so limp, so lifeless, that she was completely incapable of moving it of her own freewill. Waves after wave of visions, of feelings and sounds pushed into her brain, clamoring for her attention. Her body became nothing more than a vessel for the child to escape from, like a mere pod to be tossed away once the pea had been wrestled from deep within its worthless, hard case. The people around her showed little concern for her own well being and the pain that tore through her body as they pushed and prodded her vibrated throughout her mind.

Deanna hated them.

She was helpless to the tortures that they forced upon her body. Each time that the women around her held her up, she would wake, and each time that they would rest her body back down on the bed the darkness would seize her again. Each time her ability to focus on her surroundings became more and more difficult, more and more blurred and illusory.

One of the last visions that she held clear in her mind was waking to find Seth holding her legs against his body, her feet propped up on his shoulders as he bared down on her, pushing their child from her pain ridden body. Her sister, Bridget was standing close to him, touching him in a way that was unsettling to Deanna. It was then that her sister smiled at him, pushing the hair from his eyes in a soft, caring way and whispered something seductively into his ear.

Deanna was only partially aware of her surroundings as she was forced to push the baby from her body.

She had become the empty pod.

Without a second glance at his wife, Seth quickly handed the newborn child to Bridget as she stood next to him and then cut the thick blue cord that attached him to his mother. The child looked strange to Deanna.

Why are you handing my child to Bridget? Deanna's mind screamed. *The baby needs to bond with me...with his mother.*

Bridget turned from her, hiding the child from it's mothers eyes.

He's too quiet, he isn't crying at all. Something is wrong with my baby.

Deanna had only the vaguest knowledge that Seth and Bridget left with the child as the three remaining women closed in around her. There hands reached out to her, pushing violently against her stomach as the last remains of the placenta and its fluids were pushed from her body. Deanna could feel their remains slip smoothly from her body, her blood washing over the bottom portion of the bed to fall in crimson waves on the floor. The pain was unbearable and the thought of death surfaced suddenly in Deanna's mind.

Kind, painless death. She smiled.

As Deanna slipped into the deep, velvety blackness of unconsciousness an unsettling thought spread itself throughout her mind. Her child was different, he looked...furry.

Chapter 18

Bridget made her way out of her sister's room as soon as Seth cut the infant's cord. Her resolve towards the end had started to falter and she began to worry not only for the welfare of the wolf cub she now held in her arms, but also for that of her sister.

Deanna had fought for consciousness throughout the entire birth, something that she and Seth had not expected. Seth had assured her that the drug he administered shortly after entering the room would cause her sister to sleep throughout the entire birth. But perhaps he had merely not given her enough of Eva's potion to dull the pain successfully. Even with a sorceress as powerful as Eva there to assist with the birth of her nephew, Bridget still worried about her sister's state of physical and mental health.

There was so much blood.

Bridget looked down at the wet cub in her arms but could still only see her sister's naked body laying there, covered in her own blood.

So much blood.

Bridget had known from the very beginning that Seth had instructed the local physician, his good old friend, to inject her with Pitocin to induce labor earlier that same day. He had also told her, quite matter-o-factly, that if the child was left to grow to full term while still inside Deanna's body, the possibility, or probability, as he put it, of her death increased dramatically.

After what seemed like an eternity Eva finally left Deanna's room and wrapped the cub in a soft terrycloth towel to rub the wolf cub awake and clean, just as a mother wolf would stimulate their cubs breathing with the gentle message of her tongue.

"What took you so long?" Asked Seth from where he stood in the quickly darkening hallway. "My *son* is more important than anything else right now."

"We were having trouble with Deanna. It was hard to get her bleeding under control, but she should be fine for now." Eva gave him a stern look, but he just turned away. As she took the child from Bridget's arms the cub's body shifted from animal to human in one fluid movement.

"He's perfect," soothed Eva, as she held him in her arms. The child's features were strong and handsome; even for those of a newborn infant.

Seth quickly joined them, briskly taking the child from Eva's arms and assessing his son under a critical eye.

"He looks to be a strong, healthy boy," he wiped the child's head with his bare hand causing the damp, blonde ringlets to flatten momentarily and then spring back to there normal shape.

"How is Deanna? Is she going to be alright? Eva said that she had trouble getting her bleeding under control." Worried Bridget, the anxiety clearly showing in the dark lines of her face.

"What?," asked Seth. His eyes never leaving his son's perfectly human face.

"Is Deanna alright?" Bridget asked again, this time a bit more strained and agitated.

"Yes, yes. Of course she is. I've left Jessica and Candice to see to her needs. They will have her cleaned up and resting in no time."

Seth turned from both of them and made his way down the corridor and then out into the main entrance of the old manner. Bridget turned to Eva for guidance.

"Will my sister be alright?"

"She lost quite a lot of blood, but as Seth said, the girls are looking after her. She will be fine after a little rest and nourishment."

Bridget gazed down the hall to the disappearing form of Seth and the child.

"Where are you going? The baby needs his mother," followed Bridget, her forehead wrinkled with confusion.

"*We* are going to pay a visit to Grumhold and show him my truly marvelous success." Called Seth from a distance. "Do *not* keep me waiting."

Eva said nothing but looked quietly in Seth's direction with approval. Seth would do what he wanted for now, and she knew that they could do little to sway him, even if she *had* wanted to. Which she didn't, at least not yet. For now she was quite content to let him have things his own way. But Eva knew in her heart that the time for letting Seth have his way was coming to a swift and treacherous end. For now though, they would both continue to follow him.

As Seth made his way into the study and down the darkened stone steps

Eva touched Bridget's arm gently and held her back.

"Let him have this Bridget. He has waited a lifetime for this moment. I know you are worried for the child but believe me when I say he is in the safest place right now and no harm will come to him." She started down the steps behind him and paused. "Your sister on the other hand…you are wise to worry about *her* safety. Seth has what he wanted from her. Her usefulness has expired."

Bridget's heart dropped. Surely she was wrong. Seth loved her sister, he wouldn't…*kill her*.

When they reached the caverns below it was Seth that stood on the platform holding the still wet infant in his arms as he called out to his Lord, the mighty Grumhold, to come and bless his great success.

As he stood there Seth's other seven children slowly emerged from their dark, rancid caves to see their new half-brother; resentment heavy in their hearts for the man-cub. They had never gained their fathers love or his acceptance. The eldest creature, the one known as Grubb, would have liked nothing more than to tear the child from Seth's outstretched arms and devour him right where they stood. The thought of which brought a smile to the beasts brutal face.

"My Lord, please come to us now and bless this child of mine, come and bask in the sweet fruit of my success." Seth held his son up in front of the mirror before him and after a few moments a haze of smoke began to pool along its placid surface. The glass bubbled and twisted, pulling from its center the Lord and master with which he wished to have counsel. The beast came to tower over Seth and his newborn infant son. A look of indifference firmly placed upon his face, he would not rejoice in the child's birth.

Grumhold passed a massive, clawed hand over the child causing the small, wriggling form in Seth's arms to change from newborn human, into that of a dark furred whelp. Its small form reaching out towards the massive creature before him as the tiny ball of fluff began to snap and spit at Grumhold's out stretched hand. As Grumhold withdrew his hand the cub returned to its soft, human form.

"He seems to have your glowing personality," he growled, withdrawing his massive hand. "His destiny however is not as solidly written as you would have liked. I see turmoil, and possibly even a question of alliance. Are you sure this half-bred whelp will be worth the trouble it brings with it and all of the possible consequences?" Grumhold looked at him sternly. "Don't misunderstand me

Seth. While I applaud your desire to improve your race I must question your ultimate reasoning for such an…*unnatural move*. I do not wish to see the human race become extinct, I need them. They are a source of great pleasure for me. Not to mention nourishment. Balances must be made Seth, this creature that you have let loose upon the earth could prove to be more deadly than you had anticipated. There is always the possibility that both sides will suffer from it. Perhaps even *you* most of all."

Grumhold took the child from Seth with one clawed, reptilian hand and the animal within the small form came to the surface again. Canine features with a full set of shiny new, sharp teeth that snapped and clawed at its captor. Grumhold inspected the creature thoroughly and then tossed the whelp back to Seth, restoring its human shape as it landed safely in its fathers arms.

"It seems that your cub is suffering from an unstable balance between the human and wolf planes. It should be watched and hidden until it is old enough to control these two forms. If not, I am certain that it will be hunted down and killed by those who would like nothing more than to see your kind wiped from the face of the earth. I'm sure you haven't forgotten what man has done to your kin in the past."

"With age and the proper training he will settle into his skin. My race will no longer be forced to hide on the outskirts of Hell, and more importantly we will no longer be made slaves to races more powerful than ourselves." He gazed at his child. "And no, I haven't forgotten what the humans have done to my kin."

"Unfortunately your crosses with Eva have proven to be…less successful. They are not only short lived but they find it impossible to change into the human form." Grumhold motioned to the seven wolf-like creatures that now paced the edges of the platform. Their noses high in the air, waiting to catch a sniff of the child they were discussing so intently.

"No, indeed. We will no longer breed immortal witch to werewolf. It has proven to be too much of a disappointment for both of us. They are a liability to me, and a heartbreak to Eva. Each time one dies Eva retreats farther away from me." He bent down and rubbed the head of one of the creatures closest to him, the one Eva had so lovingly named Grubb, and then pushed him away. Disappointment radiating throughout his entire body at the sad state of his children, of his family. What an embarrassment they had all become to him. A constant reminder of the frailty of his entire race. But with the birth of his son his life had changed.

His entire *race* had changed.

"Very well then Seth, as you wish. I will bless this human cub of yours, but let it be understood between us that I will not tolerate *any* form of liability. If this creature that you have bore becomes too much for you to handle I will be forced to take it from you."

"Understood my Lord." Seth bowed, although rather rigidly.

"Remember what I have told you, and know that I will not be swayed by fatherly love."

With a disapproving look at the child that rested in Seth's arms he slid back into the mirror, pulling and rippling its stagnant form as he disappeared from sight.

Turning on his heels Seth left the platform and handed the now human child to Bridget. "You must suckle the child."

"But Seth, I have no milk to offer him." She held the baby with a wide look in her eyes, unsure of what to do next. "We need to take him back to Deanna, she has the milk he needs."

"No! I demand that *you* care for the child. Eva will assist you. She will help you to feed your new child. Now you must take him with you to her chamber, and quickly. He's becoming restless. I will sit with Deanna until she wakes. I must tell her that our son is dead."

"What the Hell are you talking about Seth? I never agreed to any of this." Bridget couldn't believe what she was hearing.

"You will do as I say or pay the consequences," Seth's eyes seared into Bridget's flesh. "How do you think Deanna will react when I make a full confession of our new-found intimacy with one another?" Anger flashed across his face, his boy-like charm had disappeared, causing Bridget's stomach to churn.

"You fucking bastard! You set me up so that I could do little more than stand by and watch you destroy what is left of my family. If I choose to speak, you have made it so that I would destroy my own family with the horrible truth." Bridget stepped forward as if to strike him but pulled back. "Be careful Seth. I'm not the only one that risks losing everything if Deanna finds out about our involvement. There is your son for instance to consider."

"*My* son is of no consequence to you *or* his bitch of a mother. Be perfectly clear on that my dear."

The total lack of emotion that shone on Seth's rock-like face stirred something in Bridget that until now had lain dormant. Was it possible for Seth to feel so little for Deanna that he would tell her that the child she had carried for so many months had died in berth? The thought sickened her.

The memories of her own lost child rushed to the surface of her mind again, demanding that they be relived. Bridget *knew* how she had felt; and yet their circumstances were complete polar opposites. Deep down Bridget understood the loss, but for every regret that her heart had felt not even *she* had experienced the movement of the child within her own body. How that loss in it's self must be devastating to a woman. For her sister to know that she had come so close to becoming a mother, only to have it snatched away from her by her very own husband, began to soften a bit of the sharp edge that she had always felt for Deanna. The heavy burden of guilt had crawled into Bridget's body like a blood thirsty parasite to hang upon her heart. There it settled down to fed upon her soul, greedy in its overwhelming desire to consume her.

Chapter 19

Reluctantly Bridget decided to go along with Seth's deception, at least for now anyway, and followed Eva back to the upper living quarters, and then on to her room with the child cradled safely in her arms. She couldn't help but wonder at the complete turn around in Seth's behavior, his personality. It was as if she had never really known him at all. Bridget couldn't help but be dumbfounded at how quickly Seth had become so harsh, so uncaring towards the mother of his child.

His child.

Seth had made *that* perfectly clear, there could be no misunderstanding him. There would be no interference from the child's real mother, or any surrogate mother that he saw fit to put in charge temporarily. Reluctantly Bridget also realized that she had just witnessed the *real* Seth Toumbs and that nothing and no one would keep him from getting what he wanted. She also began to realize, with a bit of self loathing, that she too, no matter how fleeting the thought had been, even *she* had considered only her own desires and needs, and never gave a second thought to those of her sister. Now as Bridget looked down at Deanna's helpless newborn baby she knew that she could do little more than follow Seth's instructions. At least until she could come up with some way to get them all away from Laurendale Manner and Seth Toumbs in one piece.

Eva's room was quite different from the others Bridget had ventured into and not at all what she had expected. The room had a dark, almost masculine atmosphere that hung in heavy contrast to the main living quarters of the rest of the house. Bridget could almost feel the electricity coursing through the heavily scented air, the absolute knowledge that if she were to touch something in the room, that she would surely be shocked with a bolt of electricity.

The room itself was a full two stories high, the second floor, most of which Bridget could hardly see more than what was intermittently lit by candle light, was lined with old books. As she looked around the main living area Bridget could tell the lower level itself was where Eva slept and bathed. The most curious sunken bathing pool sat at one end of the room surrounded by a low wall of stone. The pool was enticingly lit with candles running the length of it's side, casting a warm, golden light across its blackened surface. The water was as black as Hell itself and Bridget thought for a moment that the water had moved as they neared it. She gazed in, half expecting to see some sort of magical creature leisurely bathing in its blackened waters, but there was nothing. Bridget stood there and waited, but nothing could be see moving about the water so she moved farther away. No matter what the cause she was sure there was at least a steady moving current. The thought of which for some reason unsettled her nerves.

The second floor, although poorly lit, was lined with bookshelves from floor to ceiling. A single ladder on wheels was connected to a metal rod ran the length of the wall and was used to reach the uppermost shelves. As Bridget's eyes became accustomed to the low light of the candles she realized that old books were not the only things that lined the shelves. Jars filled with powders, liquids, and things that moved about their glass prisons shared shelf space with dried remains of both humans and animals alike. There could be no mistaking that this was indeed the home of a witch.

"Just set the child over there on the table. I assure you he will be fine there while we take care of your milk production." Eva said, motioning to a large, roughly made wooden table that was covered with smelly concoctions and animal bones. "I will need you to undress and stand in the center of the pool."

Bridget looked intently down at the dark, thick water with fear laden curiosity.

Eva glanced over her shoulder at Bridget and noticed the look of mild panic on her face.

"No need to worry about that my dear, I'm sure *your* bite is far more dangerous than anything still left swimming around in there." With a laugh Eva turned from her, ascending the old wrought iron staircase that lead to the second floor to scour the rows of millennium old books that stood there waiting, tattered and torn, for the ingredients that she needed.

Bridget stepped out of her wrap and into the thick, black water of the pool before her. It was warm, like a comfortable bath, and a bit slimy to the touch, causing Bridget to wrinkle her nose in disgust.

"Do you know what Seth will name the child Eva? I know he has waited for some time now to have a son of his own. I don't remember Deanna saying that they had picked out any names yet."

Bridget stood thigh high in black muck, not really paying attention to how it clung to her body, how it slid up a bit higher on her thighs each time she moved, higher than what it should have. Its smooth blackness climbing up her as if alive. Her full attention was on the child lying on the table in front of her, his plump hands grabbing and twisting at invisible fairy's in the open air.

"David is the name Seth has chosen for him." She said, not taking her eyes from the rows of books in front of her. "Seth has always been partial to that name for as long as I can remember."

Her hand stopped about halfway down a row of particularly old looking books and with a grunt of satisfaction she pulled it from the confines of the shelf.

"Right, now let's make some milk, shall we?"

Bridget looked down and placed her hands on the smooth curve of her hips. "Will I have to lay all the way down in the water?" The look on her face clearly showing her dislike of the idea.

Eva looked up from her reading. "What's that?"

"Will I have to lay down in this...this water?"

"Oh, yes, I'm sorry, I forgot to mention that. The water must cover your breasts entirely. If you move to the center of the pool there is a step, it becomes deeper there." she paused for a moment and gazed back at Bridget. "I assure you, it *can* be quite pleasurable. The water at times...has a mind of its own." Eva smiled almost wickedly.

The thought of going deeper into the water made Bridget wince, but she reluctantly stepped down into the center of the pool where the water reached the top of her shoulders, curving a bit high around her throat and touching the corners of her open mouth like a lover's fingers. The thick water massaged her body; coming alive as it caressed the softness of her skin. Bridget couldn't help but moan in pleasure as the water took on an almost orgy like sensation, penetrating the soft flesh between her legs and pulsating against every inch of her exposed skin. Bridget closed her eyes, her head leaning back as the creature took her, it's forceful touch bringing a flash of rose colored embarrassment to Bridget's face.

"The creature seems to like you," smiled Eva. "It is well equipped to help pass a boring afternoon." She laughed. "Alright, that's quite enough pleasure for one day, we have work to do." At Eva's command the waters ceased their lovemaking, much to Bridget's dismay.

Eva found the spell she was looking for, an old one, passed down from mother to daughter for generations, and glanced through the long list of ingredients. She turned to the multitude of glass jars she had brought down with her, making sure she had everything she needed. Each jar was inspected and checked to see if she had enough of each delicate ingredient.

"We're in luck." Eva smiled as she sat down on the edge of the pool with glass jars in both hands and her spell book clutched tightly under her arm. "I've got everything we need."

Bridget watched as she took what looked to be regular, everyday leeches out of one jar and dropped them into the water.

"What are you doing? I hate bugs." Bridget moved back slightly in the thick water.

"Technically they are not bugs, they are invertebrates. But don't worry, they won't hurt you." Eva didn't even look up from what she was doing to see the look of despair on Bridget's face.

Meanwhile the filthy little "invertebrates" were swinging their bodies back and forth in the water until they were close enough to connect themselves to Bridget's breasts.

"Okay, that's just nasty," said Bridget. "I thought they sucked things out, not put things in." She wrinkled her nose again at Eva.

"These are *special* leeches my dear. Now just be patient for a moment will you?"

Eva continued to pour different powders and liquids into the water, muttering under her breath what Bridget imagined to be some sort of spell, but couldn't quite understand what she was saying. No doubt it was all in her ancestral tongue, perhaps some ancient form of German but she wasn't really sure.

After Eva was finished talking the leeches began to grow at an alarming rate as their razor sharp teeth dug deeper into her flesh. Each time the dug deeper Bridget squeeze her eyes shut and clench her fists in pain. Bridget could think of nothing else but ripping the nasty little creatures from her body and smashing them against the stone wall.

But the child, the child needed nourishment.

Bridget tried to relax the muscles in her body, tried to accept the slimy creatures as they dug into her soft flesh. Then, just as Bridget was sure that the creatures had gotten too large for their own skin and that they would explode at any second, they forced their bodily fluids into the small incisions they had made in both of her breasts. Their size was returned to normal and they released their hold upon her now tender breasts.

Eva collected the small, wriggling creatures back into the jar and placed them on the table next to Seth's child. Bridget's breasts were now heavy and swollen with milk, she had grown at least a full cup size in a matter of seconds.

"Not bad. I know some ladies back home who would just *kill* to have something like this done." Bridget cupped her newly improved breasts in her hands, wiggled them a bit and smiled. "Look mom, no plastic."

"You can get out of the pool now," Eva said, rolling her eyes a bit at Bridget's humor. She held her hand out to help her, but for the moment Bridget lingered in the water.

"Do you think it would be alright if I stayed in here a while longer?" Bridget's smile was large, her cheeks had suddenly become a light shade of rose from blushing.

"Of course, if you like." Without another word the seductive water churned around Bridget's body becoming as hard as any human man she had ever know and began pushing against her flesh. The free-flowing form of the creature pulsated into her; pulling at her swollen breasts and entering the wet, hot flesh between her legs. Bridget moaned loudly, peaking to ecstasy quickly. Once her body began to settle from her earth shaking climax, she calmly rose from the water, her skin red, her breathing heavy. The water did not cling to her body but ran slowly back down into the pool. Bridget came out of the water as dry as she went in…well, almost.

Bridget went to the table and picked up the plump child in her arms, his hands clasping fists full of her hair and pulling them tightly. Bridget gently wrestled her hair from his grasp.

"You must feed him now. Put one of my robes over your shoulders so you don't catch a chill." Eva removed a black silk robe from her closet and took the child from Bridget's arms while she slipped into it, leaving it untied Bridget climbed onto Eva's bed. Eva handed the wiggling child back to Bridget, clearly not wanting to hold him any longer than necessary. She pushed several large, goose down filled pillows behind her back so that she could sit in a more comfortable position while the child nursed. After a few awkward moments and false starts, the child finally latched onto one of Bridget's nipples and began to suckle. He was indeed hungry.

"As you can see, Mother Nature helps even the most inexperienced of mothers to care for their children."

"Perhaps, but I can't help but think that you were more of a help to me than she was, along with your vast understanding of the black arts of course." Bridget said, as she snuggled down deeper into Eva's bed and held the wolf child closer to her bosom.

The changes in the small child's appearance had slowed, no longer were there the rapid waves of human and wolf form pressed upon his small body. Although Bridget realized early on that the child's shape-shifting didn't seem to cause him any discomfort, she still looked down at him in amazement. The changes of his body were so fluid, so natural, and swift that one would have to say he truly felt nothing at all. His now heavily furred body lay curled up in her arms and Bridget couldn't help but marvel at his unique beauty. There was a stark difference between him, and an adult werewolf, although Bridget had to admit that they too had a certain dark beauty about them; although much more wicked than soft.

"I never thought I would be privileged enough to feel the warmth of a child," she said to Eva. Her voice soft and full of her own private sorrow.

"Why would you think that? Most woman have the ability to create offspring. Are you unable to bare children naturally? If that is the case, I might be able to assist you."

"The physical ability is there, it's the emotional ability that I lack," she slid her index finger up the bridge of the wolf cubs nose, causing it to twitch as he continued to suckle. "When I was very young and foolish, I became pregnant. Back then I wasn't ready for the responsibility of motherhood, and the father, who was a married man, had broken off our relationship weeks before I had even realized what had happened. Deanna and I were both living with our Grandmother at the time…money was tight and we were having a hard enough time with only the three of us, let alone another small mouth to feed. I made the difficult decision to have an abortion. My body recovered, but I don't think my heart ever will." Bridget looked away in shame. "I'm not really sure why I just told you all that. No one knows, not even my sister, Deanna."

What the hell am I doing? I don't even know this woman. Why tell her anything about myself? I don't owe her an explanation of who I am or where I come from.

Eva came to sit on the bed next to them and rested her hand on Bridget's leg, squeezing it gently in support. "I'm sorry for your loss. Perhaps Seth's child will help to close that part of your life and help you to forgive yourself."

"I don't see how that's going to happen. After all, I helped Seth *steal* him away from his true mother. How can that help me to forgive myself? He's not even mine."

"Perhaps Seth feels you would make a better mother to the boy than your sister. You are one of his kin now, you are no longer merely human like your sister. That has to count for something in his book. Besides, what makes you think your sister would even *want* the child once she found out what he is, once she sees that he is not human. Once the child changes in front of her it could be all over for him, and then what? I think Seth was right to remove him from her. She would never be able to understand him."

"You're wrong. Sure Deanna would have a hard time at first, but he is still her son. I'm certain once everything was explained to her, she would find a way to make it work out for the best. I could have helped her over the difficulties, but I didn't. All I've managed to do is steal my own sisters child. Now Deanna understands my own unfortunate loss, weather she realizes it or not. The only difference between the two of us is that she didn't *choose* to do this to herself, instead *I* have inflicted the wounds of my own stupidity." Bridget gazed down at the contently sleeping cub.

"I should have stopped Seth. I should have reasoned with him. I should have fucking done *something*."

They both sat in silence for a while, looking down at the wolf cub as he quietly wiggled around in Bridget's arms as he slept.

"I never should have agreed to take this child from my sister. I should have helped her when she needed me and instead I have helped to brake her heart. I don't think she would have ever done anything as treacherous as this to me, had our positions been reversed."

"So what are your intentions Bridget? To suddenly come clean about the deception and tell her that her child is not only *alive* but that he is also a werewolf? You do understand that too much honesty at this point may do more harm than good. You are sure to destroy what little relationship you have left with her; and quite possibly her very sanity."

157

"No of course not but that doesn't make what Seth and I did right. I don't know what to do anymore. I don't think I can even bring myself to look at her anymore."

"Consider yourself lucky my dear, at the very least your sister is still alive," Eva said, seemingly almost to herself.

"What do you mean by that? Surely you don't mean Seth would kill her...do you?"

"That's not *exactly* what I meant, although you're not far off the mark when it comes to Seth. It's just that Deanna lost quite a lot of blood during the child's birth. Of the few human women that I've know to give birth to a werewolf cub, only one ever survived long enough to see it grow. Unfortunately, they were also both murdered before the cub was able reach adulthood and realize his full potential.

But as you said, Seth wouldn't think twice about killing her, not if it meant losing his child. What I had meant to say is that the last woman he seduced into having his child ended up dead, her *and* the child I'm afraid." Eva crawled into bed next to her and the baby and soothed his head as she spoke. "It's not something he likes to talk about so we don't normally discuss it around him. He's quiet the brooding type I'm afraid. Hell, sometimes, if I didn't know any better I would have to say that he actually prefers to be miserable. He was positively *unbearable* for months after his last child was killed."

Bridget frowned, "how did it happen?" The memories of her own childhood came flooding back.

My own mother was killed while still carrying my brother.

Bridget moved the child to the next breast; the feeling that the other had become almost empty of milk was strange to her, but none the less clear as to what she should do next.

"Well, from what I understand she had two other children when she first met Seth. Her marriage was troubled, and her husband had become abusive. The poor woman found Seth to be solid and understanding of her difficult situation. His charm was able to outweigh her better judgment, as I am sure *you* can attest to."

And it is also something I am learning to regret more and more as the days pass. Thought Bridget darkly.

"Yes, I can understand her weakness to Seth's...charms." Bridget forced a smile.

"They fell in love, or what passes for love these days and Seth told her everything about what he was and the many terrible things he had done in his life. He was even so bold as to tell her that he wanted her to help him realize his vision of a race of werewolf that no longer needed the pull of the moon to change form. A tenacious breed of werewolf that was until then, quite unimaginable. Its powers would be virtually unstoppable due largely in part to the fact that the creatures would be able to control the change of their bodies as they saw fit. The ability to blend in with the rest of the human race at a drop of a hat when being hunted by others would make finding and killing them almost impossible." Eva snuggled down into the blankets next to Bridget and rested her head on her shoulder like an old friend.

"This woman of his, she actually agreed to all of this? She didn't even for a moment think he was lying, or worse…a total nut job?"

"I suppose not, at any rate the woman agreed and soon she became pregnant with his *half-breed* of a child. One night, the woman's drunk and violent husband followed them as they met at a local park, there usual meeting place. Anyway, after watching their heart warming meeting, and hearing not only that the child his wife was carrying was *not* his, but that she also planned on taking her two daughters and leaving him the very next day, that he well…just lost his mind I guess.

From what Seth told me the woman's husband must have waited in the shadows for him to leave, and then he attacked and murdered his wife, along with the unborn child she was carrying. Seth said the man beat her to death with a rock and his very own hands. The hatred the man must have felt to do such a dark and horrible deed, one can only imagine.

As it happened Seth had returned just as the man stood from his lovers lifeless body. Seth admitted to me later that he though he had smelled someone near them earlier in the night, but that his attentions were elsewhere and he hadn't given it the attention it deserved. He blamed himself for the loss of his woman and child, it has eaten at him for years now.

As I'm sure you can imagine he was inconsolable.

It was just at that moment that the moon appeared in the distance. Seth's form shifted and sealed the mans fate in a matter of seconds. Seth said he ripped the murdering husband to shreds and the police deemed it the work of a homicidal maniac. I don't think anyone ever realized that it was the husband all along that had actually killed his wife and just assumed whoever killed the man also killed the woman and her unborn child."

"How horrible for him, for all of them," Bridget frowned, but looking down at Seth's newborn son she couldn't help but smile again. "I can see why having another son was so important to him, but I don't understand why Deanna must be told the child is dead. It still seems so cruel to me."

"Seth has his own way of seeing the world I'm afraid. He sees women as inferior to himself, they are just play things to be used up and then tossed away when he tires of them." Eva's tone had hardened, her jaw line tightened.

There was a sudden nagging in the back of Bridget's mind.

My mother was murdered in the park, murdered while carrying my unborn brother. It could easily be the same incident. I wouldn't put it past Seth to keep an eye on us, to watch us grow and still have his way. He could still have the half-breed child that he wanted so desperately, if not with the woman he originally chose, then perhaps one of her daughters...

Her mind turned to her sister...*and what of her? What would she do if she found out her own sister had slept with her husband and that her child was part werewolf? Would she turn to murder, or even suicide?*

"The child is asleep, set him down on the lounge and come sit with me awhile." Eva motioned to the long, heavily pillowed chase lounge that sat by the alcove of windows and Bridget did as she was asked.

"I like you Bridget. I won't pass judgment on you for what you have done in your past, for that is what it is...your past. I myself have on more than one occasion hurt those that are dearest to me. I believe the secret is to learn from our mistakes and move forward. Never dwell on should haves and could haves, a long life has taught me that. You wish to leave this place?"

Bridget nodded in response.

"I assure you that Seth will not let you go so easily; or Deanna for that matter. My fear is that he will convince her to conceive yet another child and then what? If she should be lucky enough to live through the ordeal will he try to deceive her into believing that child has also died? I fear for your sisters life...he is not the man you think he is."

"What are you saying?" Bridget sat up. "Do you think Seth would truly murder his own wife in order to keep her from her own child?"

"I have seen him do far greater tragedies than that my dear. Killing your sister would be nothing to him I assure you."

Bridget gazed after the sleeping child as he lay curled in a furry ball, the rise and fall of his chest visible from where she sat.

Could she be lying? Eva has known him longer than either of us, but still...she may just want things to go back to the way they were. Seth and her...alone.

"But perhaps I am just over cautious." Eva watched her momentarily, for what? A reaction? A sign that she had touched a nerve somewhere in Bridget? "At any rate, I would like you to meet my children," she said, her gaze rising up to scan the darkened second floor.

"*Your* children?" Bridget asked, surprised. The change in conversation spinning her mind. "I'm sorry, I just never realized that there were any other children in the house, Seth never mentioned..."

"Well," smiled Eva, her pale blue eyes flashing. "They go throughout most of their day unseen by anyone but myself and the girls. Seth...he wouldn't have mentioned them anyway, he prefers for them to stay out of sight."

"How rude!" Bridget frowned and sat up a bit straighter on the bed. "I would *love* to meet your children."

Bridget's senses had become stronger since Seth had bitten her, infecting her blood with that of the werewolf virus, and it was just then that the strong, pungent odor of Eva's children first hit her nose. She turned and looked up to the second floor, her eyes scanning the darkness for any sign of movement.

From the deep recesses of the upper room stepped several creatures, their eyes reflected the fire that burned next to Eva as they stared down at them from above. Bridget counted seven pairs of glowing orbs as their low hunched bodies slowly emerged from their hiding places. Blue-black skin shone under sparse, black hair that became thicker as it ran up their rounded spines to cover their heads.

Wolves? But they look so strange.

Wolf-like heads that were larger than what the body should have permitted teetered on thin necks that should have broke from their sheer weight, yet none the less there they were. Those immense, wolf like heads hung low to the ground as if too heavy to hold up on slender, long necks for any length of time. Their teeth were grotesquely over-sized and yellowed as they peered through from thick, blackened lips. To Bridget's surprise they had eyes as blue and as human as Eva's; beautiful and intelligent.

Bridget vaguely remembered seeing them in the catacombs under the manner the night she was infected, but she would have never imagined them to be Eva's children. Never in a million years.

The seven creatures made their way slowly down the steps to sit in front of Eva. Two of them quietly inspected the sleeping child, but soon decided it was nothing of interest to them and joined the others at Eva's feet.

Eva reached out to caress the face of the unsightly looking beast that sat directly in front of her, his massive face resting heavily on her lap.

"This is my eldest son, Grubb. He is a joy to me. He would be a joy to any mother." Eva smiled as she spoke, clearly meaning every word that she said. "He is strong and fearless, as all sons should be."

"I don't understand," Bridget blushed, not wishing to insult Eva, but not totally comprehending the marked difference between the children of Eva's and the one that slept so soundly beside them.

"You're wondering why there is such a strong difference between your sister's child and mine. Am I correct?"

"Yes."

"Seth, as you may or may not have guessed, is also the father of *my* children. Although you would be hard pressed to tell, what with the way he treats them. He is the father of all ten of them to be exact. Unfortunately two of my eldest died earlier this year, *they* are not immortal.

There is only one real difference between Deanna and myself that could possibly come into the equation, and that is that your sister is mortal, and I am not. My children will never learn to control both forms because they do not *possess* both forms. Such a limitation has turned them from Seth's favor but never from mine...*never*."

The tone of her voice had harden and her body became ridged with pride. It was clear to Bridget that Eva felt betrayed by Seth. Something Bridget herself was beginning to feel more and more with each passing day.

"Do you hate him?"

"Yes...and no. There is more going on within these walls than you can imagine at this point Bridget. The mood of the house is changing and Seth must change along with it or, well, we will just have to wait and see. Suffice it to say my dear that not everything, or everyone for that matter, is as they seem in this place. It would be wise to keep that in mind."

Chapter 20

Bridget had managed to lose an entire day talking with Eva and learning how to care for her sister's child. Jessica had assured her that Deanna was fine, that they had managed to keep the bleeding under control, and that they were keeping her sister heavily sedated until Seth had a chance to talk to her about the baby. A good deal of Bridget's conscious was thankful for that. If for nothing else than to spare her sister's weakened mind and body the horror of a child lost.

A child lost to circumstances beyond anyone's control.

Later that following night, Bridget lost sight of Seth as the moon rose high in the late night sky, pulling them both from the house to feed and changing their body's as it washed them with it's pale light. She was starving for blood and the sweet taste of human flesh began to take it's toll on her normally clear thinking mind. Seth hadn't waited for her like he had done countless times before, but what did it matter to her? Perhaps he was forcing her to think and to act on her own.

A test so to speak.

As Bridget pointed her ruddy colored muzzle to the sky she reassured her self that she *could* kill on her own, without any assistance from him, or anyone else for that matter.

Seth had become distant since the birth of his half-human son. She wanted, no, *needed* to talk some sense into him, reason with him that they could save Deanna the heartache of losing a child. It was getting harder for Bridget to focus on her human thoughts. Her human mind began to cloud with the desires of her new animal one. She needed to...she needed...

She needed to eat, and she needed to eat now.

The small, stone farmhouse that Bridget came to was well lit and the smell of human that drifted through the night sky was almost overwhelming. The soft ground around the buildings had become saturated by the day's rain and

Bridget's weight pushed her down into the muck. As she moved over the ground her legs made a sucking noise as each one was pulled from the thick mud.

Bridget caught the smell of the humans watch dog as a soft breeze drifted down alongside the house. He was close, the risk of drawling unwanted attention to herself became a strong possibility. Bridget scanned the surrounding hillside, a small box sat just to the right of the dimly lit house, a steel spike rising out of the ground just opposite it's small dark door.

Bridget was sure to stay downwind from the box as she crossed behind it, making sure to stay close to the wall of the house where the ground was drier, and her weight held quietly. The dog stretched in the opening, his snout pointed up to the sky when he froze; nostrils flaring. Bridget brought her heavily corded arms down hard upon the animal, killing him instantly. His small, high pitched yelp was cut short by the blow. Bridget waited in the silence of the night to see if anyone had become alarmed.

Nothing stirred.

If anyone had been outdoors at that very moment they would have heard the poor animal cry out in the darkness. As luck would have it though she was alone, and as she came up the side of the house she could see clearly into the dwellings main living room windows.

An older couple, possibly in there late fifties, sat snuggled closely together on the living room sofa watching television. Their fading eyes glued to the screen in mere slits, a bowl of crisps cradled in the man's full lap. His hands worked automatically, shoveling the golden fried potatoes into his mouth without thought.

Somewhere in the house a kettle began to whistle, automatically the wife slowly left the room, her eyes still intently watching the television's vivid screen until she was totally out of the room.

"Would you like some biscuits with your tea," she called out.

"The chocolate ones?"

"Yes."

"Go ahead then."

Without too much delay she came with back into the room with a tray of chocolate biscuits and two cups of tea, much to her husbands delight.

Bridget's hunched, animal form backed up far enough from the window to perch upon the stone wall that enclosed a small front porch. From that height she could see directly into the room and after several moments of waiting she was sure that they were the only two humans in the house.

Saliva dripped from her gapping jaws in anticipation of the meal laid out before her. Coiling her hind legs under her body Bridget steadied herself on the ledge of stone beneath her. In a smooth and powerful motion she sprang up and crashed through the window opposite the quietly sitting couple. Bridget's animal body cleared half the living room with ease and landed full length on the man's lap, practically crushing him with her weight. Her teeth sunk into the soft fatty flesh under his chin and tore at him. The man's head fell backwards, like a giant Pez dispenser, nearly removing it totally from his equally plump body. His wife shrieked in terror and clumsily scrambled backwards off the sofa, falling to the floor she scurried away into the corner like a frightened child. Her eyes bulging, tears rolling down her face, she watched the creature as it turned to look at her, it's head covered in pieces of what was once her husbands face, its mouth nothing more than a crimson grotto of teeth. The woman curled her wafer thin body into a ball and shook violently. Hiding her head in her arms she pulled her eyes off the now dead body of her husband Her sobs drowning out the sickening noise of the creature as it ripped through his body. She dared not raise her head to see the creature as it drew closer, and closer it did come. She could feel the creatures hot, sour breath beating against her face and then suddenly it's teeth punctured through the flesh and bone of her face. Her left eye popped from its sockets as the pressure from her crushing skull forced it out to dangle softly against her cheek.

Laughter crackled from the television as a rerun of *The Tonight Show* blared in the background. The creature that by day had been known as Bridget Manning settled down into a comfortable position and finished her late night meal.

Bridget had indeed killed successfully on her own.

Chapter 21

Early the next morning Seth sat on the bed beside Deanna as she lay sleeping. He had misjudged the complications of his son's birth at the manner, of Eva's resentment towards him, and the fact that Deanna had actually lived through the birth.

He felt he was losing control of the situation.

Eva had become cold towards him since the arrival of his sister-in-law. Now coupled with the arrival of his wife, Deanna and the birth of his son, she had become downright fridged. It's not as if he had *planned* for her to follow him all the way from the U.S. He hadn't taken into account the possibility that Bridget would even find out about his race, let alone become a werewolf herself, it had just *happened* As it turned out Bridget seemed to have complicated matters far more quickly than he was comfortable with. Obviously the same could be said of Eva. She had made it clear that she did not welcome the two new women into the manner, into their home.

Then of course there was Michelle. Eva hadn't even *mentioned* her name, not a good sign when it came right down to it. He knew well enough that no voiced opinion, was a *bad* opinion, when it came to dealing with Eva.

The idea of letting Deanna go to full term and then having the boy born at home, thus causing her death from complications, had been swept away in a rush of unforeseen events. Once Deanna had arrived at Laurendale Manner there was no way for him to allow her to return home, not her, or her sister.

He had hopped that she would die in childbirth, or shortly after from hemorrhaging like most of the other human women had done. But again, she hadn't.

Seth felt that Bridget was also becoming a liability even after he had turned her into one of his kin. Even with the knowledge that she was never going to be the same human again she continued to stir trouble. He had changed her at her own free will and in doing so he thought at the time that he also sealed her lips from confessing his sins. But for how long? Bridget had already shown signs of regret. Would she really be stupid enough to jeopardize *everything* by telling her sister what was really going on?

If she does, if she tries to betray me, she's dead. Dead and buried along with her sister.

The thought of overdosing Deanna with the same drug he had used on her during the child's birth crossed his mind. It would make matters so much simpler between Bridget and himself if Deanna were no longer alive to pray on her mind. Seth hadn't counted on his new mate to grow a conscience overnight. If his wife never woke up again then *maybe* Bridget would come around, she might then realize that her sisters death was really for the best.

He felt the left breast pocket of his dark suit.

The vile of liquid Phenobarbital was still there. Plenty left to get rid of her and still…what? Drug Bridget if need be. He could drug her and chain her in the basement until she came to her senses. Just as he was about to pour the entire contents of the glass vile into her water, Candice entered the room, distressed.

"Seth, come quickly. There is a man in the lobby demanding to see Michelle. He says he is her *husband*"

Seth reluctantly rose from the bed, placing the vile of Phenobarbital back into his suit pocket and followed Candice out of the room and down the stairway to the main hall. The man was tall, well built and clearly pissed off.

"So you're the little fucker who talked Michelle into leaving me." He stormed toward Seth, rage clearly seen in every manner of his body. Swinging at Seth's head with his right fist the man lunged forward. Seth moved just out of his reach with the ease of a cat and struck the man once in the face, toppling him into a pile of flesh at his feet. The man lay there unconscious as Seth grabbed him and lifted him easily over his shoulder.

"You should probably tell Michelle that she has a visitor. I will put him in the old garden room, she can speak with him there." Seth turned to leave, the strangers head bobbing and arms swinging behind him as Seth made his way to one of distant corner rooms of the manner.

Forty-five minutes later Todd Searight woke up in what was know as "the garden room" one of the many empty rooms that now plagued Laurendale Manner. Seth had learned not to trust jealous husbands or doubt their capabilities. Todd was chained to a large steel ring set into the stone wall with mortar, he wasn't going *anywhere*

The man pulled himself up onto his elbows from where he had lain face down on a large over-sized bed. His prison was cast in darkness, but he could still make out the sheet covered white blobs that must have been furniture that cluttered the seldom used room. The cloth that had previously saved the bed from an on slot of dust and cobwebs now lay on the floor, crumpled like spilt cream. Thick drapes were pulled closed but he could still see the long sliver of golden sunlight that managed its way through the crack in the fabric where they didn't quite meet in the middle. Its soft light catching the particles of dust in the air, outlining their shapes in early morning sunlight.

Todd's head was killing him as he touched his quickly swelling jaw, not quite broken, but very nearly. As he moved the chain that held his right wrist pulled and rattled against the stone wall.

There was no doubt about it, he was a prisoner.

Todd was seriously pissed off and in no mood for someone's sick idea of a joke. He knew his rights, and he was sure that the British police were not much different than the American ones when it came to holding someone against their will.

"Michelle!" he screamed. "Michelle!"

Overwhelming silence was the only thing that greeted his straining ears, he lay there in disgust trying to slip the shackles from his wrists. The only reward for his trouble was a raw, bloody mess left behind by the shackles sharp metal casings as they tore into his skin. Todd pulled hard against the chain…nothing, not even a crack in the mortar, he would be there until whoever it was came and unlocked his wrist.

If they unlocked his wrist.

Reluctantly Todd became resolved to his current and unfortunate situation and decided to wait it out. He sat there on the corner of the bed, waiting to sock the next bastard that walked into the room and force whomever it was to remove the steel shackle from his wrist. He sat there brooding, there was no way Michelle would get away with this one. Once he managed to get his hands on her he would make sure that she couldn't sit down for a week.

It was literally hours before he could hear the faintest of footsteps coming down the hall towards his darkened prison. A light spilled through the bottom crack of the door only briefly before it was opened. Michelle stood there alone, her face illuminated softly by the old fashioned oil lamp that she carried.

"I could hear you screaming my name a mile away Toddy, you really should learn some better manners. There are people trying to get on with the rest of their lives here."

"What the hell are you doing here with that man Michelle? How could you do this to me?" He pulled himself up from the bed and strained against his short length of steel chain. Michelle stood just out of his reach.

"Why Toddy, I'm getting on with the rest of my life, the way you should have gotten on with yours. I rather like you on a short chain. It really suites your Neanderthal-like personality," she giggled.

Todd strained harder against his chain. "Don't be such a bitch Michelle. Get me out of this and I promise not to tell the cops back home about what you did to your Daddy."

Pulling the white sheet off the dressing table she set the glass oil lamp down and turned to him. She was even more amazing than he had remembered.

It was quite an effort on Todd's part to pull his attention from her body, but he did, and instead concentrated on the *real* reason he had bothered to follow her there. Todd loved her *money,* he knew that much for sure. Hell, that had been the one and *only* reason behind his hiring of that shit of a private detective and then following her here all the way from the U.S. Michelle had made the fatal mistake of putting a freeze on all of their assets, not to mention draining their four bank accounts and closing out *his* credit cards. He wasn't leaving there without his wife and her money.

Now however things had changed, if only slightly, now he had a score to settle; no one made an ass out of Todd Searight. The son of a whore that had hit him would pay dearly for ever thinking he could put his filthy hands on him and live to tell about it. He hadn't been knocked out like that since his college days and he sure as shit wasn't going to take it lying down now, any more than he had then. Todd would make sure to take care of that ass first, and then Michelle…maybe even make her watch as he carved the man up like a Christmas turkey.

Michelle though, his loving wife she would need a good seeing to, and he was just the man to do it Maybe even a few broken bones would be needed this time to put her in her place, nothing too serious, but enough to get his point across. Todd licked his lips in anticipation, he would have her on her knees the second she came close enough, and then he would teach her what it meant to be really afraid.

As Todd began to ease back a few steps in the hops that Michelle would misjudge the length of his chain so that he could then spring out at her and take her by surprise, he looked at her face for the first time, there was something very different about her. Something almost magical.

"You never were very smart, were you Toddy. A man such as yourself should never threaten a woman that holds his tiny, withered balls in the palm of her hands. Now don't get me wrong Toddy, I'm not saying that your visit here will be totally unpleasant…just that it will be short. I have the ability to make the next few minutes of your life a truly…*orgasmic* experience." Michelle smiled that coy little smile that she always used on him whenever she wanted her own way. She stepped close enough to caress his face, brushing his hair back into place with the tips of her fingers. Todd had forgotten about the clenched fist that he held tightly behind him, the fist intended for her.

"Don't you want me Toddy?" she asked, sliding the knot of her gown and standing naked before him.

His mouth suddenly went dry and Todd's desire for his wife became rather visible from the newly formed lump his jeans, she laughed at him. Michelle stepped nearer to him, his hand falling limp as his arms pulled her closer to him. She kissed him deeply and then pulled back just enough for him to see her face in the lamplight.

"Christ!" crackled Todd, his voice becoming as soft and submissive as that of a young child's. He tried rather unsuccessfully to recoil from her iron-like grasp.

He stood there, as ridged as any scarecrow, and watched as Michelle changed before his very eyes. His wife's once cool blue eyes turned to a predator yellow, her once beautiful blonde hair became pitch as night, and her alabaster skin changed to the shinny blue-black scales of a snake.

"I honestly loved you at one time, my dear *sweet* Toddy." She hissed. "Ah, but you were deceptive to me, and unfaithful. I know all about the money you have stolen from me, and the ever growing gambling debts that you've accumulated all over town. I even know about the jewels…*my* jewels that you've switched with cheap, paste knockoffs. And then there's the women…the nasty, filthy, stinking whores you've dared to be with, all the while laughing at me; mocking me behind my back." She caressed his face with a long, smooth hand as she spoke, drawling him into her.

Todd's face had froze in terror at the sight before him; she had become nothing less than a vision of Hell.

"I won't fuel your addictions," she slithered over his body, pulling him into the cavern of her body. "But you can fuel mine." She pressed her lips against the crook of his neck, pulling in the human scent of him, filling her lungs with the sweet, heady aroma of his fear, as he fought against her inhuman strength.

But it was too late, she had already become too intoxicating to him, too desirable. The need to touch her, to be touched *by* her overriding the fear that now clouded his mind. Michelle's black lips parted to show several rows of fiercely sharp teeth, each one curving slightly inward like that of a snake's, saliva foamed and dripped from her chin.

"Please," Todd begged softly. "I need you Michelle, can't you see that!" Tears, actual *tears* welled in his eyes as she brushed her lips gently against his face, the smell of him permeated the room, and she thrived on it.

She slowly withdrew her lips from the flesh of his neck as her eyes locked on to his, he could *feel* her pull him into her, as if she were feeding off of him.

Devouring him.

Todd could do little more than succumb to his own deadly desires. Her naked body slid like silk against his as she freed him from the snug confines of his clothing. She gazed at him steadily, caressing the taunt muscles of his body and roughly stroking his already primed genitals as she pushed him to the bed. She parted her long, smooth legs and mounted him, taking from him not only his seed, but also his very life. Michelle's body had become a well oiled, human harvesting machine as she rocked deeply into him, as wave after wave of semen left his body. Each movement bringing him closer to his own death, each smooth gyration of her hips taking more and more of his essence. Todd moaned loudly, sweat beading across his chest as Michelle leaned down as if to kiss him, her mouth stopping just short of his as she opened it wide, drawling in a deep, sadistic breath she latched herself onto his mortal soul. His flesh became pale, his eyes closed.

Todd felt "himself" detach from the solidness of his body, his soul weakened, and then faltered. His mind began slipping through memory's like sand until there was only nothingness left. The last remaining wisps of his essence drifted gently from the blackened hollows of his eyes and the turned in, soured hole that had once been his mouth.

The body of Todd Searight drifted lightly back onto the bed, his seed and his life had been drained from his body. Todd's once dark brown hair had turned to a brilliant white, his skin was wrinkled and pulled like old, tanned leather. Deeper she pulled him in, deeper she drank the last remaining electrodes of his life. His body had become withered and brittle like a thousand-year-old mummy, until nothing was left of him save his lying, stealing bones.

Todd Searight was dead.

His human needs and desires had been quenched, but at a cost.

Michelle rose from her spent lover and pushed his now empty shell of a body from the bed and onto the dusty floor. She felt invigorated, empowered. She stepped nonchalantly over his dead body to gaze at herself in the mirror, adjusting her hair and wiping the glossy sheen of his essence from where it had spilled from her lips.

She licked her fingers and purred.

Her strength had been increased by the feeding and as she began to change back into the alabaster skinned goddess that she knew herself to be, she paused and looked at Todd's dried remains that were reflected in the mirror.

"That has got to be the *nicest* thing you've ever done for me Toddy," she smiled at him and picked up the oil lamp.

Outside the room Seth stood slumped against the opposite wall waiting for her to finish. He smiled warmly as she opened the heavy wooden door. His eyes moved from Michelle's naked body, to that of the misshapen form of her now *ex*-husband on the floor, and then back again.

"Forgive me for waiting just outside the door for you my dear, but I needed to make sure you could handle your first feeding on your own. Of course I'm not at all surprised that you didn't need my help in any way. I can only assume that the girls have taught you well." He pulled her to him, his mouth gently kissing the rising mounds of her breasts as they pushed against him. "But then again, I knew you were a strong woman from the very moment we met. I also knew that you would be perfect for me, perfect for making my family stronger."

Michelle leaned her nakedness against him, touching his face with her hand. "You're my lover now, and I would do *anything* to make you happy." She smiled at him. "Besides, I couldn't afford a long and messy divorce. Toddy could be so damned *greedy* at times."

Seth slid his hand down the smooth curve of her hourglass form. His fingers gently brushing the blonde corn silk hair between her legs. Michelle arced her body into the warmth of his hand, needing him to penetrate her. He smiled darkly at her as he pushed into her soft wetness of her flesh.

"Fuck me Seth. Fuck me right here," she almost cried, her body shaking with desire.

"It would be my pleasure."

Without warning Seth turned and pushed her body hard against the wall as pushed his fingers deeply into her. Michelle gasped, sucking in the air around her and smiling, her hands fighting to release him from the confines of his pants, her fingers tightly encircling the girth of his swollen male form. Seth moved his hands up to cradle her ass and support her weight as he entered into her in one strong thrust, forcing her legs up around his waist he pushed her hard against the wall.

Michelle could clearly see Todd's discarded body on the floor from where she lay propped up against the wall, she smiled wildly at him as Seth thrust deeply into her.

Too bad she had killed him first.

What she wouldn't have given at that very moment to have Todd see him fuck her brains out right in front of his ugly little face.

"Harder Seth, fuck me harder!" Michelle screamed and gritted her teeth as Seth ripped into her, her nails digging into the flesh of his back.

Delighting at the thought of her former husband laying there shriveled up into nothingness, she let herself go to the overflow of orgasmic raptures that wrecked throughout her body. Seth had feed her, and she now belonged to him. And *he*, belonged to her.

Chapter 22

Bridget had checked on the physical condition of Deanna soon after Seth had left her sisters bedside to take care of Michelle's little marital problem. Bridget had no desire to speak to him about Deanna's baby, and what exactly he hoped to achieve by keeping him from her, at least not yet. So she had kept watch by her sister's room waiting for him to come out, hoping with everything in her soul that he hadn't had a chance to say anything about the baby and his subsequent "death." Once Bridget saw him quickly ushered out by Candice, who was frantically rambling on about someone named Todd Searight and the fact that he was claming to be Michelle's astringed husband, she grabbed the opportunity and quickly slipped in to see her.

Bridget stood by her sisters bedside for some time, gazing down at Deanna, verifying for herself that she was indeed alright. Reassured only with her own two eyes that her sister had lived through such an unnatural childbirth, that it *hadn't* render Deanna in poor health, or worse, death.

She was sleeping soundly, although she was still heavily drugged as she had been told, Deanna's breathing was normal and steady. Bridget couldn't detect any fever so the thought of infection was eased from her mind, although she still looked a bit pale from the loss of so much blood. Even so, Bridget expected Deanna to make a full recovery.

She looked around the opulent room, with its heavy drapery and dull lighting. Hardly the type of sterile environment most woman gave birth in these days, but then again Bridget knew that Deanna wasn't the first woman to give birth outside of a hospital's walls, nor would she be the last. Deanna would be fine. Her and the baby would survive.

Bridget had to fight back the desire to shake her sister awake, to tell her that her baby was fine, that the child was just resting in another room of the hotel and that they would all be going home together soon.

But Bridget didn't, she couldn't, not yet.

She knew that she couldn't betray Seth, not now, not without risking her sister's life, and possibly even her own in the process. Bridget knew well enough that her sisters life was hanging by a thread, and to know the baby was alive and healthy, would, in Seth's eyes, cause her to become too much of a liability for his plans. Seth made it very clear to her that the only one he now cared for was the child, and that Deanna was entirely expendable. It was only a matter of time before Bridget would became as expendable as her sister, that is if she hadn't already. Bridget had seen first hand just how quickly Seth could change his feelings for someone he supposedly loved, to discard them like an old plaything to rot. How just uncaring Seth could become.

She left Deanna's room as quietly as she had entered it, knowing at least for the time being that her sister was alive and safe. Outside her sister's room she was met by Jessica and Candice on their way to the dining room for lunch. Bridget had lost more time sitting with her sister, watching the rise and fall of her chest as she slumbered, than she had thought, and agreed to join them.

The three of them had sat quietly for some time, discussing Michelle's visitor and his subsequent demise, when Eva entered the room looking rather pleased with herself.

"Seth has informed me that he and Michelle will be having their lunch in *her* room today. For some reason I'm sure the four of us won't find the lack of their company *too* distressing," Eva's smile was small but poignant.

"I dare say I could stand an afternoon without the likes of Michelle spoiling it," said Jessica.

"What's your opinion of her Bridget? Do you find her to be as exhausting as the rest of us seem to?" asked Eva, taking her seat at the head of the table, leaning back into the soft curve of the chairs upholstered seat.

Bridget couldn't help but feel that Eva sat at the head of the table more often than not. She had begun to get the most curious feeling about these women. The feeling that Seth was more of a venue for entertainment than the master of the house. They seemed to be almost amused by his actions and took little care in sharing their opinions of him…or his new plaything with one another. Their actions had become open and uncensored to Bridget since her arrival at Laurendale Manner.

"Well, I suppose if we are all being honest here, I would have to say that she comes across as an obvious fake to me. I'm sure that the *real* Michelle isn't quite so stupid *or* so friendly." Bridget drank half her glass of brandy, letting the smooth liquid run down her throat and warm her stomach before finishing her candid opinion of Seth's new woman. "So I suppose my answer is…yes, I guess I *do* find her as exhausting as everyone else seems to."

"She smells like trouble to me," said Candice, with a twitch of her nose. "I wish Seth would get rid of her."

"I'm quite sure that if we were to give Michelle enough rope, the little darling will save us the trouble and hang herself. She seems just the type for such a cliché travesty as that," Eva said, touching Candice's hand gently in a reassuring manner.

It was then that four of the servants entered the dining room, each one weighed down heavily with silver trays bearing lunch. The smell of roasted lamb and winter vegetables filled the air. Talk at the lunch table temporarily wavered into silence, save for the sharp clang of utensils against fine porcelain.

"I know it's none of my business Eva, but just how long *have* you and Seth been together?" Bridget asked, now that half of her plate was empty and her stomach no longer demanded that it be heard long enough to fill it.

"It's hard to track the years when so many have passed you by," Eva smiled darkly, her nose wrinkling a bit at her own dry humor. "Let's just say that I've known Seth for as far back as your great-great grandmother knew *her* mother, and be done with it. Back then I wasn't quite the stunning creature you see before you today, it's amazing what money can do to a persons looks." Her smile was wide and playful.

Both Jessica and Candice laughed, "Don't let her modesty fool you Bridget, she has always been a stunning creature, only now she can afford to dress accordingly." Jessica turned to Eva and said, "Tell her how the two of you met. I'm sure she'll find it as fascinating as we did."

"I would have to agree with Jessica, she makes the story sound most intriguing. I must say that I would love to hear how the two of you met. That is if you don't mind telling it?" Asked Bridget, downing the other half of her brandy and then refilling it.

"Very well, but don't complain to me when I've finished with my story and it doesn't turn out to be quite as interesting a tale as the girls led you to believe."

Bridget set her newly filled brandy class down and reclined slightly in her chair, truly anxious to hear Eva's account of how she came to know Seth Toumbs.

"Seth and I met at a particularly dark period in my life. In those days I lived in a small village just outside of what is now Frankfurt, Germany. It's winters were long and harsh, many people in my village died of malnutrition, disease, and more times than not, murder.

I had been unfortunate enough to catch the eye of a local textile merchant named Heiko. He was very wealthy and very powerful, although neither of which proved to increased his attractiveness, at least not enough to make the attraction reciprocated on my part. He lacked manners and anything even close to acceptable personal hygiene." Eva paused to take a sip of brandy and wave the boys in with dessert; Terra Misuse, Bridget's favorite.

"Where was I now…oh yes, his advances had became more and more obvious, almost aggressive in his desire to posses me. Yet each time I found some sort of excuse as to why we could not meet and occasionally I even managed to avoid him altogether.

Heiko, although you would have never known by his actions, was also already married to a woman named Petra. Granted, she was a particularly ugly woman; both in appearance and in personality, but that gave him no excuse for his behavior. Soon Petra became privy to her husband's unsavory advancements towards me and one night, two of her men broke into my home." Eva downed the rest of her brandy, her eyes slightly closed. "That night was the worst I have ever experienced, and for the span of life that I have lived, that is truly saying something. Her men beat and raped me; their brutality unmatched by any I had ever experienced before…or since. The bastards even burned down my home so that I would have nothing to return to once they had finished with me. The house itself wasn't much, but back then it was all I had and it was filled with countless books and papers that will never be replaced. When they had finished, there was nothing left but a blackened mark on the surface of the earth to show here my home had once sat. I believe they made their mistress pleased with their great success. While I'm quite sure that the ordeal only lasted a few hours, but unfortunately when you are on the receiving end of such cruelty, time seems to pass with tediously slow brutality." Eva paused for a moment, remembering the taste of her own blood in her mouth and the hatred that gripped her heart that night, so long ago.

"My God, How horrible for you," Bridget said quietly.

"I'm inclined to agree with you my dear; it was horrible. But in those days women had to endure a great many injustices with very little compensation. Luckily though for the most part we have managed to overcome the vast majority of them." Eva dismissed it with the wave of her hand but Bridget could tell that the old days that Eva spoke of still managed to hold onto all of their venomous sting as if it were only yesterday.

"They informed me, those treacherous men, that the lady Petra no longer found her husband's desire for me amusing, and that she wished for my immediate and permanent departure from the village. So with nothing more than the torn clothes that were on my back I was ridden out of town, bound, gagged, and blindfolded and left deep into the unforgiving wilderness where I would surely die.

In those early days, before the revelation of my *true* powers, I would have easily died from the below freezing temperatures or the ravenous wolves that were so prevalent back then. By the first signs of dawn I could barely feel my legs under me from the fridge bite of the cold, but I *had* managed to find the road. Though it was not much better than the dark recesses of the woods I'm afraid, since thieves and murderers traveled those lonely country roads looking for victims unfortunate enough to pass by them.

As the sun crested the trees I realized that I was being hunted by a small pack of wolves. Maybe four or five at the most, but just as deadly as if there were twenty. They must have circled 'round me in the night; their prints had become visible in the light dusting of snow as morning cast its pale light on the ground around me.

I had resolved myself to my death, to my fate, or whatever it was that would come my way. When a dark, brooding rider on an even darker horse passed by me on the road and then mercilessly stopped. His manner was grave and his face full of his own bitterness, but he still possessed enough humanity in him to take pity on me anyway. He lifted his face up into the air and closed his eyes, he then very calmly told me that a small pack of wolves, perhaps four or five, were hunting me. He said that he had *smelled* them, and that he had witnessed their tracks in the frozen ground as I had. He seemed rather curious that I did not panic at the information he had shared with me and so offered me a ride to the next town. I noticed that he carried little with him except a heavy purse, no weapons at least, so I accepted his warm generosity. At that moment he was my savior, my dark knight so to speak."

Bridget sat intently listening, hanging on every word that she spoke. The romance of her story managed to rekindle a bit of the love she had once felt for Seth; the desire to understand his actions clouded her judgment, but only momentarily. What had changed the man that she thought she knew from someone who at one point in his existence seemed to cherish human life, into the heartless beast she knew him to be today?

"It was several years later that I found out that earlier that very day he had lost his wife and child to the hands of several uneducated, superstitious men. His family's blood practically still on his hands; the dirt from their graves still fresh under his nails. But as it was, at that moment in time I knew nothing of *his* hardships, only that of my own suffering and bitterness. My disdain for the world of man consumed me.

We rode for what felt like hours, the winter sky had turned dark early and this dark, handsome man set up a small camp a few miles from a nearby village. A simple fire was all we had to keep warm and at first I had even considered using the heat of our two bodies, wrapped together like lovers, in order to keep us sustained until morning, after all, he did save me. I owed him at least that much. But that was not to be our destiny, at least not that night anyway." Eva smiled coyly, and continued with her story.

"As the darkness grew around us and the moon filled the night sky, I witnessed for the first time the workings of the Devil upon the body of man. I knew that such creatures existed, after all, my mother had explained the vast and dangerous creatures of the night to me when I was very young, but had never seen one with my own eyes. The horrible sounds that his body made as it twisted and reformed, the grotesque stretching of his flesh sickened me as he stood there, naked before me and changed from man to wolf.

Once again that night I had resolved myself to dying, but I must confess the thought of being torn to shreds by that towering beast shook me to the very core of my being. The beast stood closer to me than you sit now Bridget, his sour breath beating against my cold face, his red eyes burning into my soul…but he never attacked. Not once did his claws tear at my flesh or his gaping jaws snap at my body. He merely turned from me and vanished into the darkness of the night. I'm sure you can imagine my confusion at still being alive.

I'm not sure if it was shock or stupidity that kept me by his fireside that night, but I stayed. When I awoke the next morning he was washing the blood from his body with the snow around us, turning it a deep crimson red. His demeanor was calm and relaxed and we didn't speak of the nights events, but instead carried on with our journey to the next town. It was in that town where we took proper lodging at a small inn and he filled our stomachs with good, hot food and countless pints of warm, dark ale. When we came upon some of the local shops he was kind enough to purchase me warm clothing to protect me from the cold winter chill.

Seth and I have not separated since.

We will die together, for better or for worse, I am his partner in life...for as long as that may be."

There was silence around the table as Bridget and the twins looked longingly into the fire, trying to capture some of the romance of Eva's tale. It was Bridget that finally broke the silence.

"The girls were right; that *is* an amazing story. You have come such a long way since your harrowing night in the woods of Germany. I dare say that you will never have such misfortune again." Bridget smiled as she watched Eva. There was no doubt that she was a woman of substance, but not of trust. Bridget imagined that there was more to her story than she let on, but even as well rehearsed as it was, it still gave some insight to the woman who sat at the head of Seth's table, his table *and* his life.

"Nor do I plan to. I have learned that we all make our own destiny. We just need to have the strength to act upon it when it comes time."

"Perhaps you're right Eva." Bridget wiped her mouth with her napkin and rose from the table. "Well, it's getting pretty late. I'm sure my sister will be awake by now. I should sit with her for a while."

"Let us know if there is anything that she requires," said Eva, as Bridget left the room nodding and smiling in acceptance.

Just short of entering her sisters room Bridget was stopped in the corridor by Seth.

"Bridget, I need to leave immediately for London. Unfortunately that leaves only yourself or Eva to tell your sister that the child died during birth. I think it would be best if it came from you, you being her sister and all. I would do it myself, but as it so happens there is pressing business in London that I *must* attend to."

Bridget's eyes hardened. "You bastard. You *never* intended to be the one to tell her about her son did you? You expected me to do your dirty work all along."

"Listen Bridget, I don't have the time *or* the interest right now to deal with your unwarranted accusations. Now just do what it is that you do best...lie to your sister and take care of this little problem for me. Now if that's too difficult for you, perhaps you would rather I take care of your sister instead?"

The look that passed from Seth's eyes to Bridget's told her more than she needed to understand the meaning behind his words. He did have it in him. He could kill his wife without so much as a second thought.

"What's happened to you Seth? What has made you into this *monster*?" Bridget's eyes welled with tears.

"I grew up Bridget, maybe you should try a doing little of the same," said Seth, as he turned on his highly polished heels and disappeared down the quickly darkening hallway.

She hated him. Bridget hated every part of him and she suddenly became very aware of the deepening desire to taste his rancid, foul blood.

Chapter 23

Deanna woke to see Bridget sitting in the rather uncomfortable looking wooden chair that sat by her bedroom window, her body illuminated by the soft light of the late afternoon sun. Her sister's back was to her and as Bridget stared out the window to the grounds below her manner seemed quiet; reflective. Again it struck her that Bridget looked younger, years younger than she had when she first left Pittsburgh in order to track down Deanna's husband for her. Looking back, it seemed like years had passed since Deanna had walked into her sister's living room begging for her help. But then again, maybe it was just that she felt so much older.

Feeling her sisters eyes on her Bridget turned to face her, forcing a thin smile over the curve of her mouth.

"Good morning," she said, and stood to join her by the bed. Touching her arm Bridget gazed down at her sister in a strangely somber way that she had never seen before. Deanna began to feel uncomfortable.

"There's something wrong with the baby isn't there?" Deanna said. It was a statement rather than a question, her gaze had drifted out of the window and off into the distant fields beyond.

"Yes," there was a physical pause that took over Bridget's whole body. Uncertainty touched her face briefly, but then it hardened again. "I'm afraid we did everything we could...but the baby...the baby came too early. Seth called for the doctor as soon as you went into labor, but like I said, there was nothing that could be done. He died shortly after he was born. The doctor said you have a terribly high fever now due to the infection, but he has given us something for you to take to relive that."

Bridget stood by her sisters bedside, her gaze lost in the random folds of the pale cotton sheets, not daring to look Deanna in the eye, terrified that she would come apart at the seems and tell her sister everything. She stood there for some time, stroking her sister's arm affectionately, but Deanna didn't seem to have heard her. The lie, the lie she had told had come out easier than Bridget had ever thought it would, but the words left a bitter taste in her mouth. The putrid, evil lie lay there rolling against her tongue like some sort of poison candy.

"Was he…was he normal? I thought I saw something strange…something *wrong*." The words caught in Deanna's throat like fish bones.

"Yes, of course he was normal." Bridget's lie came out a bit louder than she had intended it to.

She couldn't have possibly seen the child, she was deep under sedation…and I took him away so quickly.

"He just never moved, that's all. The doctor said that it was just too early for him to come, the poor child's lungs weren't fully developed."

"Strange…I thought I heard him crying." Deanna muttered softly to herself, refusing to look at Bridget, as if somehow not making eye contact made what was happening not real, not solid.

Something critical had changed between them.

"You must have been dreaming; or hallucinating. He never made a noise, I promise you." Again the sour, rotting taste of lies.

"So my baby *was* a boy. I've been trying so hard to remember, but it seems the harder I try, the more elusive the images become."

Bridget couldn't bear to talk about it anymore, she needed to get out of that suddenly miniscule room to breathe, the walls were closing in on her. Bridget couldn't breathe, not in there, not with her sister.

"Your fever was dangerously high. The doctor was surprised that you lived through the birth at all." Bridget crossed over to the window and opened it enough to let a cool breeze in to freshen the room, to free her from the closeness she was feeling. The lies were slowly suffocating her. "We were all quite worried about you." The tone of her voice had become hard and strained, suggesting anything but worry to Deanna.

"How long until we can go home? I don't like it here Bridget." Deanna said through silent tears as they gently rolled down her cheeks. The vision of her child danced before her eyes, how she had *dreamed* of him.

"At least a few more days. He wants your temperature to return to normal and then he promised to release you from his care and we will all be free to leave." Bridget forced a short lived smile across her ashen face.

"And where is my loving husband? Shouldn't *he* be here?" Deanna looked at her now, her eyes had become red rimmed and puffy. Deanna couldn't help but feel the coldness that radiated from Bridget, the distance between them had become marked by miles, not feet.

"I just passed him in the hall, he had to take care of the legal matters, such as there are, with the death of a baby not born in a hospital." Bridget turned to the window again, sucking in a cool breath of air, wishing above all else to make their conversation short. Her body physically ached to leave not only the confines of her sisters room, but also the weight of her steady gaze.

The matter of fact tone in her sisters voice cut Deanna to the quick. She couldn't understand the sudden change in her.

"Why have you cut off your feelings from me Bridget? Do you not even *care* that my baby has died?" her voice was strained and weak.

My God yes I care, this kills me…

"What do you mean? I'm no different to you than I have ever been. I have come here of *your* bidding. I have helped to save *your* marriage. I am sorry for your loss Deanna, but there is nothing that I can do. Crying about it won't help matters, it will only make them worse." Bridget had to force the words out, horrified by them before they even had the time to leave her mouth.

They could hear the popping sound of tires gliding over gravel as a car pulled away down the long driveway. Bridget moved to the window and gazed out. "That's him leaving now. I'll tell Seth you wish to see him when he returns, he shouldn't be too long." Bridget returned and paused by her sisters bed, Deanna seemed smaller than she remembered. She resisted the desire to touch Deanna again, to hold her, and gave her a drink instead and the small pills from the clear glass jar that sat on her dressing table.

"Here, take this, it will help to reduce the fever. But I can't say that it'll do much for your emotional state."

And what about my *emotional state… if I tell you what's really going on Seth will kill you.*

Bridget's mind swam in a murky fog caught somewhere between guilt and rage. Her head began to ache with a sharp, piercing pain that flashed in her eyes as white lightning.

"Will I get to see my son…before they take him away from me?" Deanna asked, swallowing the two small pills and handing her sister back the empty glass.

"I really don't think that's such a good idea Deanna. Besides," she paused at the door, "the doctor has already taken him."

"Strange how it's like in my dreams; about the baby I mean. Something horrible *did* happen to him." Deanna was no longer watching Bridget, but laid there staring, unseeing out the bedroom window. Exhaustion began washing over her ravaged body, her limbs became as heavy as those of the long dead, her eyes became mere slits on a face full and swollen with sorrow.

Bridget closed the door behind her, leaving her sister alone to dwell with her fading dreams of a perfect child.

Her stomach churned, tears broke the surface of her once barren, cold eyes.

All Bridget could think of was her sister's broken dreams, her broken family, and her broken heart.

And how *she* had helped to cause it.

There was no mistaking that if in the end Deanna were to find out that her child was indeed alive, that her sister would see it as being all Bridget's fault. And she wouldn't be wrong, not really, she had helped to destroy her own sister with her actions, with her adultery, and with her lies.

Bridget knew the pain of losing a child. But she also knew that the loss was purely due to her own gut wrenching decision, even so, she had lived quietly with that pain for all these years. She had never felt able to voice her own sorrow to the comforts of her sister. Would she have understood? Bridget couldn't risk it, she couldn't risk the possibility that her own sister might reject her, that she might chastise her decision to terminate her own pregnancy, and instead she had buried her pain deep inside where it rotted and soured her mind against Deanna.

Only now, now she also knew the feeling of being a child's mother, of the child suckling from her breast and tugging at her hair. It wasn't the family that she had hoped for, Bridget knew that this child was no more her own than Seth was her husband. While Bridget could fool herself into believing almost anything, even she couldn't trick herself into believing that what she had done to her sister was justified…or even human.

After Bridget had closed the door behind her, Deanna lay crumpled in bed, trying desperately to fight against the sedative that her sister had given her long enough see and speak with Seth. The thought that perhaps she too was going to die made its way into her mind. Not that Deanna thought it would solve all of her problems, but to be honest, the thought of her own death didn't seem so awful after all, not now, not after losing the most precious thing that had ever touched her life.

Still, even after everything that Bridget had said, Deanna *still* couldn't shake the feeling deep down in the marrow of her bones, that her baby boy was still alive somewhere.

Deanna would come in and out of consciousness throughout the night, always alone, but sometimes, sometimes she heard the most beautiful sound far off in the distance, the sound of a newborn baby crying.

It was a baby that she *knew* had to be her own.

Nothingness had surrounded Deanna. The nightmares that had haunted her throughout her pregnancy had truly become real, and in their realness they had left her. Now she was alone; alone with the thoughts of what might have been.

Bridget stood outside Deanna's closed door, desperately breathing in the stale air around her, filling her lungs deeply with large, fevered gulps.

What have I become?

The thought sickened her, Bridget's mind raced frantically to find some sort of reassurance behind what she had just done to her sister. She *did* it to save Deanna of course, but at what cost? Seth had given her little time to do other than follow his well rehearsed orders.

I've become no better than him, no better than the animal Seth.

Bridget pulled herself along the darkened corridor to her own room where she collapsed into a torrent of tears and regret.

Later that night, the cub-child now known as David was brought to her bosom by the twin, Candice to feed, and she did so as her surrogate mother's instincts had instructed her, but her heart was not in it. Bridget gazed down at the heavily furred whelp unseeing, she focused instead on the growing hatred that had begun to germinate in her werewolf heart, fostering it along with the visions of her sister, stricken and ill at the thought of her dead child.

Along with that came a hatred of what Seth had made her. A beast that would forever comb the night in search of human victims.

Victims like herself...victims like her sister and her parents.

Her innocence had been lost there in a coven of devils and bloodsuckers, and she knew her only true and final escape would be her own death.

Her death yes; but what of the man who damned her like some righteous God?

Bridget had begun to not only enjoy her ever growing desire to taste Seth's vile werewolf blood, she began to foster it, even at the risk of spilling her own.

Chapter 24

A few hours after Bridget had finished feeding David, Candice had returned to take the small wolf cub back to her room for the night. The sleeping arrangements made by Seth all made sense to her now. He wasn't really worried that Bridget would accidentally kill the child in the night, when the moon's light took over her body and her senses; David's scent wasn't even *human*. The real truth of the matter was that Seth didn't want to risk the possibility of her suddenly becoming a reformed werewolf and steeling him, and perhaps even her sister, and returning with them to the States.

As the graying light of evening broke against the sky Bridget stood outside the warmth of her room on the cement and stone balcony, naked in the swiftly darkening world around her, and looked out over the great expanse of lawn. Seth had returned from London at least an hour earlier but hadn't bothered to come to her room and see her, to find out how it had gone between her and Deanna. Her soul felt hollow, useless.

He's avoiding me, the spineless jackass.

The coldness of the late October evening whipped against her thin human skin, but Bridget couldn't feel it. She had become increasingly distant, with each passing second, from her human self. Distant from her rational, moral, *human* thoughts and with each steady crawl of the clocks hand forward, she felt the ever maddening call of the animal that stirred within her, clawing savagely at her organs in order to free itself from the tight confines of her fragile skin. Night had fallen, and Bridget waited anxiously for the moon to rise, as if the silver sphere had been her long awaited lover, and along with its anticipated rising, came the swift and merciful removal of the human frailty of guilt and remorse.

Bridget tried to hold onto the thought of Seth and the man Eva had portrayed him to be so many years ago. Perhaps, she thought, as she looked out into the darkness that surround her, one forgets their human emotions after having them perpetually forced from them, time after time, month after month…decade after long decade of changing into the beast that she was now becoming.

Bridget ran her hand down the nakedness of her body, desperately trying to hold onto the human that was being torn from her mind. She could feel it slipping…slipping into the vast darkness the way the smooth curve of a woman's naked body slips into the depthless waters of a darkened lake on a hot summers night.

She would try to reason with him one more time. She would try to find the man that he used to be so long ago…the man Eva had described so eloquently to her in her story.

Bridget placed her hand on the cement banister and watched the long, feminine curve of her fingers as the moon rose high in the distant horizon. Her pale, flawless skin began to darken and decay around the smooth contours of her wrist. Her skins softness began to burst, at first only in a few small patches, and then in ever growing numbers they consumed her as course red hair was forced from every follicle on her body.

Bridget staggered forward, her eyes blurring as her face pulled and popped from the confines of her once modestly sized human skull, into that of the large, heavily boned proportions of the creature she was to be for an eternity.

She had changed, both in form and function, and her quickly fleeting human thoughts and emotions were becoming no more than vague memories.

Bridget then caught sight of the black, hulking from of the werewolf Seth before her. He had somehow already made it to the grounds below and was quickly making his way to the thick mass of trees that lined the property without her. She moved forward, smelling the cool night air and catching the heady scent of him on her tongue and rolling it around her mouth like sweet icing. Bridget knew that they would hunt separately tonight, and perhaps even forever if they didn't clear up this family dispute that was coming between all of them, but what should it matter to her.

"The bastard tricked me…what should I care *what* he thinks of me?" Her animal voice was thick and raspy as she spoke out into the stillness of the night, but no one was there to hear her, save herself.

She leaned farther out over the balcony and as the wolf inside her took possession over that of her human side, she forcefully clung to the anger that she had fostered for Seth over the last two days. She *had* too, the animal inside her desired the touch of her mate, to feel the steely strength of him inside her was almost as commanding as the need for human flesh. Bridget latched onto those familiar feelings of betrayal and treachery, like a prizefighter's golden glove, and kept them tucked deep inside the recesses of her chest.

Bridget felt the hackles on her back rise as a snarl escaped her deep russet lips…if they *had* hunted together on this night, she knew in her animal heart that they would have either fought or mated…and neither of those possibilities would have been to her advantage, at least not tonight.

The former Bridget Manning and one time high priced call girl, stayed just long enough to catch the last fading scent of her lover and then jumped smoothly down onto the well manicured lawn below. Momentarily the she-beast paced back and forth; unsure of the direction in which to hunt. If she were to follow too closely behind Seth, she was sure to come across his path at some point during the night causing unneeded stress. Finally the dim decision was made to hunt in completely the opposite direction that Seth had gone. Bridget turned away from the sexual temptations Seth Toumbs and away from the small, overcrowded hamlet of Odiham.

Several hours into the night Bridget had still not caught the scent of any human and the need for human flesh was becoming unbearable. Perhaps her decision to avoid the nearby hamlet, and also Seth, had been a mistake. Perhaps if they *had* mated they could have worked something out between them, something that they would have *all* been happy with.

Bridget had come to one of the main roads as it branched out from between two neighboring farms and crouched low into the thick cover of overgrown brambles that flanked the edged of the black pavement. A few meters ahead of her where she waited was a single red phone box highlighted by a flickering street light, its highly enameled form intermittently illuminated by the lamps light. The stretch of road that wound its way through this particular part of the country side, like some ridged black serpent, was exceedingly treacherous, that coupled with the fact that it was also poorly lit, caused the few cars that found there way along its dangerous path to slow down considerably at that particular bend in the road.

Bridget's mind raced as she watched the occasional car pass slowly by her, the animal's thought process was slow, but sufficient.

She knew what she had to do.

Bridget waited until she heard the steady hum of the next car's engine as it came along the roads tight bend. The driver, like all the others, applied the breaks slowly, not realizing the intensity of the turn. As the driver realized his mistake and pulled harder into the turn Bridget jetted out in front of him, causing the car to veer off and out of the turn. She had sent the human and his car swerving off the road and into the deep embankment beyond where the vehicle became stuck.

She waited for the human to leave the relative safety of the car.

After a few stunned moments the driver's side door opened and a man stepped out. Blood dripped from a superficial cut on his forehead caused when his head hit the steering wheel. He hadn't been wearing his seatbelt.

Bridget licked her lips…the smell was intoxicating.

The man touched his forehead and felt the blood, from somewhere deep inside his coat pocket he withdrew a white linen handkerchief and wiped first the blood from his hand and then gingerly from his forehead. He replaced the handkerchief and then continued on towards the phone box, his form bathed in the occasional light from the street lamp. Bridget's predatory eyes locked onto him.

Seth?

No, it couldn't be him.

Still…Bridget waited a bit longer just to be sure. Seth was out there right now, somewhere in the darkness…hunting, just like she was at that very second. There was no way in this world that he could still possess his human form, the moon was still affecting them both too strongly.

Even so, the man was strikingly similar to him. He was tall and well built, a dark dress coat just like the one Seth wore came to right above his ankles. The man could have easily passed for his twin. The mere thought of the *possibility* of it being him was good enough for Bridget…good enough to perhaps even quench the thirst she had for his blood…at least for now anyway.

The man reached the darkened door of the phone box and stopped.

His long dulled human instincts buzzed to life like a late night bug zapper. Something had passed close behind him in the night. Something large and perhaps even dangerous.

"What the fuck…"

Were the final lack luster words that escaped his mouth. They merely caught in the cold night breeze and floated away almost instantly, losing their potency as Bridget sprang from the dark, throwing the man into the brambles behind the phone box with such cosmic force that she could hear the snapping of his spine as it echoed throughout the night.

His body went through a short burst of spasmodic tensing of the muscles as his last remaining breath was forced from him. Bridget had suddenly forgotten about Seth, forgotten about her sister Deanna and the child she thought she had lost. The softness of his flesh was orgasmic to her, the sweetness of his blood like the warm refreshment of fine wine. Bridget drank and ate her fill.

She had *lived* in that moment as he had died...in total excess.

Chapter 25

Sometime in the early morning hours before the sun had managed to crest the distant line of trees, Deanna woke with a start. For a moment she lay there in the gray light of the coming dawn and wondered if it had all just been a horrible nightmare. Her eyes stared up at the ceiling, not risking the tell tail glance down at her stomach, and wished for nothing more than to be back in her home. Her one and only desire at that moment was to retrace her unfortunate steps and to have never gotten on the plane in the first place.

But this wasn't *her* bed, and no matter how hard she concentrated, she knew that this would never be *her* ceiling that she gazed at so intently.

She *was* in England; and it *was* true that she no longer carried the baby of her dreams inside her womb.

The room around her was dark for the most part but she could still make out the furnishings that cluttered the room. With each passing second the room became more and more illuminated as dawn crested her world's horizon to the east.

The world around her was waking up.

Her hair and pillow had become drenched in her own perspiration during the night. The pain that had been dulled by sleep and drugs earlier had now began to waken and demanded Deanna's full attention.

Slowly she pulled herself up into a sitting position, she felt weak and disorientated. Deanna pulled the coverlet back to reveal a large patch of fresh blood as it oozed from between her legs. The white cotton gown that she wore had settled between her thighs in the night and had been soaked through with her own blood turning it a dark brownish-red. At first her mind jumped at the sight of so much of her own blood, but then she realized that she was probably just still bleeding from the birth, although she was unsure just how much blood was normal. There seemed to be so much of it. She moved her body to the side and glanced at the sheet beneath her, to her dismay it had saturated all the way through, no doubt staining the mattress underneath as well. While she didn't think that the hotel's management would look too far down their noses at her for staining the mattress (under her current circumstances) she was still rather embarrassed. Deanna needed a shower and a clean change of clothes.

Whatever pain medication that they had given her was beginning to taper off and her body began to scream for more. The water pitcher that sat by the side of her bed was empty save for a few glistening droplets that clung to its side, making her lick her lips in desire. Deanna's overwhelming thirst overrode her body's pain, if only momentarily, as she gently pulled at her weakened legs to swing them out and over the side of the bed. Her feet dangled there, doll-like over the side of the bed, at a height of least four inches above the highly polished wooden floor. Slowly she slipped her haggard body down until her numb feet touched the ground, her head swam in a fog of white light from her sudden upright position. For a moment Deanna worried she would pass out and held on tightly to the beds high wooden post until the feeling had passed.

The sensation of hot pins shot through her legs as she stood there, braced up against the bed. The prickly sensation was caused by a lack of circulation throughout the entire lower half of her body and after a few moments, as her blood began to settle in the balls of her feet, she could feel her weight steady on them once more.

Deanna could feel the sudden emptiness of her body and it made her feel all the more ghost-like; as if she had become nothing more than a restless spirit, invisible…translucent to the world and its inhabitants that dwelled there. She reached for the light by the bed and turned it on. The room came alive with a rich, full spectrum of color but Deanna couldn't help but think that it all still looked much more like a dismal funeral home than an expensive hotel room. Perhaps it was just her current state of mind, but it still made the skin along her body crawl like it were infested with bugs none the less.

Eventually she regained most of her balance and with the empty glass pitcher in one hand and the other one now holding her suddenly smaller stomach, she gingerly made her way to the bathroom to fill it up with fresh, cold water.

My baby is gone…dead…

Drinking deeply from the bulbous form of the pitcher as she stood there in the small darkened room, Deanna made sure not to make any form of eye contact with her reflection in the mirror. She couldn't; not now, not while there was still so much guilt for what she had done staring back at her through her own eyes. She knew that directly in front of her, in that small, insignificant mirror, was the *one* person she couldn't keep the horrible truth from. The truth of what *she* had done.

I've brought this terrible nightmare all on myself. I'm the one that has foolishly suspected Seth of infidelity...and for my trouble I've now lost the one thing that ever mattered to me in this whole wide world.

Halfway back to her bed with the now full carafe grasped tightly in her slender arms, Deanna was stopped dead in her tracks. Floating up from the small crevice that ran under her door came the soft, almost musical cries of a baby and as they touched her ears they also caressed her mortal soul. Deanna's heart pounded within her chest with growing intensity as she strained to hear more of the melodious tune over the drumming in her own head.

There it was again...only this time much more clearly than before. She was *sure* that this time it wasn't just her mind wishing that she had heard the hungry cries of a child.

Deanna *wasn't* mistaken.

But what if the cries she heard bellowing up through the rafters of her ceiling were from another woman's child? After all this was a hotel, and even though she had not *seen* anyone in the lobby when she first arrived didn't mean that there weren't other guests already in there rooms or out for the night. Deanna had been out of it for how many days? She was unsure. Perhaps shortly after her own arrival someone else entered Laurendale Manner, someone with a newborn child of their own.

The soft cries of the child sounded so new, so small. Deanna had to reign her heart in on tattered strings. She reminded herself that her child was dead, and that Bridget...her own sister, had made that painfully clear.

She set the suddenly heavy water pitcher down on the table before she spilled it and listened again. Nothing this time, the child had been seen to...fed or changed perhaps, either way, the cries had stopped. She wished that the nagging in her heart would stop, the nagging that the sounds she had heard were from *her* child and not from someone else's as she imagined them to be.

Her mouth had gone dry again, a thick film of stress stuck to the roof of her pallet like soft white bread. She gulped another mouthful of water from the carafe and then set it back down, the cold water managed to help steady her breathing. Deanna went to the door and stuck her head out, beads of sweat glistened on her forehead and upper lip. The blood that oozed from deep within the cavity of her body was all but forgotten. Deanna steadied the frailty of her body against the smooth coolness of her door, her stomach threatening mutiny if she were to push it any farther but she chose to ignored it, instead she strained her eyes against the darkness. She had to be sure that the cause of the disruption was not her child.

I have to see with my own eyes that it's not my child...not mine, just my mind playing wicked tricks on me.

Closing the door behind her she stepped out into the darkness of the hall and waited for her eyes to adjust. The hall was long and punctuated with doors like her own at random intervals, but none of them had any number or letter that would make one recognizable from the other, at least none that she could see.

How did the guests find their rooms?

Deanna decided that the safest thing to do was for her to leave her door open just enough to let out a sliver of golden lamp light. That way it would make finding her way back to her own room in the darkness less difficult.

As she came to the end of the hall she could hear the muffled voices of people below her in the main hall. Not wishing to be seen, at least not in the state she was currently in, Deanna stayed close to the massive central arch that jutted out from the staircases banister and peered down into the vastness below. Several small lights had been lit around the rim of the main entrance hall, their dim illumination giving off just enough light for her to see clearly into the room, but not enough to give away her presence to the people below.

To her horror it was Bridget, her naked body covered in what looked to Deanna to be blood. Her hair was a muddy and tangled mess. Her breathing heavy and jagged as if she had been running for her life only moments before. Even from were she stood Deanna could tell that Bridget's legs and feet coved were in mud and filth. Her sister had gotten into some sort of trouble during the night. The thought of Pigglie's bar resurfaced in her mind and she wondered if Bridget had tried the same vulgar thing over here, although this time with more disastrous results.

Maybe her sister had been raped; possibly even injured from the amount of blood that Deanna could see on her body. The thought that she might have even killed her attacker struck Deanna as a very real possibility, after all, her sister wasn't the type of woman to let something like that slip by unchallenged.

Bridget was a strong woman and in good physical condition, the blood that soaked her bare skin might not have even been her own.

As Deanna leaned forward over the banister, ready to call out to her sister below, she was suddenly stopped in her tracks by the relative queerness of the vision before her. Bridget was smiling and talking quietly to another woman, as if nothing troublesome had happened. Deanna recognized her as the same woman she had seen several times before, her striking pale features and black hair had become clearly marked in her memory. The woman's voice was the same one she had heard countless times over the telephone when she had called the hotel to reserve a room for Seth.

Her name, if she remembered it correctly, was Eva Van Cruse.

Bridget hung close to her in a familiar and friendly manner. Then the woman touched Bridget's hair, pushing the wet mess out of her eyes and laughing. Bridget wasn't hurt or even upset…but the blood.

The blood had to come from somewhere, from *someone*.

Deanna shrank back into the dark shadows that surrounded her. Her sister had gone insane. There Bridget was, covered in someone's blood, naked, and laughing with that woman below like they were happily dissecting a juicy piece of gossip for further inspection.

What on God's sweet earth was happening around her? What was happening to her life and the lives of the people she loved so much?

As quickly as she could Deanna made her way back to the small slit of light that beckoned her to her room, her stomach lurching, threatening to empty its already sparse contents right there on the bedroom floor.

Something had gone *very* wrong with Bridget; there was no doubting it now, not after what she had just witnessed. Deanna suddenly feared for her own life, perhaps even at the hands of her sister, Bridget. Her mind raced as she slid the back of the small chair that had been sitting in one of the far corners of the room up and under the door knob, temporarily locking the door to her bedroom. She stood there, watching the doorknob and hoping above all else that it would be enough to keep her sister out, at least until she was able to face her again. Deanna couldn't help but think that it might be ages before she could do that again, ages before she could get what she had seen out of her mind and face her sister.

What exactly had *Bridget been doing tonight that could have caused her to be in such a tragic state?*

There was something else though, something even more unsettling about what she had just witnessed below in the main entry hall of Laurendale Manner, but she couldn't place it.

Deanna went to the room's closet and removed another sleeping gown from one of the wooden hangers inside and changed the bloodied gown she presently wore for a fresh one. She moved slowly to the bathroom, her hand still cradling her empty stomach, in order to wash the drying blood from between her legs. While she was still in the bathroom she retrieved several thick terrycloth towels from the small shelf above the tub, and placed them over the still wet patch of blood that spread out over the white sheet of her bed like some obscene ink spot.

She crawled back into the thick comfort of her bed, the stress of the night washing through her body in venomous waves. As crazy as it sounded she now feared her sister. Deanna's slowly closing eyes focused in on her room's brass doorknob, knowing that at any second Bridget might come crashing into the room and rip her to shreds as she lay there helpless in bed.

Then an even more horrifying thought came to her.

Of course Bridget wouldn't kill me, but...I feel she has already done something terrible to me.

What if her sister came to her bedside to confess?

Exactly *what* Bridget would come to confess to her in the early hours of the morning she was unsure, but the mere thought of it made Deanna vomit warm water onto the floor next to the bed. As she wiped away the thickened water from her mouth it struck her, Bridget's mouth was covered in blood...what, or who, had her sister been eating.

Chapter 26

Michelle lay sprawled out in Seth's bed, her naked form anxiously awaiting his return from the late night hunt. She continued to reassure herself that it wouldn't be much longer. The sun's rays had just peeked over the distant horizon and began to cast their pale golden light through the balcony's glass door.

Michelle had seen little of him since her liberation from her husband Todd, and she was beginning to feel the cutting edge of neglect. Seth had spent all of the late afternoon and most of the previous evening in London, but she had heard his car pull into the driveway not long after the sun had set. He had come home only moments before he had run off again with Bridget to hunt for the night, leaving her no time to spend with him. Michelle had been waiting impatiently for him to return all night...so that she might remind him of her importance in his life. After all, it was Seth that sought *her* out in the beginning of their relationship, not the other way around. Now that he had her she wasn't about to be forgotten along with the rest of the women in this house.

She heard a silent rustle on the balcony and smiled...he was home.

The door to the balcony opened and a torrent of wind swept across the room caressing Michelle's body with its invisible hands like a wistful lover. She smiled. The pit of her stomach began to grow warm with desire.

Seth stepped in through the balcony's glass door with a thick coating of cold, wet mud clinging to most of his lower body and appendages. His legs and arms were covered with enough mud and filth to hide Seth's skin almost completely underneath. His chest and face were also splashed in a mixture of well aged blood and pieces of human flesh. Some of the rancid filth was still damp to the touch, but most had dried into a thickened paste. His genitals were lightly coved with a mixture of both blood and drying mud, his normally well groomed hair had become wet and matted.

He seemed genuinely surprised by Michelle's presence in his room and walked over to the bedside.

"I can see from the amount of blood splashed across your body that last night's hunt must have gone rather well." Michelle smiled as she slid her hand suggestively over her naked body. Her smile was so wicked that even he had to appreciate it.

"I take it you're not here to talk," he smiled and pulled back from her playfully in order to stand just out of her long reach. He was still partially aroused from the nights kill, so it took very little to excite him farther.

Michelle ran her finger down the soft valley between her breasts in an equally playful manner. As she reached out to him, Seth obliged her, leaning his body towards her so that she might stroke him to life with one smooth motion of her hand.

"Be careful my dear, you may become soiled if you keep that up." Seth croaked out, his desire for her ached throughout his entire body.

Michelle ignored him, and instead pulled him down overtop of her, rubbing her naked body erotically against his, transferring the wet mass of filth onto hers.

"How dirty do you think you can make me?" she teased.

"Why don't we find out?" He dragged the mud from his body against hers causing her to giggle in delight. She licked the blood from his face, pulling his lips as she kissed him and delighting in the taste of his kill…of his murder.

Seth pulled Michelle into position, cradling the small of her back against the edge of the bed and forcing her feet on the floor so that her legs spread wide and her hips met his as he stood in front of her. Dragging his hand up slowly between the contours of her legs he felt the moisture begin to form as he fully entered her with two of his fingers. Once his body was fully aroused, Seth wasted little time and thrust himself into her hard, filling her with each rocking motion of his body as it pushed into hers.

"Harder Seth, harder," Michelle panted, wrapping her legs around him as she sealed their union, pulling him deeper into her and licking her lips. Her head tilted back into the covers, her bloody hands grasped the bedding that rippled around her for support, streaking them a muddy red as he took her as savagely as he would have if she were his werewolf mate.

With an animal-like grunt he pushed into her again and again, harder and deeper each time. His teeth and lips pulling hard on her pale, rose tinted nipples causing them to redden deeply and swell to the delight of his hot mouth, his hands wrapped tightly around her waist pulling her into him as he pushed. With a scream of delight Michelle gave way to her pleasures as a tidal wave of orgasmic vibrations shuttered deeply throughout her body. Seth too felt the wave of his passions explode, sending their tentative shockwaves rocketing through his body like a bullet.

After several moments their pulses began to steady, their breathing calmed. As they lay next to each other on the bed, content in the morning light, Michelle began musing as she played with the bloodied patches of hair on Seth's chest.

"I've been wondering Seth, exactly how old are you anyway?" She questioned, her eyes coyly blinking at him from under her long, fair lashes.

"I'm afraid that I'm *much* too old for you my dear," he teased back. "Besides, what kind of question is that to ask your lover? Didn't your mother ever teach you any manners? Not that age matters in the grand scheme of things, do not be surprised Michelle, when their comes a time in your life when the years begin to pass like mere days. And *then* you will begin to realize just how little age has to do with the mechanics of real life."

"Wow, *that* old huh?" she laughed.

Seth smiled at her, his age had long been lost in the folds of time. There were moments that even *he* could not believe his true age. Over the last few decades though the years had begun to pass slower than before, and they had now begun to cause him more pain than power. The thought of his own immortality only angered and frustrated him now.

Michelle curled up closer to him, the heat of his body comforting her. "Did you know that I was only ten, no more than a child, when I killed another human being?" She said softly, almost to herself.

"Ah, an early prodigy I see. Tell me all about it darling." His mouth traveled playfully between her full, heavy breasts. Michelle giggled in response.

"My baby sister, Shelby, was my very own personal Hell on earth. She screamed and cried constantly, demanding my parents full attention twenty-four hours a day."

"So what you're saying is that your kid sister was a royal pain in the ass. Yeah, I think I get it," smiled Seth.

"Yes, now listen to me!" she yelled at him, wiggling away from Seth's adventurous hands as they slid over the nakedness of her body, spreading blood and drying mud wherever they traveled. "*Anyway*, one night after what felt like countless hours of listening to my parents coo and coddle the creature, it was finally her bedtime. I waited a few hours after they put her down, until I was certain that my parents had gone into the family room to watch television and the servants were gone for the night. Sure enough, they had become so strongly glued to that ridiculous babble box that I could go anywhere in the house and not be detected.

That's when I crept into my baby sister's room. My mother had spent so much time getting that obnoxiously frilly room ready for her, that I honestly started to wonder if she remembered *me* at all. After all, she had one daughter already, what did she need another one for? It was quite upsetting I can assure you. My mother could be so damned greedy at times. Anyway, I never could tell what it was my parents saw in her. She looked rather plain to me."

Michelle stopped, trying to remember the small, miserable creature as it lay there sleeping in it's crib, barely remembering the color of her hair. "As I was saying; she was sleeping soundly in her crib. It was all actually quite simple. I just took the small, lace covered pillow that my mother had bought special for her, like everything else in that room, and placed it over her fat little face. It didn't take long for her to stop moving, not *really*. Hell, I wasn't even sure that I had actually *killed* the little beast until the next morning when my mother's scream woke me. My sister Shelby was dead, and now I was back in favor."

Michelle tried to ignore Seth's probing mouth and hands.

"The doctors just thought that she had died from SIDS," she continued. "My mother never even tried to have any more children after that. I think the ordeal may have broken her heart a little, but she had me, and that's all that *really* mattered in the end."

Seth seemed to pay little attention to what Michelle had confessed to doing. Instead he let his mouth trail its way down the flat plane of her stomach and followed along the slender path of golden hair that hid between her glorious legs. Her skin burned hot to his touch, his mouth expertly bringing her to climax with a few pulsating probes of his tongue. Michelle lost her train of thought and pulled him hard into her, her hands grasping fist's full of his sandy brown hair as she cried out in delight.

Seth didn't care that she had murdered at such a young age, or that her victim was a mere child, for he had done the same countless times. Seth merely continued to enjoy the new addition to his ever growing family. Secretly he reveled in the idea of filling his bed with beautiful women, of dominating them, bending them to his will and having the life of a true twentieth century king.

Seth also knew that his dream would never be realized, at least not that one. He knew the whispers that were making there way through the house even at that very moment. He knew without a doubt that Eva hated Michelle and that the twins didn't much care for her either. Seth also knew that at least for the time being Michelle could be something to help pass the time in a more enjoyable fashion.

That is until Eva found a way to put a stop to his fun, and he didn't doubt for a moment that her meddling would begin sooner, rather than later.

Eva hadn't changed, she was still the same woman he had discovered abandoned in the Black Forest so many years ago. She was jealous and deceitful, surely a woman to be coveted, but also watched. Seth knew that in the end, she would feel the need to dispose of Michelle, like she had done with so many of his *other* playthings.

He would let her of course, he always did. Eva was the one woman that had always controlled *him* and at times he even hated her for it. The hate never lasted long, and soon he would forget about the women that had once come between them.

Not long after their passions had ceased Eva came to the door asking for Seth. Michelle didn't like being interrupted, she didn't like sharing Seth or anything else for that matter. Her mind was a dark one to be sure and it was at that moment that she decided that Seth's family needed to become just the tiniest bit smaller. Seth would be hers in the end, even if it meant that she had to kill everyone else in the house, she *would* have him all to herself.

Murder it seemed, was a trait that came easily to her.

After Seth had left her bedside to join Eva, Michelle lay there brewing.

How dare Eva interrupt my time with Seth. I need time to work my way into his soul, to make him need me the way I need him.

She wanted to show him just how valuable she was to him. She wanted to make him understand just how far she was willing to go to make him hers.

Only mine.

It wouldn't be that hard, she had done it so many times before. But those were *other* men, *other* situations.

It's not something that can be done with the constant interference of these other God damned women! Somehow I need to make a rift between them and Seth, I need to make them inaccessible to him.

Her usual method of seduction wouldn't work here. The women of this house all shared his affection *and* his bed equally, that was clearly understood by everyone. Michelle would need to change her tactics. No matter what it was that the other women became during the pull of the moon or the setting of the sun, they were all still women.

That at least could never be changed.

While no one had mentioned tensions between Eva and Seth she could read their signals a mile away. Michelle knew that she could find a way to stroke the troubled fires between them with little effort on her part. She would find a way to pull them farther apart and in doing so, she was sure that Jessica and Candice would leave his bed as well. The girls deep devotion to Eva was clearly evident in everything they did. Once they were estranged from Seth, she would then turn them on each other like rabid dogs.

After all, they are no different than my sorority sisters back in college. Like them, they are no more than puppets for my entertainment. They even killed for me in the end.

In that instance it was also over a man, a man of which Michelle felt, at least at the time, to be of a superior intellect to her own.

She was wrong.

In the end, he was the one who paid the price for her desire. To this day the poor, stupid man sits waiting his fate on death row for a crime he neither committed, nor understood. The murder of his loving wife was orchestrated by Michelle and played out without a hitch by the young, stupid girls of her college sorority. How she loved each and every one of those girls, in a simple, unemotional way of course.

Michelle was sure that such a successful outcome could be recreated quite easily with this gaggle of women that slobbered at her lovers feet.

She had witnessed the hurt and resentment in Eva's eyes when she spoke of her children. Those half-breed deformities that lived below in the caverns under the manner whenever Seth came to Laurendale Manner. He was ashamed of them because they marked out his failures as a man in glorious color for all to see, but to Eva...to Eva they were everything.

Michelle's first night at Laurendale Manner she wasn't as drunk as she had let on. She needed to assess the situation she was in, the people, and her surroundings. She saw first hand the hurt in Eva's eyes when Seth called them her *pets*. It wasn't until a few days later, when she had innocently asked one of the twins as to *what* pets Seth had referred to, did she find out they were actually his and Eva's failed attempts at bearing a child. To Seth's horror and embarrassment they were never able to attain human form at all, and instead stood on four hairy legs like dogs. His dreams had vanished as his "children" stood there drooling from their gapping muzzles like loathsome curs.

While Eva had suckled each child at her breast, Seth became more and more distant. The presence of his own fatherly shortcomings flared his already short temper, and he eventually banished them to the catacombs under the old manner whenever he was in residence.

I could very well feed those feelings of inadequacy that Seth had festering deep inside him. I could even push at Eva, push the possibility that Seth's new "human" cub might very likely take his favor over her own children. Not that Seth ever really favored them in the first place, but with the successful breading with the woman Deanna, it could push Eva's children even farther out of the picture.

Michelle ran her hand over the quickly drying mud and mess that covered her body. The heat that Seth had left behind in the softness of the bed was disappearing along with her patience. Seth should be here, with her, not running to Eva's beck and call like some sort of adolescent child. Michelle's anger was growing.

Perhaps... I could even plant the seed of mistrust in Eva. Hinting to her that Seth could decide at any moment that her children had become too much of a liability for everyone involved. Perhaps all Seth really needs is one more good excuse and the next logical step would be to kill them all himself. A real mother would never stand for that. Eva would fight him first and in doing so she would also turn the rest of the house against him. That would leave Seth's bed empty for me to succeed to.

The only risk Michelle could think of was her inability to determine Eva's true powers.

Could it be possible that Eva could fight Seth and win? Even if she did manage to kill him, I'm sure the risk is worth taking. The thought of having Seth all to myself is rather exciting, on the other hand, the possibility of having to share his bed for an eternity with five other women is more than enough to soften any fears that I might have.

And while it was true that men were never in short supply for Michelle, she *did* have a particular fondness for this one.

Then again there was that horrible child... he would also have to be dealt with rather quickly if I am ever going to rein any sort of power over him. There is no way that I'm going to be stuck raising some snot nosed brat alone once the other women had vacated the manner. After all, accidents happen all the time to small children. A dangerous house like this, with all its tunnels and stairs. A child could go missing and not be found for days... if ever. The little darling might fall off of one of the balconies and bust his head open. Hell, anything could happen in the right situation.

Michelle fluffed the silk covered pillow and pulled the sheet over her breasts. A smile crept across her lovely mouth. The anger that had been slowly building up inside her had managed to escape from the open pout of her lips in a sour thrust of air. Left in its place was a devilishly evil purpose. The plan unfolded in her tainted mind the way a rose spreads its petals. Her thoughts turned to her mother, and how she would have commended Michelle on her well thought out strategy.

How she would have praised my diligence in working through a difficult situation like this and turning it to work in my favor. Of course mother never imagined all the terrible things that her only living child had done. She would have never imagined that her sweet little girl could have killed her infant sister or that years later I would push my father down the steps to his death on my very own wedding day. Although, that in all fairness was Toddy's idea. He felt that we shouldn't have to wait for an inheritance that was rightfully ours anyway. Not when we could enjoy it right away instead of having it collect dust in some stuffy old offshore bank.

Her mother was a fragile woman, fragile in body and in mind. The payments Michelle made to the convalesant home that her mother now lived in was well worth their extravagant amount. Her mother deserved the very best after all. In the end, Michelle had *always* been the one to give her mother exactly what she deserved, no matter what it took.

The thought to call her mother and see how she was doing crossed her mind, but she knew she would be heavily sedated as her instructions to the home had demanded.

Money could buy so many wonderful things.

Chapter 27

Deanna woke to the smell of bacon and hot coffee. She sat up and looked around the room, her mind puzzled by the sight before her. She could have sworn that she had wedged the small wooden chair under the doorknob of her room and yet there it sat, in its usual corner, as if she had only dreamed of moving it.

She heard movement in the bathroom, and then actual fear that it might be her sister. There was no doubting it, no pushing the reality of it away, she was afraid of Bridget, afraid of what she had seen her doing in the early morning hours.

"Bridget?" she called out, hoping to see Seth flash his broad smile at her from the now sun filled doorway.

No response.

"Hello?" this time her voice cracked. The thought of her sister running out, covered in blood from head to toe, made her feel dizzy.

Then, much to her surprise a young boy stepped out of the bathroom carrying the dirty towels she had used to cover her bed and her bloodied nightgown. Under his arm he had what looked to be several bottles of cleaning products. She pulled the covers back, the sheets had been changed. The towels were gone.

"How did you get those?" She wasn't really sure she wanted to know. If he could come in while she slept and somehow change the sheets around her without waking her...what else was he capable of? Instead Deanna tried to focus in on the tray of food but her eyes wandered back to the boys cluttered arms and the bloody towels.

"Thank you for the breakfast, it was very kind of you. Did my husband order it?"

The boy merely glanced at her but never answered.

"No need to be shy...I don't bite." She smiled but this time he didn't even look her way. Instead he set about dusting the furniture in a quick but thorough manner. Deanna's eyes returned to the wooden chair in the corner.

"Did you have trouble getting in?"

Nothing.

"I only ask because I thought I had placed that chair against the door…silly really if you think about it."

Nothing.

"Perhaps I only dreamed I did it…I do that a lot these days."

Nothing.

"Can you tell me if you changed the bed sheets? I could have sworn I put those towels that you have there under me this morning to cover quite a bit of blood. I'm so sorry about that, I guess I'm still bleeding from the labor. It's really quite embarrassing you know. Don't get me wrong, I'm not angry with you or anything for doing it. I guess I must have just passed out or something."

Still no response.

Deanna watched him and as she did the long hairs on her arms began to stand on end. The boy moved with a slightly exaggerated manner, as if his joints had become welded with age. As the sunlight settled on him through the now open window it did little to improve the color of his skin that bordered on a bloodless shade of gray.

Her throat began to tighten.

He looked at her then, looked right through her with his deep set, small eyes that made her flesh crawl.

"I would like to get up now if you don't mind," she rasped. "I would like it if you left." Her face paled.

The boy stopped what he was doing and without so much as a backward glance left the room, closing the door behind him with a click of the latch.

Deanna felt her blood drain to her toes. She needed to stop this irrational behavior that was beginning to consume her. If not, she was certain to lose her mind.

I need to get out of here before I go insane, the boy was only doing his job…

She stared at the door for a moment, wondering if he would come back in to…what? Kill her? If he had wanted to do that, he would have killed her while she slept instead of just changing the sheets under her. Even so, the thought of him bursting through the door with an upturned butcher knife sprang to life in Deanna's mind. She felt her body tense for his assault, ready to defend herself against his inhuman attack on her already broken body. She lay there waiting for him and after several moments when he *didn't* return to stab her to death as she lay helpless in the confines of her bed, she began to feel a bit better.

She glanced at the tray of food that had been left behind for her on the night stand and her stomach rumbled loudly. She was starved to the point of nausea. Deanna tried to remember the last time she had eaten, but she couldn't.

*No matter, the food is here now, and it smells delightful. But is it safe to eat...*her mind whispered.

She pulled the tray onto her lap and gazed down at it. Eggs, bacon, sausage...not to mention toast and coffee. Her stomach began to rumble again, a decibel or two louder this time.

If I eat it... I could die. It could be poisoned.

She brought the coffee to her lips, the steam opened her nostrils with its rich, heady sent. Deanna sipped it, hesitantly at first, and then waited for the poison to take hold of her body and relentlessly squeeze the life out of her.

No pains, no deliria...no poison.

What reason would anyone have to kill me...

Deanna set the cup down and began eating, slowly at first as she had done with the coffee, and then with great enthusiasm.

Half way through her meal there was a knock at her door.

Seth... at last...

"Come in," she called out, moving the tray to the side table and wiping the toast crumbs from her night gown.

It was her sister.

Don't start to crack old girl, it was only a dream...you never saw her covered in blood.

"Morning sis, I'm glad to see your eating again. I was beginning to worry about you." Bridget smiled down at her, her eyes seemed troubled.

"Yes, I'm starved. I might even call down for a second tray once I've finished with this one. I feel as if it's been an eternity since I've last eaten."

"And a bit of humor too, that's always nice to see," Bridget moved to the window and looked out. Seth's car was back and although they did not hunt together during the night, she had felt his presence. It worried her. He was watching her, just waiting for her to disobey him. Then what? Kill Deanna and possibly even herself? She needed to think of a way to get them out of there and soon.

"Has Seth been in to see you yet?" she questioned, although she had already guessed the answer.

"No, not yet he hasn't. I was hoping the knock on my door was him."

"Sorry to disappoint you," Bridget came back to the bed and sat next to her sister. "How are you feeling? I know you said you wanted to leave soon, do you think you would be able to travel within the next day or so? It's just that you look so pale to me."

"Well that's some change. I thought I needed to wait for clearance from the doctor." Deanna eyed her sister. Something had changed about Bridget, she looked worried, possibly even scared.

"Well of *course* we have wait for the doctor to give you the okay to travel. I'm not in any hurry really." Bridget got up again and looked out the window again. "I just know how desperate you are to leave this place that's all. I can't say that I'll miss this place that much either. Hell, Buster's probably moved in with the kid next door already. I'm sure I'll get the cold shoulder for weeks now for abandoning him for so long."

"Well, I suppose I feel okay," she lied. "My legs are getting stronger at any rate," she rubbed them, "they don't seem nearly as rubbery as they did before. I even managed to get up last night and get my own water from the bathroom." Deanna paused a bit and rubbed her brow with her hand. "At least, I *think* I did. I've been having some real doozies lately. The worst dreams you could possibly imagine Bridget, the kind that make you not want to sleep for a week after having them."

"Good," said Bridget, walking towards the door, "That's good to know, about your legs I mean. Not the dreams. Too bad about those. Look, I have some things to do later today. You try and get some rest now alright? If I see Seth I'll let him know your awake and asking for him."

"Thanks…and Bridget?"

"Yeah," she stopped at the door, her hand on the knob.

"Is there anything I should know about? Anything at all."

A queer look passed over Bridget and Deanna's stomach fell.

"No Deanna, you just get yourself all better and we'll be home before you know it."

Deanna nodded, she hoped with everything left in her that Bridget was right.

Chapter 28

Michelle had been keeping rather close tabs on Eva as her best bet in finding a wedge to drive between Seth and the rest of the household. She had hoped to hear Eva confide some juicy little tidbit to the twins but what she had practically stumbled into turned out to be far better than she had ever imagined.

She had been skulking about the manner for most of the day, catching bits of conversation here and there until she finally decided to go back to her own room. Everyone knows that the moment you stop searching for something, is the moment you find exactly what it is you're looking for. So, in keeping with the way the world around us works, that was precisely when she heard the hushed voices coming from Seth's quarters. Eva was with him, and from the sound of it, she wasn't too happy with him.

"How long do you think you can keep this going Seth?" her voice was low but seething with contempt. "What you fail to realize is that you have jeopardized not only yourself with your actions, but also the entire house."

Michelle pressed her ear harder against the door.

"Calm down Eva, don't you think you're overreacting? Deanna and Bridget have no family, and few, if any, friends. No one will miss them, and when the timing is right I'll go back to the states and sell both of their properties."

If Michelle could have seen into the room at that particular moment she would have seen Seth tug gently on Eva's hand as he lay sprawled out over his bed. His wolf smile that he flashed at Eva would have been almost comical if she hadn't been in such a foul mood with him. "Within a month or two no one will even remember their names."

"I remember a similar conversation I had with you Seth, not all that long ago. Instead there were weeks of speculation and police interviews," she turned and glared down at him from where she paced the floor. "Or did you forget that little fiasco you had with their mother."

"I haven't forgotten Eva. You know that I have never left a body behind to be discovered since that wretched day, nor will I again. Besides, what would you have had me do Darling? Would you have me eat them along with the body of my own child? Not even *I* have the stomach for that."

There was a slight pause and whispering. Michelle couldn't make out what was being said so she pressed harder against the door. For a moment there was only silence.

"Come in Michelle, you really shouldn't listen at closed doors," Seth's voice boomed out, causing Michelle to jump in spite of herself. "You might not like what you hear."

Michelle opened the door and stood there innocently staring in at them from the outer wall of the room.

"It's not what you think, not really. I was just wondering if you would take me shopping in London this afternoon. I heard you and Eva talking and I just didn't want to disturb you. I've only been here a few seconds at most."

"So you just figured you would listen at the door until we were done," Eva said, "how very *you* Michelle."

Michelle couldn't help but sneer at her. She couldn't wait to see the back of her…when Seth chose *her* over the very forgettable Eva Van Curse. Michelle felt she was gaining ground with Seth every minute of the day.

"Would you be kind enough to wait for me in your room Michelle? We can then discuss your shopping trip to London when I'm done speaking with Eva," said Seth. His eyes never leaving Eva's strong body as he spoke.

"Very well then Seth, I'll be waiting for you in my room." She smiled sweetly to the both of them and then made her way across the hall to her own room to wait.

Things were beginning to look up for her. Screw Jessica and Candice, Michelle would get rid of Deanna and her sister first…maybe even the brat too.

"You do realize that Michelle just heard most, if not everything, that we were discussing," asked Eva, as she watched Michelle glide down the hallway and close the door behind her before turning and closing Seth's.

"I will make sure she understands the importance of censure." He stood by Eva now, engulfing her in his arms he held her close to him. "Why have you left the comforts of my bed Eva? It has been too long since we have been together. I miss the taste of you."

"Perhaps it is the overcrowding," she pulled away from him. "Why don't you just get rid of all three of them tonight. It would be simple enough."

"Not yet…give me more time."

"Time for *what* exactly Seth?"

He didn't answer her right away, his demeanor changed into that of a child who hadn't gotten his way yet again.

"We'll do this *my* way Eva. Do *not* question me again on this matter."

"Very well, I've made my feelings known to you. Enjoy your little friends while you still can Seth, but I believe we *both* know how this is going end."

Eva left him alone to brood. She wouldn't share his bed again until the house was free from distraction, and from the way things seemed to be going it wouldn't be that much longer. Even if in the end Eva had to clean the house out herself. It wouldn't be the first time she had to fix Seth's mistakes and she knew in her heart that it wouldn't be her last.

Chapter 29

As night wrapped itself over the house the soft rain that had fallen for most of the day finally ceased it's constant tapping on Bridget's window. The moon had risen and now pulled itself from under the heavy blanket of large, slowly rolling clouds, like a child waking from a deep and restful sleep.

Bridget stepped out onto the balcony and watched it coming with a heavy heart. She didn't want to turn into the beast that now lived deep within her as the moon took over its domination of the night sky. She had too many things to take care of, too many important things. She needed to help her sister and her baby escape the dark walls of this house, and the dark hold Seth seemed to have over all of them.

The hunger that began to grow inside Bridget for human flesh was now gnawing at her insides like a pack of starving dogs. It wasn't long before the almost common sound of her own bones popping from their sockets filled her ears. Bridget's body began pulling itself apart in its feverish attempt to transform into an animal of the night. This time it was no less painful than the first, but at the very least the pain was expected. She crouched naked on the balconies floor, her hands clawing into the cement as she changed, making deep incisions in its smooth gray surface. The fleeting memory of her sister coasted through her mind followed closely on its heals by the desire to feed on human flesh.

Now in her wolfen body, Bridget stood upright once more. Her new, malevolent form was bathed in moonlight as she leaned down over the stone balcony in search of a familiar face. A cold breeze ruffled her auburn fur, her perfect night vision picked up the form of Seth as he paced the outer rim of trees at the edge of the great expanse of manicured lawn. His black hulking form crouched low so as not to be seen from the house. No doubt he was trying to avoid the risk of Deanna seeing him there in the whitewashed light of the moon. His eyes flashed up at Bridget, his impatience with her was growing.

He was waiting for her, but why?

With the ease of a cat jumping from the living room sofa, Bridget left the confines of the balcony and landed gently on the lawn below. Seconds later her long strides brought her to rest at Seth's side.

Seth stepped into the dense thicket of trees and paused. She didn't follow. He glanced back impatiently at Bridget as she lingered behind, still watching him intently as if trying to understand his actions.

"I see there is little trust between you and I tonight Bridget." Seth barked, looking back at the house he knew her worries. "You needn't fear for your sister's life. I have no desire to see her dead."

"As you said, there is little trust between us." Bridget made sure to stay out of his long, vicious reach. She no longer felt safe in his presence. He had become too unpredictable, too dangerous, like a once familiar dog gone feral.

"Perhaps the fences of our relationship can be mended, or perhaps they can not. For now that is not what is important us. What *is* important is that we hunt together. I can't afford the humans dangerous interference with mine, or my sons existence. Your hunting alone could jeopardize everything that I have worked so hard to achieve. Your inexperience could make you careless."

Bridget looked away from him. What exactly *had* he done? Nothing more than procreate, and even at that, Deanna was the one that now suffered the most from it. A smile brushed her deep brown lips, what a fool Seth was to think he was anything more than a lowly sperm donor.

"Very well." Bridget bowed her head submissively towards him. "We will hunt together then," her eyes narrowed in on him. Bridget's hatred for him seared into his flesh unnoticed. Just one drop of his rancid, parasitic blood would have driven her insane for more. The thought made her salivate heavily in spite of herself.

The physical pain of hunger was growing deep within Bridget's stomach, so she reluctantly kept herself from voicing her anger with him right then and there. Seth had already turned away from her and was making his way quickly through the woods when she realized that she was losing her grip on rational, human thought.

Bridget's human mind was fading. The animal was taking over…the need to protect her sister had washed away in the steady pull of the wind down her back. With a final look at the lit windows of Laurendale Manner and the now silver-green grounds that surrounded it, she obediently followed Seth into the woods. Seth knew that the only human scent they would pick up this close to the manner would be that of Deanna's. They both needed to move further away from the house or risk endangering her life if the hunger inside them grew too strong, too quickly.

Bridget made her way through the mass of twisted holly branches and evergreens that formed a tight barrier between the lawn and woods. The small stretch of trees changed quickly into fields that were lined with old stone walls, along their great length they had been dotted with the occasional metal or wooden fence.

The first farm they came to brought the strong smell of pigs, sheep, and humans. Bridget stopped just short of that year's planting of corn, as it stood almost ready to be harvested it brought in a multitude of wildlife; some of it even human in nature. Quietly they strode through the small passages between the towering rows of ripe corn. The heavy smell of human life, fire, and cannabis filled their senses. In a small inconspicuous section of field sat four shabbily dressed teenage boys. A small fire of straw and corn husks burned in front of them as they sat there cross-legged, getting high and guzzling down dark pints of Guinness, wincing at the bitter aftertaste. Their young pallets were not yet seasoned enough to appreciate it's strong flavor. However, what they *did* appreciate from the bottles of Guinness was the mellow stupor that it wrapped around their adolescent brains.

The boys were far enough away from the house to party in relative safety from parental supervision or intervention. Their distance from the animal pens also kept the fire's smoke and smell from alarming the animals. Any closer and they would have had every animal in the vicinity carrying on, unsettled by the smoke and fumes from the burning cornhusks. Unfortunately for the boys the distance also kept *them* from being heard, had they any reason for assistance during the night. Something they would never be able to regret later.

The two werewolves split company, each one coming to rest opposite the other. Each blackened, hunched form focusing in on their first kill of the night. The group of boys couldn't have been more than fourteen. A vast array of heavily used porn magazines littered the ground around them. Bare breasted nymphs winked out at them over torn covers and dog-eared pages. One boy was half-asleep, propped up against a bale of hay with a bottle of beer in his lax hand. The others shared a roughly fashioned joint and made dubious comments about the sex they had never had. Each boy trying to out-do the other with brazen stories of imagined copulation.

Empty beer bottles were set off to the side of the small clearing so as not to be lost in the field, and for good reason. They would need to be gathered up and disposed of so that their parents wouldn't become aware of the weekend liberties their youngest son was in the habit of making.

It was Bridget this time that made the first kill. The overwhelming desire for human flesh erased all well seeded human morals, all reserve she would normally have had scattered in the wind like the seeds of so many dandelions. At that moment nothing mattered but the kill. Nothing mattered but the warm soft flesh and the salty-copper tinged blood that filled her mouth and her stomach.

Her large muscular form burst through the dark wall of corn stalks and without pausing she tore through the first two boys she came to, killing them instantly. Fear locked one of the other two boys ridged and trembling where he stood staring down at the carnage before him. Seth stood silently behind him and in one sweeping pass of his jaws decapitated his small body, spraying his life's blood like a sprinkler, pumping himself dry with every slowing beat of his heart. The last boy had managed to find his legs and ran blindly through the rows of tall corn stocks. His young hands stretched out in front of him as he clumsily made his way in the dark. In his panic to get away, to run from the bloody visions that blinded his eyes, the boy had mistakenly run in circles. He had lost all direction in the night.

Silence engulfed the field as he paused to listen for the wolves that he had seen murder his friends. He needed to get back to the house, back to the safety of his father's home and the shotgun that sat locked up in the plate-glass cabinet in the den. His eyes were bulging from their sockets, his heart pounding in his chest as he stood there and waited for his inner campus to kick in. After all, this was *his* farm, *his* field.

He needed to think. He needed to get his bearings.

The pounding of his heart was blocking out any sound that could have been made by the assailing creatures in the dark. He focused on his breathing, he needed to hear something other than the beating of his own terrified heart. From directly in front of him the black hulking form of a werewolf stepped out from the darkness and into a flood of moonlight. Its monstrous face was covered in bits of his friend's flesh, its teeth stained red with their blood. Without even enough time to cry out the werewolf lashed out, ripping his chest apart and splitting his young body in two. Moonlight bathed the gruesome scene with it's silver light as silence once again claimed the surrounding night sky.

With her stomach full Bridget headed towards home and as daylight spread its golden wings into the sky she collapsed to the ground. Several moments passed as she lay there naked in the well manicured lawn of the manner. Thick, drying blood and flecks of skin caked her entire body, the sour-sweet smell of it sickened her. Her mind swam in filthy memories that she dared not consider possible. The true horror of what she had truly become broke upon her consciousness then and finally she wept. She had no desire to be this creature, no desire to live an eternity of inhuman hunger and murder. Bridget knew in her heart she had to somehow stop what was happening to her, and if it meant her own death, then so be it. Bridget pulled herself up from the freezing ground beneath her as the cold morning air wrapped itself around her frail human body. Steam rose from the depths of her human mouth, her suddenly insignificant body quivered in the starkness of the morning light.

Still no Seth to be seen, or smelled for that matter. He had not returned with her after their feeding but had instead disappeared into the darkness that surrounded the farm. Bridget had no desire to follow him, no interest to find out what had pulled him from her side. She desired no more than to wash the remains of the night from her body and make amends to her sister. The somber memories of the previous night haunted her and it would take more than hot water and a bar of soap to dispel them.

Only God could fix her now, and God was someone she only knew by name. God meant no more to her than a white knight in a fairytale. A fairytale that could be dispelled by the cold hard facts of life and the coming of dawn.

Chapter 30

Michelle waited in her room a good twenty minutes after she heard Bridget return home before she decided that she had waited long enough. The thought of Seth being directly responsible for Deanna and Bridget's unfortunate childhood, and the *murder* of their parents, practically dragged her from her room with glee. She was quite certain that her new found piece of knowledge wasn't going to wait for no man, not even if the man were Seth Toumbs.

Michelle giggled to herself as she made her way to Bridget's room. The vision of how she would react, the positive heartbreak that she was sure to see in Bridget's eyes, made her move swiftly down the hall in delight. She lingered briefly in the hall until she was certain Bridget was alone in her room. Bridget had returned to Laurendale Manner a full two hours *after* Seth, proving to Michelle that they had *not* hunted together after all, as Seth would have had her and the rest of the house believe.

She made sure to knock too softly on the door so as to avoid Bridget actually hearing her, therefore making it quite acceptable for her to quietly let herself in. Michelle could hear the shower running as soon as she opened the door so she sat on Bridget's bed and waited for her to finish. The anticipation of what was to come became almost too overwhelming for Michelle to control herself.

Bridget let the hot water soak into her frozen skin. The thawing of her flesh brought out a new sense of wonder as to what she had become. She hated it to be sure, but she couldn't deny the power, the strength she felt with every movement of her body. The werewolf had changed more than just her body, it had changed her mind and she couldn't help but feel a bit of loss at her own humanity. She no longer felt emotion as strongly as she had before, the human part of her was self-destructing, becoming less and less with each passing night that the wolf inside her took over. Bridget watched as the water that ran off her body turned pink as it circled down the drain. She had almost forgotten the source of the blood, the teenage boys that no longer went to school. No longer dated the girls of their dreams or played videogames until their eyes hurt. They no longer existed solely because of her inhuman hunger for flesh. She tried to focus on them, to feel some sort of remorse for what she had done, but there was none. She felt nothing inside but the beating of her own wretched heart.

After what seemed like a lifetime, the showers water finally stopped, Michelle could hear the glass doors open and close and after a few short moments Bridget emerged from the other room wrapped in a thin silk robe of the palest yellow. She seemed genuinely startled to see Michelle in her room waiting for her.

"I knocked, but you must have been in the shower," said Michelle. "I hope you don't mind my letting myself in, but this couldn't wait."

Michelle leaned back on her elbows to admire Bridget's room; it was larger than hers.

"No, not at all," said Bridget, wrapping a small towel around the bottom of her hair and rubbing the water from it.

"I thought you and I should have a talk. You know, woman to woman. There are a few things that I think you should know about. A few things that I'm sure Seth hasn't bothered to mention to you." She sat up and crossed her legs. "He hasn't been really honest with you Bridget. I think you deserve to know everything, don't you?"

"What do you mean?" Bridget questioned, her brows drawing together. "What has Seth been dishonest about?"

I mean, other than everything...

"How do I begin?" she paused, putting her finger on her full lip as if to ponder her own question. "I guess the best way to go about it is to just dive right on in and tell you what I know. The fact is Bridget that...well Seth told me just the other night, after a particularly *long* love making session, why it is he has chosen *you* and your sister to come and live here with the rest of us. Why he *really* wanted you to join our little family," she lied.

"It was to make his bloodline stronger, I think we all know that Michelle. It's hardly a secret, at least to me anyway." Bridget said, tossing the wet towel on the back of the dressing tables heavily carved wooden chair.

"Well, that's not *exactly* the reason Bridget," Michelle said, a fake pout forming on her lips. "Its because he feels *so very* guilty. You see, *he* is the one responsible for your parents' death."

Bridget stiffened at the thought. If Michelle were right it would make everything else that had happened make sense, but she couldn't be.

"I'm sorry but you don't know what you're talking about Michelle. It was over fifteen years ago that my parents were murdered. It's common knowledge that Seth wasn't even *in* the states back then."

"And you *believe* him, you poor dear. Well, that's not the way he tells it." Michelle stood and looked at her reflection in the mirror, absentmindedly fixing her hair. Her cool demeanor was untouched on the outside by what she so carelessly repeated to Bridget. Her insides however were screaming with joy at the obvious pain she was causing her.

"What are you talking about?" Bridget demanded, her face flushed with heat.

"He practically *bragged* about it to me. According to him, *he* was the one having the affair with your mother. Turns out *your mother* was the second human to carry his child, not your sister like he's told you I'm sure. Hell, he almost became your daddy." Michelle laughed, looking back at Bridget over the contour of her shoulder. "Too bad for you that your father had to go and find out about it. Seth was pretty pissed off about that. He said he should have known that your daddy had followed them that night when they met. He said he should have smelled his drunken ass." Michelle guessed of course, but she was right. Bridget knew that her father had a drinking problem. Now everyone in the house seemed to know about it too. "Seth said that he must have gone nuts once he had left your momma behind alone and beat her to death with his own filthy hands."

"It's hardly a secret how my parents died. Why should I believe you that it was Seth that caused it all." Bridget was having a hard time controlling her temper. Michelle was too smug for her own good. The vision of her ripping her face off with her bare hands cycled through her mind. It would be so easy for her. Bridget could almost feel her fingers digging into the soft flesh of Michelle's face.

"Because I *told* you it was." Michelle's voice rose an octave, it looked as if she were losing her cool also. "Ask him yourself if you don't believe me, see what *he* has to say about it."

It was at that moment a look of horror washed over Bridget's face and Michelle knew she found her soft spot.

Why am I so shocked? If there was any way that Seth could be connected with my parents murder why do I find it so hard to believe? I have witnessed first hand the cruelty he is capable of.

"Seth told me that he came back that night. He said that he had a feeling in the pit of his stomach as he drove off and left your mother there alone in the park, that your father was there watching them, but that he just didn't put two and two together until it was too late. I guess that's when he saw your father kill her. I guess he must have just lost his mind and murdered your father." Michelle looked coldly at her with that fake pout plastered on her face. "He told me he actually enjoyed ripping your fathers throat out. Like it turned him on or something."

Bridget sat on the bed with a lost expression on her face. She knew that it had to be common knowledge by now how her parents were murdered. She considered briefly how Michelle could be twisting things, making the events of her family's tragic past fit into her own scheme of things. She also had to admit that her story seemed to tie up a lot of lose ends. Bridget had known most of what had gone on back then, but not all of it. In the days and years following the death of her parents Bridget found that she was happier not knowing every single detail of that horrible night. She had told Deanna that she didn't wish to discuss it, didn't want to dwell on the past. Bridget was sure that her sister had assumed that she was being cold, even uncaring. It was more like self-preservation to Bridget. If she spent too many hours thinking of what had happened to her mother, even to her father, she would have gone insane. The very idea that Seth had actually been the one to cause all their hardships finally connected in her mind. It all seemed to make sense now, as if the last piece of the puzzle had finally been found under the kitchen table. The truth had always been close, it was just out of Bridget's line of vision.

"I know that's a lot to take in all at once, but I always feel it's best to know everything about the men you sleep with. Don't you?" Michelle smiled as she left the room, secure in the knowledge that Seth would no longer be privileged enough to share Bridget's bed again any time this century.

In the silence of her room everything began to flood back to Bridget. The TV news breaks, the newspaper head lines. She had only been eight when it happened and she and her sister had been crated off to live with their aging grandmother in New York. She knew that Michelle hadn't told her because of her concern for her or her sister. She knew that she had divulged the information solely for her own benefit. Michelle felt she would no longer have to share Seth with Bridget, not after telling her what had *really* happened on that night so many years ago. What sane woman would sleep with a man who was directly responsible for the death of her parents?

Bridget dressed and left her room to check on her sister. The thought of telling her everything flooded in on her.

By the way Deanna...your son is alive.

That would kick her in the ass alright. If she were going to tell her that then she needed to tell her everything. How would it sound to tell Deanna seconds later that she had not only slept with her husband but that she agreed to let her go on believing that her son was dead? Not too good Bridget thought. Hell, it was totally unforgivable really.

When Bridget reached her sister's room she was surprised to see her dressed and moving about the room. The small amount of high end luggage that she had brought with her was laid open on the bed.

"Where do you think you're going? We haven't spoken to the doctor yet."

Yeah, the fake doctor...what the fuck do I care what he says?

The concern on Bridget's face this time seemed genuine enough but Deanna had had enough of this place.

"I can't stay another night under this roof Bridget. I'm losing my mind, or what's left of it. I need to go home. With *or* without you."

Everything around her was starting to unravel. Bridget couldn't risk telling Deanna the truth, not about Seth *or* the baby. She certainly couldn't tell Deanna that she herself had become something truly maddening, a beast that roamed the night in search of human flesh. Bridget was certain that any mention of what she had become would push her sister right over the edge. That is if she even believed her. Bridget couldn't take the chance, at least not yet.

"Okay, okay but at least wait until Seth gets back. Then we can all fly home together."

You're stalling Bridget. You can't seriously think we can leave with him. Seth can't even find out we intend to go anywhere or he'll kill both of us. God, I can't remember one lie from the next.

"Where is he anyway? I've hardly seen anything of him since our baby came. I'm starting to wonder if I even want this marriage to work." She put the last of her belongings in her carry on and zipped it up. She looked weak and her face had become drawn and tight, but her voice was strong and unfaltering.

Bridget couldn't help but think that she was changing into the person she had known back when their parents were murdered. Resilient and unemotional. Bridget respected that, if for no other reason than she found that she could relate to her sister on a much easier level. It hadn't been long after Deanna had married Seth that she had changed into the uncertain and flighty woman she was when they first came to England. Nothing like the sister she had known all her life, but an imposter who merely walked and talked like Deanna.

"I'm not exactly sure where Seth went this morning to be honest, but I'm sure he won't be much longer. You can't really expect to leave by yourself Deanna. You're in no condition to travel alone."

"Then come with me Bridget, leave this place with me tonight. I'm not exaggerating when I tell you that I'll go mad if I stay here another night. If you only knew what I've seen, or at least…what I think I've seen. I need to get out of here. Tonight." Her voice had begun to crack, the uncertain, frail Deanna was coming back. She began to absentmindedly play with the zipper on her bag, but when she looked back up at her sister her face had hardened again.

"You *are* coming with me, aren't you Bridget? Unless of course you have reasons of your own for staying here alone with Seth. There wouldn't be any reason for you to desire his company over my own…would there?" Her tone was accusatory. Bridget felt the sting but refused to show it.

"Of course not Deanna, don't be stupid. I have no reason to stay behind without you. I'll pack my things immediately." Bridget felt the heat rise in her face. Her sister was only guessing, speculating about her relationship with her husband.

"Good. I was starting to wonder if there was more to worry about than just strangers."

Bridget sat on the bed, watching her sister closely. There could have been no way for her to know about her and Seth, unless of course Michelle had told her. Something she began to think was entirely possible.

"How could you think such a horrible thing of me Deanna? I'm your sister."

"So you are Bridget. A simple fact *I* have never forgotten."

Bridget looked away, trying to rebuild her thoughts. She tried desperately to keep her emotions from spilling over, of revealing to her sister that she had indeed betrayed her. She focused in on the death of their parents, she had to know if what Michelle said was true. If Seth *had* been the one behind their parents murder.

"While we wait for Seth to return…I was hoping to ask you a few questions about mom and dad."

Deanna was caught off guard. She hadn't expected such a change in subject.

"What about them? That was so long ago Bridget. Haven't we all been through enough death these past few days to last us a lifetime? Do we really need to talk about them right now?"

"It's important Deanna." The tone of her voice managed to shake some of the anger from Deanna and she sat down next to her on the bed.

"Alright, what do you want to know?"

"I never really had a chance to find out everything. You kept most of it from me. Something which I'm truly thankful for, but then when we moved in with Gram she forbade us to talk about it. Eventually it just became something that was never discussed between any of us."

"You have to understand Bridget that it was very difficult for Gram to cope with everything that happened. Grand-dad had died only weeks before from a sudden heart attack and she hadn't even finished grieving for him yet when her only son was killed. Everything seemed to be snowballing out of control."

The memories of that night so long ago began to filter through to her now. Each new memory bringing another close on its heals until Deanna had to shake her head and walk into the bathroom for a drink of water.

"I realize I'm only two years older than you Bridget, but I felt a need to protect you back then. I needed to protect you from seeing those ghastly photos and reading the horrible details that were plastered all over the news for weeks afterwards."

Deanna came back into the room, her face relaxed and soft, her eyes tired.

"It was like a page out of some horror novel. At least that's what it sounded like to me from what the police were able to tell me. They said mom and dad must have been sitting in the park, just enjoying the clear night air when a madman came up behind them. They suggested that the murderer must have had some sort of dog with him. They said it had to have been a big one from the bite marks on dad…at least what was left of him anyway."

A wave of nausea passed over Bridget.

This can't be true. My God, say this is all just a coincidence…I've been so stupid.

"What about Mom?" She choked out. Her throat threatening to close up before the words had a chance to escape.

"Well, they said he must have attacked mom first. They had it figured that he must have been watching them from somewhere in the bushes and when she got up from the bench he jumped out and struck her with some sort of rock that had been laying near by." Deanna paused for a moment to steady her mind.

"As you can imagine Dad jumped up to help her...and that's when the police say the guy's dog must have attacked him. The dog ripped dad's throat out, killing him almost instantly."

"And Mom?" Bridget asked, her vision becoming dim at the realization that Michelle had been telling the truth, the truth that she herself had come to know days before but didn't...couldn't except.

"Mom was beaten to death. Our unborn brother died while still trapped in her whom. The police said that they never even had a chance."

"Thank you Deanna. Thank you for telling me the truth. I know it was difficult for you."

"You have every right to know what happened that night. It's not like you're a little girl anymore Bridget. But I must say that I'm surprised you asked. You never seemed to want to talk about it before. I just assumed you would rather *not* know all the details."

"Things have changed. I've changed." Bridget got up and went to the door. "I'll go and pack my things immediately. I'm sorry Deanna, sorry for everything you have been through these last few days."

Bridget paused a moment at the door. She knew what she had to do. Even if it meant losing her sister in the long run. She knew that it was only right that Deanna knew the truth, the whole truth about the baby and her relationship with Seth. But where could she start? What words would make it sound less devastating that it really was?

"I *think* that I just might have something that'll make you feel better."

"What is it?" Deanna looked at her unseeing. Her mind still focused on the dark, unrelenting shadows of the past.

"I can't say what it is just yet. But I'm sure you'll love it, I just know you will."

Bridget left it at that and closed the door behind her.

She had something alright.

Bridget had her sister's child and she was determined to get him back for Deanna no matter what the cost was to herself, or to Seth Toumbs.

Seth could rot in Hell for all she cared, and knowing him, he would probably enjoy it.

Chapter 31

Deanna's child, up until now, had been staying in in the warm confines of Bridget's room. Thus making it simpler for her to nurse him whenever the child demanded with little or no effort on Bridget's part. However, since the gradual reduction in Deanna's medication had caused her to not only stay conscious for longer periods of time, but to also become suddenly mobile, a hasty rearrangement of sleeping quarters was implemented. The child was quickly moved to the twins room farther away from Deanna and altogether separate from that of the main hall. Just incase Deanna should suddenly move about the manner of her own free will.

At least those were the reasons that Bridget was told for the child's relocation. She however had the feeling it had much more to do with her unwillingness to cooperate with Seth's unreasonable demands. Tensions between the two of them were at an all time high, and Bridget began to get the unsettling feeling that she and Deanna were gradually being blackballed from their small, tight-knit group. Bridget also knew that if she let that happen they would lose more than David. They would undoubtedly lose their own lives as well.

Bridget stood at the top of the main hall's vast and open stairwell. She tried to visualize each step of her plan to get her sister and David out of Laurendale Manner with the least amount of conflict. While her sister seemed strong enough physically, although a little pale, she was uncertain of her mental state. Deanna herself had been the one to bring up the idea of her truly losing her mind to Bridget, and she wasn't one to overreact about her own stability...or instability for that matter. Bridget knew however that if she waited too much longer it would be nightfall and the thought of her and Seth having it out right in front of Deanna in their wolfen forms didn't appeal to her at all.

She did however realize the importance of telling her sister about David, and soon. Bridget needed to find a way to not only reveal the fact that her child was indeed still alive, but that the small boy possessed special, if not dark, powers. The words that she needed to voice wouldn't even form in her mind, let alone her mouth. Bridget thought that perhaps the best way to brake it to her would be to just let Deanna watch the child change right in front of her eyes. Deanna would have to believe her then. Bridget could then try and fill in all the blanks for her sister when she ultimately asked how, or why, the boy was so different.

The weight of the whole world seemed to rest solely on Bridget's shoulders and it was at that moment that Eva placed a gentle hand on her arm and shook her from the unpleasant thoughts that raced through her mind. "You look troubled Bridget, is there something wrong?"

There seemed to be an inability on Bridget's part to keep the truth from Eva. She had even begun to wonder if it was more than just her easy, carefree manner that got her to spill her guts and not some sort of spell that Eva had cast over her. A witch is a witch after all, no matter how attractive her casings might be.

"I can't do this anymore Eva," she gushed, "I can't continue to lie to my sister about her child. Seth hasn't any true feelings for any of us, not *really*. Not even for the child…David. The poor thing has become no more than a possession, a *thing* to be had and controlled by Seth, not *loved* by him at all." Bridget tried to hold her tongue but she continued on, "and there's more. I…I know about Seth and my parents. I know now without a doubt, that *he* is the one responsible for their deaths. I guess I've known since I came here. Since the night I was raped by him and changed into the same unholy creature that he himself had become so many years before. It was as if when he bit me, in the darkened caverns below the manner, that we became connected somehow. I *knew* his past. I *knew* that he was the one that killed my parents. I just couldn't bring myself to believe it."

Eva's brow drew up in puzzlement. "I don't mean to be rude Bridget, but it all sounds rather far fetched to me, even in *this* house. Are you sure you didn't get this idea some someone else? Michelle perhaps? You know what a bitch she is, how she would just love to drive you and every other woman from Seth's favor. Surely you don't really think that Seth killed your parents. He had never even *been* to the States until a few years ago, I can't imagine how he could have even know them."

Bridget glared at her. "Does he know anyone he murders?" Her face flushed as she cast her eyes down to the landing below. "I don't have time to go through all this right now with you Eva. We're leaving here, all of us, including David. Before it's too late."

"I really don't know what's happened to make you suddenly feel this way Bridget, but don't you think Seth deserves a chance to clear himself of these accusations that you lay at his feet? He has done so much for you and your sister. I tell you what, why don't we discuss this in my room where we can sit and talk without the worry of being overheard?" She gestured her hand in the direction of her own room, well away from the rest of the house where they could speak openly and in private.

"Very well, but my mind is already made up Eva. There will be no stopping us I assure you."

"Understood. I merely wish to make sure that you are acting on actual fact and not merely speculation." Eva smiled and followed quietly behind Bridget to her room.

When they first entered Eva's room it was pitch dark. Eva's drapes, which she always kept pulled tightly shut, did little to lighten the mood of the room. Even thought it was barely past noon, not even a single sliver of sunlight managed to make its way through the heavily draped windows. With little more than a single word Eva commanded the powers of fire, sending every candle a spark of energy and bringing them to life. Just as easily the fireplace burst into flame inside the stone confines of its mantle, sending a warm, orange glow throughout the room.

Bridget was startled to see two of the young servant boys sitting quietly in the darkness at the foot of Eva's bed like alabaster statues. Neither turned their head to welcome them or had even flinched by the sudden light in the room.

"Please, don't be alarmed by them. I assure you they are perfectly harmless…unless I command them not to be." Even with Eva's assurance that the boys were safe, there was a look of uncertainty that she caught lingering in Bridget's eyes.

"I will have them leave if you like. If they really make you feel that uncomfortable."

"I just thought you wanted to discuss this alone. I guess if you're not worried about them spreading rumors all over the house, then I'm not."

"I'm sure *that* won't be a problem. I don't think I've ever really taken the time to explain them fully to you. You see they can't speak. They're mutes. They haven't any tongues in which to wag even if they wanted to."

"My God, I'm so sorry. They must think I'm horrible." Bridget went to touch the one sitting closest to her but decided not to. The thought of touching him suddenly repulsed her.

"No need to be sorry my dear. They haven't any feelings either. They aren't even human, not really, not the way you would expect anyway. They are one of my greatest creations. They've turned out to be quite valuable to me and the others." Eva smiled warmly at them as if they were her pets.

"You're joking! They look as real to me as any other human I'd meet on the street." Bridget couldn't help but look closely at them, inspecting them like some creepy new toy. Fascinated by their sudden fake grotesqueness.

"It's a spell my mother passed down to me ages ago. We always had some poking about the house when I was young. They do all the work that we higher life forms would rather not. Even better, they don't require any form of payment or the need to voice their unwelcome opinions." Eva sat down on the chase where the child, David had once slept.

"Do you mind telling me who it was that confirmed your suspicions of Seth's participation in your parents death? Although to be quite honest I'm quite certain that it was indeed Michelle, I would like to hear it from your lips. Nothing surprises me when it comes to that girl."

Bridget realized then that she had almost forgotten her anger, she had become so mesmerized by the creatures that sat like stone sphinxes at the bottom of Eva's bed, that she felt almost relaxed.

"I guess it's no secret, you were right the first time, it *was* Michelle. She really is the only other new person at the manner other than myself and Deanna. I'm sure you realize that the twins would have little to gain from divulging such information to me, even if they were aware of the awful truth to begin with. Which I'm not really sure that they knew about it anyway, either way, it doesn't matter anymore, the truth is out."

Eva smiled, "Your right of course, at least about the twins. I don't think Jessica and Candice would have spread such nonsense. They know rather intimately the comings and goings of Seth over the years, and the flat out inability of his even being *in* the States when your parents were murdered. I hope you are smart enough to realize that Michelle is working as her own agent in this. Spreading lies to keep you from Seth's bed. She has little desire to share him or become a member of this family. Michelle thinks of little more than her own desires I'm afraid."

"Yes, I do know that to be the case. Even so, your assurance that she is wrong about Seth's guilt does little to sway my belief that she is indeed telling the truth. Even though her reasons for telling me were not really to help me, as Michelle would have liked me to believe." Bridget's face had begun to harden with anger. "The simple fact of the matter is that Seth is either directly, or indirectly, responsible for the death of my parents. At the end of the day he is the ultimate reason for all the heartache in my life and the life of my sister."

"I can assure you that Seth has indeed been responsible for a great many things, dark things, in his life, but I hardly believe you can rest all of your problems at his feet alone. No more than I can blame him for my own shortcomings. No matter how tempting the thought might be."

"What do you mean by that? How can you expect me *not* blame him?"

"What I mean to say my dear is that Seth didn't *force* you to sleep with him, no more than he forces any of us. You're a smart girl Bridget, you *must* realize that Seth couldn't have stolen the child from your sister without *your* help. Lastly, but more importantly, *if* he had been in the States at the time of your parents murder not even *he* could have made your mother have an affair with him."

Bridget looked into the fire, wishing to hide the overwhelming guilt she felt for what she had done to her sister. Wishing for nothing more than to be rid of this place and everyone in it.

"While it *is* true that Seth can not be blamed solely for all the wrong that has happened to my family, you must see that he is not *blameless*. Without his perverse persuasions I know in my heart that we would never have come to this."

"Perhaps, and perhaps not." Eva said, reclining back into the softness of the lounge. Gazing up at the blackened ceiling she watched the shadows dance across it's somber length. "So what do you plan to do about it then?"

"I'm taking David and my sister and we are getting hell out of *here*, and away from *him* and his lies."

"Seth would kill you first, you *do* know that don't you? Deanna too for that matter, now that the child is born she means very little to him. The chances of her agreeing to bear another child for him are slim. He will move on to another human, a *fresh* one. To be honest, I'm a bit surprised he has let her live this long. I was certain that he would kill her as soon as the boy was born, since the birth itself didn't kill her, as it does most humans. The only thing that Seth cares about now is David, you said that much yourself. Why not have it out with him, tell him what you *think* you know to be the truth. Give him a chance to prove you wrong, if he can. I would think that a rational person like yourself you would see how that would be better for all involved. A Hell of a lot better than snatching his son in the middle of the night and running back home with him tucked under your arm."

Bridget knew in her heart that there would be no talking to Seth. No reasoning with him. She also knew that she needed Eva to believe that she intended to stay and try, if for nothing else than to give her family the chance at living through another night. Unfortunately her sister was expecting to leave now, today. Bridget needed to find a way to tell her sister everything if she was going to get them out of there alive and in one piece. She needed her sister to know what was *really* at stake.

"Perhaps you're right, I might just be jumping the gun a little. I promise you that I'll wait and talk to Seth, you know, try and get *his* side of the story before I do anything crazy. I'm sure we can come to some sort of civilized agreement between the three of us." Bridget smiled, but the feeling that she needed to get her sister and her baby out of there was even stronger than before. Eva could not be trusted, she knew that much for sure. She was foolish for even talking to her. Suddenly the overwhelming desire to tell her what she really planed almost spilled its way from her mouth. Bridget had to bite the inside of her cheek to keep it locked up inside where it belonged. She needed to get out of Eva's room, and out from under whatever spell she had cast over her and quickly too, before it was too late.

"So you promise that you will at least give Seth the opportunity to plead his case? Very good. I knew that you were a smart girl the moment I set eyes on you. I'm sure once you two talk this out between the two of you you'll see how ridiculous this all sounds." Eva seemed to try to draw her out, to pull on her mind in an effort to see if that was indeed the case. Bridget needed her to think she would stay, that she was willing to work things out between her and Seth no matter what.

"Look, I'll be in my room for the rest of the night, you know, going over things in my head. When he gets back would you be kind enough to send him over to see me? We really do need to work all this out. Alright?"

"Of course my dear. He shouldn't be much longer, he is always back before nightfall. I will let him know that you would like to speak with him and that it's of the utmost importance."

Bridget nearly ran from the room, quickly putting as much distance between the witch Eva and herself. Her thoughts of escape, not to mention mutiny, needed to be kept to herself at any cost.

Eva had confirmed Bridget's suspicions of Seth's guilt whether she knew it or not. She had known almost word for word what Michelle had told her, and the only way she could have known that was if it were true. Bridget had only told her that Seth was responsible for her parents death, she said nothing of the alleged affair.

Chapter 32

Eva sat back and stretched her legs out to their fullest extent and considered her options. She *could* do nothing, which she was certain would result in the swift and immediate departure of not only the two women that she had become so weary of, but also that of the wiggling monstrosity Seth called a son. Unfortunately she also knew that such and outcome would cause Seth to demean himself by chasing after them. He might even be able to persuade Deanna and her cub to return with him to Laurendale Manner. He *was* after all devilishly charming.

Or, she could call him, tell him all about Bridget's recent revelation, thanks to that little bitch Michelle, and await his swift return. Seth of course would be furious, the thought of which made a thin smile spread it's long, red fingers across her pale face. Eva could practically envision Seth disemboweling them all in his anger. That would solve three of her problems immediately and she wouldn't even have to get her hands dirty. Seth's anger would be directly focused on the girls, leaving her to come out of the situation totally untarnished in his eyes. In fact, Eva would likely become the hero for informing Seth of the goings on in *his* house during his absence.

Her heroism would have been an unlikely outcome if she had insisted that Seth remove the girls immediately due to her own desires, as she had originally planed. If Eva had to be the one to force the decision to rid their home of Seth's playthings then *she* would be the one that would have to endure the brooding, angry man that he would surely become afterwards.

As it stood now in her mind, she liked the idea of calling him, of telling him of Bridget's deceit and of her plans to leave the manner and to steal his child. More than likely such a revelation would result in the immediate death of Bridget and possibly even that of Michelle for telling her in the first place. It would then only be a matter of time before she would in turn get rid of Deanna, possibly even with Seth's approval. That would then only leave Seth's half-breed child and she was quite certain that the loathsome creature could be used to her advantage anyway. The boy could become more of an asset to Eva if she kept him alive and with her. Seth would be only an occasional nuisance. He could be swayed into letting her and the girls see to the child's upbringing…and to his development.

Eva waited until she was certain Bridget was no longer in the hallway before she called the two boys to her side.

"I have a feeling that things are going to go bad rather quickly. We must turn the tables in our favor. Come to me." They stood quickly and went to her side. Eva took the hand of the first one. "I want you to stand guard by the front door. As far as Bridget knows that is the only way she is going to get her sister and that little brat of hers out of the estate. You are to let no one leave with Seth's child. Do you understand?" The boy nodded and left the room. Eva took the hand of the second boy. "I want you to follow Michelle, but not too closely. I don't want her to know what you're up to. I have a feeling she is going to be more trouble than she's worth, she's such a stupid child. Don't let her out of your sight."

Eva watched as the second boy left and then studied the fire until she was sure of her decision. The child would indeed be easier to raise as her own if his birthmother was not there to interfere with his development. No doubt wishing him to study the arts and humanities instead of corporate domination and the use of black magic. If the deadly justice was dealt by his fathers very own hands then Eva felt there would be little in the form of repercussions towards her later, if the boy grew to feel the actions towards his mother were unjust.

Eva could hardly wait to tell Seth about his perfectly indulgent little world crumbling down around his ears. Like most men he never was very good at seeing his own short comings, no matter how apparent they were to the rest of the world. She picked up the old fashioned ivory and gold phone that sat at her side and dialed the number to Seth's limo. It rang only once before his chauffer picked it up.

"Is Seth available? I'm afraid that something rather important has come up."

"Yes mum, Just one moment please."

Eva could hear their brief but informative conversation and then silence as Seth took the line.

"Yes Eva. What's the trouble? Is David alright?" If she didn't know any better she would think that he was actually concerned for the little whelp. She wanted to gag.

Eva had to control the laughter that pushed at her from deep inside her chest. How she wished to show him what a fool he had become in her eyes. He had mistakenly brought into their house the addition of so many women that seemed to want little more than to be rid of him.

"David is fine. It's the rest of the house that needs your presence I'm afraid. It seems your new bride Michelle has taken it upon herself to make a full confession on your part to Bridget. The little darling has told her all about how you are the one to blame for her family's misfortune and how it was *you* that murdered her father."

Seth was silent on the other end of the line and she knew she had his undivided attention.

"I'm sure you can imagine the upset Michelle has caused in revealing your personal involvement in her family's destruction. It's my understanding that Bridget is now bound and determined to tell her sister *everything* and leave with the child tonight. Bridget told me just a moment ago that she would wait to talk with you first before running off, but I get the feeling she's lying and will no doubt be out of here as soon as she can gather everyone together."

"Don't let anyone out of your sight." Seth practically seethed with anger. "I'll be home shortly to deal with the situation myself."

"Of course Seth. As you wish."

Eva set the receiver down and reclined back into the comfort of her chair, a smile spreading itself wide across her beautifully crimson lips. To think that earlier in the day she thought she would die from sheer boredom. Now this delightful little turn of events was sure to liven things up around the old place. The possible bloody outcome of the day played out in her head like a some sort of dark soap opera. What fun she and the twins would have this evening watching Seth clean house.

Eva pulled a crystal ball the size of a baseball from out of the depths of silken pillows and cashmere throws that graced the side of the chase she had been lying on and brought it to life with a single pass of her long, tapering fingers. She couldn't wait to tell Grumhold of Seth's mind numbing stupidity and her own newfound interest in his amazing son.

Chapter 33

Bridget closed the door behind her sharply, her mind racing. She hadn't counted on Eva pulling as much information out of her as she had. She knew that it wouldn't be long before Eva informed Seth of her and her sister's eminent departure. That is if she hadn't already. The thought of his swift and unyielding reaction to that wealth of information made her shiver. Seth would never let them leave there alive, not with his son. The possibility that he would kill all of them, even the child if it meant losing him, seared through her mind like a hot iron. She wouldn't let that happen, not ever. Bridget knew in her heart that she had been responsible for so much of the pain in Deanna's life that she had resolved herself to her own death before she would let Seth kill her son again. Even if the first time had only been a cruel and heartless deception.

Bridget was unsure of what worried her the most, the fact that she had lied to Deanna about her child's death, or the fact that she had slept with her husband. Both facts would have tremendous consequences on their already rocky relationship. One lie she could rectify, the other, she couldn't. There would be no way to take back her welcomed seduction by Seth. The mind numbing fact that she felt liberated by his touch only made matters worse.

Halfway to her room Bridget stopped, the realization that there would be no way to keep David from turning into a werewolf in the presence of her sister made her stomach leap.

How is Deanna going to react to finding out that her child is not entirely human? I'm sure that rather unfortunate little tidbit of information might just be enough to push the old girl right over the edge and into insanity. Which is something I could just as well live without doing to her just yet. As things stand now I've already done quite enough to her already, without being directly reasonable for sending her screaming off into the boobie hatch. How can I tell her that her child is a monster?

Bridget couldn't waste time thinking of that, not just now. The only thing that mattered right now was getting her sister and David out of that dreadful house and back home where they belonged. They would be able to work things out between them there, alone, and with plenty of time to heal both of their wounds. Maybe Deanna would even surprise her and accept David for what he was.

Him *and* Bridget.

It was true that she had fallen short of being a good and loving sister, but she could still try to heal things between them. There was still time.

Immediately upon entering her room she gathered what little she had left of her personal belongings and shoved them into a small overnight bag. What she *did* have to wear hardly amounted to sensible traveling clothes.

My God, what an arrogant bastard Seth is, for him to somehow feel justified in dressing me as he sees fit! As if I'm some sort of doll to be played with!

Her mind wandered to Deanna. Seth hadn't bothered to take her clothes. Perhaps he didn't account on her still being alive by now for it to have even mattered to him. The thought of her own sisters death brought Bridget's skin out in gooseflesh. Deanna wouldn't be so easy to get rid of now, not with Bridget in her corner. In the light of day she could protect Deanna, but at night…at night she would have to be on her own. Bridget forced herself not to dwell on the coming darkness, she needed to move quickly.

Bridget could always borrow one of her sister's oversized maternity sweaters and just pull it down over one of the more plain gowns that now hung in her closet. The subject of shoes on the other hand would prove to be more difficult. If they had to make a run for it, stilettos, although *killer* high fashion, hardly improved a woman's running stride. Bridget would have laughed herself sick with the thought of herself running in such ridiculous shoes if the situation she and her sister were in wasn't so tragic.

Bridget looked outside her window as she suddenly became very aware of the day's fading light. The afternoon sun was slipping away much faster than she would have wished. The warm, golden sun was slowly starting to dip behind the hedgerow at the western edge of the old manner, casting long, dark shadows against the earth as it dropped. Bridget was running out of time.

Bridget glanced down to the speckled patch of brown-black gravel below and noticed that Seth had left his black Mercedes in the driveway. Luckily for them he had taken the limo into town, or perhaps even farther on into London.

She hoped that his arrival would be delayed for a few more hours, at least until she were able to get her sister and David out of the house and far enough away to settle her nerves.

Bridget knew in her heart however that he *would* be home before nightfall.

Nightfall…what was she going to do when the sun had finally set? If they were able to wait just one more God damned night the moon would not force her body to change into that monster. Bridget would be safe until she could work something out with her sister. But tonight, tonight she would change into the beast that Seth had damned her to become. He had damned Bridget and her nephew to an eternity of cruel, senseless murder, murder without remorse or feeling and the torturous hunger for human flesh.

It was then that Bridget realized the true tragedy of her situation. There would be no winning for her or the child, even if they did somehow all make it out alive. They were all damned. She sat on the edge of her bed and sobbed.

After a few moments, past the sound of her own tears, she heard the now familiar grinding crunch of the limo as it made its way up the long driveway to park just outside the house. She hadn't expected him to return so early. Seth must have been closer to the manner than she had imagined when Eva called him and spilled her guts about what Michelle had told Bridget…about the senseless murder of her family.

Bridget stood by the window and pulled the drape to one side so that she could see his dark form from where she watched in relative safety. From the look on Seth's face as he stepped out of the car he was not too happy to be back so soon from his outing. There was little doubting the soured expression on his face or the darkness that washed over his entire being. Eva had told him everything about what Michelle had said, and now he had come back to settle the matter himself. Bridget desperately needed to get to her sister and David.

Quickly she walked to her door and peeked outside into the swiftly darkening hallway. From her location she could not distinctly hear what was being said, but there was no mistaking the boom of Seth's angry voice. Bridget crept to the end of the hall and peered over the balcony, keeping herself far enough back to be just out of their range of sight. She could see him now, talking hotly to Eva. A cool smile plastered squarely on her face as she spoke quietly to him. His frustration was growing and at last Seth turned from her and screamed for his now lackluster toy.

"Michelle!"

Her name vibrated against the walls, the house was defiant in its stillness. He screamed a second time and ascended the stairs two at a time.

"Michelle, I want you here in front of me now!"

Bridget pushed herself flat against the wall, sliding herself between it and the large Grecian statue of Venus. By this time Michelle had come to stand in front of him as he reached the top of the stairs, her mouth pouting but her eyes were cold, distant orbs that stared right through him and on into the vastness of the room around her.

"How dare you take it upon yourself to interfere with my family," he boiled. His face had become red with anger and his temples pulsed with fevered heat.

"I'm sure I don't know *what* you're talking about my dear. Has something happened to upset you?"

"Eva tells me you have informed Bridget of my *relationship* with her mother. She also tells me that you have been less than candid about the unfortunate outcome of that relationship and the death of not only her father but also that of her unborn brother." He grabbed her by the shoulders and gave her a hard shake, just enough to get his point across. "Do you realize the damage you have done!"

It was then that Michelle's true personality came spilling out in filthy waves. Her hate filled gaze burned into him as she shook the hair from her blue eyes with a toss of her pretty head.

"Then I would have to say that your little friend Eva is a filthy lying whore," her words were cold and quick like the slice of a razorblade.

Seth reached back and struck her, sending Michelle stumbling back to the opposite wall where she slid slowly to rest her ass on the floor. It was several moments before she moved, her mouth bloodied from a split lip.

"Now go to your room and lock yourself in. You'll be safer out of my site." He started to walk away from her in the direction of Deanna's room when he stopped. The urge to strike her again shook through his body but instead he looked back at her as she slowly got to her feet, spitting the blood from her mouth.

"You had better hope that the problems you have caused can be mended, or it will be *your* flesh that I dine on tonight."

Bridget was unsure of the expression that washed over Michelle's face but it was clear that she understood him and believed that he would do just as he said he would.

As Seth disappeared down the hall Bridget came out of her hiding place and walked past Michelle, she paused at the top of the steps before descending.

"Not quite the reaction you were hoping for was it Michelle?"

Michelle glared and turned from Bridget, retreating back into her room to lock the door as Seth had ordered. Fear had replaced her normally cool exterior, but there was something else mixed with it, something that they had all somehow missed.

"I see you wasted little time in telling Seth about our *private* conversation," said Bridget, eyeing Eva and one of the servants that now stood guard in front of the main door.

"I merely felt it was my duty to notify Seth of the unrest that was going on in his very own home. I'm sure even you can understand that," Eva smiled, cool and disarming as usual. The cold personality of a snake crossed Bridget's mind.

"You could have waited. You could have given Deanna and me a fighting chance."

Something was beginning to change in the room, the air seemed heavy, warm. Bridget had the feeling that she had forgotten about something that was alarmingly important. Her anger with Eva waned slightly.

"I'm going to my room to finish packing my things. I'm sure Seth already knows all about that thanks to you. I'm guessing it will be alright with everyone then if I don't stop to chit-chat."

Without waiting for a reply Bridget ran back up the steps, her strides were long and easy. *Perhaps*, thought Bridget, *stilettos wouldn't be so cumbersome to run in after all.*

Chapter 34

Michelle closed the door to her bedroom and locked it, her heart pounding loudly in her chest.

Seth had betrayed her, just like Todd had, and just like her father. He had become nothing more than a man...a backstabbing scum of a man. She would show him just how foolish he was to have struck her, to have betrayed her. She licked her lip, basking in the dull thud of pain it caused.

That damned brat of Seth's was the only thing that he truly cared for. That nasty, stinking little shit bag was the only thing he loved. If you could call what he held for his son to be true emotion and not just the realization of power. I'll kill the child, suck him dry and then he will regret laying his dirty, nasty hands on me. He will live to regret making me bleed.

Her body began to quiver with rage, she hated him. She licked her lip again, she could feel the swelling pulsate and burn as the blood began to thicken around the sliced bit of flesh that he had once kissed so passionately.

The house and its occupants seemed to have forgotten about the child, at least for the moment. Michelle knew that this would be the one and possibly only time that she could make her move, to burn while the iron was still hot so to speak. She would steal that moment, while thoughts were else ware, and take the whelp Seth had named David from Jessica and Candice before anyone even had a chance to think to check on either of them.

She slipped out of her room and locked the door behind her. If Seth were to come back for her he would assume she had done what he had ordered her to do. Michelle wouldn't answer his childish pounding at her door because she was angry at him for striking her. That is what Seth would expect, that is what *any* man would expect.

He had ordered me. Ordered me to go to my room and lock myself in...ordered...no one fucking orders me to do anything...ever!

When she reached the girls room Jessica was just leaving.

"Christ, what happened to your lip?" She asked, her finger touching her own lip to emphasize the question.

"Seth was a bit too rough this morning in bed that's all, and he ended up biting my lip too hard." Michelle smiled softly and licked it again, "you know how crazy he can get at times."

"Well, enjoy it while it lasts. Unfortunately Seth is just like any other man, once the novelty wears off, you will be filling your afternoons reading steamy romance novels like the rest of us."

"Yes well, like you said, it's bound to happen sooner or later I suppose. Is Candice in? I wanted to ask her something if I could."

"Sure, go ahead in. She's just putting David down now for a nap."

Michelle watched her as she disappeared down the hall and then let herself in. Candice was pulling the curtains closed on the fading sky when she heard someone behind her.

"What? Did you forget to ask me what *I* wanted from the kitchen?" She turned to see Michelle standing behind her, not her sister.

"Oh, I'm sorry. I thought you were Jessica. She went down to the kitchen to get us something to tide us over until supper. I'm positively starved."

"I know, I just passed her in the hallway and she suggested I stay with David so you could join her. That way she *knows* you will get what you want to much on without her having to guess."

"Really? That would be great. I've had David most of the day, other than when Bridget comes to feed him, and I really could use a bit of a break. That's if it's not too much trouble that is?"

"Not at all. Go and join your sister. Take your time." She smiled at her causing the new seal of skin to split on her lip and it began to bleed again.

"Wow, that looks nasty. How the Hell did you manage that one," Candice looked a bit closer at her and noticed that Michelle's jaw was beginning to blacken and swell in addition to the split lip.

"Seth got a bit rough that's all. We were wrestling in bed and I slipped off. I managed to hit the side of the nightstand and wound up with this. He said he would make it up to me later."

"I would think you could get a nice hunk of jewelry out of him for that one. Don't go letting him off the hook too easily."

"Oh don't worry, I don't intend to let him get away with anything. I'll make sure he *really* pays for the privilege of making me bleed." Michelle smiled a warm and tender smile, punctuating it with a soft laugh.

"Okay well, I'll be back in just a few minutes. I've got to make sure Jessica doesn't eat all the chocolate before I get down there and get some for myself."

Michelle stood over the bed watching the child sleep, lost in her own dark thoughts.

A pillow is so easy...you just place it over their face and hold it down until they stop moving.

"Would you like me to bring you some back," Jessica asked as she opened the door to leave.

Michelle didn't answer. Her fingers tracing the slice of her lip, the swelling of her cheek.

Maybe I should suck the child dry and leave its withered little corpse in Seth's bed for him to find.

"Michelle?" she said a bit louder.

"What...I'm sorry, what did you say?"

"Do you want me to bring you back some chocolate?"

"Sure, sure. That would be great."

Candice smiled and made her way down the hall to the kitchen, her mind filled with nothing more important than the smooth sweetness of fine chocolate. Leaving behind Seth's only son, alone and unguarded, with Michelle at last.

She stroked the child's soft blonde curls, his form shifted at her cold and uncaring touch. The wolfen cub began to growl.

Chapter 35

By the time Seth reached his wife's bedroom door he had managed to regain control of his temper. Adjusting his jacket and combing his fingers through his thick, wavy hair he entered. The fake smile he had used so many times before in her presence plastered across his handsome face.

Her bag was packed and resting on the bed, and yet his smile never wavered.

"And where are you off to my dear? You know you really shouldn't be moving about until the doctor has had a chance to examine you. I spoke with him earlier today actually and he said that he should be here to see you some time tomorrow morning."

"I'm leaving this place *tonight* Seth. I won't spend another night under this horrid roof." She took the small bag off the bed and moved toward the door. He intercepted her, closing the door and gently taking the bag from her. Pulling her to him gently, Seth directed her back into the room like a child.

The mere fact that Deanna was still there, still accepting his touch, indicated to Seth that Bridget hadn't yet had a chance to divulge the information about the child *or* the death their parents.

"You don't look well enough to travel Deanna. Isn't it enough that I have lost a son? Must I lose you as well?" The concern on his face made her feel guilty for ever doubting him.

"Please Seth. I'm not trying to be difficult but we need to leave here. I'm afraid if I stay another night under this roof I'll go insane. That is if I'm not already. If you only *knew* the dreams I've had, the things I've heard, you would let me go home." She sat down on the bed, what strength she had mustered began to seep slowly from her body. She could feel him taking control again, taking control of her, of the situation. To argue would only be useless and draining.

"I tell you what darling, I will call Dr. Landau and see that he gets here first thing in the morning. If he says you're fit to travel then we will all be on the next flight home." Seth eased her back on the bed, swinging her legs up to rest above an extra pillow.

He's won...again. Why can't I fight him? Why can't I stick up for myself and defy him?

"Alright darling. One more night. But promise me we will leave first thing in the morning."

"*After* the doctor my dear. I can't risk your becoming ill." He kissed her forehead like a child. "Let me just get you some more water, you really need to listen to the doctor and keep yourself hydrated."

He took the carafe from the bedside table and left the room. Deanna could hear the tap turn on and fill the container. After a few moments he returned and poured her a glass.

"Now drink this and try to get some rest. I'll see if I can get you something to eat. It's getting late."

Seth looked out the window, it *was* getting late. The sky was becoming purple in the east and he could feel the moon coming, he could feel it pulling on his bones. It wouldn't be long until he and Bridget would be forced from the house. The thought occurred to him that maybe this time Bridget might not be returning to her human form in the morning light. This time, she might not be returning home at all.

Once Seth was sure the sedative that he had slipped his wife had taken affect he left her room in search of Bridget. He was certain that she could be reasoned with as easily as her sister. He had already proved her to be of an easy persuasion, pliable in his expert hands, but he was unsure how to tackle the death of her parents. The truth would certainly be in his favor, most of it anyway.

Her room was empty. The one bag she did have left was packed and ready to go. Bridget however was nowhere to be found. He made his way over to the second wing of the manner where Candice and Jessica had the baby. Possibly she was just stupid enough to try and take the child. When he got there though the room was empty and the hour was growing late. The need to get out into the cool night air was becoming overpowering.

As he was descending the steps Bridget was coming up, her face ashen. Something was wrong and the anger he thought he would see in her eyes was not there. In it's place was fear.

"Where's Michelle? Have you seen her?" she barked.

"I sent her to her room to wait punishment, unlike *you* she obeys the orders I give her." He grabbed her arm as she tried to pass him on the steps. A snarl escaped her lips, the moon was also beginning to affect her.

"You're nothing but a fool Seth Toumbs. Don't you see what you've done?"

"You're not leaving here Bridget. Not David or his mother, not *any* of you."

She pulled away from him, her strength was increasing steadily. The muscles in her arms tightening into corded iron.

"Michelle is missing…and so is your beloved son, David."

"That's impossible, she would *never* disobey me, not after my warning." His voice full of contempt. "Not the way *you* have."

"Maybe you should find out a little more about the *whores* you fuck before you go and bring them home to meet the rest of the family," hissed Bridget, her temper getting the best of her.

"You mean like you? But I know all about *you*." Seth baited her, waiting for her to bite.

She tried to control herself but it was too late. Bridget's anger grew in running strides as her soft, human skin began to darken and pull from her body. Her once feminine jaw line burst forth bringing with it razor sharp teeth that ached to taste Seth's flesh. Her body twisted and changed into the monster she was so desperate to control. Bridget tried unsuccessfully to focus in on David and getting him away from the house before Seth could get his hands on him. She had to find him before Michelle was able do whatever it was that she had planed for him in that rancid mind of hers. Bridget was losing her concentration though, her werewolf instincts were taking over her angry human mind and as it did so, it cleared from her the memories of what was so dear to her.

Seth's body also began to change, and yet with his change, there was not the loss of mind that Bridget suffered from. He had embraced over a hundred years of practice and he easily controlled the wolf side of his brain. He had at one time hoped that the two of them would have many years of companionship together, but as it looked now, that would never be the case. Seth had already decided that he no longer needed Bridget. If anything, she had become a liability to him and he needed to get rid of her…the first of what was soon becoming one of his many problems.

He lashed out at Bridget, taking her by surprise and pushing her backwards down the steps in a tumbled heap of fur and flesh. Stunned, Bridget lay there, stretched out on the floor for a few seconds, her wolf mind registering what was happening.

Bridget could see her own murder in his eyes now.

Seth intended to kill her *and* her sister and raise the child to become like him. Bridget stumbled to her feet, her body aching from the crash of wood in her back as she hit the steps on her way down. She needed to get away from him, she needed to think. The werewolf that had once been her lover moved closer, teeth bared, he descended the steps with the intention of killing her right where she stood.

Eva stepped from the corner where she had watched the events unfold and removed the boy from in front of the door so that she could open it for them. The risk of them disemboweling her servant while lost in their own quarrel was too great, and she still needed him. The cold night air drifted sweetly in, overloading Bridget's sensitive animal senses and pulling her from the tight confines of the house. Close at her heels came the thunderous roll of Seth as he bounded down the stairs after her.

Chapter 36

Bridget stumbled from the house, her body completing it's agonizing change into the monster she was doomed to become for an eternity under the pale moon light. As she looked back, she could see Seth standing in the doorway, his image dwarfing that of Eva's as she stood next to him.

"It's time you took care of your problems in a more permanent fashion." She cold hear Eva say, as she glared out at Bridget's wolfen form with contempt.

Fear rose in Bridget, a fear that blotted all else from her mind. She turned and ran, her heavy body lumbering across the great expanse of lawn for the cover of the woods beyond. She could hear him behind her, she could *feel* the thunderous weight of him hit the ground at a run. She could imagine the heat of his breath on the curve of her back.

Bridget had to beat down the insane terror that welled up in her chest as she ran. If she lost her wits, if she became confused, she wouldn't last more than five minutes against him. Bridget knew the power he had, the shear strength of him outmatched her own in every way.

Once under the cover of the trees that surrounded Laurendale Manner, her pace slowed. She could no longer hear him behind her. Bridget stopped to catch her breath, her animal mind racing. There was no way that she could have out run him, no way she could have lost him so easily. He was hunting her, teasing her with the possibility of escape when in reality she knew full well that she was an easy target. Bridget crouched low in the brush, her ears straining to hear even the slightest noise, as her heart pounded fiercely in her chest.

The only noise that penetrated the darkness was that of a train engine. Far off in the distance she could make out the rushed pounding of a train winding it's way through the countryside. Bridget thought that if she could get to it, somehow hide herself on it, then she would be safe.

If I can just make it to the train, then I know in my heart that I'll live another night, and then I can help...I can help...who?

She couldn't remember.

Her animal mind was strong, forcing the human memories back into the darkness. She craved human flesh and she feared for her life. Nothing else surfaced. She closed her eyes, her breathing settled as she tried to remember. A glimmer of memory stirred in her mind and then...

Bridget felt the sudden weight of Seth on her back as he knocked her to the ground, his teeth ripping at her, tearing the flesh from her right side in a hideous, gaping wound. Waves of pain flooded her body as she stumbled backwards against a tree. Lashing out blindly she struck back, gripping Seth by the throat she ripped and slashed at him with her own treacherous weapons.

While it was true that he out weighted her by a good hundred pounds, she had the driving force to live another day pushing violently behind her.

The fear of death drove her on.

Digging her teeth deep into his throat she could feel the beating of his heart, she could taste the flow of his sour blood as it washed through her mouth. Her mind fogged, her ears rang with each pulse. Seth had been momentarily caught off guard, not expecting Bridget to be such a strong opponent. He stumbled but caught his balance, his heavily muscled arms smashing down upon Bridget's head, knocking her from him, momentarily separating the two dark warriors in the darkness.

For a moment they stared at each other, each assessing the strength of the other. Bridget had tasted his blood, her stomach screamed for more but her mind demanded that she escape. She broke into a run, crashing blindly through the darkened woods in the direction of the train tracks and the smell of burning coal. She could hear Seth close behind her, his body ripping through the undergrowth like a newly sharpened sickle.

As Bridget broke through a particularly dense patch of undergrowth she lost her footing on the soft ground around her and tumbled head first down a rocky slope and into a deep canal. The cold water momentarily stunned Bridget, the gaping hole that Seth had inflicted in her side was sent exploding into pain as she hit it's icy surface. As Bridget's head crested the waters cold surface she could see Seth's form outlined in the moon's silver light, his breath coming out in steaming billows as he looked down at her. The boom of his howl rang out into the night, blotting out the sound of everything else and ringing savagely in her ears. His massive body charged head first down the muddy slope and into the water after Bridget. Without a second thought Bridget lunged at him, claws thrashing, teeth ripping at anything she managed to come into contact with. Seth swung heavily at her, knocking her back under the water, the side of her face was slashed deeply from his claws. Bridget pulled herself farther under the fridged water with the steady beating of her arms, the strong current helping her to distance herself from Seth's reach.

A few moments later she broke the surface of the water under a mask of brambles and low hanging branches, the taste of her own blood heavy in her mouth. Bridget scanned the water's rippled surface and the opposite shoreline for Seth, but nothing moved. Grasping the tangle of roots that hung out and over the edge of the earth like some sort of primitive awning she stayed partially submerged as she listened for any indication that he was near by. The deep throbbing in her side had started to ease as the freezing water rushed past her. The slice in her face had gone clean through to her teeth causing her mouth to fill up with water as she stood there. Bridget tried to seal the wound with her hand, but with no luck. The wounds brought about by another werewolf could quite easily prove fatal to Bridget, if she let Seth get the better or her tonight, it could be the end of her for sure.

Bridget needed to get out of the water and she needed to stop the bleeding before there was nothing left to stop. The thought of Seth being behind her on the bank, just waiting for her to show herself kept her where she was at least for the time being. The night was still young, her wolfen body could last a hell of a lot longer than her human one in it's present condition and she knew she could stand the freezing waters that surrounded her for a bit longer.

Again in the distance she heard the sound of a train rushing through the night and the smell of burning coal. She was closer to the sound now, she felt the desperation in her rise to get to the tracks, there was bound to be another train tonight, a train that would take her far enough away to tend to her wounds and to get away from Seth's ripping bite forever.

Twenty yards down the canal was a large brick and mortar bridge reaching over the water, arching high into the night sky. Bridget quietly made her way to it's side, swimming most of the way under the thicket of twisted roots and deep, silty mud. Her fur had become a tangled mess of sticks and mud, making it difficult for Bridget to move under the sheer weight of it. The gapping hole in her side had become covered in filth but it had done so in Bridget's favor, the heavy coating of mud helped to hide the smell of her oozing blood from Seth.

251

She hadn't seen or heard Seth for what felt like hours but she knew it was only a matter of time before he found her. Bridget needed to put as much distance between herself and him as she could until day break when she could go for help…human help.

Bridget pulled herself up the bank and leaned to rest against the cold exposed brick of the bridge. Her wolf eyes scanned both sides of the canal. Her vision was exceptional in the moon light yet even *she* could only see so far into the woods that flanked either side of the canal.

On the other side of the bridge were three boats, their long forms outlined by the moons subtle light. Each one drifting quietly on the water, not a soul could be seen on any of their exposed decks. Two were definitely empty, but Bridget could smell the maddening aroma of humans wafting up to caress her senses from the one that sat harbored closest to her. Her stomach growled with a fierceness to match her own but the fear of being discovered and killed by Seth managed to temporarily keep her close to the deep shadows cast by the bridge.

Where the boats were tired off a path lead up to a small row of houses, the center of which stood an old, dimly lit pub. Each dwelling faced the canal with small, well kept gardens enclosed by either a hedgerow or a rose laden wooden fence. Bridget turned her nose towards the pub…again the smell of humans. The need to eat was becoming unbearable. That, coupled with the loss of so much of her own blood, was beginning to make her weak and nauseous.

Still hidden by the shadow of the bridge, Bridget's injured form moved to the boat closest to her. The vessel was dark and quiet but unmistakably occupied. The hunger in Bridget's stomach drove her on, compelling her to hunt even while she herself was being hunted.

Quietly she descended upon the deck of the boat, a trail of blood stained mud spread out behind her to mark her passing. The boat rocked gently as she boarded, her weight causing the vessel to move a bit more than she would have liked. Bridget stood still, waiting for the night's silence to be broken. It was at that moment when she smelled something else. Something much more dangerous than a startled human.

It was Seth.

There was no mistaking him. His blood was strong and acidic to her nose, overpowering the mild smell of human that had originally pulled her to the boat. Then the cabin door swung slowly open, Seth stood in its blackened pit, a human arm dangling loosely from his jaws. He glared at her…spitting the appendage from his mouth as he stepped closer. His clawed hand reaching up to touch his own throat, tracing the damage Bridget had left behind.

"It took you long enough Bridget…I'm afraid I've gone and eaten without you."

He lunged at her, pushing her backward and over the side of the boat, their two bodies hitting the water in a frenzy of teeth and nails. Bridget felt her shoulder blades hit the jagged rocks beneath them as the weight of Seth's body forced her down into the deep sediment that lined it's bottom. The icy water began to fill her lungs, she struggled against him…trying desperately to get to the surface to breath. Seth held tightly, his grip as strong as ever, his claws digging deep into the wound in Bridget's side. Desperation grew in her chest as her lungs pounded for the slightest breath air. Bridget struck out at him wildly, her teeth sinking into the side of his face where it sliced deeply into his eye, pulling the small orb from it's socket as she pushed away from him. Seth recoiled sharply in pain as she broke away from his grasp, both of them putting enough distance between the two of them that Bridget was able to surface at a safe distance. Her long, smooth snout crested the water as she sucked the night air in, her massive arms pulled her halfway out of the water like a cork before the weight of her body pushed her back down again and she began to swim to the other side. Seth also had surfaced but he stayed where he was, a deep growl emanating from his throat as he clutched the side of his bloodied face, an empty pit of a hole stared out at Bridget where there had only moments before been his eye.

Bridget pulled her body from the water, bringing herself to rest in the cold mud on the opposite bank where it sloped down to touch the waters edge. Her chest rising and falling rapidly as she desperately gasped for the air that had been denied her. After several moments her breathing began to slow and she rose to her feet and stood by the waters edge.

Seth was gone.

Her eyes scanned the water and the steep rise of land on the other side. Nothing.

He was gone, and she had won…at least for now. Bridget looked to the east, the sun had begun to crest over the distant breath of trees. Her form changed, shrinking into it's weak, human shell. Bridget rested her naked, bloodied body against the nearest tree, shaking viciously from the cold and exhaustion.

Deanna.

She remembered now…she needed to get to Deanna before Seth did. Before it was too late.

Chapter 37

Eva stood in the doorway and watched as Seth disappeared into the woods after Bridget.

"Things are going to change around here my dear, and they change tonight." She half said to herself, half to the disappearing form of the werewolf she knew as Seth. She had overlooked his indiscretions long enough.

She closed the door behind her and bolted it. Eva would have no more interruptions, not tonight. She would take care of this business with Michelle herself.

First things first though; she needed to find her. Eva considered that to be easy enough. There would be no way for Michelle to leave the manner with David in tow and it was obvious to her that Michelle hadn't left by the front door. To which left only one alternative; Michelle really was stupid enough to try to get out through the catacombs. The poor girl would never make it out alive.

"Let me know if someone *other* than Seth returns. If you see the woman called Bridget find me immediately," she said to the manufactured boy that stood guard. He nodded in understanding as Eva started up the steps to look for the twins. No more than two steps up the girls came to the banister at the top of the staircase, both were out of breath. "She's not in any of the rooms upstairs," Jessica called down.

"No luck on my end either. Also, it looks as if Seth must have given Deanna something to make her sleep, but from the way she's moving around it's not going to last to much longer. She was waking up just as I left her room. I'm can't be sure if she saw me or not," Candice puffed as they reached the bottom of the steps and stood by Eva. "What do you want us to do now?"

"I've had enough of these humans and their petty problems. I want them out of my house for good. I've let Seth run things his way for far too long." Eva's temper began to show.

"What's going on?" A haggard voice demanded from above them. Deanna stood at the top of the stairs glaring down at them from above. "Where is my sister, Bridget?"

For a moment the three just stood there, looking at Deanna with blank expressions on their upturned faces. After a moment of repose Eva quickly spoke up.

"Your sister should be back shortly," she smiled. "She and your husband needed to take care of a few things."

Deanna looked at her suspiciously.

"She promised me that we would leave tonight. I must have fallen asleep while I was waiting for her." Deanna's hand rubbed her forehead, shaking the last remaining signs of sleep from her face. She started down the steps and then stopped. A queer look washed over her face.

"What did you mean when you said you'd had enough of these humans?"

The last few days came flooding back in a tidal wave of emotion. The visions Deanna had of the birth of her child, and then of her sister's drastic changes both in personality and in body forced their way to the front of her mind. The things she'd *thought* she'd seen and heard were all true.

The uneasiness she'd felt within these walls since her arrival were suddenly amplified. She was certain, more than ever before, that her child *was* alive. Alive and somewhere in this God forsaken house.

"*Where* is my baby? And don't you dare lie to me! I've had enough of that to last me three lifetimes!"

No one answered. The younger twins looked quietly at Eva with cool, placid faces; a small smile touching their distinctly full lips. It was a direct question, blunt and to the point, but Deanna was never so certain about anything as she was at that moment. Her child was alive and they all knew it.

Eva moved forward, her hand touching the carved wooden spindle at the end of the stairs.

"To answer your question as truthfully as we can Deanna, I can honestly say that we are not entirely certain *where* your child is at this point. While you are quite correct in your assumption that your child was born alive and well, I am sorry to inform you that at this particular moment the child is missing. Although, if it is any consolation to you, I am quite certain that he is still in the house. To be perfectly frank, I must admit that I'm not even sure if he is still alive for that matter." Eva's voice was cold and steady, no emotion lingered on the sharp edge of her words.

"You're lying! Now tell me where he is!" Deanna stood firm, her heart pounding in her chest. Her only thought, now that she knew that he was indeed alive, was to get him into her arms at any cost.

"Do you remember that *delightful,* full figured blonde harlot that captured your husband's heart, not to mention his genitalia?" Eva smiled.

Deanna turned a bit white.

Bridget told me there was nothing going on between them, that they were just business partners.

"From your reaction I would have to say that you *do* remember her. Well as it turns out, *she* is the one that has kidnapped your son."

Deanna was halfway down the stairs before she finished her sentence, her eyes full of parental desperation. "She wouldn't. I mean, you don't think she would..."

"Hurt him? Well my dear, I'm afraid she plans on doing just that if I've read her correctly. She's got a thing for small, defenseless children." Eva's manner was cool and uncaring.

Deanna stood in front of her as she fought to keep herself under control. Her desperation to see her child, to hold him, outmatched her sense of self preservation that had suddenly sparked to life in her gut. The thought, no...the knowledge, that she would soon be fighting for not only *her* life but the life of her child, came as quite a shock to her already weakened system.

"Do you know where she has taken him?"

"There's only one other place left to look for her. Jessica and Candice were kind enough to have already searched the upper levels." Eva eyed Deanna strongly, "are you sure you're even up for this Deanna? It could be quite difficult, and from the looks of you, you don't look like you have the strength to stand let alone fight."

"Yes, I'm alright. I would do anything to get my baby back." Deanna stood a bit higher, a bit straighter than she had before. Her fists were clenched in tight, hard balls.

"Good. You just might have to do that."

Eva turned and whispered something into Jessica's ear and the two girls left through the front door.

"Where are they going?" Deanna watched them leave, the cold night air rushing in as they opened the door.

"They're what I like to call my insurance policy. In the unlikely event that Michelle does manage to get out of the manner alive they will be waiting for her. She is little more than an inconvenience to them I assure you."

Deanna watched as the boy that had cleaned her room and brought her food for most of her stay there stood looking out the side window. His body language seemed strange to her, and as he stood there by the reflective glass of the blackened window, he held himself at a rather odd angle. The boy's eyes scanned the vast darkness, intently searching for something beyond the stale air of Laurendale Manner.

The hair began to rise on Deanna's arms and the back of her neck as she watched him. The sudden thought that she wouldn't want to have to get past him, forcing those dark, unfeeling eyes upon her. The idea was more than she could stand.

Deanna thought again about what Eva had said about humans. Human...she was human, but what about him? What about Eva and the young, attractive twins? Suddenly the overwhelming desire to get away from the old house and it's inhabitants almost crippled her. She wanted to get away from here. Away from here and these...people.

"So what do we do now?" Deanna said, her mouth suddenly as dry and as brittle as old parchment.

"We go and get your child back. There *are* however a few things that we will need to discuss on our way."

"What do you mean?" Deanna followed her into the study where the desk had recently been pushed back to reveal a stone stairwell leading down into the darkness below. Eva stopped to pick up a small kerosene lamp that graced one of the small tables, a waft of black smoke puffed through the top as she moved it. Light danced across the walls and Eva's face, making her suddenly seem ancient to her.

My God, I've been here before. But...when?

Deanna had that *familiar* feeling that she sometimes got when she looked around the other rooms of the manner. Perhaps it was just the unmistakable feeling that she was dreaming again that was getting the best of her.

Only this time she was awake and everything that was happening was real.

The images that floated in her mind, in her dreams, were foggy, unformed thoughts as she tried to remember what would happen next. Deanna's body was feeling strangely light, as if she would blow away if there was a strong wind. She felt small and insignificant, her legs suddenly shorter than she had remembered.

"Your child is not like the others of your race...the other children I mean. He's special. You will do well to keep him with you at all times. I can't guarantee his safety once you are out of my house." Eva said as she led the way down the steps. Danna stood there for a moment, her mind trying to understand what Eva was saying. Fighting to make some sort of sense out of what she was trying to tell her.

"My God, there *is* something wrong with him then. My son was born with something horribly wrong with him, wasn't he?" Deanna's face had suddenly gone ashen. Her mind raced with the possibilities. Then Deanna remembered the fur that she had *thought* she had seen. She wanted to vomit.

I should have stayed at home. I've caused terrible damage to my baby by flying so late in my pregnancy, and that's why Bridget told me he was dead. She actually thought it would be better than knowing that it had been all my fault.

Deanna stood in the room, watching Eva disappear into the darkness below them, the light growing fainter with every second her mind raced. Her son was deformed; or sick.

"Wait," she called out into the darkness. "Wait for me."

Deanna's hand skimmed the side of the wall to steady herself as she descended the stairs. Cool, smooth rock lined the walls, her eyes focused on Eva and the light she carried.

"No my dear, don't get yourself in a panic. How do I put this, other than just to say it flat out? Your baby...your son, is a werewolf. Seth is a werewolf, and for that matter, now so is your sister." Eva glanced back to see if she had heard her. Half her face glowed in the warm light of the lamp.

Deanna stood rock solid, her mind echoed Eva's words in the vastness that surrounded her. She was going insane, or was it only Eva that was nuts?

"Why would you say such a thing? Why would you lie to me?" Deanna tried desperately to hold onto what was left of reality as *she* knew it to be.

"*Why* precisely. I have no reason to lie to you Deanna. I am only speaking the truth and I am sure if you stopped to think about it, you would know that."

She didn't. She couldn't. Nothing so ridiculous had ever been said to her. She would have laughed if it hadn't been such a horrible thing to say. She was going to get her baby and get the hell out of here. She knew now that no one could be trusted. Not even her sister.

"By the end of the night Deanna you will know that I'm telling you the truth and you will finally understand everything that has been going on here. You will then be forced to make a rather difficult decision on your part. Do you take your *special* son from this house and return home with your sister? Or do you leave them both here and return to your normal, hum-drum human life. While the decision is entirely yours, it may be harder than you think."

"Honestly, what kind of question is that? Of course I'll be taking my son home."

The decision wasn't hard at all. At least not from where she stood. Deanna would take her normal, healthy baby boy from this wretched place, and go home to where they belonged. She would leave her bitch of a sister here to continue fucking her husband and whatever else it was that they had been up to together.

Bridget told me that my baby was dead. How stupid could I've been? They were screwing around right in front of my eyes and I didn't even see it.

The deceit, the mind numbing deceit had to stop. There was *nothing* wrong with her son.

There just couldn't be.

Chapter 38

"Look you little bastard, bite me again and I will snap your neck *right* here, *right* now," whispered Michelle through clenched teeth.

David had changed moments before Michelle had taken him from the twins' room and had done little but squirm and snap at her ever since. She now held him by the scruff of the neck, at arms length, in order to keep him from bloodying her any farther. Halfway down the steep steps that lead down into the catacombs below she had almost dropped him when he bit into one of her breasts.

Michelle had decided soon after he bit her that the eviscerated body of Seth's son needed to be found in one of the caves where Eva's children lived. Everyone knew that Seth already hated them, one last push would send him on a killing spree while she disappeared to someplace warm and sunny. The south of France seemed as good a place as any to conquer wealthy men. The old fools would be easy pickings for a woman as beautiful as she was.

"Hell, I won't even need the help of those stupid mirrors to sneak into their rooms and suck them dry. They will beg me to take it from them, their money and their lives." Michelle looked intently at Seth's cub and shook him vigorously again. "God your ugly. What on earth did Seth ever see in you?"

Michelle knew that she had all night to take care of this little problem and get out of the country. Seth and his little bitch would be out hunting until the early morning hours. Tonight would be the last night that the moon would be able to effect them. It would also be the last night that Seth's powers would be greater than her own, and it was also the last night she needed to fear him.

It wasn't until she reached the bottom of the smoothly carved steps that she realized someone was following close behind her. She shook David again until he settled, his heavily furred limbs hanging limp in the air, his teeth still barred in a constant snarl. David's gums had been pulled back to reveal surprisingly large incisors for such a young cub.

Michelle touched her breast, a dull ach thumped where he had bitten her. She would enjoy disemboweling him, but first she needed to get rid of whomever it was that was following so closely behind her.

What if it's Seth? What if he hasn't yet left the house to hunt with Bridget, and he saw me take the little brat? What if he's followed me down here to kill me?

Her body began to tense as she looked for someplace to hide. The soft light from the torches didn't make their way far enough into the corners of the room for Michelle to feel safe. *Anything* could be down there with her, or *anyone* The platform and mirror that sat in the center of the room were well lit, but that was about the extent of it. Along the perimeter of the room stood each of the seven caves, all of them still lost to the darkness.

Michelle stepped quietly into the first cave she came to. The smell of urine and rotting flesh stung her nose and she had to breathe through her mouth to keep from gagging. She slid up against the inside wall and flattened herself against it's cold surface as best she could. Making sure she was still able to see the steps from where she hid and waited. Not more than a minute passed before a shadow was cast against the dirt floor, growing in mass with each step that brought it closer to the landing. Michelle bit her lip trying to steady her breathing. The cub whined softly and she shook him again wildly.

It was one of Eva's servant boys. Michelle smiled to herself. What could a mere adolescent boy wish to do against her? She felt her courage return to her.

Michelle stepped from her hiding place ready to kill him if he dared to interfere with her work, just as a second shadow crested the opening. The servant had turned to look back up behind him when he caught sight of Michelle. His black eyes burned into her, his mouth moved as if to speak but no words erupted from between his thin, pale lips.

Eva now stood behind him, a lamp in one hand and the other reaching out behind her to help Deanna down the last step. Deanna's body seemed pale and withered with the weight of her child's perceived death resting so heavily upon it.

Eva caught Michelle's eye. "Not a wise thing to do Michelle. Did you really think that Seth would just let you take his child?" Eva handed the lamp to the young boy. Deanna stared out at Michelle in confusion…but where was her child?

"What makes you think I want it?" she shook the cub hard. "I have no need for this nasty, half-bred deformity…other than to spill it's blood, to split it's tiny body and devour it entrails at your very feet."

"Ah my dear, sweet Michelle, unfortunately for you, your end has already been written. Why make it any harder on yourself? Give me the child. Seth no longer wants you in his bed. He no longer wishes to have you in his company. Not that his fleeting desires are of any importance to me really, but the child is more powerful than even Seth realizes at this point." Eva stepped closer to her, her eyes hardening. "Do you really think that Seth, a mere *man* is the master of this house? Do you really think I would let some slut come in and ruin what *I* have created here. My dearest Michelle, I have been in this house for far too long to let you jeopardize it all now."

Eva again moved closer, this time her body began changing with each tentative step. Her skin became reflective like liquid silver, her body fluent and seductive as she moved. With each step Eva took she began to rise slightly above the ground, she had become a dangerous Goddess in her own right. A strong current of cold air whistled throughout the room, coming from every possible direction and bringing with it the sounds of Eva's children as they poured into the room around her. Eva pointed a smooth, reflective hand out to the cub and he was instantly forced from Michelle's tight grasp. Michelle stumbled forward as the child was whisked from her arms, almost toppling over into the sandy dirt that covered the cave's floor. Michelle's eyes grew wide with fear as sudden understanding filled her mind.

All around her Michelle could see them coming, Eva's children filed in around her, pacing the floor with their malformed bodies. Each creature coming to rest only an arms length from Michelle, saliva dripping from their oversized jaws as their heads hung low to the ground, waiting patiently for their mother to give the sign to attack.

The cub that only seconds before had been in Michelle's grasp now rested in the crook of Eva's arm. As Eva turned toward Deanna, she stepped back, recoiling from the small creature that the woman held in her arms. Deanna's foot slid back behind her, searching desperately for the steps that she knew had to be there. All the while her eyes were locked onto the small cub as he slowly turned from animal to human.

Her limbs froze, the child was beautiful. Deanna knew in the depths of her heart that the child was hers, their could be no mistaking him. Blond ringlets caressed his chubby face, pale blue eyes mimicked his fathers. Deanna began to cry as she reached out to him, her whole body shaking. The child reached out to accept her and Deanna clutched him to her chest, her breath coming in sharp, ragged gasps.

It was at that very moment that Deanna's eyes caught sight of the eerie, stomach dropping vision that came from behind the woman who had taken her son. The large mirror that seemed to hang from the air had begun to bubble, its smooth surface became rippled with a sinister, inner movement that caused Deanna's very soul to shudder. She grasped her newfound child tightly against her chest as her legs unknowingly pulled her up another step. Backwards she moved, with each step bringing her a bit farther from the room and its inhabitants, a bit closer to safety. Deanna watched in horror as a creature emerged from the mirrors reflective depths, half man, half reptile it pulled itself from the liquid womb of silver to stand behind Michelle. The creatures heavily muscled body was covered in a thick, blue-black skin that reached all the way up to it's massive, dragon-like head. The beast was crowned with a mane of heavy scales, as reflective and as impenetrable as any knight's steel armor around it's face.

Michelle turned to face the creature and as she did so, her eyes changed to yellow, her skin turned to reflect that of the creature's very own. Her lips pulled back to reveal her own set of deadly weapons.

The mighty beast bowed down and addressed the creature that Deanna had know as Eva.

"Daughter, so good of you to come. I see that you have brought me yet another fine gift," the massive creature gestured toward Michelle.

A troubled look crossed Michelle's monstrous face. "*Daughter?*" she looked at Eva, "you mean to tell me he's your *father?*"

"I told you that this was *my house*" Eva's arms rose above her head, her hands clapping hard only once as she produced a small ball of liquid blue flame. The ball floated a few inches above her outstretched palms where it began turning and churning between her silver-reflective hands until it grew in size similar to that of a bowling ball. "Unfortunately Seth has a tendency to forget his place here...with me and the girls. Sometimes he even lets his playthings get out of control. Luckily for him though, I'm *always* here to set things right again, with my fathers help of course."

Michelle stepped back from the glowing vision of Eva before her, only to be met by her children as they began to drawl closer around her in anticipation. She could *feel* the heat of their sour breath on her back as they pressed towards her, aching for a taste of her soft, luscious flesh. Eva began to laugh in a deep and inhuman voice as she coiled her arm back and thrust it forward, sending the ball of steel blue flame whirling into Michelle. Her body igniting into a blue torrent of flames on impact, as if she had been coated in gasoline. The flames clung to her body and for a moment it looked as if Michelle had been unaffected by the heat of the flames. Seconds later pain seared across her grotesquely illuminated face. Michelle screamed, stumbling forward her arms flailing relentlessly at the flesh eating flames as they devoured her, her once again human body shaking and contorting in pain. Her vision blackened as she dropped to her knees, she groped forward, reaching out to Eva. Michelle could feel her flesh as it was split from her body and her innards were turn to soot. It was then that the claws of Eva's father reached out and ripped Michelle's once beautiful head from her shoulders.

The spell, that until then had frozen Deanna in her place, was finally broken and a scream hurled itself from deep inside her throat as the flaming head of Michelle came to rest at Deanna's feet like a burning marshmallow dropped by a careless child. Turning from the horror before her Deanna raced up the stairs, her baby clutched tightly in her arms as the sound of ripping flesh met her ears; Eva's children had begun to gorge themselves on the remains of Seth's dead lover.

Chapter 39

Bridget slowly climbed to the second story balcony of her room, her naked body covered in blood and half frozen mud. She felt numb clean through to the bone and weaker than she had ever felt in her life. Her only thoughts were of her sister and the child, David. She needed to help get them out of there and then she would deal with Seth on her own terms. Bridget stopped short of the door. She couldn't let her sister see her like this, there would be no way that she would never be able to explain what had happened to her, why she was so badly injured and covered in blood.

She looked down at the hole in her side, blood flowed freely down her leg at an alarming rate. She touched her face, the pain it brought was immeasurable and the swelling around it had begun to blur her vision. She needed to see to herself quickly and then they would leave together, *all* of them, before Seth had a chance to do anything about it.

At this point Bridget was unsure if Seth had managed to get back to the manner before her, or if he was still out in the woods, nursing not only his wounds but also his injured pride. She hoped that he hadn't returned, that Seth still rested somewhere in the deep, cool cover of the woods. Bridget knew however that her small victory over him wouldn't last long and that she would have to settle things with him, one way or the other in the very near future.

As quickly as her body would allow her she stepped into the shower, the heat from the water hit her like knives but helped to wash away the feeling of death that hung over her. Bridget used one of the thin slip-like dresses as a bandage and dressed as best she could. Her face was another matter, there would be no hiding the gaping slash across her cheek or the purple bruise that had formed around it. There was nothing large enough in the medicine chest to cover it and nothing heavy enough in her make-up bag to soften its hard lines. Bridget would have explain it later, *after* she took Deanna to her baby. Deep down in her heart Bridget needed to know that her sister could forgive her for what she had done. She *needed* to believe that Deanna was capable of forgiving her for sleeping with Seth and stealing her child. She needed to tell herself that everything *would* be forgiven, or risk the chance of not telling her sister at all. If not, she might let Deanna continue to believe that the child was dead and just leaving the house with her, letting Seth keep the child if he truly wanted him so badly. The child that was neither werewolf nor human.

Bridget opened her bedroom door, the hall was quiet. Nothing moved, no sounds could be heard emanating from the main hall of the house. She made her way quickly to her sisters room to find that the door was locked. She tried the handle again, she knocked quietly. There was a rustling of noise on the other side of the door. Bridget's caution grew. There was someone in there but it didn't sound like Deanna, her normal animal senses had been dulled by the mind numbing pain of her wounds and the steady loss of so much blood.

"Deanna," Bridget whispered, "It's me…we need to get out of here."

Nothing but silence answered her. Gently she forced the lock, her strength making the job easy and almost silent. The room was still clad in darkness, the morning light had been kept from entering the room by the use of heavy drapes. Two steps in Bridget felt the hot pain of metal as it sliced through her arm. She stumbled back crying out in pain as she fumbled for the light switch. Deanna clutched the steak knife that she had taken from her dinner plate the night before for protection. She stood against the wall, her eyes wild as she stared back at Bridget, her mind still not knowing if what she saw was real. She was still not sure if the "being" that stood in front of her was truly her sister, or just another creature disguised as her, that had come to kill her in the morning light. Deanna cradled her sleeping child in her arms.

"It's me Deanna. It's Bridget," she held out her hand, "I'm not going to hurt you *or* David."

"David." She looked down at the child in her arms. "You've named him David?"

"Yes, now put the knife away. We need to leave before Seth comes back. He won't let us go Deanna, he'll kill us before he'd let us take David from him."

"Why did you tell me he was dead Bridget? Why did you try to make me believe that my baby was dead?" Her words were weak but sharp and full of pain. "Is it because he's not human? Not really anyway. I saw with my own eyes what he can become. I've seen the animal that lives inside him."

"Then you know." Bridget sat on the edge of the bed as forgotten blood trickled down the side of her arm from where her sister had just stabbed her, soaking the heavy yarn of her sisters borrowed sweater. "Seth tricked me into believing it would be best for everyone if you believed the child was dead. He didn't want you to know that he was different, that he was a werewolf."

"From what that woman says, he's not the only one Bridget. From what she said you're now a werewolf too...don't forget that. Eva told me, she told me that Seth is a werewolf and that he has made *you* one of them. At first I didn't believe her, couldn't believe her. Then I watched as she changed in front of me, changed into some disgusting creature. I saw *my* baby change from a wolf cub into this beautiful human child. I also saw creatures I'd rather never see again. I saw them kill and eat the woman that I saw leaving Pittsburgh with Seth. The woman *you* said I had nothing to fear from."

"I don't know what to say Deanna. I never meant to hurt you. Everything just seemed to spiral out of control."

"Where is Seth?" Deanna stepped closer to her, still holding the knife between herself and her sister. "My God, what happened to your face?"

"Seth and I...we had a little disagreement. I told him I thought you should know about David, about everything really. I guess he didn't agree with me. We fought last night and he almost killed me Deanna, but I managed to injured him enough to buy us some time...but he is still very much alive. I'm worried that if we don't leave here now, that we might not ever get the chance again."

Deanna stood there for a while watching her sister, looking for the slightest reason not to trust her, but it wasn't there. For the first time in days she felt like she could actually believe what Bridget was telling her. Deanna trusted her for the most part, but only because she felt she had a bit of control back in her own life now. Even with the way things had turned out, she felt able to deal with almost anything at this point. Nothing mattered now that her baby was safe and in her arms where he belonged.

"What guarantee do I have that you won't turn into some hulking beast and kill me, or even David for that matter?" she looked down at him.

"The full moon is over for now. I may even be able to control myself more the next time I change. Besides, David has nothing to worry about from me. You're the only one that now runs the risk of being hurt by me. You've got human blood, the one thing I have trouble denying myself. But I've given that quite a bit of thought recently too, and I figured that and we can make some sort of living arrangement that will keep us all safe," she paused. "I'll make sure you have a gun, you can shoot me if you think there is any danger for yourself or David. I love you Deanna. I love you *and* your son. You're both part of me, you always have been."

Deanna softened, her eyes began to well with tears.

"Okay. I'll trust you…for now," she dropped the knife to the floor and hugged her sister.

Bridget felt a flood of emotions but held them back. Seth would be on his way here if he wasn't already and there would be Hell to pay for what she had done to him.

"I can't even begin to express how important it is for us to leave right now Deanna. Do you think you are strong enough to travel? It's just that you look so pale to me."

"Don't worry about me. Now that I have my son back. I think I could do anything."

"Good. You might still need that," Bridget pointed at the knife on the floor. "I'm not really sure what good it will do against the creatures out there but you never know. Hell, I'm sure it can't hurt."

Deanna nodded and picked it up. She placed it in her back pocket and grabbed her overnight bag.

"I have the keys to Seth's Mercedes. I picked them up last night on my way through the lobby. I recognized his key chain."

Bridget smiled. "You always were the smart one."

Deanna stopped at the open door, "I don't hear anything."

"They still might be out there, waiting to stop us. I don't know where Eva fits into all this, or the twins. I don't know how loyal they are to Seth, even with all that's happened. How about you give me the knife, it's going to be too hard to fight and hold David at the same time if it comes down to it."

Reluctantly Deanna handed the knife over to her sister and held David tight against her chest.

The hall was dark, Bridget strained to hear but there was nothing. Slowly they made their way to the main hall's staircase when Bridget stopped abruptly. It was Eva, she never even heard her enter the hallway. She was leaning casually against the railing, waiting for them.

"Let us pass Eva, we have no quarrel with you. We only want to go home."

"You'll be leaving *without* Seth then I take it Bridget? Have you killed him or have you just beaten him at his own game? It's been some time since Seth has been bested. But then again, he always was a sucker for the taste of human flesh…in more ways than one."

Bridget glanced at Deanna uneasily.

Why can't she just keep her damn mouth shut? I don't have time for this now.

Bridget had slept with Seth and Eva was trying to make that point painfully clear, although she was unsure if Deanna had caught onto her innuendo.

"He was still breathing the last time I saw him, if that even matters to you. I think he was a bit worn out is all." Bridget brought Deanna up beside her, guiding her past Eva and down the first few steps. As she passed by her Bridget whispered into her sister's ear.

"Don't stop for anything. No matter what happens just keep going until you're in the car. If I get stuck behind just go on to the airport and I'll catch up with you later."

Eva reached out and gently touched Deanna's face. "Such a pretty little creature. So devoid of bitterness for her sister, it's almost hard to believe that she still trusts you after you fucked her husband while she lay alone in her bed, thinking her only child was dead."

Hurt flashed across Deanna's face.

"Go to the car Deanna. She's just trying to keep us here until Seth gets back. I will be with you in a minute."

Deanna did as her sister asked, her steps slow and cautious. It was more than just Eva that she feared in this house, much more, and she didn't want to risk running into any more of them.

"Stop it Eva. You have your house back and you even have your man back, such as he is. We want nothing to do with you. If you're so worried about Seth why aren't you out looking for him. He was quite a mess when I left him." Bridget leaned in close to Eva, a snarl rose to her lips, she could smell the foul witch blood that coursed throughout her veins. "He may not be as pretty as he used to be Eva. You might want to get a younger, fresher model."

Eva moved her long, tapered hand along her hips to the small of her back, producing a thin, inwardly curved blade made of the finest silver. Deadly to Bridget in *any* form.

"I could kill you right where you stand Bridget. If I did that, I can promise you that your sister would never see the light of another day," she glanced down at Deanna. "But as I've told you before, I like you." She placed the blade close to Bridget's face, Bridget could feel the poisonous heat radiating off the blade.

"Maybe you should just go ahead and slice my throat now, spill my immoral blood right here for my sister to see. It won't matter to me much longer anyway. Not once I get her and her baby home and safe. I hate what Seth has made me into. I know I will burn in Hell for what I've done to my sister and all those other innocent people. I will burn for an eternity for the monster that I have become. Even though it was through no fault of my own."

Eva withdrew the knife and slipped it between her hip and the slender belt she wore just below her waist. "He will come looking for you you know. He won't let this rest. Not as long as the child lives."

"Then let him come to me so that we might finish our conversation. I will be better prepared for him next time I lay eyes on him," Bridget turned from her to descend the stairs.

"You overestimate my level of interest in Seth Toumbs," called out Eva.

"As you do mine," smiled Bridget. Her fingers tracing the slice in her face that he had made a few hours earlier. The hatred that Bridget now spawned for him began settling in the crevices of her bones.

Deanna came to the bottom of the landing, her way clear save for the lone servant boy who stood by the front door, his blank face looking at her in his usual creepy manner.

"We are leaving now…if that's okay with you."

Deanna moved toward the door and the boy held out his hands, his fingers tightening like vices around her shoulders. Deanna struggled against the coldness of his flesh, her own skin repulsed by the feeling of it…cold and lifeless to her touch. There was nothing human about the greasy feel of it, the way it gave way like clay to the pressure of her hands. Grabbing at his face Deanna watched as the flesh gave way, pulling from the bleached bones beneath, his blank expression never changing, never showing pain or fear.

Deanna pulled away from him, a chunk of what was once his cheek still in her hand. A gapping hole stared back at her, bloodless. Nausea shook through her body, her head grew light and dizzy. Gradually the realization of what she still held in her hand finally registered and she dropped it to the floor, her mind slowly coming to terms with the creature that stood before her. It was as if the boy were made of magical clay…brought to life by the dealings of a witch.

Deanna gripped David close to her breast and withdrew back into the main hall. She could hear Bridget's feet hit every step behind her as she came down the stairs at a run but couldn't take her eyes from the creature before her, terrified that he would reach out and touch her again. The boy just stood there, guarding the front door like a grotesque store mannequin. Bridget gripped Deanna's arm to let her know she was behind her and moved her gently to the side. Blood had begun to trickle down her right side, the hole left by Seth's ravenous bite had begun to worsen.

"Bridget," whispered Deanna, a worried look following the train of blood down the steps to where her sister now stood. It began to form a small pool around her feet.

Bridget turned, placing a hand against her side, trying to hide the blood from her sister without luck. "It looks worse than it is. It will heal in a few days Deanna, no need to worry." The words were strong but Bridget looked pale and weak.

Bridget turned her attention to the boy.

"We'll be going out now," she touched his shoulder. "Eva understands what needs to be done. She has given us her permission. You have done well."

Expressionless the boy stood still for a moment, perhaps trying to understand the demand. Eva spoke from above them, bending her slender body over the railing to make eye contact with the boy.

"Let them go. I have no need to keep them here any longer."

The boy moved to the side of the door to permit Bridget to open it. She held out her hand to Deanna and motioned her to come.

"Walk Deanna, don't run," her voice was firm.

Nodding quickly Deanna made her way slowly to Bridget and took her hand. Once outside the fine mist of rain went unnoticed as the three made their way to Seth's black Mercedes. Deanna looked back at the boy, half his face still missing, watching them leave with that blank stare she had been so terrified of this past week. The urge to run nearly taking over her body, but she was held in check by her sister's firm hand on her own.

Taking the keys from her sister, Bridget unlocked the passenger side door and helped Deanna and the child in and then closed the door. Bridget looked back at the house, Eva stood where only seconds before the boy had been, her expression unreadable in the growing gloom of the day. Bridget felt a pang of regret touch her heart. She had in some twisted way enjoyed her time there at Laurendale Manner. She had felt a part of something unique and wonderful there that was unlike anything she had ever know before A dark and distant part of her felt loss, maybe even sadness at leaving them behind. Perhaps it was just the animal part of her heart that felt the breaking of ties as she closed the drivers side door and started the car in an dull explosion of exhaust.

Halfway down the winding gravel driveway Bridget briefly caught sight of a naked man lingering on the outer rim of the woods. He had paused there just long enough for her to recognize him as Seth Toumbs, his eye missing and his body covered in both their blood. He looked smaller somehow. Perhaps by beating him she had somehow broken the spell he had over her.

"I think we're going to be alright now Deanna. There's no way that Seth will be able to get to us now." Said Bridget, her eyes watching the curve of the road as a cold morning fog floated across their path.

Deanna said nothing but slumped down farther in her seat.

"Deanna. Are you alright?"

Still nothing.

Bridget slowed the car to a crawl and looked over at her sister where she lay folded around her child and the passenger side door. Blood oozed heavily from between her legs and the color from her face had all but disappeared. Bridget slammed on the breaks causing David to suddenly wake in a fit of tears. It was as if the thread of her life had been cut the second they had left the cold grounds of the manner.

"Deanna!" Bridget grabbed her sister, desperately feeling for a pulse but there was none.

Her sister was dead.

The desire to turn around, to go back to Laurendale Manner and kill everyone still standing exploded in her mind. Bridget gritted her teeth, grinding them slowly against each other as her pulse quickened, and then she stopped. David's cries had finally penetrated her own heart wrenching screams. She had to go, she had to get away from that Hell on earth for David's sake.

She would have to raise him as her own. Bridget was once again his mother, as if nothing had ever really changed between them. Bridget took the child from her sisters dead grasp and cradled him against her. She would be his protector...his...mother.

Bridget knew in her heart that it was only a matter of time before Seth mended his wounds and followed them back to the States. Perhaps a new location would do her and David some good. A place warm and comfortable, maybe even by the sea. Bridget brought the car back into drive and headed towards the east. Towards a new life and a new beginning.

A few hours later, after entering a particularly deep patch of forest in the northeast corner of England, she buried her sisters body. Bridget wept, not only for Deanna but for David, her parents, and even for herself. They had all suffered from the ill effects that Seth had inflicted over their lives, but she was determined not to let it continue.

The thought of conquering Seth one day excited her as she smiled down at her sisters child, holding him loosely in her arms. His name would have to be changed of course, but for now she would just call him Little Cub.

"Next time Little Cub, I will be ready for Seth, next time I will kill him." Bridget knew in her heart that Seth wasn't a man that could be beaten easily.

At least not by a mere woman. *Never* by a woman.

But then again, Bridget wasn't just *any* woman.

IN THE NAME OF CHURCH

By Edmund DuBois

In 1572, there is an uneasy peace in the bitter religious wars between Catholics and Protestants in France. Madeleine, daughter of a nobleman, and Colette, her bright but unlettered maid, find themselves fending off strange attempts by a Catholic bishop who is determined to take control of the maid because he professes to believe she is bewitched. A royal wedding in Paris provides the opportunity for Madeleine to seek excitement and shield Colette from the bishop. Madeleine and Colette have romantic affairs, but the Saint Bartholomew's Day massacre of Protestants turns the happy royal marriage into macabre tragedy and gives the bishop the chance to attempt his evil intentions- yet once again, Colette escapes. In a final confrontation, the bishop's true motive is unmasked, and believing himself possessed by the Devil, he goes insane. Madeleine, because of the terrible happenings "In the name of church," disavows affiliation with any church, and takes her worship directly to God.

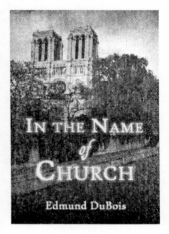

Paperback, 531 pages
6" x 9"
ISBN 1-4137-1763-2

About the author:

Edmund DuBois is a retired Army officer. He served in the Pacific during World War II and subsequently had assignments in the Pentagon and with NATO. He has co-authored one publication and is working on a sequel to the present novel. He resides in Sonoma, California.